Marilia, the Warlord

www.MorganColeWriting.com

© 2013 Morgan Cole

Morgan.Cole.Writing@gmail.com

Cover design by ebooklaunch.com

Map design by Nalja Kay

Marilia, the Warlord

Morgan Cole

"Please, help me. I don't know what to do."

*Marilia knelt on the floor of the tent, staring into the candle-flame.
It was a blue candle, for clarity and wisdom. She needed some now,
more than she ever had.*

*"Father," she begged. "I need your help now. Anything you can
give. The Tyracian army is here, and if we don't stop them…" her voice
faded into silence. She couldn't bring herself to speak the words out
loud.*

Come on, *she urged herself.* All those games of strategy you used to
play…all those war-books you used to read…what good was any of it
if it can't save you now?

*But the spirits and gods felt far away. Though she stared into the
light until her eyes watered, though she breathed in the smoke until it
tickled her lungs and scratched the back of her throat raw, no clarity
came. No wisdom. There was only fear. A dread that burned inside her
with a heat far greater than any candle's flame.*

You're going to die. You're all going to die.

*She rose and made her way outside the tent. She listened to the
sounds of the army; the rattle of armor, the cries of horses, the faint
buzz of nearby voices. Considering she was surrounded by almost ten
thousand men, it was remarkably quiet. The soldiers of Svartennos
were subdued; they huddled close to their campfires, casting anxious
gazes towards the south, where a smear of red like a blood-stain
scarred the ashen face of the sky. The wind carried the smell of charred*

wood; a gray river of smoke rose from somewhere behind the southern hills and flowed upwards to join with the sea of gray clouds.

Svartennos City was burning.

Once it was gone, the Tyracian army would come for them.

Her husband was dead. Her home was turning to ashes before her eyes.

What's next? What will the Tyracians take? Maybe tomorrow they'll march up this hill and kill your friends. Then tomorrow they'll sail to the rest of Navessea. Who knows how far they'll get? How many they'll kill? Your father? Your brother? The empire itself? At least you won't be around to see it, except as a spirit. Because if they make it that far, you'll probably already be dead.

In the valley around her was an army of weary, heartsick, outnumbered men. If the great Emperor Urian was right, and hope was worth a thousand swords, then they were even more outnumbered than they looked, because after the sudden loss of their prince and their greatest city, the soldiers of Svartennos had run short of hope.

In the command tent was a general who was no match for the enemy he faced. A man too proud to listen to reason, who had sent away his strategoi so that he could pace and fret alone, doing his best to convince himself—wrongly—that his strength, bluster and courage would be enough to save the day.

There was a chance—a slim chance, but still there—that he might listen to her.

But only if she had an idea worth listening to.

In truth, she needed more than one idea—there was no way to know exactly what the Tyracians would do, so she had to be ready for several contingencies. And she had to be ready now—*for all she knew, she might have only one chance to make herself heard.*

3

"Marilia." She turned to see Camilline standing next to her. Her friend—her sister-by-marriage—but her hand on Marilia's shoulder. "You look like you're about to rip out your hair."

"I feel like I am. Camilline…I don't know what to do. I can't think."

"Just take a moment." Camilline drew close, close enough that Marilia could feel her warmth. It was a greater comfort than the warmth of the candle had been. "Just breathe."

Marilia took a deep breath.

She pictured herself standing in her father's shrine, listening to the deep, soothing rumble of his voice as he ran her through the Stoics' trance. Empty your mind. Find your center.

She took another breath in and out.

This is just another game of Capture-the-Emperor, *she told herself.*

It's not. These aren't some pieces on a game board. They're men's lives. It's not the same.

Then pretend it is. If it was, what would you do? Just sit back and let yourself lose?

No. Your father always called you stubborn, because you are. You'd fight to the last piece. You'd make sure that if you lost, you could sit back and comfort yourself with the knowledge that no one could have done any better.

You have to do this. You were meant to do this.

"I thought there would be more time," she muttered under her breath. The Tyracians would be there before the sun set again.

Well, there isn't. Make do with the time you have.

In a way, she had been preparing for this moment all her life. She thought back to all those little moments that had led her here, a long and dizzying path to this cliff's edge. From those first, innocent games in her mother's pillow house to those years in her father's villa, to her

4

marriage to Kanediel, lord of Svartennos—a union which had been so suddenly cut short.

She'd watched him fall. She'd been helpless then. She wasn't now.

She closed her eyes, let the world around her fall away, let the noise of the camp fade to a distant murmur like a river. She forgot the taste of the smoke, the bite of fear in her chest.

It was just her and the Tyracians, trapped in their game—the only game that mattered.

Life or death.

Winner take all.

Somewhere far—but not too far—to the south, a war-horn echoed through the hills.

They were coming.

Part I: Childhood

Nine Years Ago

CHAPTER ONE

"Come on, before Tyreesha comes back." Annuweth took Marilia's hand and pulled her along the hallway.

Marilia hesitated. Truth be told, she didn't really want to *come on*. She wasn't sure what waited for them at the end of the hallway, but the sounds coming from the rooms on either side made the hairs on the back of her neck rise, and she would have much rather gone back downstairs to where she and her brother were supposed to be working with the other children, serving drinks to Oba'al's buyers.

But she wouldn't let her brother see her fear. So, with one last, uneasy glance behind her, she followed Annuweth down the hall.

The ceiling was hung with paper lanterns. The hall was red, the color the sun made when it shone through her fingertips. Annuweth's face glowed with the same bloody color, as if he was a traveler who had just emerged from a storm at the edge of the Red Wastes.

Hand-in-hand they went. On either side, silk drapes hung across open doorways. Dark shapes flickered on the other side. There were sounds, too—the voices of men and women.

Then they heard Mother's voice. They paused outside the curtain.

"Maybe we should go back," Marilia said.

"Do you want to?" Annuweth turned his eyes toward her.

There was a pause as they waited. From inside came a sound like feet landing on wet clay.

"No," she said, holding his gaze.

"Me neither. Let's see."

7

It was, after all, what they had come for. Why they had sneaked away.

Annuweth reached for the curtain but Marilia's hand was faster; she took hold of the edge of the curtain and, ever so slightly, drew it back.

They peered in through the gap.

It probably wasn't the first time Marilia had caught a glimpse, but it was the first time she would remember. Before she had been too young, and the memories of that time were already going, slipping away like a dream forgotten upon waking. This memory would be different. It would burn on like a prayer-candle in the night that refuses to fade.

Marilia knew that what the buyers and the painted ladies did was called loving (the buyers had another name for it, but Mother didn't like them to say it), and she had gathered that it was some kind of game, perhaps not unlike the street games she and Annuweth played with the other children of the pillow house—except that this game was only for two. What form such a game would take, she'd had only the vaguest idea.

Mother was on her knees on one of the pillows. She was naked, and in the light from the candle that guttered in a lantern overhead she was the same deep bronze color as the coins the buyers paid her with. Her skin was shining and slick. Her dress lay tangled to one side. Her head hung down, and her hair dangled to the floor, except for the few strands that were still stuck to her forehead. Her eyes were closed.

A man was bent over her from behind. He pushed his face into her neck as a shudder coursed through him. His thick dark beard rasped against her skin. Mother sucked in a slow breath. The candle flame fluttered like a trapped thing. The man started to turn his head, and Marilia quickly let go of the curtain. She and Annuweth stared at each other.

Marilia's face had grown hot. She wished she hadn't looked. She wished Annuweth hadn't been there to see.

Mother's room would be hers someday.

That was the way of things; the daughters of painted ladies became painted ladies themselves.

"Let's go back," she whispered. "Please, let's go back."

Without another word, the two children tiptoed back the way they had come.

The pillow house was busiest in the night. The buyers came in droves. Oba'al sat at the doorway, smiling, greeting them with a voice like melting honey. They paid him for the food and the drink. They paid his painted ladies to be loved.

The common room was vast, filled with big, round tables and colorful cushions. Thin drapes the deep red color of arandon berries hung from the ceiling. At one end of the room was a bar where Tyreesha, Oba'al's cook and medicine-maker, poured drinks for the buyers. Near the bar Oba'al's painted ladies stood in a long line, brightly colored in their dresses with habithra sashes wound around their waists, waiting to be chosen.

"Where were you?" Tyreesha demanded when Marilia returned, eyeing her suspiciously.

"Just…just had to take a piss," she lied.

"Well, hurry. There's orders that need filling. He's here tonight, you know. Your one-eyed friend. He said he had something new to show you."

"What something?" Marilia asked. She stared up at Tyreesha, feeling a shiver of excitement. He had brought her many things before—stories of Tyrace's king, who, like him, had only one eye; stories of killers and desert battles; once even a set of dice carved (or so he claimed) by a wanderer all the way from the Red Wastes. But these words—*something new*—suggested a thing more marvelous, more exciting than all those others. Something special.

Tyreesha shrugged. "You think I know? Go and see, girl."

It was Marilia's task—and the task of the pillow house's other children—to carry food and drink to the buyers while they talked and gamed, their raucous laughter so loud it almost drowned out the sound of the minstrels, who stood on their stage at the far end of the room, gamely singing on through it all. Though some of the other children grumbled about it, Marilia liked serving the buyers. It was much better than her other chores—namely, cleaning and working the kitchens. In the common room, you got to hear things, stories about the sand-people and lava ghouls and far-off places. You got to see things—games of chance and people from distant lands and, apparently, whatever it was One-Eye meant to show her tonight.

She made her way over to him now; he was sitting close to the window, only one companion with him tonight. Behind them, she could see the glowing lights of Tyracium spread out at the base of Oba'al's Hill like a thousand fireflies, the last glow of the setting sun kissing its way down the darkening face of the sky.

"Ah. There you are, girl. Come here." He gestured for her to approach, and she did.

At first, she'd been frightened of him. He looked frightful enough; three long gashes marked the side of his face, a wound he had earned in Horselord Castaval's service, years ago. The left-most gash was deepest, a furrow like one in a farmer's field, bisecting his eye. He wore a patch to hide it, but had shown it to her once. It was white like

10

the moon.

She wasn't frightened of him anymore; she much preferred him to the other buyers. Most of them cared little for the pillow house's children—they had eyes only for the painted ladies. They took their drinks and waved her away and went back to their games, paying her so little mind she might as well have been one of the lanterns or silk drapes. One-Eye was different. Sometimes, he invited her to sit with him and his friends. Sometimes he even let her join in their games.

At first Oba'al had frowned at that. But One-Eye had passed him a few coins—for the pleasure of the young one's company, he said—and after that, Oba'al never frowned again. Oba'al never said no to more coins.

One-Eye took his cup. There was an empty cushion nearby and Marilia took it. "Look at the view," One-Eye said, pointing out the window. The moon was full and huge, like a silver-scaled dragon egg resting high above the city. "Magnificent. It's moments like this that make life worth living."

"This is the fourth-highest hill in the city," Marilia informed him. Oba'al, she knew, was very proud of this fact; the height, he'd told her, meant *distinction.*

"Is that so? Well, aren't you full of interesting little secrets," One-Eye laughed. "A perfect spot, isn't it, then? High enough to see the lights and the moon, but not so tall that a man could get tired out walking up here." He took a sip of his drink. "How's your brother? Annuweth?" That was another thing; to the other buyers she was just *girl* and her brother just *boy.* But One-Eye had learned their names.

"He's well," she said, her feet tapping restlessly on the floor. She could no longer wait; her eagerness was a feeling like an itch on the palm of her hand. "Tyreesha said you had something to show me?"

One-Eye's companion rolled his eyes. "Do we really need the company of a five-year-old dress twirler?" he asked One-Eye in a low voice.

"I'm nine, sir," Marilia informed him. "Almost ten."

One-Eye beamed. "There you have it. Almost ten, and that makes all the difference. This girl is a ghoul at dice, Derrion, she'd surprise you; and even when she's not playing, she's good to have around. She's my Lady Luck. Aren't you?"

Marilia nodded.

"Well, we're not playing dice today, but maybe you'll prove lucky all the same. Here's what I wanted to show you, girl; take a look."

Marilia scooted up onto her knees to get a look at the table, and sure enough, there were no dice there that night. Instead there was a board, eleven squares by eleven squares, with a cluster of white stones in the middle and four smaller clusters of black stones arrayed around the edges.

"What is it?" she asked.

"This is a new passion of mine. It's quite the thing at the markets these days—a game all the way from Navessea."

"Land of the fish-eating bast—" Derrion started.

"Have a care. This girl's father was from Navessea, isn't that right?"

Derrion raised an eyebrow. "Is that so? Who was he? Traveling merchant? Or one of those scum priests from Dane who come to speak shit about the Horse God?"

"My father was a prefect, sir," Marilia said. She stared at Derrion, willing him to choke on his drink. She had only a vague notion what a *prefect* was—some kind of Navessean Horselord? —and hoped he wouldn't press her for details and make her look stupid. Thankfully, he didn't. Maybe—probably—he didn't know what a prefect was, either.

"A prefect," One-Eye repeated. "Yes, indeed. Well, this might have been the kind of game he would have played."

She looked at the board and tried to imagine her father hunched over it. She had never laid eyes on him, but she had crafted an image of him, piecing him together from the things her mother had told her. Handsome, with rich hair and a proud chin, the sort you would find on a statue. He'd been one of Navessea's best warriors—until a giant killed him.

"How do you play it?" she asked.

"It's like a battle, you see? A battle that's gone poorly for white, and now all white's enemies are closing in. The white stone in the center is the king, and his goal is to escape to one of the corners. The black stones are his enemies, trying to cut him off and trap him."

She watched them play. She watched the pieces move, and she could almost imagine that she was seeing knights in dark armor— cresting a dune, rising above the sand like a sudden storm-cloud as they prepared to fall upon the heathen king. The crystal blades of their swords glowing red, blue and purple, capturing the sunlight until they shone as bright as the pillow house's paper lanterns. *A game a prefect might have played. A game my father might have played.*

It was much more interesting than dice.

One-Eye soon defeated Derrion. He turned to her with a satisfied smile. "I see your good luck holds, girl. Here; have a try."

She leaned in over the table, reached out, and took one of the black stones in her hand. Her brows narrowed. She sucked in one cheek and chewed on it as she thought. There was a pattern to the game, she saw, though she couldn't quite make out what it was. And as she tried to find it, the game swallowed her. The noise of the common room fell away as if she'd plunged her head underwater. She stared at the pieces as they moved until trails of black and white blazed like threads of fire across her vision.

In the end, she lost. She sat back, disappointed.

"What did I tell you?" One-Eye said to Derrion. "See how she played? She's sharp as aeder crystal. Too clever for this place, I think." He smiled at her. "You keep practicing, and if you ever beat me, I'll tell you a secret."

Marilia blinked. The threads of fire faded. Slowly, the room returned; she became aware of where she was. A painted lady was walking past, dancing on the tips of her toes, the hem of her dress spinning around her ankles in a wheel of color—the walk that let the buyers know she was ready to be loved. Tynaeva's minstrels were heading into a quick new tune, one that had the buyers at the next table over banging their cups on the table in time to the rhythm. One of the lanterns overhead was fizzling out, making the shadows on the walls flicker.

And One-Eye was watching her, brows raised, waiting for her answer.

She found her voice. "What kind of secret?"

"What kind do you want?"

She considered this. She sensed it was the sort of question that was not to be answered in a rush, all at once. Annuweth or one of the other children might have done that—over-eager, carried away by their excitement—but it wasn't her way. At last she said, "Do you know anything about the giant? The one that killed my father, I mean?"

One-Eye raised an eyebrow. "You'd do better to ask a trader from Navessea. I don't know much about that."

She chewed the corner of her lip, thinking. What she wanted was a

14

good story; one she could be proud to trade with Annuweth. It was a game they had—each night as they served drinks they listened to the chatter of the buyers and when they awoke the next morning, they shared the best story they had heard. Yesterday, for instance, Annuweth had told her a story he had heard from a group of soldiers—how Horselord Castaval had defeated Chief Malack of the Kangrits in battle and mounted his head atop a spike. In return, Marilia had told him a grisly tale she'd heard from a trader, about how a mysterious man named the Night Killer had claimed another victim in the East Quarter, leaving a smile like a bloody moon carved into the neck of a charm-seller's daughter. Everyone knew the bloody tales were always the best.

An idea came to her. She leaned in to whisper in One-Eye's ear, feeling bold. "Do you know how the king lost his eye? How he *really* lost it?" She had heard a few options—a battle with the Tigrits, a duel over a lady, that he'd cut it out himself to save his wife from a dremmakin's curse. But she wanted the truth.

One-Eye coughed. "You'll hear lots of tales about that," he whispered back. "But it just so happens I know the true one. Is that the tale you want?"

She nodded. It would be the kind of story the other children in the pillow house would almost have been willing to cut out an eye of their own to hear. She felt rather pleased with herself.

One-Eye chuckled. "Fair enough. All right, girl. If you beat me at this fish-eater's game, I'll tell you how our king lost his eye. So it goes. But I won't play easy, so you'd best practice well."

A thought occurred to her. "How can I practice? I have no board and no stones."

"I guess you'll have to find them, then."

He leaned back, staring at her for a long moment before he frowned

15

and tore his gaze away. "Best run along now. I've kept you longer than is fair; Oba'al will start grumbling. Go send Raquella over." He smiled and touched her arm. Raquella approached at Marilia's beckon, the hem of her dress swirling around her ankles, her body swaying as she came. *A painted lady moves like water*, Marilia thought, remembering something her mother had told her. *Not stiff like aeder. Always like water.*

One-Eye took Raquella up to the silk hallway and loved her. Marilia returned to the bar, gathering another tray of cups. And as she poured jala juice and wine and night-tea her mind was elsewhere, far-away. In the fish-eaters' game.

At night, when the buyers came, Marilia served drinks. In the mornings she slept. In the early afternoon she had lessons with her mother—she taught Marilia and Annuweth sums, and how to light candles to seek the aid of the dead, and how to know if a ghoul had laid a curse upon you, things that everyone, even painted ladies, needed to know. In the late afternoon she swept the halls, and when that was done, she played at dice or tag or wooden swords with Annuweth and the other children. In the evenings, she helped Tyreesha in the kitchen—chopping carrots and yams for stew, making jelly from baby kwàmmakin, grinding asahi nuts for the paste that stopped the painted ladies from bearing child.

And in the stolen hours between one chore and the next, Marilia practiced.

With chalk, she drew a board on the worn flagstones of the pillow house's courtyard. At first, she practiced with asahi shells gathered from the pillow house's kitchens, but that felt wrong, somehow. The cracked and ugly shells were a poor substitute for the One-Eye's beautiful polished stones. She asked Mother to purchase some from the market, but—as she'd feared—Mother cut that idea down; they had other things to spend their coins on besides colored rocks. So Marilia decided she would find game-stones of her own. Her chance came on the first Seventh Day after her first game with One-Eye.

Every Seventh Day afternoon, the women of the pillow house went to wash their habithra sashes in the waters of the River Tyr. Before they headed back to the pillow house, Marilia wandered the riverbank, gathering pebbles. Some dark as midnight stone, some light as limestone. After two such trips, she had enough.

At first, she practiced with her brother, but Annuweth quickly grew tired of the game. Hoping to spur his enthusiasm, she told him it was a prefect's game, the kind their father might have played. That kept him at the board, as she'd known it would, but she could tell his heart still wasn't in it. He began to fidget, his arms and legs twitching like the legs of a chicaya. Her brother had never been much for sitting still.

In any case Annuweth was easy; no real practice. She turned to the other children of the pillow house. Of these, there were ten, but two were already in training to become painted ladies and—as they said—would not stoop to playing games with a young un-flowered girl. Three children were too young to grasp the game's rules. Damar was a year older than Marilia, and reasonably clever, but he was a cheat, prone to taking moves back when things didn't go his way. That left Nyreese, a girl only a little older than Marilia was, and, her brother excepted, Marilia's closest friend.

They played a few games together, the pieces dancing back and forth across the checkered squares like armies of ants at war. But it quickly became clear that Nyreese, while better than Annuweth, just didn't *see* the game the same way Marilia did.

So she played against herself.

It was a thing unheard of among the other children, and it earned her many stares. After all, what was the point of a game where no one could win, and no one could lose?

But Marilia was possessed. She was driven, not just by the desire to hear One-Eye's secret, but by the desire to beat him. And, last but not least, she was driven because he had said she was *sharp as aeder crystal*, and she desperately wanted to prove him right.

Perhaps her heart had been touched by the sense of optimism that seemed to have possessed Oba'al and so, by extension, the other members of his housel. It had been a good year for Oba'al's pillow house. Midnight stone had been discovered in the mountains to the east, and Oba'al had invested a good many orets in the Midnight Mining Company; he hoped to receive even more in return. Better still, Aldavere, Oba'al's closest competitor, had fallen on hard times; one of Aldavere's painted ladies had come down with the Sweats. And it was rumored that hard times had fallen on Dane to the north as well, which was good because everyone knew the governor of Dane was, as Oba'al once put it, an evil heretic imp-fart.

Marilia, being only nine, was only vaguely aware of all this. What she was aware of was the energy in the air. It was something fierce and sharp like dry lightning before a desert storm. She felt it, and though she couldn't have explained why, she knew what it meant; this summer was a time of promise. What better time to beat One-Eye at his own game?

CHAPTER TWO

Once, when she was very little, Marilia's mother had taken her and Annuweth to visit a caravan of traveling rhovannon with their colored carts. One of the men had boasted that he had trained a wild silvakim, a worm of the desert. It was a small one, its weathered, craggy body little longer than Marilia's leg. She had shrunk back at the sight, for everyone knew silvakim were dangerous; inside their mouths they had five rows of teeth, and each was as sharp as an arrow-head made of aeder.

But this man had stroked the silvakim's back, unafraid. And the creature made a noise like a cat, a purr, while she and Annuweth watched, fascinated.

It kept on purring right up until the moment it turned and bit its owner's nose off.

None of them would ever know why the silvakim had turned vicious so quickly and so suddenly; it was a creature of the desert, with moods as changeable as the winds that scoured the sands.

Sometimes Marilia thought her mother was like that, too.

Marilia's mother hadn't always been a painted lady. Once she had been the daughter of a trader, but her father's ship had sunk at sea. She had grown up an orphan in one of the gods' houses, tended over by the red-robed sisters who served Almaria the Blessed.

She was possessed of no great skill that any craftswoman would desire her as an apprentice, and hardly a single copper to her name (which meant that few husbands would want her) but she did have her beauty. And so, she made her way to the only logical place: Oba'al's house. A stroke of a pen, and he became her new father, at least as far as the magistrates of the city were concerned.

One day, Mother found Marilia in the courtyard while she was practicing the game—she had learned its name was Capture the King—against herself.

"What is this, sahiyya?" Mother asked.

She stood with one hand resting lightly on her belly, where it swelled against her habithra sash. Tyreesha's nuts had failed to work, as they sometimes did, and even the Ghoul's-Head brew she had made after the baby had taken hold had not shaken it loose, though it had made Mother terribly sick for three days. Tyreesha had thrown up her hands in defeat; the Fates had spoken. The baby would come by the end of the year. Marilia knew Oba'al was eager for all to be over with; ever since the baby had come and Mother's belly had started to swell, fewer and fewer buyers had asked for her—not even One-Eye loved her much these days, and she had always been his favorite.

At first Marilia had been concerned about how a new baby brother or sister might change things for her and Annuweth, but her mother had explained that she meant to put this child out, rather than name it—two to care for was more than enough for her.

"A game," Marilia said, in answer to her mother's question. "Father played it."

"Let me see this game, my sahiyya, my desert flower. Show mother."

In that courtyard, enclosed by high walls the color of cream, grew an old tree with cracked gray bark. Its thick roots strained against the dusty soil like the humped backs of silvakim as they burrowed through the sands. Marilia's mother took her seat on one of those roots, gathering the hem of her dress around her knees to keep it out of the dirt.

They played for a while, and it was going well until Marilia captured three of Mother's pieces in a row, pinning them between her own.

Mother's face soured. She swept her hand across the board, scattering the pebbles across the courtyard. They clattered like a baby's rattle. "I'm tired," she said. "I don't have time for silly games." She rose to her feet. "You'll see. When you're a painted lady you will have no time for these games of yours."

Marilia thought of her mother, bent double atop a cushion as the buyer hunched over her, the sweat on their skin shining like the surface of a river. She imagined what that would feel like—the bristles of his chin scratching her back, the heat of his breath blowing in her ear. "Maybe I don't want to be a painted lady," she said.

"You will," Mother said.

Marilia frowned. She was thinking of One-Eye's words. *Too clever for this place, I think.* "Maybe I could be a weaving lady?" she suggested. "Or a rhovanna?"

"The daughters of painted ladies are painted ladies. So it goes."

"Annuweth doesn't have to stay…"

"Your brother has nothing to do with it."

"But *why?*"

"Why?" her mother mocked. "Why? Why? Always why with you. Why do you ask so many questions?" Her voice was stiff. "You're going to be a painted lady. Or do you think that's not good enough for you? Maybe you'd like to be a courtesan? Or you could be a gods' woman, what about that? Is that what you'd like? Maybe you'd like to be the queen's handmaiden?" Still Marilia said nothing. She felt her mother's nails dig into her arm, pricking at her skin. "I'm tired right now. Do you care about that? No, all you care about is your questions."

"I'm sorry."

"I'm tired of listening to these questions. You'll be a painted lady. You understand?" The nails dug in harder and Marilia felt herself start to cry.

"I understand."

"You'll be a painted lady, and you'll not whine about it. No one likes a whiner." Mother released her arm and walked back inside the house.

Marilia gathered up her stones. She walked to the trunk of the gray tree. Seven sticks were leaning there; the wicker-wood sticks the children of the pillow house used in their sword games. Marilia took hers and walked around the tree until she found a place where the cracks in the bark made a shape like her mother's face. Then she lunged, striking again and again until the wood was marked with little scars like the bites of a viper.

"Tell us again about father," Annuweth said.

It was three days after the incident in the courtyard—long enough for Marilia's anger to have cooled somewhat. She lay with Annuweth and Mother in the little room they shared in the silk hallway. It was just after midday, and the three of them were just waking up from a deep sleep. The sun had risen above the roofs of the buildings outside. It made a pool of gold light on the floor. A gentle breeze made the curtains whisper secrets to each other.

Though both twins had heard the stories of their father before, Annuweth never tired of them. Marilia knew that the idea of having a prefect as a father excited him—so many of the games they played together involved prefects and battles and the occasional wicked, murderous giant.

Their father had come from Navessea to ask the Tower's one-eyed king for help in a war. He had stayed for a month before he had ridden away to his death, leaving Mother behind with Marilia and Annuweth in her belly.

Mother sighed. She lifted a hand to her brow to shield herself from the sun. "Not this morning," she said. "Mother's tired."

"Please," Annuweth begged.

"Why? Haven't you heard those stories enough times before?"

Annuweth looked crestfallen. "Maybe I forgot."

"You didn't forget."

"I just like hearing them."

Mother sighed, easing herself up into a sitting position, her back against the same cushion that she'd lain on when the buyer had loved her. She put her hand on Annuweth's head. Her eyes were far away. "Well...you know how he was a knight from the Order of Jade. The best knights in Navessea. They have dragons on their banners—he told me so. The reason for that is when a man becomes prefect, he has to kill a dragon. That's how he shows he deserves to lead them, see? And I don't mean the little dragons that people have for pets, but one of the great big ones, the ones that live in fire mountains. The ones that have hot lava for blood. So the prefect, he climbed up the mountain..."

Her words died. Her eyes were far away. "What happened next?" Annuweth asked.

Mother looked at him. "Oh, he stabbed his spear down the dragon's neck, and it died."

That wasn't how you were supposed to end a story, Marilia thought.

23

It was over too fast. You were supposed to draw it out, make it exciting, make your listener beg to know what happened next.

But she could see mother's heart was not in the story today. "You know, he had eyes like yours," she said to Annuweth suddenly. "Gold-green. He said I was very beautiful. The most beautiful girl in all of Tyrace." She giggled, her face brightening like a flower opening in the sunlight. "The whole time he was here, he loved no one else but me," she said proudly. "He said he was going to come back for me, to take me away so I'd live with him in his tower forever. If he hadn't died, he would have come and taken us all away and we'd all live together in Navessea."

"Where is Navessea?" Annuweth asked, his eyes alight.

"Remember when I took you out the north gate? To watch the victory parade?"

Annuweth nodded; Marilia remembered, too. To the north the sand rolled on in hills like the waves she'd heard the northern traders tell of. The sky over the north road shimmered with heat like wet gossamer so that, try as you might, you could not see what lay at the end of it.

"Farther than the sands go," Mother said, touching the tip of Annuweth's nose with one finger. "That's where he was going to take us. I know it."

This was what their mother had told them before, and Marilia had never questioned it. Now, though, the shadow of a doubt was coiling through her belly like cold river-water. Something a buyer had said to her the night before had put it there. Marilia had told the buyer the same thing Mother had just said—that her father would have taken her away, if he had lived—and the buyer had laughed at her as if it was the stupidest thing he'd ever heard. *There's a thousand men told a thousand ladies the same thing*, he said to her. *I'd wager a man's told*

24

that to every lady in this house. And where are the ladies now?

He leaned in and grinned at her. *Still right here.*

"How do you know?" Marilia asked, and Mother turned to her.

"Know what?"

"Know that Father would have come back?"

"He told me so."

"But one of the buyers said that lots of times people say that, only it's not true."

"It was true. He loved me."

"Like the other buyers?"

"Not like them. He was different. You're a silly girl. You can't understand."

"But..."

"He would have come back," Annuweth said hotly. The heat of his glare surprised her, made her shrink back. "Why are you asking so many questions? Mother already said he was coming back for us. That's the end of it, all right?"

Marilia understood that Annuweth *needed* to believe Mother's story; he had fashioned her words into a warm night-quilt he'd wrapped around himself. And here she was with her probing questions like a little silvakim, biting pieces out of that fabric until it was full of holes.

She felt an unaccountable, savage desire to speak again, to ask more questions, if only because she knew it would bother him, and bother Mother even more. But Mother's mood was already off, and Marilia feared that to speak again would probably earn her a striking. So, she held her tongue. She gave Annuweth one last, cold look, then rose and pulled the curtain aside. She left the two of them cuddling there and made her way down into the courtyard, where her river-stones were waiting for her.

25

Every time One-Eye returned to the pillow house, he and Marilia would play while his companions listened to the minstrels or made their way upstairs to the silk hallway. Each time Marilia would fall into the game until the noise around her faded and all that she saw were the stones.

One-Eye was slippery as a dragon, wriggling free of her traps, snatching her pieces one by one as she fought to hold him back. But although she continued to lose, each time, it took longer, and each time she claimed more of One-Eyes pieces.

She came to realize that she could see where the pieces would be— they were all connected as if bound by invisible threads. If she moved a piece there, then One-Eye would move another, *there*, and she would move hers to a third square, *there*. And on and on it went. But there were too many pieces, too many threads. They joined and blurred in her head until they were as tangled as the strands of a kwammakin's cocoon.

She stared at the pieces until her eyes burned, trying to draw the strands apart, to make sense of the board. One-Eye watched her, and he chuckled.

"Can I make a suggestion?"

"I don't need a suggestion."

He shrugged. "As you like."

She moved another piece, and three moves later One-Eye took it. She gave in. "What suggestion?"

"You're staring at the board too hard. Trying to play all the pieces. And you're sharp, but you're still just ten years old, and you're quite not sharp enough for that."

26

"What else am I supposed to do?"

"First rule of battle—know your enemy," One-Eye said. "Something my uncle—and he was a wise man—told me during the war. Don't play against my pieces, girl. Play against me. You don't have to figure out everything I could do, every way I *could* move. You just have to figure out how I *will* move. And that's a much smaller task."

And sure enough, she came to see that though One-Eye was clever, he let himself be carried away by his cleverness. When he saw a move that seemed cunning, he would take it. When he had a plan that excited him, he was too slow to abandon it when it wasn't working.

She offered him traps, and he fell into them.

In the week leading up to Horse God's Day, she became entirely absorbed. She knew One-Eye was coming to the pillow house later that week, and she had determined to beat him then.

"Let's play pirate's dice?" Annuweth suggested one hot afternoon, but she turned him down.

"Maybe next week," she said, and he stuck his tongue out at her. "I have to..."

"Practice for One-Eye?" he made a face. "I don't like One-Eye."

"I don't care."

"He's creepy."

"He is not. He's just missing an eye."

"It's not that," Annuweth said with a huff. "It's just...him. He acts creepy."

Marilia had no time for this. "I'm going to practice."

"Don't be an imp-fart," he warned her. "I think you're starting to turn into an imp-fart."

"I am not."

He shrugged innocently. "If you say so."

"He's going to tell me a secret if I win," Marilia reminded him.

"One secret," Annuweth said doubtfully. "Not really worth it, is it?"

"A good one."

"I had a good secret off a small-lord yesterday." Annuweth smiled, evidently very pleased with himself.

Marilia paused at setting up her stones, curious despite herself. "What is it, then?"

"I'll only tell you if you play pirate's dice with me."

Marilia hesitated. Annuweth bit his lip. She saw the triumph in his eyes; he knew he had her.

"Oh, all right, then. One game."

"Two," he said, ever the haggler.

"It better be a good one, then."

"It is. You know how there was an earth-shake in Dane?"

"Yes?"

"Well, the governor of Dane blamed it on the Horse-God's faithful. He said they put a curse on his country. So what he did, he rounded up a bunch of the faithful and took them into his arena and fed them to tigers."

"The governor of Dane is always feeding people to tigers," Marilia said, shaking her head in disgust. He truly was an imp-fart, as Oba'al always said.

"That's not all, though. King Damar was really upset about it. He wrote a letter to the imp-roar of Navessea, saying he was going to send an army to attack Dane if they didn't apologize for what the governor did. So, the imp-roar of Navessea..."

"The what?" Marilia interrupted.

"The imp-roar. That's what they call their kings up there."

28

"The emperor," Marilia corrected him.

"Whatever. He sent down some people to meet with the king."

Marilia stared at him blankly, thinking: *that's it?* It was hardly the sort of secret she'd thought would make Annuweth's eyes light up.

"That's not all," he said, leaning closer. "One of the men the improar is sending is the new Prefect of the Order of Jade."

"He isn't!" she gasped.

"He is," Annuweth insisted. "He's one of the same knights who came with father last time he was here. He's going to be staying up on Tower Street. One of father's friends!"

Now Marilia understood Annuweth's enthusiasm. Even if they might never see him or speak to him, the thought of a real prefect, one of their father's friends, being inside the city, less than a mile away, was certainly exciting to think about.

"Maybe we could meet him!" Annuweth suggested eagerly.

Marilia laughed. "Don't be silly. They don't let painted ladies' children on Tower Street. Everyone knows that."

"You're right," Annuweth said, looking deflated. "But still...I wish we could. Well, we might see him if he passes by Market Street. You never know."

"Maybe." Marilia chewed her lip thoughtfully. "What's his name?" She wasn't sure why it mattered. But for some reason she found that she wanted to know.

"Something foreign. Karthy something."

"Karthy," she repeated, trying it out. It wasn't the sort of name she'd expect a prefect to have—but then again, even though she wouldn't admit it to Derrion, she hardly knew much at all about prefects.

One thing was certain—it was a piece of news that was worth at least two games of pirate's dice. She let Annuweth lead her back inside, where Nyreese and the others were waiting.

Two days before Horse God's Day, One-Eye returned to the pillow house, just as he'd said he would.

It was a night full of promise.

The air was cool but not cold, dry but nicely so, the breeze like the brush of soft river-grass against your arm. In the corner, Oba'al's lead minstrel was plucking at her shamiyya, testing it, readying it for the night to come.

One-Eye was early to the pillow house. He came in with Derrion and four other men, all smiling, all happy. She soon learned the reason for One-Eye's smiles—he had just been promoted to the post of Lieutenant of the City Watch. He had caught the Night Killer.

"Is today the day, girl?" One-Eye asked as he set up the pieces. "Or will I get you like I got the Night Killer?"

"Maybe I'll get you like Neravos got the ghoul king," Marilia said. Her mother had told her that she shouldn't talk that way to the buyers, but she didn't think One-Eye would care.

Sure enough, he didn't. He smiled. "What's this? A bit of fire? Come and get me."

Their first few exchanges were quick, ferocious, nothing held back; a flurry of movement that left three of his pieces and four of her own captured as he tried to break for the right corner of the board. He was playing close to his best today, and she found herself reacting to his moves, her pieces trying to contain his king as he pressed her again and again.

"I've got you running," One-Eye said. "If your enemy's running, he can't attack you. If you never give him a chance to hit you, you never have to fear the killing blow. Did I tell you how I killed the Night Killer?"

"No," she said. *Know your enemy.* She tried to see what he meant, tried to trace the lines of his pieces. She was aware of the eyes of his companions watching her. She wondered what they were thinking.

No; that didn't matter. Only one man's thoughts mattered—One-Eye's.

"It was a trader's death that tipped us off," One-Eye said. "The trader had a strongman protecting him, but all the same, the Night Killer got them both in an alley. It was the *way* he killed the strongman that gave me pause. It was different from the usual; the body had a slice to the throat, quick and clean, straight across. And from the *front*, not behind. The sort of cut a skilled swordsman might make. It meant the night killer wasn't just some ruffian. He was a trained fighter."

Slowly, Marilia began to assert control over the board. The net of her pieces, stretched thin at the beginning of the game, began to close again. She let One-Eye run ahead of her, his king nearly to the top-left corner now, but that was all right; *nearly* counted for nothing. His eagerness made him sloppy; at the last moment, she cut him off.

"Do you know what it was that let me catch him?" One-Eye asked. He raised his eyes from the board between them, and for a moment they met hers. "It was chance. Chance made me a lieutenant. Call it what you will, the spirits or the will of the Fates, but when it comes down to it, it was luck. You see, the Night Killer was one of my very own guards." He found a weakness in her formation, taking two more of her pieces, widening a gap for his king to slip through and escape. "I knew the Night Killer was a trained fighter—I knew my man Fendon had a night off each time a killing happened—strange pattern, that. I knew when I asked Fendon what he thought of the killings that his answers weren't quite straight. And I knew the look in his eyes when he went to the fighting pits—like a rabid dog slurping at water—like he can't ever get enough. I knew all that, and I put it together, and I followed him one day and caught him at his bloody business, and here I am."

"Clever bit of work," Derrion remarked.

"Clever, yes," One-Eye agreed. "But if he hadn't been one of my men? I never would have figured it out. So let that be your lesson for tonight, my friends." He raised his cup. "To the greatest goddesses of them all—the Fates." His smile spread across his face. "And the Night Killer wasn't the only thing we found. He talked before he died. We found his stash."

"The Captain let us keep some of it," Derrion grinned. "A bonus for good service."

"So now I'm lieutenant, and rich, and about to win another game of Capture the King," One-Eye said. "The Fates are good."

Indeed, One-Eye's king was dangerously close to the corner now. At least it appeared to be—only three moves away from a victory—and a lesser player might have worried about it. But Marilia saw that it was irrelevant; he would never have a chance to move there, because in two more moves she would block him, and two after that the game would be over. She saw it—the inevitability of her victory—and the vision burned before her eyes with the intensity of a summer sunset.

It had taken the Lady of Four Arms, wife of the Sun God, ten days to make all the beasts that walked the earth and all the fish that swam in the rivers. It took Marilia ten games to beat One-Eye. There was a kind of beautiful symmetry to it.

She felt eyes on her, buyers at the surrounding tables staring her way. "There's noble's blood in her, sure enough," she heard someone mutter, and her heart leaped.

For a long while One-Eye himself said nothing. And when he did speak, it wasn't what she'd been expecting to hear. "You should have had a different mother," he said. And he downed his cup of night-tea so fast he dribbled some down his chin.

"What does that mean?" she asked.

"It means that you're clever, like I said before. Too clever for this place."

Marilia's smile swallowed her face. She felt as if tiny sparks were dancing up and down her arms. "The secret," she reminded him.

"Of course. But this is no place for secrets. Too many ears."

He led her out into the courtyard where the gray tree's branches wound overhead, cutting pieces out of the silky black of the night. The music of the minstrels played in the background, a new song, one she hadn't heard before. It was a Navessean song, she realized, and that felt right, fitting for this night.

"The king lost his eye in a fight," One-Eye said. "But not the sort of fight you'd expect—otherwise the story would be no fun. He lost it as a child, in a practice fight with a Horselord's son; a boy named Sethyron Andreas. That boy was banished along with his father, and now no one speaks their names."

"Is that it?" Marilia asked. She was a little disappointed. She'd been hoping to hear it had been poked out by the tail of his pet dragon, or that it had been cut out by sand people.

"That's the truth," One-Eye said. "Not what you were expecting?"

"No!" she said hurriedly, not wanting to seem ungrateful. "No, it's good…"

But she could tell from the look on his face that he sensed her disappointment. He laughed. Then the laughter died, and for a moment, with the moonlight limning the contours of his face, he looked almost sad. "Be careful of the truth, girl. Sometimes it's not as much fun as the lies we tell ourselves to fill its place. Take this." He handed her something small and smooth before he walked away. At first, she thought it was a coin, but when she held it up to the fire-light coming from the window she saw that it was a white stone, larger than the rest, and perfectly smooth. A horse's head—the symbol of the royal house of Tyrace—had been painted across the top.

It was the king she had just captured. She slipped it into her pocket. And though it would have fetched only a copper at the market, to her it was worth as much as an oret of midnight stone.

CHAPTER THREE

Though she didn't know it then, the day Marilia won the king-stone from One-Eye marked a turning point in the fortunes of the pillow house. That evening, even as she basked in the glow of her victory, dark forces were conspiring against them; maybe Oba'al's rival, Aldavere, had finally succeeded in doing what he'd long threatened and laid a curse upon the pillow house. Maybe it was the work of some disgruntled buyer, or maybe it was simply the Fates themselves, playing games. The troubles came one upon the other, all in the span of two weeks. First a trader was murdered over a game of dice, Oba'al's strongmen too slow to intervene. Oba'al was forced to pay the trader's aggrieved family.

Then one of the painted ladies became sick, and she in turn made a knight sick. She was put out, and more coin was spent to soothe the upset buyer. The knight told his friends to stay away, and they told theirs. Business grew slow.

Then the news came that the stories of midnight stone to the east had been highly exaggerated. Oba'al's investments there were all for nothing. No one knew for sure just how much money Oba'al lost in that ill-fated venture, but they knew it was *too much.*

But the worst blow the Fates saved for last.

Marilia, Annuweth, and Mother were in the silk hallway, resting together, Marilia curled up under the window beneath the hazy morning sunlight when her mother stiffened, frowning and sitting up. Her hand went to her belly.

"Is it the baby?" Marilia asked. "Is the baby come?"

"Yes, child." Mother rose. Sweat sprang out across her brow like gooseflesh. "Call Tyreesha. Quick! Run along!"

Marilia ran, banging down the stairs. Behind her, her mother groaned. The sound made the hairs on the back of Marilia's neck stand on edge.

She hurtled through the kitchen, down the staircase to the room where Tyreesha slept. The old woman roused herself, blinking. "Child! Take hold of yourself! What in the name of the gods...?"

"The baby is come," Marilia said breathlessly, pulling to a halt.

Tyreesha was up in a flash, businesslike. She raced up the stairs, Marilia hurrying after, pausing to bark orders to the bewildered painted ladies that she passed. "Tynaeva—the birthing chair. Raquella—there's some medicines on the top shelf in the kitchen. Fetch them, will you?"

Marilia's mother walked from the room. Her habithra gown was damp, plastered to the insides of her thighs. Annuweth followed her, looking hesitant, unsure what to do. Tyreesha took Mother's arm, guiding her along the hallway. As Marilia made to follow, Tyreesha put a hand on her shoulder, stopping her.

"You children stay inside," she said. "And don't fret. Everything will be all right."

They went back to their room. Slowly, the red curtain over the window grew brighter as the sun came up.

Marilia reached into her pocket and found the little piece One-Eye had given her. She ran her fingers over its surface as if it were a good luck charm, feeling the cool, soothing smoothness against her skin.

Screams came from below. Marilia flinched. She felt as though her stomach had tied itself in knots.

Tyreesha had said that everything would be all right, and she knew that there were always cries when babies came. All the same, she couldn't help but feel that the sounds Mother was making now were not *all right* sounds. They were the opposite of all right.

Time crawled on. Morning changed to noon. Annuweth got up and began to pace around the room.

The hours slipped by. After what felt like an age, Tyreesha appeared.

"Come, children," she said. "Come quick."

The first thing Marilia noticed was the blood. The flagstones were painted with it; the cracks between them were clogged with it, and the dry earth of the courtyard had swallowed it like a drunkard. Mother sat in the shade of the gray tree. Her lips were empty of color, flaky like paper. Her eyes seemed to be sinking into her face, as if her skin was made of heated wax. She lifted her head weakly and stared at the children. The baby was nowhere to be seen.

Marilia froze as her mother lifted a blood-stained arm towards them. Everything looked wrong; some evil sand person had reached into her mother's belly and scooped out all that was red, hollowing her like a gourd. Marilia had the fleeting thought that if somehow she could gather up all the blood and put it back inside her mother, everything would be all right.

Numbly, she walked across the courtyard.

She and Annuweth stopped beside their mother. Mother's trembling, bloody fingers reached out and found Annuweth's hair. They left it stained with crimson. "Oh, my children." It was the last thing she said. Something went out of her eyes; her head fell back, and Marilia found herself staring at blind glass—a stare as distant and lifeless as that of a figure painted on the aeder window of a temple.

Oba'al's strongmen laid a sheet over Mother's body and carried it away.

Marilia and Annuweth clung to each other in the shade of the gray tree while the world swept past, forgotten. The day wore on. Their grief rolled through them in waves and all they could do was sit it through.

Mother had been cruel sometimes, and frightening when one of her moods took her, but she was still Mother. She was still there to keep them safe, to tell them stories of lava ghouls and prefects, to light candles for them when they got sick, to lie with them through the late hours of night and the early hours of morning and keep the bad dreams of the sand people away.

Now she was gone.

It was a loss Marilia couldn't begin to measure. She felt as though a sword had slashed through the thread of her life, dividing it neatly into two halves—before and after. Nothing would ever be the same after this. Nothing could.

One by one, the other children came to them. Damar promised to light a black candle for Mother every Seventh Day for the rest of the month, to guide her spirit to the House of White Sands and guard it from the ghouls. Saleema promised that her own mother would help look after them and offered them a cup of water so that the faints didn't take them. Nyreese said nothing, but simply wrapped her arms around Marilia and held her close; Marilia buried her face in Nyreese's hair and sobbed until her grief, like a sickness, passed to Nyreese, too. Soon both of them were weeping together, huddled in the courtyard's lengthening shadows.

It was late afternoon when Oba'al finally came. The day's heat was settling in with the slow authority of a cat curling up on a doorstep. Dust hung like a thin curtain of silk in the air, turning the light yellow and diffuse. The warmth of the air struck Marilia like an open palm, stealing the last of her strength. She stared up at the seller with eyes swollen with the dust and with grief. She hadn't eaten anything since she'd awoken, and, besides the cup of water Saleema had brought her, hadn't drunk anything, either. She felt dizzy; she felt as though the act of rising and walking back inside the pillow house would be far beyond her.

He stood above her, chewing his lip, his mustache twitching like the antenna of an insect. "Children," he said, with a gentleness Marilia hadn't seen often before. "Why don't you go inside? Tyreesha's made supper."

Marilia looked up at him. Suddenly, it occurred to her that without Mother, their ties to the pillow house had been cut. She had heard that when one of Aldavere's painted ladies had died, he had put the woman's children out. A new fear struck her. "What will happen to us now?" she asked, her voice quavering.

"They have to stay, sir," Nyreese burst out. She bit her lip as Oba'al turned his gaze upon her, momentarily cowed. Oba'al didn't usually like the children addressing him directly, not unless he spoke to them first. Nyreese swallowed and pressed on, undaunted. "They have to. Please. They're my friends." Buried as she was in her grief, Marilia still felt a powerful rush of affection for Nyreese.

"They will," Oba'al assured her. "You children can help with the cooking, the cleaning, the serving of buyers, as always. When you get older, girl, you can take your mother's place. Your brother can join the miners, or the pit fighters, or even the city watch. Or might be there's a place for him here."

"He's fierce like his father," Marilia promised. "He'd be a good strongman." All she could think was that she didn't want to lose Annuweth, too, didn't want him to be taken away—not now, not in a few years, not ever.

"Someday. Go on. Come inside."

That night she and Annuweth slept with Tyreesha in a windowless, cramped room beside the kitchens. The walls were bare white stone. They lay on bedrolls spread on the ground, and the air felt dank and stale. Marilia tossed about; despite her weariness, it took her an age to fall asleep. She missed the room upstairs; the cushions, the night air that made the curtains flutter, and most of all the warm bulk of Mother beside her, her white night dress a brighter shape in the darkness like a cloud passing before the moon.

The next day they burned Mother outside the city walls. The gravers took her eyes first, to let her spirit out. Marilia stared at her as they lit the flames, at those two dark holes as big as the space between stars. The noise she made when the fire washed over her was like a log cracking beneath Tyreesha's cooking pot.

A last gush of sparks; a final flurry of smoke and a rain of ash the color of a yoba's shell. That was the end of Mother.

Marilia stood there, close to the heat, feeling her skin itch, until Tyreesha took her by the arm and pulled her back.

After it was done Tyreesha gathered Mother's ashes into a clay urn and carried it south, to the place where the River Tyr exited the city through a grate beneath the walls.

The gravers let Marilia and Annuweth carry the jar together, Annuweth holding one handle, she the other. They passed beneath the shade of Tyrace's walls, the shadows of the battlements stretching like black fingers across the plain. The painted ladies and Oba'al followed. There were even a couple of buyers who had liked Marilia's mother. As she passed around a bend in the wall, she saw One-Eye standing atop it in his armor, looking down. He caught her eye and offered her a solemn nod.

She and Annuweth stood before the rushing water. It felt strange, holding what was left of Mother between them, imagining that somewhere above she was looking down at them. To think those little flakes of ash had once been legs, hair, hands, a face that could frown as a dark mood came or giggle with girlish delight.

What she did not yet realize—but what she would soon come to understand—was that Mother had been a suit of armor around her, her presence a wall between Marilia and the worst of what the world held.

Now the wall was gone. It had fallen without a sound. It had turned to ash and blown away on the wind.

CHAPTER FOUR

The pillow house re-opened the following day. Marilia wandered the tables without speaking, serving buyers their drinks, taking their orders with little more than a sullen nod. The place was buzzing with gossip—the Navesseans were bound to arrive in the city that day, and some men were placing wagers as to whether the negotiations with King Damar would end in war, or whether an angry mob would descend on the fish-eaters and exact vengeance for the slaughter in Dane. Once, these types of stories would have set her pulse racing, would have had her hovering beside the buyers' tables, feigning clumsiness with her tray so that she could linger and hear as much as possible.

Tonight, Marilia found it hard to care. She just wanted the night to end so she could crawl back under her blankets in Tyreesha's kitchen, where she could pretend that the last few days had been a dream, that she would wake up the next morning and find herself back in her room in the silk hallway, Mother beside her.

One-Eye came to the pillow house that night. He went with Oba'al across the courtyard to Oba'al's private quarters and stayed there a long time. That, at last, cut through her torpor and caught her attention; Oba'al never let anyone inside his personal quarters except his friends.

After a time Oba'al returned. He came to her and put a hand on her shoulder. "Come with me, girl," he said.

He led her out into the courtyard. Overhead, clouds were gathering; the wind was crisp, and the air smelled of coming rain. Somewhere far off, a flicker of lightning split the belly of a cloud, a bright laceration like a wound carved in the heavens by the sword of a god. She felt a drop of rain tickle her cheek.

"Where are we going, sir?" she asked, though she thought she already knew the answer. There was only one place they could be going—the small house where Oba'al lived alone, set right up against the edge of the hill, overlooking the street far below. The small house where he lived alone. Neither she nor any of the other children had ever entered it. She felt a small flutter of nervousness in the pit of her stomach.

"There's someone wants to see you." Oba'al did not look at her.

"But why…?"

"I've always been good to you children, haven't I? You and your brother."

"Yes, sir."

"When your brother was a baby, he caught the Sweats. I might have put him out then. But I got him a physick instead, a good one. Paid for him with my own coin. That was more than I had to do, the gods know it was."

"Yes, sir."

"Well, now I need you to help me."

"I do help. I cook with Tyreesha, and I clean…"

"A whole oret, girl. That's the kind of help I need." Oba'al laughed morosely. "More than a whole oret, truth be told, but the one will do to start with."

"I don't understand."

"Gods help me, I think I do." He shook his head. "Well, it may be better, in the end. Who's to say?"

Marilia reached into her pocket and her fingertips found the little piece One-Eye had given her. She squeezed it tight.

The inside of Oba'al's quarters was decorated in pale silk drapes that stirred with each breath of wind, like an audience of spirits soundlessly dancing overhead. The walls were the color of wet sand. There was a bedroom off to one side, and there were cushions on the floor. A latticed doorway opened onto a balcony that overlooked the steepest part of Oba'al's Hill. A fine view. *Distinction*, she thought, distantly.

One-Eye was sitting on a cushion beside the window. He rose as she entered and came to her. He took her hand as Oba'al tool his leave.

"I am sorry about your mother," he said. "She was a good woman."

Marilia swallowed. Her throat felt tight, and her eyes prickled. Just the mention of her mother threatened to bring tears. "Thank you," she managed to say.

"Sit with me, girl." He led her to the cushions. He took one, and she another beside him. He studied her face. What he was searching for, she wasn't sure. She felt the hairs rise on the back of her neck, an uneasiness she had not felt before in his presence.

"Oba'al's house has fallen on hard times. Maybe you know that already. There's debts that need to be paid. There's room enough in a place like this for the children of the master's painted ladies, but for two orphans…"

"Is Oba'al putting us out?" Marilia's heart jumped with fear.

"I'm doing this all wrong," One-Eye muttered to himself. He took a deep breath, staring down at his hands. "How would you like to come stay with me?" he asked.

She blinked, puzzled. "Stay with you?" It took her a moment to fathom what he was saying. She had never truly thought that her home could be anyplace other than the pillow house. What he was proposing seemed somehow incongruous, as if he'd told her he'd come here on the back of a flying horse like the First King of Tyrace. "You mean...at your house?"

"That's right. Well, I'm not finished moving in yet, but let's say...in a couple of days. It's a nice place. Not as big as this one, but there's fewer to share it with, eh?"

"But Oba'al..."

"I just spoke with Oba'al. He thinks this is what would be best for everyone. I'm a lieutenant now. A lieutenant needs servants to clean, to cook. Seems to me you've done some of that work already, under your...what's her name?"

"Tyreesha," Marilia offered.

"Tyreesha," One-Eye repeated. "You could stay with me. I wouldn't put you out, child. We could play Capture the King as often as you like. You'd be the best damn player in the city, I bet."

"What about Annuweth?"

"Well...your brother would stay here," One-Eye said. "But he wouldn't be so far away. You can visit him, sometimes."

Her mind whirled. "I...I don't know..."

"It's a big change, eh? I understand. It wouldn't be until next week. I'm too busy these days to see you settled in proper. Besides, you should have a few days to say goodbye to your friends."

"But...the daughters of painted ladies become painted ladies," she said.

"Most of them do, right enough. But not all. Sometimes they find a man who cares for them, a ...benefactor. He might be a Tyrennis or a merchant. And he takes them away. There's some courtesans who started out as painted ladies, you know."

"Like...like father was supposed to take mother away."

45

He beamed. "Exactly. Just like that. I could be that for you—your benefactor." There was a spark in his eyes she had seen there before, a look he'd had during their games together, but now she saw something else beneath that spark—a smoldering hunger. Maybe it had always been there. It was a look she knew, one she'd seen in the eyes of the buyers before they loved her mother.

"Think about it," he said. "Most of the buyers don't care a shit for the painted ladies they lie with. It's just a game to them. You should have someone to take care of you. To love you."

The world outside was a shimmering blur, lost behind a sheet of black water that fell from the edge of the roof to the street far below. The sound the water made was like the River Tyr speeding on its way beneath the city walls.

"You gave Oba'al an oret for me," she said, her voice shaking.

"And you're worth it. You are beautiful," he told her. "It's written all over you. It's there in your smile, in your eyes, in your hands and your hair. In your smile most of all."

He took her face in his hands and kissed her. His tongue tasted of smoky wood. His hands ran through her hair, and she felt the roughness of the stubble on his chin as it scraped against hers. Her heart was pounding. *No*, she thought, *this is all wrong*. He was speaking to her, holding her the way the knights in the songs and stories spoke to their ladies, but it was all twisted, not the same at all. He was *One-Eye*, the man she played Capture the King with, the man who had told her she was a clever girl, the man who had told her Know Your Enemy, who had helped her to win.

"You'll be *my* lady, don't you see?" he said, looking at her earnestly as his hands caressed her back, beneath her shirt. "Only mine."

She shivered. No one had never called her *beautiful*, had never looked at her the way One-Eye was now. But she didn't want to be his lady. She knew what waited there, in the private space that only the buyers and their ladies shared.

The thought came to her that this was all there was, all there could be between them. This was what all the games of Capture the King had been leading to. This was what he had meant for them all along. He was a buyer, and she was her mother's daughter.

She could not breathe, could not speak; it was as though her body had turned to water—or rather, as though she had discovered that beneath the frail shell of her skin it had been all along.

Finally, after what seemed like an age, she remembered how to move. She squirmed away from him. There were tears on her cheeks. In the silence between them she listened to the sound of the rain beating itself against the roof.

"Don't cry," he said. He ran his fingers through her hair. "It's going to be all right. You'll see."

"This isn't right," she said. "I'm not a painted lady yet."

"I told you—you're beautiful. The most beautiful lady in this house, seems to me. I like you just as you are." His voice was low, soothing, like a man trying to calm an angry silvakim.

"I don't want to go."

He drew back as if bitten, and for a moment something harder showed in his eye. "And what do you want? To stay here and follow your mother? To be a dirty painted lady like the rest of them?" He shook his head. "Don't be stupid. What we have is something special, girl. All those games we played together, all those nights. Don't pretend you didn't feel it, too."

She took a step back, afraid that her legs would buckle.

"I gave Oba'al an oret for you. You're coming with me, girl. It's the

47

best thing for you, and if you were thinking straight, you'd see that."
He got brusquely to his feet. "You think on it, girl. You just think on it.
I'll see you on Second Day."

She fled from him on shaking legs, expecting at any moment to feel
the rough grip of his hand on her shoulder, the tug of his calloused
fingers in her hair. But it didn't come. When she was halfway across
the courtyard, she risked a look back. He stood in the doorway of
Oba'al's house, watching her. The rain fell like a curtain between them.
It ran down her neck, plastering her tunic to her body. She shivered, the
chill settling deep inside her, in the hollow places between her bones.

The white king he had given her was tucked in her pocket, as it
often was. She took it hurled it over the courtyard wall.

CHAPTER FIVE

"What happened?" Annuweth asked. "Why won't you tell me?"

Marilia lay beside him on her cot on the floor of Tyreesha's room next to the kitchen. Tyreesha was fast asleep; the sound of her gentle snores rumbled through the room. Through the small window set high in the wall, the moonlight entered the room like a spirit. Annuweth's eyes were filled with it; they shone silver as he turned his head to look at her.

What happened? It was a question that seemed to encompass the entirety of her, the entirety of everything. It was a question beyond her reach. Like the Tower of Tyrace seen from the street below, it was too large to fit in a single glance, a single answer. So she did what she could: broke it down into pieces she could look at and begin to understand.

"Oba'al took me into his rooms," Marilia whispered. "When I went in One-Eye was there."

"One-Eye?"

"He said he's going to take me away and that I would live with him as his servant."

"Take you away?" Annuweth stared at her, uncomprehending. "He wants to be your father?"

"No. It's not like that." She remembered the feel of his hands, his lips. She stared at the window, at the moon that was white like the king he had given her. She couldn't make herself look at Annuweth. She was afraid of what she'd see if she did. She forced the words out. "He wants to love me…like Mother."

He said nothing, but she heard the sharp intake of his breath. A sound of fear, that sharpened her own to a killing edge.

"'Weth…What do I *do*? I don't want to go with him."

"We have to leave."

"But go where?"

"Somewhere," he said. "Anywhere. I don't know. We could go to the gods' houses, maybe. They take in children who have lost their mothers, I heard a Horse Priest say it once."

"One-Eye paid Oba'al a whole oret, I think. Oba'al would come after us, 'Weth. He'd make them give me back and they'd have to listen to him. He's our father."

"He isn't," Annuweth said hotly. "Our father is Nelos Dartimaos."

"That's not what the papers say. They say it's Oba'al. There's nowhere to go," Marilia said, feeling the silky blackness of her despair rising up her throat, thick enough to choke on. She began to cry. She knew the truth, same as he did. The children of painted ladies were marked, just like their mothers. Stained by a grime that would never wash clean. "No one is going to help us."

"I know someone who might," Annuweth said suddenly, his voice an urgent whisper. "The prefect Karthy."

She rolled onto her side, staring at him. "He wouldn't. He doesn't care."

But Annuweth was alight with the idea. His voice rose dangerously, and Marilia glanced worriedly at Tyreesha, who was snoring not that far away. "How do you know?" Annuweth demanded. "He's one of father's friends. That's what the small-lord said. Father would have helped us. He would have come back for—"

"Father left us," Marilia said harshly. "He left us and he never came back and he was never going to come back, either."

Annuweth pulled away from her. She could tell she had hurt him. "Fine," he said tersely. "Stay if you want."

She squeezed her eyes shut, feeling the tears squeeze between her lids and roll down her face.

She was remembering a time she had watched a rhovannon show where a man had blocked an aeder sword with his bare hand. She'd thought it a marvelous feat of magic, until Annuweth had convinced her to help him steal a piece of the broken blade. She discovered that the shattered crystal had a sweet taste—the taste of kwammakin sugar, just like the candies the street-sellers offered during festivals. That feat of magic had been just a cheap trick.

She felt a deep ache in her chest, one that made each breath hurt. In some ways, hope was even more painful than despair. What she dreaded most of all was the moment when the hope was taken away, when it turned out to be just a lie like the rhovannon's sword.

"He wouldn't help us," she said again.

But truth be told, she had no better ideas. She stared up at the flat white circle of the moon. Like a pebble rolling downhill, gathering speed, her mind, frozen since that terrible kiss in Oba'al's room, stirred to life again.

"Tomorrow's Seventh Day," she said quietly, chewing her lip. "We could slip away then, maybe. When everyone goes to the river to wash the habithras." She looked over at him. "I'm scared 'Weth."

If he had spoken a word of doubt, if he had looked away and said *maybe you were right. Maybe this is crazy,* she felt that that would have been the end of the whole thing; their dream of flight would have broken apart like the thin, threadbare thing it was.

But he didn't. Instead—even though she could see her own fear

51

reflected in his eyes—he reached out and took her hand. In that moment, she truly loved him.

Prefect Karthy was waiting out there in the city, somewhere on Tower Street. She didn't know yet how she would reach him. She couldn't know what would happen when she did. But she had the sense, somehow, that Annuweth might be right, after all.

That he was waiting for them.

"It's going to be just us, isn't it?" Annuweth said. He tried to sound brave, but she could tell he was shaken. "Like in that rhovannon song. Us against the world."

A cloud passed before the moon. In the darkness she squeezed his hand.

The River Tyr was the greatest river in Tyrace, maybe the greatest river in the world; it stretched for a hundred miles, beginning in the mysterious land of the Tigrits to the south, passing right through the center of the city, and flowing on past the city into the northern sea. Where the river left Tyracium, its waters were muddied and fouled, but where it entered it was clear and pure, thanks to one of the king's laws that said that no one could pollute the sacred water with refuse upstream of the city's walls. The river-water was said to be blessed by the Horse God, able to keep off the curses of the ghouls—the *dremmakin*—that dwelt in the lands beyond the sands. That was why the women of the pillow house came to bathe their habithra sashes there every Seventh Day. And they weren't the only ones; the banks outside Market Street were filled with people—women laughing as they laid their sashes out to dry, their children frolicking in the waters or along the banks, dicing and battling with wooden swords, hurling sand at each other and chasing each other through the grass.

It would be an easy place for two children to disappear, especially with help.

Marilia caught Nyreese's eye. Of all the children in the pillow house, she was the most *discrete* (a word Marilia had picked up from Oba'al). She was the only one Marilia had told, because one whisper from anyone to Oba'al or his strongman and the whole thing would be over.

Nyreese had cried when Marilia told her, and that in turn had caused Marilia to break down in tears again.

She felt her eyes prickle again, dangerously, as she looked at her friend now. She didn't know what would happen when she and Annuweth found Prefect Karthy, or if they even could; but one way or another, it was a very real possibility that she might never see Nyreese or the others again.

"Are you coming in?" Damar asked her. "The water's nice."

"Maybe later," Marilia said, forcing a smile. "My belly hurts."

"Suit yourself." And he dove beneath the surface. Down, she guessed, to touch the iron grate in the city walls that allowed the river to pass through Tyracium. Since Marilia had discovered it two years before, the grate had become a hallmark of all their river-games. There were so many things it could be—the jaws of a giant kraken, the entrance to a sunken ship filled with treasure, the home of Yalaeda, the Goddess of Mysteries. Today, Damar, Nyreese, and Saleema pretended it was a secret passage into a Horselord's castle and that they were ghouls, sneaking in in the dark of night to steal away the Horselord's baby as punishment for his evil deeds.

Marilia felt a lump form in her throat as she watched them play, sitting on the grass above the bank, digging her toes into the soft sand at the water's edge. Annuweth sat beside her. She saw his lip tremble.

Behind them, traders hawked their wares in brightly-colored tents.

"Cloud bread! Cloud bread at three coppers a piece! The finest you've ever tasted!"

"Chicayas from the north hills! The sweetest songs you've ever heard!"

"Habithras! Hand-woven! Only the strongest charms to keep the ghouls away!"

River-water beaded on the grass, making it glitter in the sun. In the distance, the Tower of Tyrace stabbed like a spear against the swollen bellies of the clouds—an immense shape of red stone with a bronze dome at its peak that flashed as it caught the light. It was a beautiful sight; a beautiful day. In so many ways, it felt just like all the other Seventh-Days Marilia had passed with her friends over the years. But it wasn't. It was the end of something, the start of something new.

The enormity of what they were about to do came crashing down on her and for a moment she forgot how to breathe. For ten years, the pillow house had been the only home she had ever known. She had thought it always would be. Sure, she had dreamed of other things—of being a cortey-san in the Tower, or a rhovanna playing tricks, or even a prefect, though of course she knew that was impossible—but dreaming and doing were two very different things. She felt sweat crawl down her back. The palms of her hands were slick with it and she stuck them in her pockets, her fingers curled tight.

I have to go, she told herself, for what might have been the dozenth or the hundredth time. *I don't have a choice. If I don't, he'll come for me.*

She remembered the feel of his hands on her back, her legs, the smoky taste of his breath, the oily shine of his gaze in the gray rain-light of Oba'al's quarters. She shivered.

She hoped Damar and Saleema would understand.

Nyreese surfaced, climbing up onto the bank, brushing the wet locks of her hair back from her face. Again, she caught Marilia's eye. In the look they shared, Marilia tried to say what she couldn't say with words.

She got to her feet. Annuweth rose beside her.

Nyreese shrieked. "A grave beetle! It just crawled up my leg!" The painted ladies, who had been chatting as they sat beside their habithra sashes, waiting for them to dry, sprang to their feet at the sound of Nyreese's cry. They rushed to her side.

In that moment, Marilia and Annuweth turned and ran.

They ran past the children tussling on the bank, past the painted ladies and their brightly-colored sashes, past the street vendors and their stalls, up into Market Street. They kept running, following the curve of the street up the hill towards the Tower. Marilia ran until her legs burned and the dust clawed at the inside of her throat like a trapped animal, and only then did she and Annuweth stop, winded, hands on their knees.

They must have crossed half the city. They had come to the edge of a plaza. A bronze statue showing the First King of Tyrace atop his rearing winged steed graced the plaza's center, and in its shade, they stopped and took stock of their surroundings. To the north was what she guessed must be Tower Street—it ran straight to the walls that encircled the Tower, and in the distance, she could see the blood-red horsehair crests on the helmets of the one-eyed king's guards.

She swallowed. Oba'al's pillow house was, she knew, one of the finest in the city, but still its luxuries paled next to this. Huge palm trees—she thought they must have been hundreds of years old—lined either side of the broad road ahead, their shade covering the flagstones, which had been polished so that they were a rich, perfect shade of yellow-gold. Beyond the trees were houses enclosed within walls hung with creeping vines. Marilia could hear fountains running. A couple of rhovanna were singing not far away, one cradling a shamiyya so tenderly it might have been her child. Their music put Oba'al's minstrels to shame.

She and Annuweth made their way as close to the Tower as they dared and waited in the shade of one of the palm trees. The prefect had come to meet with the king, and the king was inside the Tower; but sooner or later the prefect would come out, surely, to head to whatever boarding house he was staying at. When he did, they would see him— from where they stood, they had a clear view of the Tower's gates.

Marilia was very conscious of the stares of the passers-by. She was dressed in a simple beige tunic with brown pants, frayed a little at the knees where she'd fallen a few times while playing; Annuweth was dressed the same. Meanwhile, to their left was a sweet-shop that catered to Tyracium's nobles; to her right, a store that sold real wicker-wood practice swords, not the crude sticks she and Annuweth sparred with.

These were the sort of people, she thought, who had their own private baths (rather than the big public houses most of the city used, or the heavy buckets of water that were lugged up the hill to Oba'al's pillow house). They were the sort of people who dined on silvakim and antelope meat and the freshest fire yams. She'd seen rich men often enough before when they came to the pillow house, but being here, in their world, outside the protection of Oba'al's walls, was something else entirely. She knew she and Annuweth were out of place. They might have passed for servants, but why two servant children would be standing idle in the middle of Tower Street she had no idea.

A gruff voice made her jump. "We don't take kindly to thieves or vagrants here." A guard had drawn near, staring down at them suspiciously.

"We're not thieves or vagrants," Annuweth said, his voice full of such righteous indignation she almost believed him; he'd always been better at her than bluffing. "Our mother is here."

"Who's your mother, then?" the guard demanded.

Annuweth hesitated, and Marilia saw the panic in his eyes; he might be good at bluffing, but only once he'd had time to think up a bluff in the first place.

"Right over there. Tynaeva." Marilia took over, pointing to one of the nearby minstrels. Tynaeva was the name of Oba'al's best minstrel, the first name that came to mind.

"Your mother's a Tyrennis' own rhovanna and you're dressed like *that*?" he raised his eyebrows, looking pointedly at their shabby clothes.

"It's Seventh Day," Marilia said, as if that explained everything.

The guard cocked his head to one side. "So?"

"So, boys and girls are supposed to dress simple every Seventh-Day. Like our own first king, the Horse God, when he first came to Tyracium."

"Who told you that?" the guard looked more amused now than suspicious. A definite improvement.

"One of Tyr Jalai's best priests," she said with complete confidence. Tyr Jalai was the kingdom's western-most land. Distant enough—and odd enough—that who knew for sure what silly things the Horse-God's priests spouted there?

"Tyr Jalai." The guard snorted. "Well. That explains it. You from there?"

Marilia nodded. The guard grunted and moved on, and Marilia let out a long breath. Her hands were shaking.

"That was *brilliant*," Annuweth breathed, nudging her arm.

She didn't answer. They might have dealt with one guard, but they couldn't loiter here forever. She glanced at the sky. The sun was disappearing behind the city's walls and the stones on the western side of the tower were a deepening shade of red like a guilty blush. It couldn't be much longer, surely?

As if in answer to her unspoken thought, the gates to the Tower's courtyard swung open, and *he* appeared. It could only be him.

The prefect.

There were other men, there, too, but she hardly spared a glance for them; her eyes were fixed on the man in whose hands their fate rested. She knew him by his green yoba-shell armor, by the green cape that hung from his shoulders. *Jade* meant green, and her father, she'd been told, had worn a cloak just like that. He was tall, one of the tallest men she'd seen. He towered a full head above Oba'al and was crowned with a fringe of curled dark hair that circled his balding head. His jaw was jutting; his brows dark and fierce as two thunderclouds. His skin was a shade paler than was usual for the men of Tyrace or Navessea—perhaps, Marilia thought, he was one of those northlanders she'd heard the buyers tell of.

"Prefect Karthy," she whispered.

As she looked at him, she felt a chill crawl down her back—the beginning of fear. He was a strange man from a strange land with strange friends, with a sword on either hip and a horse that matched his size—taller and grander than any she could remember seeing. He was a fighter; he'd killed men. The idea that she would be safe with him

58

suddenly seemed highly suspect.

He wasn't safety. He was an unknown, the magician's box before
the lid was opened. Inside might be something wondrous and magical,
or nothing at all.

She told herself that the unknown was still better than what lay
behind.

She and Annuweth followed the procession at a cautious distance. It
turned right near the end of the street, entering a building surrounded
by a smooth stone wall and acacia trees. An iron gate, crafted to look
like flowering vines, opened into a central courtyard hung with ribbons
of silk. Lanterns glowed invitingly in the windows and from the open
door came the sound of singing. It was one of the city's finest boarding
houses. Which meant guards, of course; two right behind the gates, no
doubt more inside.

She wondered if it might be better to catch Karthy out in the open
street, before the gates to the boarding house closed. She opened her
mouth to call out to him, but the sight of all those armored guards stole
her tongue; she lost her nerve and with it, her chance. The boarding
house's gates swung closed behind him. He disappeared inside the
building, the rest of the men following him—six men in the green
armor of the Order of Jade, four more in the blood-red armor of the
king, and one man in strange white robes the likes of which she'd never
seen before. Another fish-eater, she supposed. Maybe their leader. One
of the imp-roar's men.

Heart hammering, Marilia approached the gates, Annuweth
following behind her. The guards paused their conversation as she drew
near. The closest man stared at her from beneath heavy brows with
dark, narrow eyes like two shards of flint.

"Please, sir," Marilia said, doing her best to sound calm and dignified, the way the ladies talked in rhovannon stories. "I have a message for the prefect."

The guard laughed. "Like shit you do."

"I mean it. I believe the prefect will want to hear it, sir. He might even reward you if you tell him." She had no idea if this was true, but it sounded right. Possible, at least.

"That right?" He sounded unconvinced. "You'd better be on your way, girl. The lieutenant's making his rounds, and if he finds you here, I doubt he'll be in the mood to listen to your horse-shit story. He's been in a mood today."

"It's about the prefect's friend, Nelos Dartimaos," Marilia said desperately. "Please. Just tell him that. Tell him that I have news about Nelos Dartimaos and his children."

"What's your news, then?" the guard demanded.

Marilia hesitated. But she could see no way around it. "We're Dartimaos' children and we need help. We…"

"You, the children of a prefect!" the guard laughed. "Not likely. 'Less of course your mother was a slattern or a painted lady, and if that's so you'd best move off." The mirth faded from his face. "There's no place for you here."

"Please, sir. I…"

"Didn't you hear me, girl? Get. Lost."

She retreated from the gates, grinding her teeth. She hadn't come all this way just to be turned back by a guard too stupid to listen to the truth when it was shouted in his face. But the sky was darkening fast now, and stars were showing; they couldn't just stay in the street. There were, as she had been so helpfully reminded, no vagrants allowed on Tower Street. Besides, Oba'al had probably put the word out by now; his strongman might be searching the city for her and Annuweth right at that moment. If Oba'al found them that would be the end of it; he'd drag them back to the pillow house, and…

She shuddered, the hairs on her arms standing on end. No. There had to be another way.

And there was. The acacia trees that ringed the compound had not been trimmed in a while, and their branches stretched out close to the top of the wall. One in particular caught her eye; a branch grew so close to the wall that it grazed the stone.

"Come on," she said, tugging on Annuweth's arm.

They slipped around the side of the building into the deepening shadows. Annuweth went first, and she followed, hugging the bark tight, wriggling up a branch like a worm inching its way across the street. What she would do when she reached the top, when she dropped down to the other side into the boarding house's courtyard, she had no idea. It was rage that drove her, rage at the thought of that guard's sneer, of the way he'd waved his hand to shoo her away, as if he were brushing away a fly.

Suddenly she stopped, her heart pounding. She was halfway out along the limb that reached to the edge of the wall, but there were figures approaching below; she glimpsed them through the leaves. Three of them, two boys and a girl, older by several years than she and Annuweth. They looked as if they were on the verge of turning into grown-ups.

The boys wore richly-patterned red-brown robes with wicker-wood swords hanging from their belts, the girl a dress with a child's habithra sash around her waist, the sort that only nobles wore. To Marilia's dismay, they stopped right beneath the branch where she and Annuweth now clung.

"The fish-eater isn't *really* leaving tomorrow, Castaval," the girl

61

was saying. "Is he?"

"That's what I heard." Castaval did not try to keep the disgust from his voice. "They're going to make peace, after all. Our king's a fish-belly coward. The Governor of Dane feeds the Horse-God's faithful to his tigers and we make peace treaties with their emperor." He spat derisively.

"Castaval..." the second boy glanced around uneasily. "Be careful...you shouldn't say such things..."

"Oh, come on, Oberal," Castaval said dismissively. "Don't be a fish-belly yourself. No one can hear us."

"The Bull Priests will be furious, won't they?" the girl insisted. "Once they find out about the peace treaty, they'll be so angry..."

"I hope there's an uprising," Castaval said, his voice savage. "I hope there is."

"We don't *know* they're going to make a treaty..." Oberal began.

"My father said he was almost sure of it. He *knows* these things, Oberal. He's well-informed, all right?"

Marilia heard a soft creak. She froze, horrified. Ahead, the branch was beginning to bow under Annuweth's weight. A hairline crack ran through the wood between the two of them. Annuweth looked back at her, wide-eyed. But he didn't dare move, not with the noble children standing just underneath. Any motion would rustle the leaves, and Castaval and the rest would surely hear it.

Please, Marilia begged silently. *Leave. Just leave.*

But they didn't. Instead, Castaval and the other boy pulled out their wooden swords. They had come to spar; the girl settled back to watch.

No, she thought. *No, no, no...*

It was too late to go back; the branch she and Annuweth were resting on broke with a resounding snap. Annuweth gave a cry of dismay; he pitched forward into the air. Marilia lunged for him. She missed, her hand brushing against the leg of his trousers. She lost her bearing and she fell after him, slipping sideways off the branch. She tumbled. The stars tore free of the blanket of night and spun around her, a million blazing fireflies. In the brief span of time between the moment her fall began and the moment it ended she had just time enough to realize—with horror—that she was coming down right on top of Castaval.

His shoulder drove into the small of her back; his elbow collided with her head. She rolled sideways against the trunk of the tree, winded, the world spinning.

Castaval rose from his knees, brushing dirt off the knees of his pants. His eyes were dark and forbidding.

His girl companion was crying and clutching her arm; the jagged end of the branch had hit her on the way down and left a scratch that had torn right through the thin silk fabric of her dress.

Annuweth struggled to rise, tangled among the leaves. "I'm sorry, my lord," he stammered. "I'm so sorry…"

"They were listening to us," Oberal said urgently. "They were *spying*, Castaval."

Annuweth managed to get back on his feet. There was a leaf caught in his hair, a scratch along one forearm where a stray twig had cut him. "We didn't mean to," he promised. "We were just…we were just climbing…"

"Just climbing," Castaval repeated. He was rubbing at his shoulder where Marilia had fallen on him. There was hurt on his face, and the beginnings of something more dangerous than hurt. She saw his eyes moving up and down Annuweth's body, taking in his disheveled hair, his dirty, simple clothes. His eyes traveled upwards, to the broken branch, and followed it to the edge of the boarding house's wall. He wasn't stupid, whatever else he was. "Were you trying to sneak in? Is that it?"

"No, my lord…"

"No? So, if I go and tell the guards you two just fell on my head, they'll know who you are?"

"Please," Marilia said. The thought of him calling the guards made her queasy. The guards had already turned her and Annuweth away; what might they do when they found out she'd disobeyed a direct order? "We're sorry. We'll go."

"Go?" Castaval shook his head. He moved like a snake striking, seizing hold of her wrist so suddenly that she gasped. "You hurt my lady friend. You're not leaving until you tell me what you were doing here."

"We just came to see someone," Annuweth said before Marilia could speak, before she could stop him.

"See who?" Castaval's grip on her arm tightened. He was older than she was by at least two years, and much stronger. He gave a sharp tug, causing her to stumble to her knees. She gasped with pain. "See *who*?"

"The prefect," Annuweth said hurriedly. "He knew our father. Our father was the old prefect, and so…"

"Hold on. Your father was a prefect?" Castaval's eyes narrowed still further. "I don't believe it."

"It's true. I swear it is."

"What are you, then, some painted bastard boy? Some fish-eater's spawn?"

Annuweth said nothing, but the tips of his ears darkened with shame.

"You *are*," Castaval said, his eyes widening.

"Please, just let my sister go."

"I don't think so. You hurt my lady. I ought to do the same to yours."

Marilia's heart was pounding. Castaval's hand was still tight around her wrist, but he wasn't looking at her. She might have seized a pebble from the ground and smashed it against his face. She might have flung herself on him and borne him to the ground. But to strike a Horselord's son by accident, as she had done, was bad enough. To do it on purpose would be far worse.

While she was still considering what to do, Castaval released her arm. He took a step towards Annuweth. "Unless…" he pursed his lips. "I suppose you could fight me for her. Yes." His eyes brightened at the idea. "Let's see how a prefect's son fights. Give me that, Oberal." He snatched the wicker-wood sword from his friend's hand and hurled it at Annuweth's feet. "Pick it up, prefect's boy."

"My lord…"

"Pick. It. Up." Castaval's tone brooked no room for argument. Reluctantly, Annuweth did as he was ordered.

Of all the children in Oba'al's pillow house, Annuweth had always been one of the best fighters. Not as strong as Damar, but quicker and smarter. He was at least as good as Marilia herself was, maybe even better (though she wouldn't have told him so).

But Castaval was older, and a horse-lord's son, trained from the time he could walk, the wicker-wood as natural to him as if it was an extension of his own arm. It was no contest. With a flick of his wrist he sent Annuweth's sword wide; his stick rapped against Annuweth's knuckles, hard, and Annuweth dropped his weapon with a muffled cry of pain.

"Pick it up."

With his hand shaking, Annuweth reached for the sword. Castaval kicked it out of reach and whipped his own sword into the side of Annuweth's knee. Annuweth's leg buckled; he fell.

"Pick it up."

Marilia looked into Castaval's eyes. The casual malice she found there took her breath away; it was something she'd seen before, once—the look in the eyes of an old alley-cat pawing at a chicaya with a torn wing as it struggled to fly away. Chipping away at its body piece by piece, each swipe of its paw leaving more of it broken until, at the end, it was nothing but a quivering lump between the cat's claws.

She tried to run to her brother but Oberal shoved her from the side and she went sprawling, tasting dirt in her mouth.

Annuweth ran for the sword but Castaval blocked his way. His wooden sword whistled as it cut the air, flicking like the tongue of a serpent, reaching out to touch Annuweth's head, his back, his other leg. Annuweth staggered. He wiped blood from his nose.

"You're not a prefect's son," Castaval said, twirling the stick in his hand. "And your sister is not a prefect's daughter. You're not anything, all right? You're both dirt. Don't forget it."

The wise thing to do then would have been for Annuweth to hang his head, mumble an apology, and limp away. Maybe that was what Castaval had expected. Instead, Annuweth bellowed and rushed the Horselord's boy.

Castaval plainly wasn't expecting it. He was slow to dodge. Annuweth's fist cracked against Castaval's face, whipping his head to one side. Annuweth might have had him then had he not stopped, brought up short by the shock of what he had done—striking a Horselord's son.

"You little bastard!" Castaval's hand tightened on his stick; he smashed the handle of it, fist and all, into Annuweth's face. Annuweth's eyes went somewhere far away. He fell and Castaval sprang on him. The sword whistled down again and again, and the sound it made as it struck her brother was like a butcher's hammer landing on soft meat.

There were tears in Marilia's eyes. "Please," she sobbed. "Please stop..." She struggled to reach him, but Oberal had her tight in his arms. He was even bigger than Castaval, and he had her head in some kind of fighter's lock. The harder she struggled, the tighter his grip grew. No matter how she tried, she couldn't pull away.

Castaval's teeth were bared. He swung his sword like a wheat-cutter with a scythe. He wasn't going to stop, she thought, not now that his fury was at its peak. He was going to keep on hitting and hitting until her brother was dead, and it would be all her fault for leaving the pillow house, for thinking she could ever be anything other than One-Eye's painted lady.

"This is what we do to fish-eating sneaks in Tyrace," Castaval said, and he took a two-handed grip on the sword, raising it high above the back of Annuweth's head.

Marilia screamed.

"What is going on here?"

Castaval froze mid-blow. He, Oberal, and the girl turned as one to face the newcomer—a lieutenant, dressed in yoba-shell armor with a rust-red cape about his shoulders, his voice muffled, and his face hidden in the shadow of his helmet.

"These children were trying to climb over the wall," Castaval said imperiously, drawing himself up. "When we came here to spar, they attacked us, so I fought back."

Through eyes blurred with tears, Marilia stared at her brother. He was shivering on the ground, curled on his side at the base of the tree.

At least the shivering meant he was still alive.

"I know these children," the lieutenant said. "There's a small-lord who's been looking for them, my lord. They're wanted as witnesses to a crime. If I might speak with them…"

"They're yours," Castaval said, shrugging, tucking his practice sword back into his belt. "Come, Oberal. Let's not waste any more time on these painted bastard children." As quickly as it had come, his wrath was gone. In its place was a smooth mask of decorum. Apart from the sweat on his brow and the heaviness of his breathing, there was little sign of his recent exertions. He might have been calmly discussing the weather over a cup of jala juice.

Oberal released her and she rushed to Annuweth's side. "Oh, 'Weth," she sobbed. He gave a feeble groan.

Her rescuer approached, his brow furrowed as he looked down at her.

Marilia felt as if she was being torn in two. On the one hand, her relief was deeper and fuller than any she'd experienced before. Castaval was gone, and her brother was alive.

But on the other hand, she knew the voice of her rescuer. And now that the starlight had found the gap in his helmet, she could see his face. The despair the sight brought her was of equal measure with her relief.

The lieutenant who had been assigned to watch over Prefect Karthy was One-Eye.

CHAPTER SIX

One-Eye stared down at her. The deepening shadows cut swaths of darkness out of the rough scars on his face. She knelt by Annuweth's side, her limbs trembling. It felt as though a great weight were descending upon her…and she was crumbling beneath it the way the asahi nuts slowly cracked beneath the weight of Tyreesha's pestle. It seemed foolish to imagine that she ever could have run away. *This is my life,* she thought. *Now and tomorrow and for all the tomorrows after.*

"What are you doing here, girl?"

"We came to see the prefect Karthy, all right?" she spat the words at him, her fists clenched. "We came to ask him to take us away. But now it's all ruined."

One-Eye did not speak for a long while, and when he did his words were slow and measured. He sounded like a child, struggling to make sense of a strange piece of the adult world glimpsed for the first time. "You mean to say that you came all this way…that you would have run all the way to *Navessea*…just to get away from *me?*"

"Yes." Her eyes prickled with tears.

He looked at her with beetle-shell eyes, glittering dark in the twilight. "Stay where you are," he said. "I'll be back."

She had thought he might strike her. Instead, he turned on his heel and disappeared around the corner of the building, leaving her and Annuweth alone.

She took his hand. He had rolled onto his back and stared up at her

69

through tear-filled eyes. He was bleeding from his nose; the left side of his face was red and swollen, and his left eye was the most frightful sight of all—it was red with blood and swelling shut even as she watched.

"'Weth," she said brokenly. "I'm so sorry. We should never have run. It's my fault." She wished she had candles to light for him. The best she could do was whisper the prayer she'd heard Mother say a hundred times before. "Spirits of the ancestors, watch over us. Give us your strength. Give us your wisdom. Help us."

She waited for some sign of her father's spirit. All she heard was the night wind whispering through the trees. It was cold against her damp skin and she shivered. That couldn't be her father's spirit, she thought; he would have offered comfort, not chill.

"I'm going to kill him," Annuweth muttered through bloodied lips, spitting out half a tooth. "Someday I'm going to kill him. The giant, too."

She had her doubts, but she kept them to herself. "Sure you will," she said, squeezing his hand.

"And One-Eye. Curse them all."

"Curse them," Marilia agreed. She reached around until she found a stone. Her luck that it was a full moon tonight; it would give her curse strength.

She carved out a hollow beneath one of the tree's roots. She lay the sharp stone against her palm and cut. The pain shot through her, fierce and hot. Annuweth had no need to cut; his blood was already flowing freely down his face.

Marilia gritted her teeth and laid the stone beneath the tree, covering it with dirt. Having spent ten years in a pillow house, she had heard her share of curses, and though she was by no means an expert,

70

she did her best.

"Spirits of the dead, I call upon you for revenge," she said. "May Castaval's blood boil and turn to dust, may his heart burst in his chest, may his eyes turn to stone. And One-Eye. And the giant, too. May the dremmakin take them all. May they walk the black sands until the end of days."

She waited beside Annuweth. From inside the walls of the boarding house, she could hear the sounds of revelry: the shrill sound of women laughing, the low rumble of voices, the light, echoing notes of the rhovannon song. It seemed so un-real, so unfair that people could be laughing with joy only bare feet away while here in the night her heart was breaking.

There came the sound of footsteps. She rose to her feet, her heart pounding, to face One-Eye again.

One-Eye was not alone.

Prefect Karthy stood with him, the crown of his balding head blocking out the moon as he towered above them all. Marilia felt a lump form in her throat; she couldn't speak. Now she knew where One-Eye had gone: inside, to fetch the prefect.

His voice carried a strange accent that Marilia had never heard— almost Navessean, but with a slight bend to it. It was deep and low, like the purr of a cat mixed with the rumble of a gate opening.

"Do you know who I am, children?"

"Prefect Karthy," she whispered. Her eyes traveled from the green cloak about his shoulders to the two swords, one long, one short, bound to his waist. The swords would be of green aeder, she knew, as were all the swords of the knights of the Jade. A bright green like young river-grass pierced by sunlight. Of all the colors of aeder crystal, only gold was rarer and more costly.

71

His face twitched. "Karthy? Close enough, I suppose. I'm Karthtag-Kal Sandaros of Navessea. The real question is…who are you?" He stepped forward until he was close enough to touch. He knelt before them. His eyes studied her face—so intense was his stare that she longed to look away, to cover her face with her hair. She didn't dare. He studied Annuweth next, squinting as he examined his swollen face, his bloodied lips and nose.

"Please. My brother needs help, sir," Marilia said.

"Then let's get him inside."

A physick came with a stretcher and a couple of assistants. They bore Annuweth through a servants' gate set in the back of the boarding house and up a flight of stairs to the prefect's quarters.

The room was hung with silk drapes of green and silver, the colors of the Navessean flag; the quarters were much larger than any of the rooms in the silk hallway of the pillow house, littered with cushions, vellum panels dividing the bulk of the room from a raised dais at its end, beside the window, where the prefect slept.

They laid Annuweth down on the carpet and the physick bent to tend to him. He held a cup of night tea to her brother's lips; Annuweth's eyes clouded, then drifted shut. His labored breathing grew steady and even as sleep took hold.

"Two cracked ribs, a broken finger, a dislocated shoulder, and of course, bruises everywhere," the physick said. "But I can mend him."

Marilia let out a deep sigh of relief. As the fear left her much of her remaining strength went with it. She sagged against the wall.

"I take my leave," One-Eye said from the doorway. She turned to look at him and he met her gaze. His eyes sparkled curiously; she realized that he was almost crying. "Good luck, girl," was the last thing he said before he bowed his head and disappeared.

She stared at the empty space where he had been. He had betrayed her, had driven her to flee the pillow house and nearly been the cause of her brother's death. But he had also saved her and led her to the prefect. She didn't know what to think of him, and maybe would never know, but she did know that the curse she had set on him didn't sit well with her anymore. "Spirits of the dead," she whispered, "I take it back, if you're listening. Just the part about One-Eye. If that's all right."

She jumped as she felt a hand on her shoulder. "All right, girl. Time to talk."

Karthtag-Kal seated himself on one of the cushions and motioned for her to sit beside him. She did. Once again, she was keenly aware of the intensity of his gaze, of the way he was studying her—as a Horselord might study a fine steed in the marketplace. She felt the hairs on the back of her neck prickle. The physick was gone; they were alone now.

"The lieutenant says you're telling the truth," Karthtag-Kal said. "I can't see why he'd have any reason to lie. Yet I never knew Nelos to keep the company of painted ladies."

"He loved my mother," Marilia said. "I promise I'm not lying." The words came tumbling out of her—how Mother had died, how she and Annuweth had run from the pillow house to look for the prefect, how they had tried and failed to scale the boarding house's wall and been set upon by young Horselord Castaval and his friends. The one part she left out—without fully knowing why—was One-Eye and the kiss he had stolen from her in the rain-dark confines of Oba'al's room. "Nelos Dartimaos was your friend, wasn't he, sir?"

Karthtag-Kal answered her question with one of his own. "What do you know of Nelos Dartimaos?"

She told him all she knew; that her father was a knight, handsome

73

and tall, who had come to the city to seek help in a war. That a giant had killed him. That he had killed a dragon so that he might be named prefect, that he had come from an island filled with savages and giant crabs and women taller than men who ate horses and had fingernails made of aeder.

Karthtag-Kal's mouth twitched; it might almost have been a smile. "Well," he said slowly. "At least some of that is true. Enough, I think. What's your name, girl?"

"Marilia."

"And his?" Karthtag-Kal rose, moving to stand beside Annuweth's stretcher. The physick had finished tending to him and had set a red candle on the floor beside him to lend him strength. The smoke curled towards the ceiling, winding ribbon-like around Karthtag-Kal's craggy head.

"Annuweth."

"Annuweth?" Karthtag-Kal frowned, sounding a little disappointed. "A... distinctive name."

"It's a Navessean name," Marilia explained. "It was the name of a great warrior. They called him long-spear."

"Is that what your mother told you?"

She nodded, feeling suddenly uncertain.

"And who told her that?"

"One of the buyers."

"I see." Karthtag-Kal pursed his lips. "To tell you the truth, girl, Annuweth was a poet, not a warrior. Though the part about his nickname is true. He was called long-spear. Though it might not be for the reasons you imagine." He coughed. "Well. In any case, it's not the name that matters, it's the man that carries it. He's brave, to fight a Horselord's son. And loyal, to do it for you."

74

"He is brave, and loyal, and all the rest of it," Marilia promised.

"High praise. And completely unbiased, I assume, you being his sister."

She wasn't sure what to say to that, so she said nothing. In any case, he didn't really seem to expect an answer.

"Tell me; what were you hoping for, when you came looking for me here?" Karthtag-Kal's eyes were still fixed on her brother's face. It seemed he could not tear them away.

"That you could help us, sir." She took a deep breath. Now they had come to it, at last. "I don't want to be a painted lady," she said bluntly. "I was thinking maybe you might know someone, or could put us somewhere, in one of the gods' houses, maybe. Where the children go who have lost their parents. Or even with the rhovannon, maybe."

"I will do no such thing," Karthtag-Kal said, and her stomach plummeted.

But then, to her surprise, he laughed. At last he turned to look at her. Now he was smiling in earnest. "I'll tell you what I would like to do, girl. I'd like to take you with me to Navessea. I have no children of my own, and no wife. I'd like to be your father. You and your brother would bear my name—Sandaros. You would live as noble children in a villa near the Jade Keep. How does that sound to you?"

It sounded as though he was jesting. But he didn't look it; his eyes did not have the twinkling look that One-Eye's had when he was in a playful mood. They were as serious as any eyes she had ever seen.

Marilia felt herself begin to shake. She felt as though something that had been pressing on her shoulders had finally been lifted off and she was uncoiling, rearing up like a dragon rising from a cave and searching for the light. What she found there was a world she had never truly let herself believe was real.

Navessea, she thought, and it seemed to her she had slipped and fallen, without warning, into a beautiful dream. Her mother's words came back to her. *As far as the sands go, and farther.*

"*Yes*," she said, and just like that, her world changed forever.

The following day, she and Annuweth rested in the cool confines of Karthtag-Kal's quarters while the prefect rode to the Tower to speak with the king.

The day after, Livenneth—the emperor's brother-by-marriage and ambassador, with whom Karthtag-Kal had traveled to the city—rented them a fine carriage. One of Karthtag-Kal's green-clad knights helped Annuweth limp his way up the steps. Her brother looked a terrible mess; his left eye had swollen shut, and his face was puffier than one of the cloud breads Tyreesha sometimes brought back from the market. His arm was in a sling and his hand in a splint. Still, as he took his seat next to her, he smiled. It was a smile of triumph. *Us against the world*, he had said to her that night as they lay on their cots in Tyreesha's room, and it seemed as though maybe they had won.

Side-by-side with the victory came the ache of loss—the knowledge that she would never again swim the River Tyr with Saleema, or cross swords with Nyreese, or face Damar across a cup of dice. Those days were over. She felt strangely still inside, as if she were a candle someone had forgotten to light. As if her body had forgotten how to feel. The sorrow of leaving their friends clashed with the joy of escape, and the two canceled each other out.

They made their way back through the city to Oba'al's Hill. Karthtag-Kal went inside first and exchanged a few words with the seller. Marilia didn't know what he said, but when he returned to the

76

carriage, he had a signed paper in his hand, and he told them that Oba'al no longer had any claim on them.

He helped Annuweth inside; it took a while, each step measured and painful. There, in the common room, their friends were waiting for them.

When they told Saleema she simply stared. Marilia hugged her.

When they told Damar all he said was "that's fine, that's all right, then." He gave them each a stiff hug; a few seconds later he burst out crying, threw his arms around them, and then ran from the room. There were tears in Marilia's eyes, too. They traced their way gently down her cheeks and fell soundlessly to the floor.

Tyreesha embraced them both and said "gods keep you, children."

As for Nyreese, she took Marilia's hand and squeezed it. "I knew you'd make it," she said.

As for possessions, she and Annuweth had few enough. A wicker doll, a few toy knights, Marilia's river-stones, a couple of dice, and their clothes. Karthtag-Kal insisted they leave their sticks behind; they'd have proper wooden swords when they arrived in Navessea.

They bundled all the rest into a pack that Karthtag-Kal had brought and followed the prefect out the door.

It turned out that she and Annuweth had reached the boarding house just in time; the negotiations with the king were over, and it was time for Karthtag-Kal and his companions to leave Tyracium.

Livenneth and his green-armored knights met them atop Oba'al's Hill; two of the knights led an old yoba for Annuweth. Livenneth himself helped her brother up onto the beast's back. They made their way down into the city, towards the river-gate, where a ship would be waiting to carry them to the sea, and their new home.

The sharp sunlight stung Marilia's eyes. The day was cloudless, the sky a bright blue field as if the world had been ripped open. She stared up at it and a wave of dizziness passed through her.

There were times that she had thought Annuweth a little silly, clinging to dreams of a father that they would never see, of a land they would never reach. But now she saw he had been right; and not just for himself—for both of them. She was her father's daughter, too, not just her mother's. It was a glorious realization, and beneath the fresh pain of parting from her friends, her heart sang with it.

The only question was whether they could trust Karthtag-Kal. She stared up at his grizzled head and felt a tremor of unease. He seemed gentle and kind—certainly better than Oba'al—but One-Eye had seemed that way, too. She decided the best thing was to keep to the background. Most of his attention seemed to be on Annuweth for the moment, and she let it stay that way. She let her brother do the talking, following along in silence, taking her measure of the man who had proclaimed himself their new father.

Ahead of them walked two knights of the Jade and four men from the Tower that the one-eyed king had sent to escort the Navessean party to the docks. With Karthtag-Kal and the two men following at the rear, that made nine men in armor, plus Livenneth—a large number. Yet the nervous way they all kept glancing around made her wonder if something wasn't quite right. When she asked about it, Livenneth only waved a hand and said that they'd be out of the city soon enough, not to worry. But the way he said it made her think that maybe he was the worried one. She recalled what Castaval had said— *I hope there's an uprising*—and her unease deepened.

The way ahead grew increasingly crowded. The knights from the

Tower that walked ahead of Karthtag-Kal had to tug at people's shoulders, elbowing a path forward. In the distance, Marilia could see the shine of the River Tyr, and to the left, up a side street—the very one where she and Annuweth had fled two days before—a troop of the city watch was approaching: ten more men in armor.

Atop a pulpit that had been erected by the riverside market, a man was yelling, his arms waving. He was wearing the dark red-brown robes of a Horse Priest. "The pleas of our northern brothers have been forgotten! In Dane they have shed the blood of the chosen. Their governor throws the faithful into his arena, he feeds them to his monstrous beasts. And what does our king do? I will tell you; the false king sits in his tower and shuts his eyes—or should I say *eye*—to the cause of rightness. For that, he shall walk the black sands. For so it is written, only the true of heart will sit in the House of White Sands! Only the true!"

"Only the true!" the crowd echoed. Some of the townsfolk they passed turned and gave them black stares.

"Oh, by the gods…" Livenneth muttered. "This can't be good."

Karthtag-Kal's narrow, dark eyes became even narrower and darker. "Hurry along," he said.

"And to those who take up the cause of the chosen, the sword of the righteous against the bloated dragon of lies, how great shall their reward be?" the Horse Priest yelled.

"What's wrong?" Annuweth asked.

"They are unhappy about the treaty Karthtag-Kal and I negotiated," Livenneth said tensely. "Your one-eyed king was thinking about invading Dane, or at the very least seizing all Danish ships and goods in his kingdom. I convinced him not to. The problem is, most Tyracians hate Dane almost as much as they hate good food."

79

Marilia could see that the crowd was growing more and more restless by the second. The men of the city watch were trying to calm them, but their presence seemed only to be making the people angrier.

"Keep calm, my friend," Karthtag-Kal said. "We are nearly to the docks."

But the road ahead had closed. There were too many people. The knights walking ahead became more insistent, pulling and shoving roughly. "Make way! Make way in the name of the king!"

Marilia couldn't see the River Gate through all the people. The sea was closing around them, wave upon wave of human flesh, clinging and soft, pink and hideous. *Too close! S*he wanted to lash out, to push them all away from her. Sweat beaded on her palms.

"See!" the Horse Priest cried, close to tears. "See as they come, the servants of the dragon, to silence the voice of our god, the protector of Tyrace! See the dragon's men—there they are! They walk among you now!" Marilia's stomach fell away as he pointed right at them. "The Governor of Dane persecutes our people, he murders them, he blames them for the misfortunes caused by his own wickedness. Every time the earth shakes, every time the sand people send a plague, what does he do? He spills the blood of our brothers!"

"Murderer!" someone in the crowd screamed, in a voice so impassioned it bordered on ecstasy.

"And *still* our king makes pacts with that governor's master—the emperor of Navessea! He lets the emperor's men walk our streets!"

Several men of the city watch were fighting to ascend the pulpit. One of them managed to lay a hand on the Horse Priest's shoulder, dragging him backwards off his perch. He continued to shout as he disappeared into the crowd.

"Out of the way!" One of the king's men growled, and he shoved a man so hard that he fell. A woman came up behind, reaching for the fallen man—maybe he was her husband, or her brother. The guard reacted on instinct; his elbow shot back, catching her in the nose, and she fell too, spitting blood. There were cries of outrage. "Bastards!" the woman shrieked. "You ghoul-spawned bastards!"

"A plague on Tyrace," Livenneth muttered. "Wish I had bothered to wear armor."

The townspeople were too close. The men of the Order, the king's men, Karthtag-Kal, she and Annuweth on his mount—all of them were being slowly crushed together. She thought briefly of the asahi nuts in Tyreesha's kitchens, ground to powder between pestle and table.

She couldn't see the Horse Priest anymore. Couldn't hear his voice over the yells around her. It was like drowning.

"Annuweth!" she gasped, reaching for his hand.

"By the gods!" one of the men of the Order yelled. "Get BACK!"

"Bastards!" Someone yelled. "Fish-eating, heretic bastards."

"Kill the heretics!" someone else took up the cry.

"For Dane!"

And like a great wave cresting, the crowd roared and surged forward. One of the king's guards stumbled and fell. He knocked into Marilia. Annuweth's hand was torn from hers.

No! She thought. *Not now! It's not* fair!

Some of the townsfolk were holding weapons—clubs of wood with jutting nails, butcher's knives, stones. She saw a man, his arm raised back to throw, his fingers hooked like claws around a big yellow brick. It looked like he was aiming at *her.*

He wouldn't, she thought. But he did.

The brick seemed to sail through water, slow as a dream. It whipped right past her. As one of the king's men turned it struck him right in the

81

face. Teeth and droplets of blood spattered Marilia's arm. The guard fell groaning, and one of the towns-people snatched up his sword. "Get them! Get them!" he screamed, waving it over his head.

A man with a heavy plank came at Karthtag-Kal, face locked in a vicious snarl.

With a sound like a snake moving through the sand, Karthtag-Kal drew his sword. Its bright arc cut across the chest of his attacker. The aeder blade opened him from right hip to left shoulder and tore the plank of wood right in half.

The way Karthtag-Kal did it, it looked easy, fluid, almost elegant. It reminded Marilia of the way Tyreesha cut yams for her stew, each movement of her wrist practiced, so that she could do it even without looking. The Tyracian fell, and his insides slid out of him.

People screamed and drew back and for a moment the way ahead was clear. Karthtag-Kal forced his way into the breach. A brick bounced off his armored chest. A man with a long knife lunged at him—Karthtag-Kal twisted away, sword flashing down. The man screamed, clutching his severed arm. For a second his agonized face swam before Marilia—then he was swallowed by the crowd.

"To the gate!" Karthtag-Kal yelled. "Everyone, to the gate!" Marilia stumbled, tripped on something. She fell. A severed hand was just a hair's breadth from her face. A foot struck it and it went spinning out of sight, leaving a trail of blood behind.

Feet stamped and shuffled all around her. One caught her in the side and she doubled over; another slammed into her head, and lights flashed before her eyes.

The buzzing of the crowd all around her sounded like a swarm of flies. As another foot came down on her head, she heard an answering buzz inside her own skull. She screamed.

She saw her future, her life, teeter on the edge of a cliff. All her struggles and fears and final victory in reaching Karthtag-Kal, erased in a single moment's awful tumble. To have come so far only for it to end like this—swallowed by the rage of a mob with the gate within sight.

A foot found her ribs. Another hit her in the back. She thought she understood a measure of the pain Annuweth must have felt, huddled on the ground beneath the blows of Castaval's wooden sword.

Then an armored hand caught her by the wrist, pulling her to her feet. It was Karthtag-Kal.

Their eyes met. The relief she saw on his face might not have matched her own, but it was close. "On your feet, girl," he said, his voice choked. He sounded shaken.

She felt as though something changed between them in those few brief seconds. But she didn't have time to ponder it. A man ran at Karthtag-Kal from behind, a sword—taken from one of the fallen Tyracian guards—held aloft in his hands.

"Look out!" she screamed, pointing over his shoulder.

Karthtag-Kal whirled. He caught the man by the wrist, stopping the sword's descent. The prefect's other hand, holding the hilt of his sword, smashed the Tyracian in the face. His nose flattened, sinking into his cheeks. He fell.

"Come!" Karthtag-Kal yelled. "Stay close!"

They stumbled together towards the gate, where men of the city watch were assembling in lines, spears lowered towards the crowd. Marilia saw a man at the end of one of those spears, wriggling like a fish, the hole in his belly tearing wider and wider.

"It's the emperor's ambassador!" one of the city watch yelled. "Let him pass! Let them pass! Hold back the others!"

The guards' lines opened to receive them. They passed through, numb, battered, with the screams of the crowd hammering at their ears.

She felt herself shaking with shock. Ahead the city gates creaked open. She glanced back, caught a glimpse of the guards jabbing at the crowd, which was slowly retreating.

Livenneth was wiping blood from his face and the edge of his sword. "Oh, gods, those bastards..." He clenched his teeth. "I hate this city."

Karthtag-Kal put a hand on his shoulder. "Then let us leave it, my friend."

As Livenneth made for the ship, Karthtag-Kal knelt in front of Marilia. "Are you all right?" he asked.

She nodded.

He put his arm around her. For a moment she flinched; the smell of blood was thick on him, and his armor was rough and hard. But he spoke gently, his voice a soft rumble near her ear. "I won't let them hurt you," he said. "You are the daughter of Nelos Dartimaos...*my* daughter. I promise, I will never let them hurt you."

CHAPTER SEVEN

The wind came from the west. It was dry and warm like a blanket of fine sand.

The Navessean ship sped away from Tyrace. The sail cracked in the wind. The Tower of Tyrace shrank behind them until it was the size of a toy.

The rocking of the ship proved too much for Marilia; she spent much of her time at the rail, hunched over, trying not to be sick. It took a lot of getting used to—the way the wood would move back and forth under your feet, the way the sky and earth would tilt ever so slightly. *The world is moving. Everything is in motion, and we most of all.*

The ship was called the Lady Narinia. It had been named for the emperor's wife. It was a big galley, with four rows of oars, a long deck with a big cabin at the stern. The cabin was divided into two sections; in the first, Karthtag-Kal, the children, and the ambassador slept. With memories of Tyreesha's kitchen still fresh in her mind, Marilia was quite pleased to now be sleeping in the best part of the ship.

Or, at least, she would have been, if not for the nightmares.

For all the brightness of the days, at night, Marilia's dreams were dark. She found herself back in the pillow house, the rain pounding outside the window, the streets outside turned to a river by a storm that seemed as though it would never end. A woman stood in the shadows of the room, head bowed—Mother. Marilia reached for her and the swinging red lantern cast its light upon Mother's face. Where her eyes should have been were only two smoking holes. The skin around those

85

holes was crumbling gray ash. Marilia tried to leave, stumbling to the doorway, but she tripped and fell, thrashing in a pool of silk ribbons that clawed at her like fingers.

"Sahiyya," Mother crooned, stroking Marilia's hair as she slipped farther and farther into the silk; it was thick and soft as the inside of a beast's mouth. "My northern flower. You're my lady. Only mine."

Marilia sprang awake, her skin clammy and her heart racing.

The sound of the tide lapping against the hull outside sounded like rain rolling down a roof, like water cascading down a hillside. It reminded her of Oba'al's room. The galley's cabin felt suddenly too small and the air too stale and heavy in her lungs. She pulled back the blanket that covered her and stepped out onto the deck.

They had anchored off the shore; the ship bobbed with the river's current. A single lookout sat by the prow, stretching his shoulders and looking out over the surrounding hills. He glanced her way, briefly, then gave her a shrug and a nod and turned his gaze back to the river, whistling a slow tune to himself.

She took a deep breath. The night wind helped to still the heaving of her guts.

"Did you have a bad dream?"

She turned to find Annuweth limping onto the deck behind her. She nodded.

"I have them too," he said. "Sometimes I dream I'm falling. Sometimes I dream about what happened with Castaval. What was yours about?"

"About the pillow house," she answered. "And Mother."

He took her hand and they made their way back into the cabin. They lay side by side on their cots, their hands touching. All around them the ship creaked and groaned. The air tasted of old wood and dried salt.

"It sounds hungry," Annuweth said. "Like a dragon's belly rumbling."

"I suppose so," Marilia said. The sound didn't seem quite so frightening with Annuweth there to listen to it with her.

"We're going to be together," Annuweth said. "Together in Navessea. They're all gone, all the rest of them. But it's still us. Just like we said."

"Us against the world," she said softly, remembering the words he had spoken to her back in Tyreesha's room. Bit by bit, her fear slipped away.

They fell asleep like that, hands joined, and did not wake again until the morning.

Slowly, hour by hour, the sickness in Marilia's stomach subsided. By the afternoon of their second day upon the river, she felt well enough to begin to enjoy the journey. It was the first time she'd been outside of Tyracium's walls (not counting that brief excursion to throw Mother's ashes in the river), and what she discovered was that the world outside of Tyracium was *beautiful.*

On either side of the river, hills of yellow grass stretched away into the distance, where the mountains of the Neck of Dane bit at the sky like a hound leaping for a treat. Herds of yoba roamed the grass, the hunched shells of the insects each the size of one of the galley's row-boats. Their long legs pawed the earth and their deep cries echoed out across the water.

Annuweth joined her and they passed the time by assigning stories to each place they passed, bringing a face to the tales of their childhood. There, that spire of rock, was where the First King had fled to escape the sand people; there, atop its peak, Sothia the Artificer had sent him aid in the form of a great red horse, to carry him over the sands. There was the grove of weeping trees where Almaria the Blessed had laid Neravos to rest and had been so stricken with grief that she'd nearly lain down to die beside him, only for the power in her tears to restore him to life. And there, in the distance, to the north, an even greater mountain that might have been the fire mountain their father had entered to kill the dragon and make himself prefect.

"Are you starting to feel better, boy?" Karthtag-Kal's voice from close behind made them jump.

"Yes, sir," Annuweth said.

"Good. You have a strong constitution, it seems. Like your father."

"Can you tell us about him?" Annuweth asked. "Mother told us some things, but not everything. Did you know him well?"

"I would say so." Karthtag-Kal stared out past the rail of the galley, to where the river-water flashed like liquid aeder. "Where to begin? I suppose I can tell you how we met. I come from a land called Cardath. It's a place far to the north, beyond the Sea of the Lost. I was once a warlord of that land; I spent my days training men and leading them against our old enemy, Thyre. It was a time so long ago that I can scarcely remember it. Well; at that time there were three great clans in Cardath. The other two allied against mine and cast us down. I found myself in exile, with most of my family dead. I fled to Navessea, where I did the only thing a man like me could do—skilled with a sword but of foreign blood and hardly any wealth to my name. I joined the Order of Jade. In the Order, I had heard, it did not matter so much who a man's father was, or where he came from. All that mattered was whether you could fight and serve with honor. Honor and swordsmanship were the two things left to me at that point."

"It was hard at first. I could barely speak the tongue of Navessea, and the promise of the Order did not quite live up to the reality. I soon learned that such things never do. There were men from old, proud Navessean families in the Order, and they mocked me behind my back. But I persevered, and eventually I caught the eye of the prefect. He saw that for all my difficulties with the Navessean tongue, for all my…strangeness…I was not a fool, as others thought me; I had experience leading men, brief though it was. He made me a captain of my own company. Still, though I admired the prefect for that, I did not really *know* him—not yet. It was Kanadrak that truly brought us together."

"Who is Kanadrak?" Marilia asked.

"A warlord from the plains of the northlands who succeeded in uniting the northern tribes and cities under one rule. With the north in his hand, he turned his eyes upon the greatest prize of all, the land everyone said could not be conquered—Navessea."

"Kanadrak…was he a big man?" Annuweth asked.

"Quite the opposite," Karthtag-Kal said. "He was small. But he was fast. One of the best fighters I have ever known. Why do you ask, boy?"

"I thought…I thought maybe he was the giant," Annuweth said. "The one who killed father."

"It was no giant that killed Nelos Dartimaos," Karthtag-Kal said. "There are no giants, at least none I have seen. He was just a man…Sethyron Andreas. The Graver, they call him."

Marilia gave a start. *The same man who put out the king's eye*, she thought, remembering what One-Eye had told her.

"He fights for our side, now." A muscle in Karthtag-Kal's right cheek spasmed; there was a cold bitterness in his eyes. "He fought for Kanadrak and bought himself a gold aeder sword with the money he won burning Navessean towns. Eventually, our emperor convinced him to turn on Kanadrak, and for that act of betrayal—for his cowardice— he was made a lord of Navessea." He shook his head. "But that is not the story I was going to tell. I was telling the story of Kanadrak. Do you want to hear it?"

Both twins nodded at the same time.

"Kanadrak's army attacked at a time when Navessea was very weak. Her emperor was a coward who cared more for fine dining and parties than he did for war. Those were dark days; some people whispered that Kanadrak was the king of the dremmakin—the ghouls— come to take back the world they had lost. He did very well at first. He destroyed the city of Korennis. He hoped to use that city as a staging point to attack the island of Svartennos, the birth-place of your father. The emperor sent the Order of Jade to help protect the people of the island. It was your father who led the Order—and I was not far from his side."

"During the first battle, your father was knocked from his horse. It seemed that he would be lost. But I and a few others managed to fight our way to his side. We forced back the hordes until your father revived and rallied our forces to victory. I myself slew one of Kanadrak's greatest chieftains with my bare hands, though his spear pierced me." Karthtag-Kal rubbed at his shoulder. His eyes were distant; he did not seem to be aware of the movement. "Battles are not entirely what the songs would make them, you know; they are bloody, and painful, and brutal. But that one—at the end, when the sun came out over the fields of blue flowers and Nelos and I stood watching the enemy scatter like ants across the hills—it was almost like a song. We saved Svartennos

90

together. And afterwards, in recognition for what I had done, he made me lieutenant of the Order—master of a thousand men. And later, he did even more than that. He passed my name to the emperor of Navessea. He recommended me as his successor. That emperor didn't listen—he chose another man—but when he was replaced and it came time for the next one to choose a prefect…he remembered Nelos' advice, and followed it. Nelos Dartimaos is the only reason I—a northern barbarian—ever became Prefect of the Order of Jade."

"What was he like?" Annuweth asked eagerly. "Father, I mean?"

"Not now, boy," Karthtag-Kal said. He looked suddenly weary, as if the story, the remembering, had taken a toll on him. "Another time." He left them there, staring out at the river and the sky, dreaming of great battles and their father's heroic charge.

The shore began to change. The dunes disappeared. The ground began slowly to rise, as if the whole earth were a quilt that some giant hand in the sky was pulling upward from one end. There were hills taller than Marilia had ever seen, covered in trees, bushes and yellow grass. The peak she had thought so impressive from a distance—the one Marilia had imagined was the place where their father had battled the dragon—she realized was just one of many, and not even the grandest of the many.

Soon they were out on the open water. The sea revealed itself, and for several seconds Marilia forgot to breathe.

It was as endless as the sands to the south-east of Tyracium's walls. It was nothing like the muddy yellow-brown of the River Tyr; this water was deep blue shot with green, dashed here and there with specks of white. It was like a thing alive, waves rising out of nothing and then ceasing to be in an instant. She felt herself trembling; she backed far from the railing. Even Annuweth, who seemed to enjoy the galley, huddled near the center of the deck, cowed by the sheer immensity of all that water.

"Deeper than five Towers stacked on top of each other," Livenneth remarked, grinning a little when he saw Annuweth's eyes widen even further.

"What's down there?" Annuweth asked. Livenneth chuckled.

"Krakens. Razorfish. The castle of the dremmakin. What the low-born call ghouls." He seemed to take a perverse delight in being as frightening as possible.

"I thought the ghouls...the dremmakin...lived to the east," Marilia said. "In the black sands."

"No doubt they have many homes," Livenneth said. "The Book of the Gods says that they inhabit the dark places of the earth, does it not?"

Marilia nodded; she remembered hearing a Horse Priest say such a thing during a festival.

"Well, the Tyracians live near the desert, and they believe the dremmakin come from the barren lands beyond the River Tyr. The Navesseans live near the sea, and they believe the dremmakin live down there, that their king, Mollagora, has a chariot drawn by razorfish with which he hunts the souls of the damned for sport. Maybe both are true. When the gods and Neravos banished the dremmakin for their crimes, who says they chose only one prison? Maybe their homes are all places that men fear." He frowned. "Did your mother teach you of the gods?"

"A little," Marilia said.

"A little won't do," Karthtag-Kal said, coming over to join them. "Not where we're going."

That was the beginning of their lessons in the gods of Navessea.

One of the men traveling with Karthtag-Kal was his steward, Stellos. Stellos had once been one of the Order's warriors, but a deep wound to his leg had left him with a permanent limp. Now he served the prefect; he, Karthtag-Kal informed them, would also serve as their teacher, at least until they reached their new home, and another could be found.

The steward had an earnest face, the sort one might expect to find on a kindly toy-maker, and as a result, every word he spoke seemed true and right. Marilia and Annuweth listened intently. They had never heard the god-stories as Stellos told them. His voice was like the soothing sound of the waves rolling past the galley's hull.

He spoke to them of how Viveos the Lantern Bearer had created the earth out of boredom; he'd wanted there to be something for himself and the other gods to marvel at, a creation of beauty that would reflect the beauty of his own home in the clouds. He carved the rivers and formed the mountains with his power the way a potter might form a clay pot with his hands. With his tears he made the seas and with the heat of his breath the desert sands.

But the world, beautiful as it was, was not yet complete. Not until Sothia, the Lady of Four Arms, the great craftswoman of the gods, created beasts to walk it and fish to swim in its seas. To tend the earth, she created the dremmakin, giving them the gift of wisdom, the power of speech and understanding that set them above the beasts.

But as time went on, the dremmakin grew lazy and forgot their duty. They stopped making offerings to the gods. They built a tower to reach the halls of white sand and they stole the greatest secret of the gods— the creation of life. They made mankind to be their slaves.

The gods saw what the dremmakin had done, and their hearts filled with wrath. Almaria, sister of Viveos, descended to earth, where, in secret, she gave knowledge to Neravos, a human slave, and filled his

93

heart with anger. He rose up against the dremmakin, and, after a fierce war, he defeated them and banished them.

"They tell those stories in both Tyrace and Navessea," Stellos said. "Both lands were once part of the same great empire, and so both share the same gods. But here's the difference between them, the reason behind all that hate you saw on your way to the docks. In Navessea, the gods are the gods and the emperors are emperors. That is how it is supposed to be. In Tyrace, though, they believe their first king was chosen by the gods, that he was guided to Tyrace on the back of a great red horse." He snorted, as if to show how likely that was. "They believe that when he died, he actually joined the other gods, and now he's Tyrace's special protector. And does that not seem like arrogance, to make offerings to one's own dead king, to believe there is a god for one people and one people alone?"

Annuweth frowned. "Mother always said the Horse God watched over us."

"Did she? Well, my boy, the Horse God belongs to Tyrace. It's a Navessean galley taking you home. It's a Navessean father who's given you the chance to become a knight or something even greater. Seems you'd do best to put your faith in Navessea."

Marilia chewed her lip as she pondered that. Stellos was right, of course. The Horse God would have left her back in One-Eye's hands. He would have been content to watch her live her days as a painted lady, stained with her mother's curse, hardly ever to leave the walls of her home, never to see the mountains or the sea.

Goodbye, Horse God, she thought. *You had your chance.*

She was a Navessean girl now.

The clouds returned as they made their way to Surennis, a city on Navessea's eastern coast. There they found a couple of yoba to carry them north-west. Wooden platforms, covered to keep off the sun, had been built atop the giant insects' backs, and it was there that Marilia and Annuweth sat, gazing out at the world. Perhaps the gods had a sense of suspense, because they spread a thick blanket of mist across the ground, hiding the great plains of Navessea from sight. The new world revealed itself piecemeal, one tree, one river, one farmer's hut at a time.

At first Marilia was frightened—the swaying of the yoba beneath her was almost worse than the rocking of the ship's deck—but as they moved on into the mist, her fears lifted, replaced by excitement. Ulvannis lay ahead.

At last, after several days of travel, the mist pulled back, and Navessea was revealed in all its glory. On either side fields of yellow grass whispered promises, and tall, narrow trees bent in the wind. In the distance mountains clawed the bellies of the clouds. Some of the mountains were so tall that ribbons of white cloud wrapped around their upper reaches like habithra sashes.

"There," Karthtag-Kal said, tapping her shoulder. "See?"

Tall stone walls lay flat across the horizon as far as they could see, cutting off the plain as if a giant knife had descended from the sky and sliced the world in half. Pennants showing the imperial dragon hung from the walls, where the helmets of the knights of the Jade glittered in misty half-light.

"Ulvannis," she whispered. The capitol city of Navessea.

She reached for Annuweth's hand, felt his palm hot and sweaty against her own.

They had come home.

CHAPTER EIGHT

Not for nothing was Ulvannis called the greatest city in the empire. Its stone walls were half again as tall as those of Tyracium and thicker than any Marilia would have believed possible. Since their construction three hundred years ago, Stellos informed her, they had never been breached.

Karthtag-Kal led them through the north-western gate, through a market teeming with life (it made even the river market in Tyracium look shabby by comparison), to a beautiful street flanked by cherry-blossom trees. She learned the place was called White Street, for the color of the well-swept tiles they rode over, and that the walled homes they passed on either side were the villas of the nobles of Navessea's great houses. Marilia's eyes widened at that; they widened still more when they came to the end of the street, into a huge courtyard rimmed in towering pine trees.

There the emperor of Navessea lived inside the Jade Keep, a vast fortress of red-white stone, a maze of arches and columns that may have lacked the height of the Tower of Tyrace, but made up for it with breadth and simple, overwhelming immensity.

Below and to one side of the Jade Keep was the barracks of the Order of Jade, a compound enclosed within a small wall of its own. Inside that wall was a field of trampled earth where the men of the Order trained, the long, squat limestone buildings where they slept and ate, the stables where they kept their horses and the armory where their weapons were stored.

At the back of the compound, a steep stone staircase led up to a building perched high above the rest of the complex: the villa where the prefect and his family had their home.

There were a hundred steps in all, Stellos informed Marilia as they approached.

"So many," she breathed.

"It's said that when the prefect can no longer make the climb, he knows it's time to step down and let another take his place. I'd guess Karthtag-Kal has a good many years left before that happens."

Marilia's heart quickened as she looked up at it. It wasn't all that large (in fact, Oba'al's pillow house was probably larger) but it had a feeling of importance about it that the pillow house did not. *Height means distinguished*, she thought as she made her way up the steps, remembering Oba'al's words. By the time she reached the top, she was breathing hard. *Very distinguished.*

She paused, staring at the entrance to Karthtag-Kal's home. The doorway was framed with an intricate, flowing writing, the same that she had noticed over the entrance-ways of the other homes they had passed on their way through the city. She pointed. "What is that?"

"Water-script," Karthtag-Kal said as he pulled open the door. Unlike the doors in Tyrace, these slid open sideways. "From the Book of the Gods. To keep the dremmakin away. Legend has it that they crawl from the sea at night and try to infest men in their sleep, though I must admit I've never seen one." He winked.

They stepped inside the villa. The silence stung Marilia's ears. She slipped off her sandals and felt the smooth, cool tiles of the floor against her toes.

She was standing inside a long hall. It was mostly empty, save for a few pillars of stone that stretched upwards, joining together to form three big arches that supported the ceiling. Above those arches, the roof was a distant shadow. Misty light entered through the doorway and the windows on either side. Silk drapes hung from the ceiling, but these were different from the ones at the pillow house. Where those had been bright, vibrant red, these were white, with the same kind of black, flowing script that had framed the doorway.

Karthtag-Kal showed them their bedrooms first. Servants were still at work in Marilia's room, laying chests upon the floor, filling wardrobes with dresses. The dresses she could see through the open drawers were a lady's clothes, brightly patterned, with silk that glimmered like dragon skin. That alone would have been enough to leave her speechless. But the fact that there were *servants* hanging them there made her head spin, and she put a hand on the wall to steady herself, struck by the feeling that this was all a dream, that if she didn't hold on, she might break free of the floor and float away.

Though she'd known that leaving her old life behind meant embracing the noble, Navessean part of herself, she hadn't really *felt* it until now. In the pillow house, the women bought their own clothes; they washed and mended them themselves. Here, in Karthtag-Kal's villa, there were servants that Karthtag-Kal could command by the simple virtue of the gold the emperor paid him. Servants that, one day, when she was older, she might command, too.

"You'll want to change for dinner, I expect," Karthtag-Kal said. He smiled. "You'll have no more need of those Tyracian rags. I'll have them burned, and…"

"No," Marilia blurted quickly, and Karthtag-Kal paused.

"No?"

She had brought almost nothing with her from Tyrace. The thought of giving up this last piece of her mother's land was too much to bear.

Nervously, she looked up at Karthtag-Kal. "I was wondering if I could keep them? Please? I'll put them somewhere out of sight, in the bottom drawer. I won't wear them, I promise."

He looked puzzled. But to her relief, he shrugged. "All right, girl. As you wish."

He showed them the shrine—a pit of white sand ringed with candles and statuettes in the form of the gods—and the garden—which overlooked a steep drop into a swift-flowing stream that wrapped around the northern side of the villa

Finally, he took them to the armory. As they entered it, Annuweth gasped.

Standing at the far end of the room was a man in full armor, helmet lowered, two dark eyes glaring angrily at them out of the polished helmet.

Marilia took a quick step back.

No, she realized; the armor was empty, a suit of yoba-shell plates propped up on a wooden post.

"This was your father's armor," said Karthtag-Kal. "He left it to me, along with his sword, since he had no true-born sons."

Marilia felt the hairs along her arms prickle at the sight of it. Annuweth spoke in a shaky voice. There was an eagerness on his face that was almost a physical force. "Can I touch it?"

Karthtag-Kal nodded.

Slowly, Annuweth stepped up to the armor of Nelos Dartimaos. Marilia followed just behind. The armor was beautiful; whoever had done the paint had been a master of his craft. It had been done the same way as Karthtag-Kal's—a dark green that was almost black around the edges, but lighter in the center—like the color of the grass she'd seen growing along the side of the river near Surennis. It looked almost as if it was lit from within; as if it was made of the same green aeder as Karthtag-Kal's sword.

Marilia laid her palm against the smooth breastplate, right where her father's heart would have been. She almost imagined she could feel life beneath the cold, smooth shell.

"Nelos has an older sister," Karthtag-Kal said. "On Svartennos, the elder child inherits the land, regardless of whether that child is a boy or a girl...so his sister got the land. But Nelos' spirit, as well as his armor and sword...that passed to me, and someday, it will be yours, boy."

On the wall above the armor was that same sword, sheathed in black wood. Almost unconsciously, Annuweth reached up to touch it.

Karthtag-Kal chuckled and took him by the wrist, gently pulling his hand away. "Not yet. Come."

As they made their way to the door, Karthtag-Kal paused for a moment, his gaze lingering on the armor. His eyes seemed to shine with the same light as the polished plates; for a moment she imagined there were tears in them. Then he blinked, turned away, and ushered them out of the room.

Sleep did not come easily that night. The shadows seemed to press in upon her; in the moonlight, their edges were jagged like knives, like the grinning teeth of silvakim.

She knew she was safe; the best knights of Navessea were right outside, their best warrior, the prefect himself, only a few rooms away. There was nowhere in the world safer. Yet she missed Annuweth. She had never slept without him by her side.

She threw off her covers and went in search of him, stumbling blindly through the darkened halls of the villa, feeling her way along the walls. She paused when she caught sight of a flickering candle. Someone was in the armory.

It was Karthtag-Kal. He was dressed in nothing but a loincloth. The scarred muscles of his back were slick with sweat; a wooden sparring sword lay on the ground beside him. He was standing before the armor of Nelos Dartimaos. As she watched, he raised one palm and laid it against Dartimaos' cheek—or, at least, the side of Dartimaos' helmet. He stood there for a long while.

"I'm sorry I could not save you," she heard him whisper. "But the gods have given me a chance. I can do this. I was meant to do this, I think."

Marilia eased back. But he must have heard her, because he turned. "Marilia. You should be abed."

"I'm sorry. I was frightened. I was wondering..." she took a deep breath. "I was wondering if I could sleep in Annuweth's room."

"Well, it's proper for young ladies and knights to have their own bedrooms," Karthtag-Kal said, and she felt her heart sink. He must have seen the dismay on her face, for his own softened. "But it's your first night in a strange place...I think, at least for a few nights, that might be best."

He walked with her towards Annuweth's room.

"What will happen to us now?" she asked him as they went.

"In five months, the Solstice Festival will take place. The emperor, the senators, the great magistrates and councilors and the finest ladies and knights of Navessea will gather here at the Jade Keep. I want you to be there, too. I want to introduce you to the nobles of the empire. And to the emperor."

"The emperor?" She felt a sudden pressure in the pit of her chest. *I can't meet an emperor*, she thought. *I'm only Marilia, the painted lady's daughter.* "I...I don't think I'm ready. I'm not a lady. I'm just..." She trailed off, unable to find the words.

"Just?" He laughed. "You are *just* the daughter of a prefect and I think you will surprise yourself."

He found a cot and a blanket for her and laid them on the floor of Annuweth's room. He gave her a brief touch on the back, whispered in her ear, and slipped away into the night. "Get some rest. Your training begins tomorrow."

She lay down and pulled the blankets up to her neck. As she turned her head sideways, she saw the pale shine of Annuweth's eyes, open in the dark. "I couldn't fall asleep," she told him.

She heard his sigh, a flutter of air in the darkened room. "Me neither."

She closed her eyes, waiting for sleep to take her. The way Karthtag-Kal had said those final words—*your training begins tomorrow*—she had a feeling she'd need as much of it as she could get.

CHAPTER NINE

Marilia had initially imagined that Karthtag-Kal would teach them everything himself; she soon discovered she was wrong. The Order of Jade served as both the emperor's elite fighting force and the city's guards and peacekeepers; managing them all required a great deal of time. Instead, he found what he told them was one of the city's finest instructors.

Marilia wasn't sure what she'd been expecting, but it certainly wasn't what they got. Karthtag-Kal's instructor certainly didn't look impressive; he was a thin, balding man with watery eyes. He had a long name that both Marilia and Annuweth both quickly forgot; they just called him Teacher, as he ordered them. He was a priest dedicated to serving Yalaeda, goddess of mysteries and knowledge; he and his brothers tutored the children of the nobles of Navessea in return for donations to their temple.

Though he wasn't anything much to look at, he had a voice like Stellos', and, as Marilia soon discovered, he knew a great deal about *everything*—more than Mother and all the other painted ladies combined, more than Oba'al, more even than One-Eye, who she had once thought wise.

For eight hours each day, he taught them. Marilia felt as if her head were like the grate in the walls of Tyracium after a heavy rainfall, the river rushing through it at frantic speed. She had, after all, over ten years of learning to catch up on.

The priest told them who the great families were, who the emperors

103

had been, how to speak as befitted children of noble birth. He taught them which city was which, over and over again, until Marilia could hear the chant of his voice as she lay herself down to sleep at night.

Naxos, land of horses. Surennis, where the draleen swim in the sea—we use their oil for the lamps. Antarenne, where the herds of yoba roam, and where medicines grow by the fire mountains on the northern coast. Dane, full of gold, midnight stone, and aeder. The Sunset Isle, full of spices and dyes...

More importantly, he taught them letters. "A man who knows how to read can teach himself," he said. He made a mark on a wax tablet and handed the stylus to Annuweth. "This is the first letter of your name."

Annuweth's face was full of awe as he made his mark next to Teacher's.

"And you, girl..." He showed her the first letter of her name, too, written on a line below Annuweth's. She stared at it, chewing on the corner of her lip. She thought it looked like the mountains she had seen on the road to Ulvannis. That pleased her. It made her feel that she belonged.

In a strange way, the letters reminded Marilia of Capture the King. It was a puzzle, putting them together into the right order, making meaning out of a bunch of simple lines. She felt she could make them do and say whatever she wanted, in time. Just as Teacher said, there was power in them.

Annuweth did not share her enthusiasm. His brow grew dark and cloudy as he scratched at the wax. He would sit there with a frown on his face, toes curling and uncurling restlessly as his eyes darted towards the open window, through which came the distant sounds of the Order's knights at their drills. He was no doubt wishing he could be out there with them instead.

After a few weeks, Karthtag-Kal brought another teacher to the villa—a woman named Nelvinna, who began to teach Marilia the lady's graces. It turned out that Navessean noble-women, like painted ladies, had a special way of walking—a graceful arch of the foot, a step that lifted the knee just higher than felt natural. "Imagine you are stepping over a river," Nelvinna told her. "The toes land first, then the heel. Keep your chin up, and your ack straight."

And that was just the beginning.

Marilia couldn't shake the feeling that, in Nelvinna's eyes, she was something of a disappointment.

At singing, she was no rhovanna; at needlework she was decent, but unexceptional.

It was at water-script painting that she finally proved talented.

Water-script was a Navessean invention that was half art, half poetry. It was a form of painting with words—primarily fragments of the Book of the Gods, verses to banish dremmakin and speak with the spirits of the dead.

Scrolls of water-script painting flew on pennants during funerals and hung from the ceilings of family shrines. They graced the main hall of the prefect's villa, and even, she was told, the emperor's private quarters.

A good piece, Nelvinna informed her, was like music for your eyes the same way a minstrel's song was music for your ears. The trick was to open yourself to the spirits, to let them guide your hand where they would. That way, it wasn't just your own wisdom that found its way to the canvas, but the accumulated wisdom of generations.

Marilia was never entirely sure if she actually felt any spirits, but whatever it was that was guiding her hand seemed to know its business.

Her first water-script lesson was the first time that Marilia saw Nelvinna's eyes light up, as if something she had been looking for— some sign of Nelos Dartimaos' greatness, perhaps—had finally revealed itself.

She proudly hung her first painting on the wall of her room. It depicted a mountain and was composed of the words of a psalm describing Neravos' climb out of the dremmakin's pits. She thought it was the most marvelous thing she had ever done.

A few days later, she tore it down, appalled by its simplicity, by the shabbiness of its craftsmanship, amazed that she had ever thought it great. She composed a second painting, this one in the shape of a flower. But Nelvinna ruined that one for her when she told Marilia that most of her young wards began by painting flowers; when she looked upon the painting after that, she saw something common, distinguished only by its embarrassing lack of originality.

The following week, she tore that one down, too.

She spent a full week on the third, poring over it for so long that even Nelvinna started to become impatient. But when it was finished, she knew she'd made something special; this was by far the most intricate thing she had yet done, an object of wonder to her, rivaling the brutal beauty of her final game against One-Eye.

Her latest creation showed a galley at sea, tossed by roiling waves. The words she'd chosen to form the image were from a psalm describing the spirit as a wandering ship. The soul was a ship; the dremmakin lived in the sea; and the dremmakin attacked the spirit the way waves attacked a ship; it was perfectly clever, Marilia thought, brilliant in its layers of meaning.

For the first time since she'd come to the villa, she felt like what Karthtag-Kal had called her—the daughter of a prefect. She hung the

106

scroll on the wall of her room so that she could look at it each night before she fell asleep.

She loved water-script painting; it might have become her passion, had it not been for Annuweth.

Though Stellos walked with a limp and was no longer fit to protect the city, he had been a skilled swordsman once, and was still fit enough to put her brother through his paces. While Nelvinna worked with Marilia, Stellos took two wicker-wood swords from Karthtag-Kal's armory and run Annuweth through his drills, driving him up and down the length of the villa's main hall. Sometimes they would duel with the longer, two-handed swords knights used for dueling and fighting from horseback; on other occasions they would use the shorter, one-handed sword meant for fighting in the shield wall, coupled with a child-sized yoba-shell shield that Annuweth buckled to his arm.

At times Marilia would catch glimpses of them, feet shuffling over the floor as they moved back and forth past her doorway, wooden swords clacking together. Annuweth's eyes were always narrowed in a look of fierce concentration, his brows drawn in, his lips pressed tight together.

"High guard!" Stellos barked. "Low guard! High!" And Annuweth's sword went up, down, up.

In the evening, after he returned from his business, Karthtag-Kal would stop in the main hall and watch as Annuweth showed him what he had learned that day, making him go through the high and the low guard, nodding his great, craggy head as he watched.

After, he would go to where Marilia and Nelvinna were waiting. He would glance briefly at Marilia's work, smile at her and tell her she was learning well. But his eyes were always distant, his mind somewhere else. When she showed him the galley, certain that he would perceive its specialness, he simply nodded his head the same way he had for the flower and the mountain.

So, she began her final task, the creation of something that was not a mere image, but a work that would hold meaning for him.

She had learned from Nelvinna that the banners of water-script that hung from the ceiling of the villa's main hall were writings from the Book of the Stoics, a group of philosophers of whom Karthtag-Kal was especially fond.

"The stoics believe that since we were once mere beasts crafted by the dremmakin to serve them as slaves, there is still something of the beast within us," Teacher explained to her when she asked him. "A piece of our spirit that we have to master through discipline and strength of will." With Teacher's help, she gathered writings from the book, picking those she thought most beautiful, even if she didn't fully understand all the words.

Over the course of two weeks, she fashioned those words into an image—Karthtag-Kal and Nelos Dartimaos standing upon a vast plain, the dark tide of Kanadrak's invading army scattering away around them.

At last, her work complete, she unveiled it for him. She held her breath as his eyes narrowed, studying the dark lines, the words that formed shapes that were memories.

"Knights," he said with a nod. "Very nice, girl." And he left her there.

Not just knights! she almost shouted after him. *It's you! You and my father!*

She had thought that such a sight would please him the same way Annuweth's high-guard did.

But now she understood.

Karthtag-Kal's library was not filled with books of poetry nor his halls with things of beauty; no chicayas sung in his bedroom. His paintings were the words of Stoic philosophers, his books the histories of the empire's greatest battles. Every day he awoke, it was to the sound of wooden swords battling outside his window.

His heart was the heart of a warrior.

The only way into it was to cut your way there with a sword.

That same evening, she stepped out into the garden with Annuweth. The stars were like a sprinkling of wind-scattered sand as the sky turned from orange to violet.

"He says I'm getting better," Annuweth said, his eyes bright. "One day, I'm going to be the prefect, Marilia. I'm going to be the prefect, like father, and I'm going to kill the Graver."

Marilia tried to muster up some enthusiasm, but somehow even the prospect of the Graver's death—while it ought to have been exciting—failed to move her. "The Graver's on our side now," she pointed out. "Karthtag-Kal said so."

"There's still duels," Annuweth said. "I could challenge him and cut off his head."

"He's supposed to be very good at sword-fighting."

"That's why I'm practicing."

"Will you show me what you're learning?"

It was strange, learning from him. He had always been a shade better than her at stick-fighting, but only a shade. Now a distance had opened between them.

After he took her through the lessons he'd had with Stellos, she took him to see the work she'd done— the same work she'd shown Karthtag-Kal. She'd added a touch of red to the black now; the smear of the setting sun, the blood on the field and the edge of Karthtag-Kal and Dartimaos' swords.

She offered Annuweth the brush, but he shook his head and told her it was girls' work. The way he said it made heat rise to her cheeks. Suddenly, her painting seemed nothing at all; a silly thing, a child's fancy. She snatched the brush from his hand and stood to block her work from his view.

"Come on," she said. "Let's go play pirate's dice."

One afternoon Karthtag-Kal took Annuweth to the shrine. He made Annuweth kneel in the pit of white sand.

"What I am about to show you is called the Stoics' trance," Karthtag-Kal said. "It clears the mind. Helps prepare it for battle—I always use it before a tournament. It's part of the reason I've been blademaster six times."

Marilia had come to the shrine, intending to light candles for the spirits—she enjoyed the way the smoke smelled. She hadn't realized it was full.

She eased back, pausing with the door still open a crack, watching her brother and her new father as they sat side by side, Karthtag-Kal a great hunched shape in the dimness, Annuweth small and slight beside him.

"You move well during training," Karthtag-Kal said. "But sword-fighting is also about discipline of mind. Just as we do exercises to strengthen the body, we also exercise the mind."

"How?"

"By emptying it, by focusing on our body and what's around us. That way, we open ourselves to the spirits, to their wisdom and clarity. And calm. It helps in battle; it helps in life."

You've got it all wrong, Marilia thought. *Annuweth's not disciplined or patient or calm. He can't sit still for long. You'll see.* She knew, without a doubt, that she could have done the Stoics' trance better than Annuweth.

When they were finished with the trance, Karthtag-Kal took two wooden swords from the rack on the armory wall and dueled Annuweth down the length of the great hall.

She watched them, studying the way they moved. It was almost like they were dancing. There was no mistaking the look on Karthtag-Kal's face. It reminded her of something she'd read in Teacher's Book of the Gods.

For a long count of years Neravos wandered through the desert of the dremmakin, and his spirit slept in the fortress of his loneliness. Then at last his lost brother came back to him, and Neravos' heart was like a flower opening at dawn. He rejoiced; that was the end of his loneliness.

She stared at the pair of them, chewing the corner of her lip until it began to sting.

It was natural that Karthtag-Kal should prefer Annuweth, she supposed. Mother had preferred him, too; he had been her golden child. He had the look of Nelos Dartimaos.

Still, as she stood there and watched them, she felt a sawing in her chest like a dull knife. The first bite of envy, and something darker that she couldn't name. At last, when she could watch no more, she turned and walked away.

"Can't I learn sword-fighting, like my brother?" she asked Karthtag-Kal after dinner.

He raised an eyebrow. "Sword-fighting is not for girls," he said.

"But if I learned..."

"What would the purpose of that be?"

"I could protect myself."

"You have me to protect you, and the Order, and your brother. Listen; each thing has its purpose, the thing for which it is made." He sighed, walking along the side of the house, she following beside him. "Tell me, girl, what would happen if you tried to drink soup with a fork?"

"It wouldn't work," she said blankly.

"And what would happen if you tried to eat a piece of razorfish with a spoon?"

"It wouldn't work, either," she said, beginning to grow annoyed. *I'm not stupid. Don't talk to me like I'm stupid.*

"Tell me, what do you think would happen if you mother had tried to raise a sword against me? Even if I taught her all I knew?"

Marilia pictured her mother, with her flowing dress swishing around her ankle, then stared up at Karthtag-Kal, with his thick arms, his chest like a slab of stone. She felt heat creeping up her cheeks. She said nothing.

They passed into the shrine. Karthtag-Kal reached into a ceramic pot and drew out a long stick of incense, the sort you set aflame to measure the passing of the hours. "Take this." He handed it to her, and she took it, not understanding.

"Bend it so one end touches the other."

She looked down at the thin stick of wood in her hands, then up at his face, not understanding. "I can't," she said. "It will break."

"Just so," Karthtag-Kal agreed. "You cannot make a thing other than what it is. It is foolish to try." His face softened as he looked down on her. "You will marry a great lord someday, and you will bring his children into the world. That is a great gift. It is written in the Book of the Gods that each half, man and woman, has its own purpose. They are different, but both worthy. A warrior has his honor, but a lady has hers as well, and it is no less."

No less. Then why is it you only have eyes for him and his sword? Why is it that all your books are only filled with the names of warriors and commanders? But she said nothing. She nodded and waited until he walked away. When he was gone, she snapped the stick in half, touched one end of it to the other, then threw both halves down off the villa's balcony into the river.

CHAPTER TEN

Sooner than she would have imagined came the Solstice Festival, when the greatest offerings were made to the gods—and when, as he had promised, Karthtag-Kal finally took her to meet the emperor of Navessea, Moroweth Vergana.

To her surprise and relief, the moment she'd been dreading was over in a flash; a servant read out their names, she curtsied to him (feeling her knees shake) and he lifted his hand in acknowledgment. As she walked out of the Jade Keep's Great Hall, she realized she was almost disappointed. She knew Karthtag-Kal admired the emperor—they were both followers of the Stoics, and Karthtag-Kal was often quoting one of the emperor's wise sayings—and she had imagined that a man who could command so much respect from the prefect would have to be some sort of god-like figure, a giant with piercing eagle-eyes and the face of a statue. Instead, there had only been a man, uglier than some of the buyers she'd seen in Oba'al's pillow house, with crooked teeth and a hooked nose.

Much more exciting, to her mind, was the celebration that came afterwards.

All across the city, people lit candles and sang songs of the creation. In the Great Arena of Ulvannis, they slaughtered and burned yoba so that their smoke could reach the House of White Sands where the gods were watching. Outside the walls, in a huge, man-made lake fed by Almaria's River, men in small ships battled sea beasts—krakens and razorfish—to the roars of the crowd. When the monsters were slain their blood turned the water inky dark. The red coils in the water reminded Marilia of a water-script painting. Afterwards, they hauled the carcasses out and burned them, too.

When the games were finished, there was a great feast at the Jade Keep. A double-row of iron braziers lined the length of the great courtyard where the pine trees grew, sparks leaping up from the roaring fires—little points of red against a backdrop of deep blue and violet. There were banners everywhere, flying from every point of the keep, one for each province of the empire—a snarling tiger against a field of blue, a black and red beetle, a blue kraken, a gold spear on a field of green, and above them all, the black banner with its green dragon, and the red banner and gold chariot of House Vergana.

The throne room was filled with glowing paper lanterns of every color imaginable. They hung from long, invisible threads affixed to the rafters. To one side, minstrels sang, and silk-dancers twirled.

A long table had been set up in the center of the room, long enough that it stretched from the doors all the way to the emperor's throne. The table's cushions currently stood empty for the moment; the nobles had not yet taken their seats. Instead, they glided about the room, greeting one another, bowing and curtseying, chatting of wars or races or who would win the tournament this year.

Marilia's head spun. Lady after lord after lady passed in a blur— women with brightly-colored dresses, men in trim white, gray, and black robes.

And then, suddenly, Karthtag-Kal pulled up short, his back stiffening.

A white-robed man stood before them—short, with close-cropped hair and a face that was handsome, in a personable, commonplace sort of way.

"Lord Prefect," he said, with a bow.

"Lord Andreas," Karthtag-Kal replied in a tight voice.

Marilia felt cold run through her, as if icy snakes had been poured down the back of her shirt. *Andreas.* The man who stood before them was not so very tall, maybe a few inches shorter than Karthtag-Kal. But she supposed the stories must have made him bigger than he really was; there was no mistaking the name Andreas, nor the sword at his waist. She caught a glimpse of the pommel. It was a rich, deep gold, the color of honey.

The Graver.

The man who'd killed her father.

He knelt before them. "You must be the children of Nelos Dartimaos," he said. He looked Annuweth in the eye. "A handsome boy. Your father was a great swordsman, one of the best. Do you take after him?"

"Yes," Annuweth said boldly.

"Good. I'm glad to hear it. Tell me...what are your names?"

They told him.

"Marilia and Annuweth. Good names—though if I thought they were bad, I don't suppose I'd tell you." He smiled, as if at some secret joke that only he understood, and touched Annuweth's shoulder. "I am..."

"The Graver," Marilia said before she could stop herself.

Andreas laughed out loud. "Yes. Some men call be the Graver. A little lurid, I know. The common folk do love their nicknames, and every so often they stick, no matter how fantastic they may be. But since we are all nobles here, my name is Andreas. Sethyron Andreas." He glanced at Karthtag-Kal. "Did you know, children, that tomorrow marks a very exciting occasion? Did your father tell you?"

Marilia shook her head no.

"Years ago, the prefect got lucky and bested me on the field of battle," Andreas said. "Since then, I've wished to test myself against him in a proper contest but, alas—I haven't had the chance."

"Why not?" Annuweth asked.

"Well, you see, six years ago, I was involved in a terrible accident. My practice-sword broke during a tournament when I was facing Scallios, Captain of the Order of Jade, and the broken end was just jagged enough that it pierced my opponent's throat and stole his life." Andreas made a face of regret. "As I said, a horrible accident. But accidents do happen in tournaments...it's not unheard of. Scallios died with honor—a warrior's death. But the uproar his death provoked...well, it was unusually fierce. I even got the impression that some in the Senate came to believe I'd *meant* to kill Scallios." A sharp glint appeared in Andreas' eye as he stared at Karthtag-Kal. "Which of course is absurd, isn't it? I can't understand where anyone would get that idea—*who* might have put it into their heads. Can you, lord prefect?"

"Who knows?" Karthtag-Kal said after a long moment's silence.

"It's a ridiculous notion. Killing Scallios, knowing the furor that would result...it would have been the act of an idiot. And I am not an idiot."

"No," Karthtag-Kal agreed. "You are not that, my lord."

"In any case..." Andreas cleared his throat, finally moving his stare away from Karthtag-Kal's face. "Out of respect for Scallios' family, I did the proper thing—I offered to withdraw from all tournaments in this city for five years. I think the prefect was pleased by that...one fewer to oppose him on the field. Indeed, Sandaros?" He gave a hearty laugh that sounded strained, like a note played on a string that had been stretched too tight and was now near breaking.

This time, Karthtag-Kal said nothing.

"Five years are up," Andreas said. "It is time to look forward. Tomorrow, children, will mark the first time in a long time that both the prefect and I take the field together in the same tournament." He raised his eyebrows. "Perhaps we will find ourselves face-to-face once again."

"Perhaps," Karthtag-Kal said. There was no warmth in his voice; there was not much of anything there at all.

"We will see, Sandaros," Andreas said. "We will see. Well; I won't keep you. Good night, children."

Andreas moved away, and Karthtag-Kal steered them in the opposite direction.

"*That* was the Graver?" He wasn't at all how Marilia had pictured him. In fact, what had struck her most was how completely *regular* the Graver seemed. It was almost disappointing; she felt much as she had after laying eyes on the emperor.

"He has no honor," Karthtag-Kal said. "He cares for nothing but his own glory. I saw it on his face the day Scallios died...Andreas' practice-sword was broken nearly in half, and he ought to have stopped, but he didn't...he couldn't. I think the prospect of winning a tournament with a broken sword was simply too alluring." Karthtag-Kal's lip curled. "The old emperor may have honored Andreas with the name *lord*, but he is not one. He gave away his nobility the day he let himself become a mercenary...the Scorpion Company. A fitting name for his army of filth. Despite his background, he's managed to crawl his way up to the Senate, with a mixture of luck, bribery, and, I imagine, blackmail."

"What is blackmail?" Marilia asked curiously.

But this time, Karthtag-Kal did not answer her; he appeared to be lost in thought. After a moment, he blinked and shook his head, seeming to remember where he was. "Come; let's take our seats."

As fortune would have it, they found themselves seated beside Beniel, the Prince of Svartennos, and his wife, Catarina—the oldest daughter of the emperor.

They were the sort of couple whose images might be found in paintings of old heroes. He was lean, with muscled forearms and hair that looked as if it had been lightly kissed by a sea wind—it was well-groomed enough to show that he was a lord but ruffled enough to suggest he was a man of action. His smile was never quite straight; it leaned this way and that, like a house left askew after an earthquake. Marilia wasn't sure what to make of him, but Annuweth seemed to like him at once. His wife was as beautiful as he was handsome, though she seemed small beside him, as if she were a spring flower struggling to grow in his long shadow.

"The children of Nelos Dartimaos, is it?" Beniel Espeleos said, and bumped his fist against Annuweth's, the traditional warrior's greeting, before kissing Marilia's hand. "I won't stand on ceremony, not with you. Call me Ben. Or Prince Ben, if you like."

"Prince?" Annuweth asked.

"That's right. All these lords here, but only three princes; Vergana's two boys, and me. Quite a trick I managed? Want to know how?" He winked. "It's because I'm magic."

Catarina rolled her eyes to the ceiling. "Oh, Ben..."

"No, truly. Allow me to show you." He pulled a small coin from somewhere in his robes and held it up between thumb and forefinger. It was a simple copper, battered around the edges. "I will make this...disappear." He made a fist.

Marilia stared at his closed hand, chewing the corner of her lip. After a moment she gasped; there was a sound like a snake hissing, and

119

green smoke curled from between Ben's fingers. She drew back despite herself.

Slowly, his eyes sparkling, the Prince of Svartennos opened his fingers. The coin was gone; where it had been was merely a gray-black smear across his palm. He took his napkin and wiped it away.

"Very decorous," Catarina said. Marilia didn't know what *decorous* meant, but the tone of Catarina's voice made her think that Ben was far from it.

"That was...I don't...how?" Annuweth spluttered.

"First time they've seen Daevish acid, is it, Karthtag-Kal?" Ben dug an elbow into their adopted father's side. "I thought so. They don't have much of that in Tyrace, do they? Good show, then. You should see your faces."

"Are you really magic?" Marilia asked, wide-eyed.

"No; Ben is toying with you," Karthtag-Kal said.

"All right; I'll confess," said Ben. "I've no magic—I made the coin disappear with the help of the Daevish metal-eater, and as for the part about being prince...well, that's simple to explain. Svartennos was the only province in Navessea never to be conquered. We joined ourselves to Ulvannis willingly. And that comes with its benefits. For all intents and purposes, I'm really just another governor, but I get to govern all my life instead of five years, and I get to call myself prince. And I won't lie, I rather like that part." He waved a hand to clear away the green smoke, which held an odor like singed hair. "Come; let's eat."

They took their seats. Karthtag-Kal was smiling despite himself.

"So, I saw you already met Andreas. That greasy-haired ghoul-fucker," Ben said calmly, rolling back his sleeves.

"Ben," Catarina said patiently. "We're in the middle of the great hall. You're talking about a lord of Navessea."

"Well, then he's a lordly ghoul-fucker, but his passion for the grey-skinned bastards burns just as hot."

Marilia had taken a drink of jala juice. She choked, nearly snorting it over the table.

"There are children here," Karthtag-Kal reminded Ben with a pointed look.

"I'm sure I haven't done the little ones any lasting damage." Ben turned to Marilia. "Will my lady please accept my sincerest apologies?" he asked, bowing his head to her. She nodded. "I swear, my lord prefect, you blush every time a horse sh... *relieves itself.* I apologize. I meant no offense to your daughter. Who, I must say, is a most rare and beautiful lady." Marilia felt her face grow hot. Flustered, she stared down at the table-cloth.

Servants brought them plates of steaming rice topped with heart-berries glazed with honey and spices. Beside the platter of rice, they set down bowls of kwammakin jelly. Marilia had to resist the impulse to stuff her face. She dug in with her spoon, forcing herself to remember Nelvinna's lessons—straight back, chin high, a lady at all times.

"You'll want to save room for what's coming," Ben said. "Kraken, I'd guess, and maybe even a bit of razorfish. Have you ever tried razorfish before, boy?" Annuweth shook his head. Ben grinned at him. "It's the food of warriors. Did I tell you my father was once nearly eaten by a razorfish? He was in a shipwreck, was clinging to the galley's mast with another one of his knights when he saw that beast circling—its red hide moving beneath the water like a blood-stain." He made a circling motion with his hand.

"What happened?" Annuweth asked.

"It went for the other man instead. It was big enough it swallowed him in one bite, the way a man might swallow a heart-berry." He

121

popped one of the glazed berries into his mouth.

Catarina coughed. "One bite, you say? That was some fish."

Ben shrugged. "Maybe two bites. The exact number of bites isn't important, Catarina. I wasn't there to count. At any rate, once my father got back to land, he led a galley out, and he hunted down that razorfish. He found it, and he killed it, and he took one of its teeth and wore it around his neck as a trophy. Because *that*—" and he smacked one fist into his open palm— "is how we handle things on Svartennos."

"How did he know it was the same one?" Marilia asked with a frown, perplexed.

"What?" Ben asked.

"How did he know it was the same fish?"

"He just knew it in his heart, no doubt," Catarina said with an arched eyebrow.

"Ah, to see such a breathtaking tale picked apart by ladies. It makes the heart bleed. Well, maybe it wasn't quite the same one, but it's the gesture that counts, isn't it?"

Sure enough, the servants soon brought the fish, dark red slabs seasoned with a dusting of spices from the Sunset Isles. Karthtag-Kal cut off a piece and put it on Marilia's plate, then got another for Annuweth. "You'll learn soon enough not to believe everything you hear from *Prince* Espeleos," the prefect said.

A chorus of flute-players struck up a tune, and dancers came into the hall, stepping so lightly and with such perfect balance that they seemed to float across the floor. Long ribbons of silk streamed out behind them. A woman began to sing, in a clear, high voice that made Marilia turn and stare.

Catarina's face brightened. "Do you know this song, children?" she asked. "It's a song of Svartennos."

The tiger lord of westerland stood gazing out to sea
Golden clouds and golden sun, my lady's gone from me
Her hair was black as midnight's cloud, her eyes like living flame
Now I wake weeping in the night; with tears I call her name
A hundred men my spear laid low, I sent them to the pyres
I turned their broken halls to ash, the brave sons and their sires
Where'er I rode on my white horse, dark Zantos rode as well
Death's pale banner upon the hill, my battle-horn, Death's knell
The war was won, the battle done, the crown upon my hair
While in my gardens children laugh, and women's voices fair
The western trees are tall and strong, the rivers bright and clear
Yet none of them so dear to me as my Chrysathamere

"Just beautiful," Ben said. "It tugs at my heart every time."

"It's about Queen Svartana," Catarina said. "She fought the Valdruk slavers off Svartennos. The Tigerlord of Westerland was Aryn, the Great Emperor, who fell in love with her."

"The people of Svartennos have a prophecy about Queen Svartana," Ben said.

"What prophecy?" Marilia asked.

"That someday, when the island is in peril...on the brink of destruction or some such thing, I can't remember the exact words...the spirit of Svartana will return in the form of another, to lead our people to victory and save our island."

Karthtag-Kal chuckled. "I thought you didn't believe in prophecy, Ben."

Ben's face was serious—a first, Marilia thought. "That prophecy is different. It was made by an Elder of Mount Phelkos, not some

123

soothsayer earning coins in a market tent. Everyone on Svartennos believes that prophecy."

Catarina cleared her throat. "Emperor Vergana's peace has lasted longer than any in our history. Let's hope we have no need for such prophecies to ever come true." She gave Ben a stern look.

"No peace lasts forever," Ben said. "War is in man's nature. Tournaments can keep that impulse at bay, but only so long. Then…war." He didn't sound too disappointed about the prospect.

"Is that so?" Karthtag-Kal asked.

Ben speared a chunk of razorfish and chewed it. "It all comes back to nature. I'm of the opinion that man has a natural thirst for glory. Take this razorfish—king of the sea. Three rows of teeth as sharp as a sword. Two tentacles on its head that can paralyze with a touch, a tongue strong enough to crush a man in armor. The hounds of the dremmakin themselves, if you believe all that. And here I am, eating him." He chewed, closing his eyes momentarily. "Truth is, razorfish isn't even all that tastier than other fish. But emperors pay talents for the stuff. Why? It's all about the power. Eating the king of the sea, knowing that strong as he was, you got him. And *that* is delicious."

"Profound," Karthtag-Kal said dryly. "Maybe you should have been a philosopher."

"I think not, my friend. I like stabbing things too much."

CHAPTER ELEVEN

The talk turned to the coming tournament. Though Karthtag-Kal frowned upon large wagers, he was not above a few small, friendly bets. He and Ben each bet on themselves for the win, and then began to discuss how the other competitors might fare. It was to be Prince Ilruyn's first tournament, and he was rumored to be skilled with the sword; Karthtag-Kal gave him three rounds, and Ben four.

As dinner ended and the lords and ladies of Navessea began to drift apart into groups to speak with one another, Karthtag-Kal took Marilia by the arm and guided her into the Jade Keep's gardens, where a group of girls was standing inside a gazebo above a small stream.

"It's about time you children made some friends your own age," he said to her. "And what better friends than these? Their leader, so to speak, is the princess Petrea, Emperor Vergana's younger daughter. I'm told she collects interesting ladies." He chuckled. "I'll leave you to them." He gave her a pat on the back and drifted over to speak to Livenneth.

Marilia approached. She was wearing a new gown that Karthtag-Kal had bought for her—black, with green sleeves and a fine green habithra sash bound around her waist—but next to these ladies she still felt as out of place as if she were dressed in the clothes she'd worn in Tyrace. She introduced herself, conscious of their eyes on her—and of one pair most of all.

A girl that could only be the princess smiled at her and beckoned her forward. She was perhaps a year or so younger than Marilia, but she seemed somehow older, more assured. She was clad in a white dress, with sleeves and sash died pink, as if she were a cherry-blossom petal that had taken human form and come to life. There was a pink flower tucked behind her ear. Her hair was combed perfectly straight, and it shone where it caught the torch-light. Marilia thought she was the most beautiful lady that she had ever seen.

The princess' companions introduced themselves; there were six of them in all.

"You're the prefect's new daughter," Petrea said.

"Yes, my princess," Marilia said.

"Welcome. Well, then; tell us a secret."

"A secret?" Marilia repeated blankly.

Petrea laughed. It was like the sound of wind chimes ringing. "Here we trade secrets," she said with an impish smile. "You must have one to join us. Something about a lord or lady, or even a knight, if you like. Just so long as it is interesting."

Marilia chewed the corner of her lip, her mind racing. "I've only been in the city for five months," she said. "And most of the time I was inside my father's villa. I don't know many secrets."

"Ah, well," Petrea said, with a touch of disappointment. "That's all right, then. You are the prefect's daughter, so of course you can join us all the same."

There was a strange power to Petrea. She was like the gentle current of a cool river on a hot summer day—you wanted to simply fall into it and let it carry you where it would. Though she couldn't have explained why, Marilia knew that she wanted this girl to like her. And so, frantic, she searched inside herself until she found an answer.

"I have one," she said hastily. "It's about the Graver—the Lord Andreas, I mean."

126

"What about him?"

"He used to be from Tyrace, but he was banished after he poked out the king's eye in a duel. That's why the King of Tyrace has one eye."

"He didn't!" One of Petrea's girls gasped.

"He did!" Marilia insisted. "They were only children, so it was with a wooden sword. A practice fight. It's true." She waited, chewing her lip.

Petrea's eyes lit up. "That *is* interesting," she said. "How did you come to learn of it?"

"I heard a guard lieutenant say it—that a boy named Sethyron Andreas put out the king's eye."

"Maybe it's a different Sethyron Andreas," one of Petrea's friends suggested, casting doubt on Marilia's story.

"It's not," Marilia said. "It's a noble name, and there's only one noble house with that name in all of Tyrace." She remembered, a moment too late, that Karthtag-Kal had told her not to speak too much of Tyrace or the pillow house. Luckily, it didn't seem that Petrea or her friends even noticed; they were too busy considering the information Marilia had just shared with them.

"That was well-remembered," Petrea said, and Marilia felt her heart lift. "Let me talk to our new friend for a while," she said to her companions. She led Marilia away from the others. Marilia's breath quickened. The princess was close enough that she could feel the warmth of Petrea's arm as it brushed against hers and could smell the jasmine perfume she wore.

"I know you are new to the city," Petrea said, "but you mustn't feel out of place with us. I appreciate clever friends like you."

"Thank you, princess."

"You can call me Petrea, since we are friends. I hope I haven't upset you; I did put you on the spot back there."

"No, pri—Petrea."

"My mother once told me that secrets were a lady's weapon; our brothers have their swords and we have our secrets. So I collect them."

"She sounds wise, Petrea."

"She was. She died a few years ago."

"I'm sorry," Marilia said. "My mother died, too."

"I'm sorry also. Who was your mother?"

Marilia hesitated. Karthtag-Kal had also told her not to tell the truth about her mother. But with the princess standing so close, she could not think of a lie. "A... a painted lady, Petrea." She regretted it at once; she felt her face grow hot.

Petrea gasped. "That was brave of you to tell me," she said. She put her hand on Marilia's arm. "Don't worry; this can just be our secret. But anyway, let's not talk about mothers or other sad things. This is a festival—it's meant to be happy."

Marilia tried to think of something to say, something the other girl would not think silly. "I heard your brother is going to be in his first tournament," was what she came up with. "I wish him luck."

Petrea rolled her eyes. "Oh, come now. *Everyone* has been saying that tonight," she said. "Yes; it's his first. He's so very excited about it. But Prince Ilruyn is not really my brother—he's adopted. My father took him in as part of a deal so that the old emperor's prefect wouldn't fight him for the throne."

"I...I didn't know that."

"Yes, well, you're still new here. I can't expect you to know *everything*. But if Ilruyn was my *real* brother, he couldn't even compete—neither the emperor nor the heir is supposed to be in tournaments." Her eyes gleamed suddenly, as if they were lit from within by a lantern. She bit her lower lip. "Anyway, I don't think Ilruyn is going to do very well. That's my secret for you; if you're going to wager, don't wager on him."

"He's not good?"

"Oh, he is. He's very good. But I heard him say over dinner that his belly was upset. I don't think it's going to get better by tomorrow. I think it's only going to get worse."

Marilia stared at her, uncertain. "Why?"

Petrea gave a careless shrug. "Oh. I don't know. I just have a feeling. Anyway, let's get back to the others."

The day of the tournament dawned bright and clear. Men in padded suits of draleen hide struck at each other with wicker-wood swords while the crowd cheered. When Karthtag-Kal took to the sands, Marilia and Annuweth leaned forward in their seats. Whenever it seemed that the Prefect might fall, Annuweth gripped Marilia's arm so hard that she gasped.

Just as Petrea had predicted, Prince Ilruyn did not fare well. Though his sword-work was precise, his movements seemed slow, and his blows lacked conviction. He fell within his first round. He stormed off with a black scowl on his face. Marilia raised her eyes to the royal box. Petrea was sitting there, staring down at her adopted brother. Marilia saw a white flash of teeth as she bit her lower lip, just as she had the night before.

Soon there were only four combatants left—two pairs of two: the Graver and a man named Septakim, and Karthtag-Kal and Ben Espeleos. Marilia had eyes only for the second of the pairs.

It was sword-work such as she had never seen. Ben was fast, but

Karthtag-Kal was a tower of strength, raining blows on him from on high. For a while it seemed the two were evenly matched.

Then at last Ben missed a thrust. His foot skidded in the sand. Karthtag-Kal struck him hard across the chest, driving him onto his back. Ben raised a hand to show that he yielded.

The crowd exploded. Marilia found herself on her feet, cheering, her hand in the air.

Next came the final round. The Graver against the prefect. A hush fell over the crowd. The two squared off, the wind stirring the sand around their feet, as the judges stepped closer, as if sensing that this final round would require all their scrutiny.

Marilia squeezed Annuweth's hand tight, forgetful of everything but the spectacle before them.

Then, to her surprise, Karthtag-Kal let his sword fall to the ground.

Marilia and Annuweth exchanged a glance. "What is he doing?" Marilia whispered, baffled. "Aren't they supposed to fight?" She looked to Stellos, sitting on her other side, but even the steward looked perplexed.

A murmur swept through the crowd, like a storm-wind slowly gathering strength.

Karthtag-Kal turned to the imperial pavilion and dipped a bow to the emperor before he walked away.

The Graver stood alone in the center of the arena, looking somehow small despite his victory. The herald found her voice and called out, in a ringing tone, "Lord Sethyron Andreas, blademaster!" She presented Andreas with his prize: a bracelet made of dragon's bones, carved with runes from the Book of the Gods that described Neravos' conquest of the dremmakin. Slowly, with what might almost have been reluctance, the Graver placed it upon his wrist.

130

"Why didn't you fight him?" Annuweth asked Karthtag-Kal as they made their way up White Street towards the Jade Keep.

"Because I chose not to," Karthtag-Kal said.

Marilia's mind was racing. "Will you be in trouble?"

"No. No man is obliged to fight to the end of a tournament. Anyone may withdraw at any time."

Then they heard Andreas' shout. "Karthtag-Kal!"

Slowly, Karthtag-Kal turned.

Andreas strode swiftly towards them. The calm of the previous night was gone; there was a twitching energy to his features, as if beneath the smooth mask of his skin something hot and liquid was moving, disquieted. His left hand toyed restlessly with his right wrist, where the dragon-bone bracelet hung.

"Why did you withdraw?" he demanded.

"My children have been asking me the same question. I did not wish to fight," Karthtag-Kal said.

"That is no proper answer," Andreas said.

"Does it matter? You have your victory, *blademaster*. Isn't that what you wanted?"

A low noise, almost a growl, escaped Andreas' throat. "Does it so amuse you to insult me? You owe me an answer."

"Owe you? I owe you nothing—and that is the point," said Karthtag-Kal. "I am a knight; I have nothing to prove. I entered the tournament as a chance to hone my skill, and because it is an honorable tradition. I sought only to test myself against my fellow knights and lords of Navessea."

"*I* am a lord of Navessea!" Andreas insisted. "The same as you."

131

"You are a lord of Navessea; you have a villa on this street, sure enough."

"Do you know what I think?" Andreas said. "I think you are afraid to face me!"

Marilia chewed her lip. Fear didn't sound like Karthtag-Kal; he would have battled a lava-ghoul, she thought, if his duty had demanded it. As she looked at Karthtag-Kal's face, it wasn't fear she saw there now. The prefect's lips stretched into the vague semblance of a smile. "Do you really?" he asked, holding Andreas' gaze. "Well, my lord, if that is what you believe. Come, children. Let us head back to the villa."

"You cannot avoid it forever, Karthtag-Kal."

"Six years ago, you challenged me to a duel right here in the city streets. My answer now is the same as my answer then; I duel only with whom I choose, my lord. And I do not choose to duel with you, not with aeder, and not with wicker-wood."

"We both know I'm better!"

"Know it and be glad, then."

He turned and ushered Marilia and Annuweth on up the road towards the Jade Keep's courtyard, leaving Andreas seething behind them. Marilia cast a glance back at him as they went. He had paused just outside the white stone wall that encircled his own villa. A hot wind swept down the street; pink and white petals from the cherry-blossom trees fell like a silent rain around him, dancing around his feet. He stared down at the blademaster's bracelet on his wrist, and, with a sudden fury that surprised her, tore it off and handed it to one of the knights who followed behind him.

CHAPTER TWELVE

The months went by. Piece by piece, the world of Ulvannis opened before Marilia.

Karthtag-Kal took her to the theater, where silk-dancers trailed ribbons like painted fire from their arms, singing of old battles and lost loves. He took her to the race-track, where chariots tore up the earth to the screams of the watching crowd. He took her to the arena, where the wicked were put to justice and where beasts battled men before being burned as offerings to the gods. He showed her marvels that the little Tyracian girl she had once been could scarcely have dreamed of.

Her lessons continued all the while—and new lessons were added. She and Annuweth learned to ride horses (despite Annuweth's initial fear of the beasts, he soon proved himself as good at this as he was at most physical exercises), to do sums, to dance.

One day, just a little over a year after they'd arrived in Ulvannis, after Karthtag-Kal and Annuweth had finished sparring, the prefect sat her brother down at the table in the garden and vanished into the house. He returned carrying a familiar board of white and dark squares.

Marilia watched from the window of her room; she was finishing another water-script painting, even though she wasn't sure her heart was really in it.

"I thought we might try a little game," Karthtag-Kal said to Annuweth, smiling. "It's called Capture the Emperor."

He seated himself on a stone chair across from Annuweth and set the board between them. "Your father and I used to play this together,"

Karthtag-Kal said. "I learned to play it from a Navessean man who came to my homeland of Cardath. A fur trader, who dealt in snow-tiger pelts. He told me it was a game for fighters. At first, I didn't believe him, but after a while, I came to enjoy it." He grinned. "I daresay I made an impression on your father the first time we went against each other." He opened the cloth pouch and began to set up the pieces.

Marilia set aside her quill and canvas and rose from her cushion by the window. Moments later, she was out in the garden, standing not far from the board, watching the opening exchanges of a duel between father and son. Annuweth took black, attempting to trap Karthtag-Kal; Karthtag-Kal took white, attempting to escape to one of the board's four corners.

As they went, Karthtag-Kal spoke, offering pieces of advice.

The board is like a battlefield—each piece a company of knights. Always defend the avenues of escape..

Yes, good; when you can, take the quicker path. Maybe you're a natural, boy.

Karthtag-Kal won, in the end. "Well, no one wins their first game," he said to Annuweth as he scooped the pieces back into their pouch. "But you did well."

As they had played, Marilia had studied Karthtag-Kal almost as much as she had studied the board. There, in those pieces, was the key—a game that Karthtag-Kal had played with Nelos Dartimaos. Something the two of them had shared, just as they had shared the heat of the battlefield, the dancing of swords.

Karthtag-Kal had not looked closely enough at Marilia's paintings to see what she had tried to offer him, and he would not teach her the sword, so she could not reach him that way. But he was trained to see the pieces, to understand the ways they moved; this was something he

134

could not miss.

She spoke. "Can I play?"

Karthtag-Kal turned to look at her. He seemed surprised. He chuckled, a deep, throaty sound. "I doubt you'd find it to your liking."

"I do. I like it."

"You know how to play?"

"I played a few times. I learned from a Tyracian man."

"You really want to?"

"Yes."

He shrugged. An amused smile tugged at the corners of his mouth. "All right, then." He set the pieces back up.

Marilia walked forward to take her brother's seat.

She felt Annuweth's warmth on the cushion, lingering even after he rose, the same way the warmth of the moment still lingered even though his game with Karthtag-Kal had ended. It was a warmth perfectly matched to the warmth of the garden.

The sun was setting, its center orange as the heart of a jala fruit; its rim red like the edges of Dartimaos' and Karthtag-Kal's blood-dipped swords in the painting that still hung in her bedroom. Between two proud cherry-blossom trees, a large swath of violet sky was visible. Clouds spanned the length of it, a white, god-spun habithra wrapped around the waist of the world.

It was a beautiful scene that might become the foundation for a beautiful memory—Annuweth's first game with his new father.

Marilia had a savage urge to take that memory and shatter it, erase it. She would tear it down and put something else, something better, in its place.

This game was *hers*; of all the things of their father's—sword-fighting, the Stoics' trance, Dartimaos' armor, his sword—*this* belonged to her; she had staked her claim to it long ago. Annuweth had made a mistake when he had sat down at that table, when he had let Karthtag-Kal tell him he had played *well* and said nothing in reply, offered no denial.

Now she would offer one for him.

She lowered her head so that her eyes were almost level with the pieces as she leaned forward, resting her chin on her forearms; she chewed the corner of her lip.

It had been well more than a year since she'd won the white king from One-Eye. But as she looked at the pieces, as she reached out and took one in her fingers, she felt it beginning to come back to her—and how good that felt! Like stepping back into a familiar, unfinished dream.

She was still afraid, of course; afraid that too much time had passed, that she had forgotten what she'd used to know. For a moment her pieces looked like a pile of white bones—cold, forbidding, threatening.

She tried to forget her father and her brother, to think only of the board. The board was enough; in its one hundred-and-sixty-nine squares, there was enough complexity to fill a hundred lifetimes and more.

"Are you ready?" Karthtag-Kal asked.

Marilia nodded.

He moved and she moved after him. "Good," he said. "Clever. Just like your brother—defend the means of escape. Good, girl."

She said nothing.

After the first six moves Karthtag-Kal seemed to straighten in his seat. His amused smile wavered like a candle about to go out.

After twelve moves, the smile was gone altogether.

And after eighteen Karthtag-Kal was leaning over the board just like Marilia.

After what seemed like an hour, Karthtag-Kal's pieces formed a ring which steadily closed around the few pieces Marilia had remaining until she could move no more. She frowned and turned over her king to signal defeat.

He stared at her. "Who did you say taught you?" he asked.

"A captain in Tyrace. One of the buyers."

Karthtag-Kal nodded. His hand slowly reached out, scooping up the pieces. There was something new in his eyes as he looked at her, something that hadn't been there before, as if a heavy curtain had been drawn back and he was seeing her now for the first time.

She let out a long breath and wiped her trembling palms on the legs of her dress.

They played again the day after that. This time Karthtag-Kal offered suggestions and advice, and she nodded, studying the board, learning its secrets. He was good, and it took every ounce of her concentration to hold him at bay.

"You have an instinct for it," Karthtag-Kal said.

"Thank you," she said. What else could be said?

"There's something I want to show you."

That something was another game, one with many different kinds of pieces. Marilia studied the carvings. Horse-head, spear, bow, helmet.

"This is a game that is played by the lords of Navessea," Karthtag-Kal explained. "Its name is Sharavayn. It is meant to simulate battle. See—each piece is a different kind of soldier. Shield-men, light cavalry, knights, archers. Some of the pieces are stronger than others—those are the ones marked with a sword. The sword is carved on only one side of the piece, the side facing you; I will not know which soldiers are your best, nor will you know mine. One of your cavalry pieces should have a crown on it; that is your commander. Guard him well, for if he dies, your troops will struggle." He shook a cup of dice, rattling them. "Shall we play?"

"How can we play?" Marilia blurted. "There is no board!"

The board was the floor of the villa itself; the movements of each piece measured precisely with strips of wood of different lengths. She had thought Capture the King to be complex, but it was nothing, she saw, next to this.

By the end of their first game, Karthtag-Kal was beaming. "You play well, girl, better than any child your age I have heard of. I think someday you could be better than me. You have a keen mind."

"What does keen mean?"

"Quick. The mind of a commander."

She felt herself swell inside. They played a second game. She lost again, but it took longer than the first time.

The mind of a commander, Karthtag-Kal had said. His words had unlocked something in her—as if somewhere buried in her bones there had been a slumbering fire that had been stirred to life.

Marilia found herself drawn to the books inside Karthtag-Kal's library—books that told of old battles, of Young Aryn's war against the usurper Cossotos, of the conquest of the Sunset Isles, of the liberation of Svartennos and the struggle with Kanadrak. She liked to imagine that each game with Karthtag-Kal was a battle, and that she was Svartana, or Aryn, or Nelos Dartimaos. Though the game was not quite the same as the battles she read about in Karthtag-Kal's books, there were many times when she was able to use what she read against her father—a false retreat, a flanking maneuver, a sudden push through the

138

center.

Such was the nature of Sharavayn that it could be played in an infinite array of locations. Books placed on the floor became mountains her soldiers had to skirt around; one of her blue habithras was a winding river that bisected the battlefield.

She battled Karthtag-Kal across the plains of Naxos, across the hills of Svartennos, through the forests of Vaerennis, and in the mountains of Dane. On the floor before her eyes, little wooden pieces pecked at each other. In her mind, great armies clashed to the sound of yoba-shell horns.

Karthtag-Kal was a better player than One-Eye, though, and even when she caught him in one trick, he managed to fight his way out of it and strike back with two of his own. The games always ended the same way—her hand raised in surrender. Though she tried her best for the better part of a year, she could not beat him.

Still, each game lasted longer than the one before; she could tell that Karthtag-Kal was impressed—more impressed, perhaps, than she had ever seen him.

He continued to play against Annuweth, too, of course, but Marilia knew that it was not the same.

He played against Annuweth for Annuweth's sake—to teach him, to better him.

He played against her for his own.

"What do you two talk about?" Annuweth asked her one day. "When you're playing together?"

"What do you mean?"

"I don't know. You talk and talk for hours. I've seen you."

Strategy, tactics, tales of father, stories of commanders and old campaigns...

"Nothing," she said with a shrug. "I don't know. We just play."

He frowned, his brows narrowing. She could tell he was not satisfied; he was aware enough to know that he was missing something, that there was some subtle, fundamental difference between his games with Karthtag-Kal and hers. "It doesn't matter," he decided at last, but from the way he said it, she thought that it mattered a great deal.

Things had changed.

She was the golden child now.

Though Karthtag-Kal would never say it in so many words, there were moments that said it plainly enough: such as when Karthtag-Kal brought Livenneth over for dinner, setting up the Sharavayn table into a re-creation of Young Aryn's doomed last stand. Livenneth (and Annuweth) watched as, against all odds, she nearly saved the heroic young emperor's life. "If she were a boy, she'd be the next prefect," Livenneth said, laughing; but Karthtag-Kal didn't laugh.

"Maybe so," he said, staring at the board.

Then there were several occasions when, absorbed by a half-finished game of Sharavayn, Karthtag-Kal even went so far as to cut short his sparring practice with Annuweth to finish the game before supper.

When it came to the game (and, for that matter, the rest of his studies), Annuweth applied a singular, brute force of will that kept him moving relentlessly forward, like a heavy galley following the current of a river. Marilia saw the effort her brother made to fashion himself into the model of a perfect knight, but it was like looking at a midnight stone statuette that had been born from a warped mold. Annuweth memorized the outcomes of battles because he knew he must, he kept at his books though she knew he hated them. But brute force could only take you so far. Mastery of Sharavayn required imagination and passion—the hunger to keep searching for the next ploy that might finally tip the scales of battle against Karthtag-Kal.

She finally found it.

One day, as she wandered through the library, she chanced upon the greatest discovery of all—the writings of the poet-general, Emperor Urian. Though she did not yet know it, his words were the bread and water of strategy; all commanders and governors were required to study his teachings.

Allow your enemy to believe he sees your deception, Urian wrote. *If an enemy expects a trick, the best thing is to show him one. Then he will not look further. Nothing is quite so dangerous as the promise of an easy, glorious victory to an overconfident general.*

She confronted Karthtag-Kal with Urian's words fresh in her mind, and (partly due to the luck of the dice, but even so) she had her first victory.

"Beaten by a twelve-year-old girl," Karthtag-Kal murmured. "Who would have thought it?"

"Almost thirteen," she said.

Karthtag-Kal chuckled. "I suppose that makes it better."

"You were tired," she said. "you said so yourself."

"Do not diminish your achievement. I have no doubt you will win again someday soon, when I am rested and with the Fates on my side." He shook his head. "I knew you would do it. From the first time we played. I knew that if you could do *that* then, I would not be able to keep winning forever. You can study and you can train for many years, as I have. But at some point, the Fates who spin our life-threads will have their say. At some point we all are who we are. And you are your father's daughter."

There were other things she learned from Karthtag-Kal's books, pieces of knowledge she chanced upon.

"The ladies of Svartennos train like the men," she said, confronting Karthtag-Kal one day after lunch, while Annuweth was having an extra reading lesson with Teacher. "It says so. Septakim Nervyn wrote it in his Blue Book. Will you not teach me the sword?"

"If you've read to the end of Septakim Nervyn's Blue Book, then you should know that the women of Svartennos' training, such as it is, is limited to riding and tests designed to build physical endurance. They don't learn the sword."

"They do in Cardath," she said, undeterred. "That's where you're from. The women spar with wooden swords—isn't that so?"

"We are not in Cardath," Karthtag-Kal said. "I have not been there in many years." He considered her for a long moment. "Why sword-fighting?" he asked at last.

Because Annuweth knows it.

Although the games of Sharavayn had brought her and Karthtag-Kal closer, something was still missing. For two years, she had watched Karthtag-Kal battle Annuweth through the villa's halls and around the garden terrace. Watching was like feeling an itch in the small of her back; those sparring lessons were a reminder that, despite all she had done, she and her brother were not the same.

But of course, she didn't say all that to him. She didn't know what to say, so she simply bit her lip. "I don't know."

To her surprise, she saw him soften. "I suppose there's no harm in a lesson," he said with a shrug. "Come with me."

He took her into the great hall and put a wooden dueling sword in her hand. She took up a fighting stance, gripping the wooden handle so hard her knuckles went white. He shook his head. "Not like that," he said. "If you stand like that you won't be able to move away fast enough when I attack you. Spread your feet more." She did what he said. "Loosen your grip. You're too stiff. You'll hurt your wrists. Let your arms flow...like water."

Marilia frowned. *Like water?* She thought. *But water is weak.* She tried to do as he said, softening her grip, loosening the muscles of her forearms and shoulders.

"If you catch my sword and try to stop it full on, you or your sword will eventually break," Karthtag-Kal said. "Instead, take my sword's energy and make it yours."

They battled across the main hall of the prefect's villa until Marilia's palms tingled all over and her muscles burned.

"Need a rest?" Karthtag-Kal asked. She shook her head, wiping sweat from her forehead, clenching her jaw. But after a few minutes more she sagged against one of the pillars, gasping.

Karthtag-Kal sat beside her. For a while neither of them spoke. Marilia turned the wooden sword over and over in her hand. Her eyes moved across the hall, to the white banners with their flowing black script that adorned the walls. Now that she'd studied water-script painting, she found she could make out the individual letters that made up each banner. "A knight does what he can for the good of the empire," she read aloud. "He does his duty; that is what makes him a knight."

Karthtag-Kal followed her gaze. "Words to live by," he said.

"Who wrote that?"

Karthtag-Kal smiled. "Neravan Vergana," he said. "An uncle of our emperor, and one of the greatest philosophers the Stoics have ever produced."

143

"What is a Stoic?" she asked. "You always talk about them, but what does it actually *mean*?"

Karthtag-Kal was quiet for a long time. When he spoke, he might have been answering her question, or he might not have been. "There is much for us to long for in this world, but doing so will bring no lasting peace. The only way to find peace is to turn inward."

"I don't understand," she said.

"Let me tell you a story."

"You like telling stories."

His laughter rumbled. "And you like hearing them. A perfect match, aren't we?"

"Is it a story about the Stoic? Neravan Vergana?"

"No. It's a story about something that happened to me. One day, I was riding through the hills of Svartennos with Nelos. It was shortly after the battle where we drove Kanadrak away. Despite our victory, my heart was troubled—I'd just lost many friends. As I rode with Nelos, hoping to clear my mind, I heard the sweetest singing you can imagine. I'd never heard anything like it before. I felt as though a huge weight had been lifted off me.

"It was a peasant girl. She was harvesting milk-yams out in the field. I don't even remember what she was singing...some work song, a child's tune about night monsters...but I've never heard a sweeter song since. Now think; if that girl had been born in this city, she might have been the best singer of the emperor's court. She might have lent her voice to festivals, might have performed in the Jade Keep. Instead, a farmer's wife, born out in the fields of Svartennos, with scarcely anyone to hear her. An incredible waste, I thought."

He pursed his lips. "Some men believe the gods have a plan for all of us, that the Fates put us where we can do the most to serve their purposes. They believe emperors are born to rule, farmers to toil, knights to fight. That it's all set up like a game of Sharavayn, each on their proper path. Then there are those who think that when we're born, the Fates roll the dice, and spin their strings, and..." he shrugged. "That seems to be the truth of it, because I have known cowardly, dishonorable knights and foolish emperors. Our lives are not planned for us, girl. We are put on this earth where we are as the threads spin out. We are here to do our duty and honor the gods so we can join our ancestors in the House of White Sands someday. To seek more explanation than that...that is the way to make yourself suffer."

Marilia considered that. "It must be sad for her," she said. "The girl in the field, I mean. In your story."

"Must it?" Karthtag-Kal raised an eyebrow.

"I only mean...if she hadn't been a farming girl, people might have loved her voice. She might have been a great singer and earned many talents."

"Yes, she could have won a great deal of gold...and that would have been very nice for her, is that the way of it?"

Marilia chewed her cheek and did not know what to say.

Karthtag-Kal shook his head again. "Some men also spend all their lives searching for a thing, thinking it will make them happy. Gold, mostly, or power. If only they were a knight, or a merchant, or a magistrate, or a governor, or the emperor himself, *then* things would be better. But that is a lie, too. The last emperor was proof enough of that. He went near mad before the end, seeing shadows around every corner. When he finally jumped to his death and Vergana stepped up before the Senate to take his place, many called it a mercy. Serenity does not come from the world. It comes from us. All this is but a fleeting glimpse—what comes after lasts forever."

"I still think it's sad," Marilia said.

"Do you?"

"You said the girl's song made you happy. Maybe if she was the emperor's singer, more people could have heard it. It could make them feel happy, too. Wouldn't things be better that way?"

"Yes. I suppose they would." His eyes crinkled. "Sometimes it's easy to forget you're only twelve years old. You have a lot of your father in you."

She looked down at the mats of the hall, feeling the blood rise to her face. She knew that coming from him, that was high praise.

"I never really told you what he was like," Karthtag-Kal said. "There are two kinds of warriors, girl. Kanadrak was one kind. War was in his blood. He was a man who lived to kill, to burn and rape and take what others had built. That was what I had been, too, in those days when I brought terror to the villages of Thyre. But Nelos Dartimaos showed me another way. He showed me a man could be a warrior, but that he could be other things besides. That the only way *to* be a great warrior was to find something beyond blood-lust—to master oneself." He snorted. "But all that is to say nothing. Nelos was brave; he was studious; he was a great knight. Anyone could tell you that. It doesn't say what he was really like…as a man." He paused, frowning slightly, his brows furrowed in thought.

"Nelos Dartimaos was the second child of a noble family of Svartennos. No one expected greatness from him; his father was far from one of the island's finest. He was a glutton, a man who whiled away his time watching others race horses, spar, hunt, perform the feats men whispered he should have performed himself. I think that was what led Nelos to the Order of Jade, what drove him to work himself so hard—he did, you know. Body and mind, he worked himself as hard as

146

a man could, trying to shape himself into the perfect knight. And he was, in many ways—Prefect of the Order of Jade, blademaster of six tournaments. Men envied him for his dedication...but I don't think many realized that his dedication wasn't something he chose; he couldn't have been any other way. For Nelos, it was a need; he needed to be great the same way other men needed to drink or to eat. Yet I think that struggle, all that effort...it cost him something. He had admirers, and he had many acquaintances, but few friends. Fewer still who he could say he loved."

Marilia frowned; something was troubling her, a nagging question turning in the back of her mind. At last she realized what it was.

"Mother used to say he would have come back to the pillow house and taken us away," she said. And that was what she, too, had once believed. But she had learned more of the world since the day she'd arrived in Karthtag-Kal's villa. She knew what the word *bastard* really meant—the bastards of Navessea's senators were scattered across the city like petals after a storm. There was one thing almost all of them had in common: they did not live in their fathers' villas on White Street. "Would he really?"

"He would have provided for you," Karthtag-Kal said. "He would not have left you in Tyrace to become a painted lady."

"But would he have raised us? Would he have taken us as his own?"

Karthtag-Kal looked away. "I don't know," he said quietly. "Perhaps not. Not because he wouldn't care for you, but because of how things are."

"Why did you take us, then?" Marilia asked. Now that she truly considered it, she realized how odd it was—a man who had taken no wife, who had forsaken the chance of having any offspring of his own, adopting another man's children.

147

The question seemed to catch Karthtag-Kal off guard. "Because it was something I had to do," he said at last. "You are Nelos Dartimaos' children—as far as I know, the only children he ever had—and you didn't belong in that pillow house. For what it's worth, if he'd known you as I do, I think he would have loved you."

Marilia felt herself grow warm. She reached out and touched his hand—it was like touching an old rock. She felt his skin jump under her fingertips as he looked at her, surprised. "Thank you," she said. For what, she didn't specify. He didn't ask.

Marilia stared across the field towards the fifteen thousand men who were coming to kill her.

The stalks of tall grass bent in the wind. The sky was gray, clouds hanging heavy and low as if the gods had descended close to the earth so they could have a better vantage of the coming battle.

The army of Tyrace approached, glittering, implacable.

At her side Camilline let out a long sigh. "That is a lot of soldiers," she said.

"Yes," Marilia agreed faintly. "A good many."

On the flanks, Tyracian cavalry thundered over the hills, the whinnying of the horses muffled by the thin layer of fog that hung, shroud-like, across the valley. In the center, the footmen continued their slow, steady advance, shields locked together, feet, trampling the blue chrysathamere flowers, leaving a trail of bruised and broken petals to mark their passage.

If there was any comfort to be found in the sight of that army coming to meet them, it was this—that Marilia had done all she could. It wasn't much, as comfort went. But it was something. This battle was out of her hands now.

"We've done this before," Camilline said. "Well, not us, specifically, I mean, but...Svartennos."

"Done what?"

"The whole mad-victory-against-bad-odds, smaller-outnumbered-force-take- on-larger-army-and-wins thing. With Kanadrak. When your fathers were here."

But that's just it, isn't it? *Marilia thought, chewing her lip.* How much like my fathers am I, really? *She had the blood of one and some training from the other, but she wasn't either of them. Maybe it was too much to ask that Svartennos would get lucky twice.*

She wished Karthtag-Kal were here with her, to lead the charge, to cut his way through the Tyracian lines. Not Zev...but Zev, like she, was all they had.

The height and the wind were with the men of Svartennos; their arrows traveled farther than those of their enemies. Some found their marks, and Tyracian shield-men fell and vanished, swallowed by the sea of their own army. Most shafts caught in the thick wall of yoba-shell shields. The Tyracians kept coming, on up the hill until they met the wall of Svartennans who were waiting for them. Shields ground together; swords glimmered in the dull light like fish darting beneath the surface of a river.

The blue flowers and green grass of the valley slowly turned to red as men began to die.

Part II: Bride of Svartennos

Three Years Ago

Chapter Thirteen

By the time Marilia was sixteen years old, she had become a full member of Petrea's circle of ladies. While Annuweth spent more and more time afield, riding with his new friends, Marilia passed many of her hours visiting the villas of Petrea's friends—Praxia, the daughter of a newly-minted governor; Claria, who giggled almost as much as she spoke; Isenia and Aveline and of course Petrea herself, the center of them all, the axis around which the others revolved. Marilia never felt entirely at ease with them. When they talked of the oddities of the other young nobleman and ladies of the city, she could not help but be conscious of her own peculiarities. Petrea and the rest seemed to age naturally and gracefully, whereas Marilia felt like one of the street-performers' puppets: long-limbed, awkward, spidery, with red marks upon her face that kwammakin cream could not completely hide. Her breasts too small, her hips too narrow, her jaw too square—as if she had been shaped out of clay by a clumsy potter who tugged and prodded too much in the wrong places.

Petrea and her circle of friends talked of handmaidens (they were all excited by the prospect of having one when they were wed someday) of races (Petrea favored the reds and so of course all the rest of them favored them, too) and, above all, of secrets—the city's many scandals. By this time, Marilia had picked up a few scandals of her own. She knew, for instance, that Livenneth's wife and he didn't get along, and that she resented how much time he spent at Karthtag-Kal's villa; knew that more than one senator was fonder of dicing and betting on the races than was proper; knew that one of the Order's captains had loved a sister of the Sacred Flame (loved the way a buyer loved a painted lady, that was). That last one, especially, was quite popular with Petrea's friends.

But in the face of her companions' stories, Marilia's often seemed disappointingly un-exciting. Her disadvantage, of course, was that she lived in the prefect's villa, surrounded by men, with no sisters and no mother. Nelvinna was there to teach her the lady's graces, but there was no one to teach her those things that transpired in the corners of gardens, in curtained rooms behind closed doors, in whispers and laughs between young ladies when no one else was there to see them. Karthtag-Kal simply didn't, as Petrea put it, *get out;* he spent most of his time with Livenneth or the captains of his Order, and tended to avoid parties and large gatherings. And there were only so many scandals she could pick up in his house.

"Let me go first," Claria begged one day as they were sitting together around a stone table in the garden of her family's villa, sipping jala juice and watching the bees hum among the flowers.

"All right," Petrea agreed. "What is it?"

"Petriel Lathaos of Svartennos *likes* me," Claria said, leaning in over the table, her voice hushed. It was clear she'd been burning to share this news for some time. "\He's been following me around. I make him do things for me sometimes; I told him to pick a chrysathamere flower for me from the garden. He looked for two hours. They don't even grow in this city." She laughed, and the others laughed, too.

"Boys don't know anything about flowers," Isenia observed.

"He wanted to kiss me," Claria said. "I asked him, and he told me so."

"And did you let him?" Petrea asked.

Claria flushed and looked down at her hands. A small, satisfied smile touched her lips.

Petrea, too, had kissed a boy (she wouldn't say who; that secret was her prerogative, as their leader. All she would say was that he was just a little older than her, and very handsome). Praxia had done so with the Harbmormaster's son. And now even Claria, who was, at just shy of fourteen, the youngest of the group, had tried it. Marilia felt dread fill her as she realized what was coming next.

"What about you, Marilia?" Claria was the one to ask the inevitable question. "Have you ever kissed anyone?"

Marilia wished she could fall away through the ground. Close her eyes, and open them to find herself back inside the prefect's villa, safely tucked away in a corner of Karthtag-Kal's library with her Sharavayn figures arrayed before her. Somehow that game, in all its complexity, seemed simpler than Petrea's dimpled smile.

She shook her head. "My father wouldn't be happy if he found out."

Petrea laughed. "That's why you keep it from him," she said patiently, as if explaining the matter to a small child. "It's only a kiss. It's not like you're taking them to your bed."

Marilia felt her face burn still hotter.

"It's not so frightening," Petrea said. "I can show you, if you want."

Marilia did not *want*. Not here, in front of Claria, Isenia, and Praxia. But the others were giggling, and Claria was smiling eagerly, and she knew they would all be terribly disappointed if she said no. So she said yes. Beneath the garden table, her hands were shaking.

"Close your eyes," Petrea said.

Marilia felt soft lips touching hers, and a lock of Petrea's hair tickling her cheek. There was that smell again—jasmine—and Marilia felt heat like a lightning strike crackle through her chest. She pulled back, wide-eyed, feeling her heart flutter like a fire-moth's wings.

"There," Petrea said. "That wasn't so bad, was it?"

Marilia simply nodded; there was a knot in her throat that made speaking impossible. The colors of the trees and the white-gold walls of the villa seemed too bright. Petrea was talking again, but Marilia could hardly concentrate on whatever it was she was saying.

It was a mercy when the meeting ended and one of Karthtag-Kal's knights came to escort her back to the prefect's villa.

She made her way into Karthtag-Kal's shrine, hoping the Stoics' trance would clear her head. She sat among the candle smoke, and tried to remember the prayers of the ancestors, but her thoughts were scattered, distracted. When she closed her eyes, she could still feel Petrea's lips.

She shivered; a tremor like a wind-blown leaf swept through her body from the crown of her head to the tips of her toes.

She sat there in the shrine until her heart slowed.

To her own surprise, she felt her eyes hot, damp with tears. The moment she and Petrea had shared had been so *much* to her; yet even now, in the Jade Keep, the princess was no doubt sitting down to dinner with her family, readying her knife for a slice of razorfish, the afternoon already forgotten. What to Marilia had been as bright and sudden as a glimmer of reflected sunlight had been to Petrea, she guessed, just another game. That something could mean so much and so little at the same time—it seemed incredibly wrong.

She envied Claria and Praxia for their perfect smiles, for their clear, un-blemished cheeks, and of course for the many stories and scandals they always had to offer. With them around, she could never be anything more to Petrea than a shadow. What she wanted was to re-create that first moment in the Jade Keep's garden when she and Petrea had stood apart from the others, bound by the realization of a bond they shared, by a hushed exchange of secrets.

She lit blue candles for clarity and insight, almost ashamed that she needed to trouble her ancestors for something that Karthtag-Kal would probably think extremely petty; but to her, in that moment, it seemed vital. She needed to impress the princess.

She waited and waited, but clarity did not come. All she felt was a growing restlessness, one that she would have thought more natural to Annuweth than to her. At last, frustrated, she blew the candles out.

But though she at first thought that her prayers had gone unheeded, it turned out that perhaps some of her ancestors had been paying attention, after all. Her chance to impress Petrea came sooner than she would have imagined, though it would end up costing her more than she could have guessed.

As it turned out, Marilia and Petrea had more in common than dead mothers. Just as Marilia had always been close to Annuweth, so too was Petrea close to her brother Rufyllys, even though in Petrea's case her brother was quite a few years older than she was.

Rufyllys Vergana, the emperor's true-born son, was nothing like Ilruyn, his adopted brother. He had the same deep, intense eyes as his father and brother, but they were not the kind of eyes that were made to glare a rival swordsman into submission. They were weak eyes with poor sight, set in a narrow, pinched face. He was thin, with limbs more knobby and awkward than Marilia's own, and unlike Marilia, he had finished growing; there was no hope that the Fates might sort him out in a few years.

Although Rufyllys was the son of the warlike Moroweth Vergana, he appeared to be the kind of man who would have been more at home during the reign of the previous emperor, Secundyn. But Secundyn's poetry parties were a thing of the past; they had been replaced by Vergana's tournaments. While Secundyn had been emperor, rhovannon troupes sang ballads and performed comedies in the halls of the Jade Keep. Vergana's tastes ran more towards the epic, the somber, and, of course, the Stoic.

It was, in part, out of love for Rufyllys that Petrea's resentment of her *other* brother was born. Ilruyn was the impostor, the interloper who had inserted himself into the Vergana family and fashioned himself into the emperor's prodigal son. Though she took care to smile at him and play nice, Petrea took delight in wounding Ilruyn in small ways, as she had during his first tournament. As she did again with Marilia's help a couple of weeks after their kiss.

It was a beautiful summer day. Marilia and the princess were walking through the gardens of the Jade Keep. "Are the others joining us?" Marilia asked. "Claria and the rest?" Petrea was almost never without her full retinue of ladies.

"Not today," Petrea said. The way she said it made Marilia think that she had something special in mind. "Only us. Is that all right?"

"Yes." Of course it was.

They continued to walk. Orange-red tiger-lilies lined the path on either side, making it seem as if they were stepping through the halls of the mountain of fire where the Tyracians believed the dremmakin king had his home. "You're very good at Sharavayn, isn't it so?" A few weeks before, Marilia had mentioned to Petrea her games against Karthtag-Kal, hoping to intrigue her.

"I am," she said.

157

"Ilruyn is good at it, too. He has a little group of his friends that he plays with. They play in tournaments against each other, and the son of Crescens the game-master runs a betting pool on the whole thing. Ilruyn is the best of them all. He thinks himself very clever. Are you better than he is?"

"I don't know."

"But do you think you might be?"

"Maybe. My father says I am." She paused, considering. This was no time for modesty, she felt. "One of the best he's ever seen."

"There's this girl Ilruyn fancies," Petrea said, her voice low, conspiratorial. "Would you try to beat him for me? Would you try to beat him in front of her and the rest of his friends?"

Here was Petrea, the princess, asking for her help. Marilia would have done anything she wanted. "Yes," she said without hesitation.

Petrea led Marilia into the center of the garden. There, in the shade of a gazebo, Prince Ilruyn was sitting with his circle of friends—six of them in all. There was a young woman, there, too, not far from the prince's side, smiling as she wound a lock of her hair coquettishly around her finger. Marilia loathed her at once.

On a huge round table in the center of the gazebo, battalions of Sharavayn figures had been set up. Two young men were seated across from each other. The prince was just finishing a game, demolishing the remnants of the opposing player's army. Marilia lurked at the bottom of the gazebo steps, watching. Measuring. He was good, she saw, and felt a small flutter of nervousness in the pit of her stomach.

Still, she thought she could match him.

"Ilruyn, victor," a man announced when the game was over. A few gold coins changed hands. Ilruyn began scooping up the pieces. He paused as Petrea skipped up the steps into the gazebo.

158

"Well done, big brother," she said, and there was such false sincerity in her voice that Marilia almost believed she meant it. She shivered; Petrea could be almost as good at acting as a rhovanna, when she wanted.

"Sister. Come to bring me good fortune? You're late; that was our last game."

"Actually, no." Petrea's voice was light and playful. "Remember how I told you I'd find someone good enough to beat you? And if I did, you'd buy me a dress of the finest Daevish silk?"

"Have you found this champion?" Ilruyn asked, raising his eyebrows.

"Karthtag-Kal's child. Will you play?"

"Karthtag-Kal's child," Ilruyn repeated. "Well, that makes sense, I suppose. The prefect always did love his Sharavayn. I was about to head to the baths, sister…"

"Oh, come on. We had a wager on it, Ilruyn."

"Well," he said. "If you insist."

Petrea smiled. Marilia stepped into view, ascending the steps of the gazebo.

One of Ilruyn's companions laughed, delighted. Ilruyn shot him a stern look and he subsided. "What is this?" he asked, looking, bemused, at Marilia. "Is this a joke?"

"Karthtag-Kal's started teaching her," Petrea said. "She's good, I promise."

"Karthtag-Kal's been teaching her," Ilruyn repeated slowly. "Well, I suppose the prefect always did have his own way of doing things. Petrea…no." He shook his head.

"But you said…"

"Come on, be serious."

"My prince." Marilia took a step forward and all eyes fell on her. A distant, forgotten part of her warned her that she was being rash. She was certainly being unladylike. Karthtag-Kal had advised her not to speak much about her painted lady mother; it would surely have put a frown on his face to see what she was up to now.

All those inner warnings paled against the simple fact that the princess had asked her for help. Now Petrea's plan was crumbling in the face of Ilruyn's disregard. Marilia wasn't going to let that happen. "I've heard you're one of the best players in the city," she said, bowing her head to Ilruyn. "Father talks about you all the time. He says you're like the next Nelos Dartimaos."

Ilruyn blinked. "Did he really say that?" She detected a touch of pride in his voice.

"He did. He said you did things with the board even he never thought of." Marilia bit her lip, doing her best to present the image of a sheepish, awestruck girl in the presence of her idol. "I would be honored to have a game with you."

The man who had laughed before laughed again. "Oh, go on, Ilruyn. Play her," he urged.

Ilruyn hesitated. But he couldn't very well back down now, not in front of his sister, his lady, and his friends. "Very well. A quick game."

It won't be quick, Marilia thought. *It won't be quick at all.*

She took the seat across from him. She took a deep breath. As the prince set up the pieces, she fidgeted nervously with the sash of her dress. She was acutely aware of the eyes of the others on her—of Petrea's eyes, most of all. They were burning with an intensity she reserved only for special occasions.

Ilruyn leaned in over the table. He *was* good. His first few moves were skilled, lethal—as if a snake that had been basking in the sun had suddenly come alive and was moving to strike. By the end of their first exchange, he had captured several of her best pieces. It took all her focus to match him.

She gritted her teeth. She could not let herself fail the princess.

Breathe, she told herself. *Find your focus. Forget them. It's just Sharavayn—nothing you haven't done before.*

The garden fell away. Petrea and Ilruyn's friends were gone, as was the rustling of the cherry-blossom trees, the tiger-lilies beside the pond, the wind and the sound of chicayas singing. All that was left was the game, her, and Ilruyn.

He was good, but she had been trained by Karthtag-Kal, and he was no Karthtag-Kal. She could tell by the rigid way he kept his chair that he had not been expecting such resistance.

She stalled his attack as her eyes scanned the board, searching for an opening.

One of the books she'd read came back to her then. The account of Prefect Valennos and his battle against the First Legion of Dane. He had allowed his center to collapse, feigning a retreat by his commander to draw his enemies in before enveloping them on all sides. It had worked in part because of the overconfidence of his adversary; until that day, Dane's First Legion had never been defeated.

Marilia knew she couldn't re-crate the maneuver in all its complexity here on this gameboard; the game was not a perfect simulacrum of a true battle. But she could create her own, modified version—a trap for Ilruyn to fall into.

Marilia let the prince carve his way forward towards her general. She began to pull back. He sensed her weakness. His best battalions pursued, driving their way into the center of her formation even as she played around the edges, doing her best to make her movements look random, reactionary, when they were anything but.

Her counter-attack, when it came, was brutal. The Valennos Maneuver left him trapped. Her pieces, though, were free to move. They regrouped and came for him, hard.

"She's good, Ilruyn," the lady laughed, laying a hand on his arm. The prince started, distracted; Marilia noticed sweat on his brow.

He did his best to recover, but it was too little, too late.

In the end he was forced to raise his hand in surrender.

He offered her a crooked smile, as if to suggest that the game was an indulgence he had granted her, a careless bit of amusement into which he had invested no true effort. "Well, look at that," he said. "The lady has some skill." But she wasn't fooled; the struggle had been real, and so had his defeat. She saw the knowledge in his eyes—and when she looked, she saw uncertainty in the eyes of his companions.

"Thank you for playing with me," Marilia said politely. She couldn't deny that she felt a cold, fierce joy at seeing his discomfort. She helped him pick up the pieces. He and his friends left, Ilruyn muttering some excuses she couldn't hear. Marilia leaned back in the chair. She felt simultaneously elated and exhausted.

Petrea beamed at her. "That was brilliant," she said. She leaned in to kiss Marilia on the cheek. Marilia smelled her jasmine-scented hair oil.

Struck by a sudden boldness, she rose to her feet, took Petrea's face between her hands, and kissed the princess on the lips. It was a quick, stolen kiss. Petrea did not object. She merely laughed and took Marilia's hand, pulling her away from the gazebo.

They wandered through the garden, dipping their feet in its cool streams, feeling the warmth of the sun as it filtered through the branches of the willow trees. The wind made the leaves rustle like a lady whispering her secrets.

"I'll never forget that," Petrea said. "You are a marvel."

Marilia felt a sudden rush of warmth. "*You're* a marvel, Petrea."

Petrea sighed and glanced back towards the Jade Keep. "I suppose I ought to head in. It's almost supper time. Father just abhors it when anyone's late."

Petrea started to turn away. Marilia frowned. That didn't seem right; this moment couldn't just end that way, so unremarkably. It was the kind of golden moment that was meant to last.

"I love you," Marilia blurted. As soon as she had spoken the words she froze, stunned by her own boldness. She feared she had spoiled the moment, taken things too far.

Petrea turned to look at her. She laughed lightly, touching Marilia's arm in farewell. "Why, thank you. You are a good friend. One of my favorites."

On any other occasion those words might have made Marilia's heart sing with joy. Now, they cut as painfully as a physick's scalpel. The golden splendor of the moment was dimmed; she felt her joy vanish like a firefly disappearing inside a child's palm. She had hoped for more. Maybe she had been foolish to hope, but she had hoped all the same.

Petrea drifted away, and Marilia made her back to the prefect's villa. The climb up the stairs seemed longer than it normally did.

Karthtag-Kal was waiting for her at the top. As soon as she saw the look on his face, she realized she had erred—badly.

He led her into his room and slid the door shut behind them. In the narrow confines of the bedroom, with both of them on their feet, she became aware of just how tall he was; he seemed as tall, in that moment, as he had the first time she'd met him back in Tyracium. Vast as the shadow of a mountain.

163

"Is this how you comport yourself?" he demanded. "Interrupting Prince Ilruyn's Sharavayn league? Humiliating the emperor's son in front of his friends? Do you know who those men are? One is the son of our Head Magistrate. Another is the son of the High Priest of Zantos. The rest? Senators' boys, all. And the girl is the sister of one of my own lieutenants." His hands clenched into fists. "You made a spectacle of yourself in front of all of them."

"I'm sorry." Her voice came out in a feeble croak.

He stepped close, towering above her. "I am the emperor's prefect," he said, each word slow and measured. "And you are my daughter. How you act reflects on me. This is how whispers begin, girl. Do you know what they may say of you now? Do you know what they may say of me?"

She shook her head.

"They will say that you are a bastard child, that you have a bastard's wildness in your spirit. They will say that there is too much of your Tyracian mother's blood in you. They will say that I—a foreigner myself—could not fashion you into a proper Navessean lady without a mother's guiding touch."

"I didn't know you cared so much what they thought."

Karthtag-Kal's eyes flashed with anger. "Only a fool wouldn't care," he growled.

Marilia felt her own anger rise in answer. She had defeated Ilruyn, one of the city's great champions. She deserved praise; she deserved all the gold from the wagers that the Crescens boy tallied. She deserved to shout her victory far and wide. Instead—this. Cowering against the wall in the face of Karthtag-Kal's wrath. "A fool or a coward," she snapped, before she could stop herself.

Karthtag-Kal's brows narrowed in anger and he took a step before

164

her, gripping her by her shoulders. She felt the immense power in his arms, enough strength to fling her across the room like a doll. "You have your father's stubbornness," he said. "And I am done encouraging it. I swear it by all the gods. No more sparring. No more games. No more *Sharavayn*."

Marilia stared at him in horror. "No…please…"

"Perhaps some of the fault is mine. I took things too far. You're not a little girl anymore, Marilia. You just turned sixteen years old. You have your own reputation to consider. Do you think you'll find yourself a good husband if you act like a fool in front of the emperor's family?"

Marilia felt an icy chill slither through her gut. She knew, of course, that he was right; for girls of her stature, there were only ever two real choices: marriage, and the Order of the Flame, the followers of the goddess Shavennya who kept alive the enchanted fire that protected Ulvannis.

But the followers of Shavennya were very particular about who they admitted into their ranks. As a bastard girl born in Tyrace, her chances of joining the Order of the Flame were next to nothing. Which meant there *was* no choice.

She'd always known the day would come, but she'd chosen to forget. To busy herself with distractions and postpone the moment she'd have to think about her future.

"I made a mistake."

"Your mistake is the talk of the Jade Keep. So much so that I learned of it within three hours. You hurt my honor, risked your future—and your brother's too—and for what? These games, Marilia…they're pointless pursuits."

"If they're so pointless, why do you spend so much gold on the best tutors to make sure my brother masters them? To try to make him as good as me, even though he never will be? They're pointless pursuits for a lady, I think you mean."

Karthtag-Kal was silent for a moment. "Yes," he said. His voice was hard and flat.

"So that's it, then? No more Sharavayn?" her voice shook. "All because I beat the prince?"

"No," he said. "Because you're not sorry in the slightest. Are you?"

She stared at him. There was a hot ache deep within her throat that made speech impossible.

"This is for your own good, you know. Maybe someday you will come to see that."

CHAPTER FOURTEEN

Marilia rushed from the room. She found Annuweth standing in the middle of the hallway; he must have just returned from his day's ride with Victaryn Livenneth and his other friends.

She froze, her face burning. "How much did you hear?" she demanded. Annuweth hesitated; that hesitation, coupled with the look in his eyes, was answer enough.

She returned to her room. She found her Sharavayn pieces waiting for her, set up in one corner of the room in a formation she'd been studying from a book she'd borrowed from the Imperial Chronicler's collection.

"No more of you, I guess," she said to the pieces, kneeling beside them. "I'm a lady now. I'm supposed to get married, and who would marry a girl who once beat a prince at a game of figurines? What a *scandal.*" She scooped the pieces into their box, erasing her complex formation—a half hour's worth of preparation—in the blink of an eye. There was a bitter, masochistic pleasure to be found in the act of destruction. When at last the Sharavayn figures were tucked out of sight, she seated herself on the edge of her bed forced herself to face the thing she'd been avoiding for the past year—the prospect of her marriage.

There had been several occasions when Petrea's friends had spoken of their future weddings, their handmaidens, their husbands-to-be. They had fashioned futures for themselves, painting them stroke by stroke with the same meticulous attention they might use to paint a scroll of water-script to grace their villa's walls.

Marilia had no painting of her own.

She sat on the edge of her bed plucking at the sheets with her fingernails, if only for something to do. A year ago, she'd stained those sheets with her first bleeding. She recalled the moment now, hot-faced; the quick, furtive rush to carry the sheets outside while Karthtag-Kal and Annuweth still slept, to hand them off to a couple of servants to be cleaned before either of them could see.

She tried, at last, to look ahead. Would she stay in Ulvannis? Marry, perhaps, a senator's son? Surely Karthtag-Kal would prefer her close. Maybe it would be a career soldier—a lieutenant, a captain of the Order? Or the child of a member of the emperor's council?

None of it felt real; none of it had any substance. The images of her future were as formless and indefinite as shapes glimpsed in the stars.

She knew what she ought to do—speak to Karthtag-Kal. But the thought of facing him again, of talking with him about her marriage, made her stomach turn over. She would be cursed by the dremmakin before she'd go crawling back to him after what had happened.

The weeks passed in grim, stony silence. Her anger still simmered inside her; it was too fierce to respond to Karthtag-Kal with anything more than the obligatory daily niceties—*I'm well, father. Thank you. Could you please pass the bread? No, I don't feel like going to the games. I'm weary. But thank you.* And when it came to Annuweth, she was ashamed—he had witnessed her humiliation

Luckily, she saw him little. He spent more and more time riding with his friends in the fields beyond the city, visiting the games, and, above all, training for the Trials of the Order of Jade, which he would take that coming summer.

She spent her time much as she had before. When she wasn't with Petrea or her friends, she was studying water-script or the ladies' graces.

Not swordplay.

Not Sharavayn.

One day, as she was sitting alone in the villa's shrine, Karthtag-Kal came to her. "I know things have been…tense…recently…" he began.

She almost laughed at how absurd that sounded. It sounded like the sort of thing she'd expect one senator would say to a rival he was trying to sweet-talk before a vote. "They haven't not been," she confirmed. "What do you want, father? Why not get straight to the point? That's what a stoic ought to do, isn't it?"

"I think I've found someone," Karthtag-Kal said. "A man for you to marry."

That got her attention. She turned to look at him, her belly lurching unpleasantly.

"Already?" He hadn't wasted any time.

"You're sixteen years old, and…"

"Petrea's father hasn't even started to look at suitors."

"Princesses marry later than other girls, you know that. Besides, if a good man is ready now, here, and has expressed his interest—why wait for one who is only fair?"

"Who is he?"

"His name is Kanediel Paetos. He's older than I had imagined your husband would be—twenty-three years old now, twenty-four by the time you turn seventeen—but already a lord of Svartennos; his father died just two years ago. He's a younger cousin of Ben Espeleos, and one of his favored strategoi—that's what they call commanders in

169

Svartennos. I knew his father—he fought beside Nelos, Ben, and I against Kanadrak. He was a good man. From all I've heard, I believe his son is the same."

"Svartennos?" she shook her head. "That's miles and miles from here." It would mean leaving most of those she knew behind. Not just her family, but Petrea and her other friends, too.

"I know. But the Paetos family has ties here. Kanediel has cousins in the capitol that I am told he's fond of, and he visits often."

"How often is often?"

"About every other year."

Marilia drew back. That didn't sound *often* at all.

"I know," he said, reading the look on her face. "But I think you could be happy with him on Svartennos. It's different from Ulvannis. It's a wild land. But things are...freer there. Besides, you have relations there. Your father's sister and her son."

An aunt I've never met, who never paid us a visit. Karthtag-Kal had explained that the Lady Dartimaea had a deathly terror of ships, but from gossip she'd picked up over the years Marilia had come to suspect that her aunt had also been less than pleased by the revelation that her brother had two children born from a Tyracian painted lady.

"If I go..."

"If you go, it will mean leaving your world behind a second time," Karthtag-Kal said bluntly. He sat beside her on the bed. She did not draw back, but neither did she move closer. She hadn't yet forgiven him. "But it could also mean you might be happy. Happier, I think, than you would be here. And believe it or not..." he gave her a keen look out of the corner of his eye "...and maybe, lately, you don't believe it...I do want you to be happy. That more than anything. Even if it means sending you away." She saw his throat bob as he swallowed.

170

She looked away. She felt something soften inside her, and was angry at herself for feeling it. "You want me to meet him," she said. It wasn't a question.

"He'll be here in the city in eight weeks. You could meet him before he returns to Svartennos."

"Fine. Let's do it." She did her best to sound calm, controlled. But inside, her heart was pounding.

After Karthtag-Kal had left her room, Marilia stripped off her clothes, and studied herself before her mirror of polished midnight stone, examining each part of her body with the cool dispassion of a commander considering the battalions of his army.

Her jaw was a little too hard for true beauty. She was unusually tall. Her breasts were too small. In her right wrist there was a vein that bulged against her skin. She stared at it. It had always been there, but in the last few years it seemed to have grown unnaturally. She thought it looked rather like a worm's back pushing up through the earth.

Her hips were narrow. Too narrow for birthing children? She remembered her mother's fingers smearing red in Annuweth's hair, the last glassy flutter of her eyes.

Would she go the same way?

Her stomach knotted. She pulled on a dress and headed into Karthtag-Kal's shrine, where she lit candles and tried to fall into the Stoics' trance.

It didn't work. She became aware of the air in her lungs, the sluggish beat of her pulse, like the slow creep of a river drained by the sun. Her throat tightened as if an invisible hand had found a grip there—One-Eye's fingers, reaching for her out of the depths of time.

She rose, furious, and blew out the candles, glaring at them as if they themselves had offended her. One resisted her. It fluttered but would not go out; it hung in the air, a single, mocking point of light.

Driven by an inexplicable impulse, she reached out until her hand hung above the flame. As she lowered her arm, she felt its heat against her naked skin, a stabbing pain like the point of a sword. Her eyes were wide; she bit her lip.

She held herself there, one second, two, three, counting in silence. Breathless, she stared at the shiny red mark the flame had left on her skin. Her hand closed slowly around the wick, snuffing it out. The pain of the fire still clung there like the ghost of a dream.

"I win," she whispered, and stepped out of the shrine, leaving the candle smoking behind her.

Two months passed in no time at all.

She waited for Kanediel just inside the door of the prefect's villa, clad in a white dress with a blue habithra sash around her waist—the colors of his house. She'd thought she'd been nervous when she'd faced Ilruyn down in front of all his friends, or when she'd first dueled Karthtag-Kal across a board of Capture the Emperor to prove herself to him. But those occasions were nothing compared to this. Sweat traced its path down the back of her neck. Her stomach felt the same as it had when she'd followed Karthtag-Kal onto the galley to Navessea. Fitting, maybe. That had been the start of her first great voyage; this could be the start of her next.

Karthtag-Kal opened the villa door, extending his hand in greeting, and then it was her turn.

Kanediel's eyes fell upon her. She saw them move up and down and knew that he was seeing what she had seen in the midnight stone mirror that morning. She felt her face heating as she stepped close.

He himself was neither handsome nor ugly, but exceptionally average. His face had a slight gauntness to the cheeks, his mouth seemed to be locked in a perpetual half-frown—not of displeasure, but perhaps preoccupation. His hair was cropped short. He was thin, and only a little taller than she was.

"My lady," Kanediel Paetos said.

She dipped a curtsy and offered him her hand. She tried to angle her arm so that the vein in her wrist faced away from him.

They made their way out into the garden. The silence stretched on. The weight of the rest of their lives hung between them like a stone block.

Kanediel sighed and stretched, rolling his shoulders, a gesture designed, she guessed, to prolong the moment when one of them would have to find something to say.

"It's a good wind we're having," she said. She was glad for it. Without it, she might have been completely covered in sweat. She was afraid he would feel the heat from her face. *The weather,* she thought, appalled. *I'm talking about the weather.*

"Yes. A fine wind. You can smell the northern sea." He gave her the impression of a physick toiling over a man afflicted with a deadly illness, gamely trying to keep the conversation alive, even though one foot was already in Zantos' fields. "Did you know they call Svartennos the windy isle?"

"I've heard that. I hear it's a very beautiful place."

"Oh, it is. Savage, at times. There are earthquakes, as there are in Dane. Gentler, but more frequent. The Elders say it's Shuvakain, the Pale One, trying to escape from beneath the earth." He seemed almost as relieved as she was to finally have found something to talk about. "The earth rattles our castles and houses from time to time, but our homes are built to last—to bend with the earth, rather than to break. We use the wood from the long-neck trees along the northern coast. It's very supple." He shook his head with a rueful smile. "My apologies. I must be making it sound quite horrible. It's not. There are hills, rolling hills with pools of water where the fog hangs in the mornings...and fields of little blue flowers. Chrysathamere flowers."

"Like the banner of Svartana the sword-maiden," Marilia said.

"Exactly so."

She shook her head. "Forgive me, my lord."

"Please—Kanediel."

"Forgive me, Kanediel. I'm usually a better conversationalist."

"Nothing to forgive," he said.

"I hope you don't think ill of me."

He touched her arm, his fingers lingering uncomfortably close to her vein. "Marilia, you are the daughter of Nelos Dartimaos. The blood of one of Svartennos' greatest families flows through your veins. Not to mention that Karthtag-Kal's told me much about you, and if there's any opinion I trust, it must be his." He smiled. "Believe me, I do not think ill of you."

Dinner—thank the gods—was a less uncomfortable affair. Annuweth had returned from wherever he and his companions had roamed off to, and Kanediel's sister was present, as well. The presence of more people acted as a buffer between her and Kanediel; when the two of them ran out of something to say, someone else stepped up to fill the void.

Kanediel's sister was called Camilline. She was slight, with long legs and straight hair that had been cut so that the ends were even as a razor's edge. The rest of her was all angles; she carried herself with one hip jutting, her head slightly cocked to one side, her mouth slightly quirked. She might have seemed odd, but the glimmer in her eyes seemed to suggest that perhaps it was the world that was a little odd, off-center, and she was the only one seeing it clearly. She was beautiful, Marilia thought, but not in the way that Petrea was. The princess' beauty was of a classic, story-book sort, while in Camilline there was something sharper, like the graceful efficiency of a well-made sword.

After dinner, while Kanediel spoke with Karthtag-Kal about the Order of Jade, Camilline approached Marilia. "How about a ladies' ride?" she asked. "Just the two of us. If you're willing?"

"Won't Kanediel mind?"

Camilline laughed. "Of course not. It was his idea."

Truth be told, Marilia didn't feel much like riding. Ever since she'd met Kanediel, her stomach had been tying itself in knots and she wasn't sure the saddle would help. But she didn't want to tell Camilline that. "Let's go," she said.

"I have to warn you," Camilline said with a grin. "I like to go fast."

That much was true; soon enough, Marilia found herself racing over the fields outside the city, her hands tight around the reins, the stalks of the tall grass tickling her ankles as she flew over the hills. To her surprise, she found that the open air *did* help; it was hard to keep worrying about marriage when she was busy concentrating on not falling off her horse. She'd always fancied herself a fair rider, but next to Camilline, she was an inexperienced child. In the capitol, most ladies used yoba-drawn carriages for most journeys, and riding was purely for leisure. On Svartennos, the ladies rode everywhere they went, the same as the men.

On either side, flooded fields of milk-yams sped past, a blur of violet leaves and glimmering blue water. In the still water Marilia could see a perfect reflection of the clouds and the distant mountains.

Beside her, Camilline laughed, a wild, breathless sound. She leaned forward over her horse's neck. She sped past swift as an arrow. Just when Marilia began to wonder if she might simply ride on over the hill and out of sight, Camilline wheeled her mount about. She charged back the way she had come—incredibly fast...recklessly fast, as if she were running away from something that was just at her back. Marilia caught sight of her face.

Camilline's lower lip was held between her teeth so tightly that Marilia feared she might draw blood. The look on Camilline's face was familiar; it took Marilia a moment to place it, and when she did, she felt a quick shock of recognition. It was the same look she had seen on her own face in the mirror after she touched the candle-flame in Karthtag-Kal's shrine to her skin.

Camilline drew her horse to a halt beside Marilia, the hooves carving long gashes in the ground. She brushed the dark tangle of her hair back from her face.

"Are you all right?" Marilia asked, uncertainly.

"Sorry," Camilline said, sounding sheepish. "I sometimes forget myself. Well, that's why my cousins call me Mad Camilline."

"Do they really?"

"And they're not the only ones."

"Aren't you worried about your reputation?" Camilline was only a couple of months younger than Marilia herself was; she'd be married, too, before too long.

Camilline rolled her eyes. "Oh, I don't think I need to worry too much. See, I have good tits and an important name. And the number of things one can get away with increases tenfold if one is the possessor of those two things." Marilia snorted despite herself.

They stopped at a place overlooking the northward-flowing river, both winded, staring out at the evening light sparkling on the surface of the water. "If there's anything you'd like to ask me, ask me," Camilline said. She glanced around meaningfully. "No one's here to listen. You're nervous, aren't you?"

Marilia bit her lip. "Is it that obvious?"

"Maybe I'm just observant. Go ahead; ask whatever you like."

"What is he like?" Marilia said after a moment.

"Well, I am his sister. So of course, you have to understand that you can't really trust anything I say. That being said…" Camilline's eyes turned inward, and her smile faded. "He's good. I suppose that sounds rather unhelpful, but it's true. He's kind. He might not have turned out that way, either. Our father always had a short temper. Our mother wasn't much better. And growing up, Kanediel was always around our cousin Zev, who did his best to turn my brother into a little shit like himself. But none of that took. I suppose because his spirit's strong." She shrugged. "I love him," she said simply. "I'm lucky to have him. I wouldn't marry him myself, of course, but I wouldn't feel bad for whoever did." She gave Marilia a side-long glance that made Marilia's heart beat faster. "I'd be glad to have you as my sister-by-marriage. If that helps."

Camilline's words touched something in her; the way she talked of her brother reminded her of herself and Annuweth; or, at least, she and Annuweth as they had been before they'd begun to drift apart.

"I think it helps," Marilia said.

Something about Camilline—the ease of her smile, the quickness of her laughter—reminded her of Petrea. But with Petrea, Marilia had always felt just a little on edge, somehow out of her depth. With Camilline, things were simpler. She felt only warmth. If Petrea was a sweltering bonfire, then Camilline was the steady, comfortable glow of its embers after a long night.

"It's up to you, of course," Camilline said. "Don't feel pressured."
She smiled. "Well, maybe just a little."

Marilia returned to the villa to find Kanediel and Annuweth sitting
cross-legged in Karthtag-Kal's garden.

Now, to complement his trim black noblemen's robes, Annuweth
wore two green aeder swords belted at his waist. Almost seventeen
years old, he had completed his trials and become a knight of the Order
of Jade. At the moment, he was engaged in a pastime appropriate for a
newly-minted knight of the Order. Sharavayn figures were set up on the
ground between him and Kanediel. Marilia paused in the villa doorway,
watching them from the shadows, Camilline beside her.

"Good swordplay *and* good strategy…you could make captain
early," she heard Kanediel say. "Your ambition, I suppose?"

Annuweth nodded. He moved a couple of his figures on the board.

Kanediel laughed ruefully. "I always thought I had a knack for this
game, but that is just brilliant. Old Prefect Valennos would be proud."

Marilia felt her heart skip in her chest; her eyes traveled
downwards, to the figurines arrayed on the ground between the man
and the boy. It was the Valennos Maneuver, the same one she'd used
against Prince Ilruyn. Rougher, undeniably; a crude simulation of her
own stratagem—as might be expected from a re-creation based on
second-hand knowledge of her game. One of Ilruyn's friends must have
shared it with him.

She watched, frozen, as Annuweth demolished the edges of
Kanediel's formation. Just a few scant weeks ago, she had
congratulated him, had endured an hours-long celebratory dinner with
Victaryn Livenneth, Thoryn Cyrdoreth, and the rest of his friends in the
Order, listening to them all talk on and on about their bright, glorious

future. He hadn't deserved that from her then. And he didn't deserve the way Kanediel was looking at him now. Watching him reminded her of the story of Margameth the charioteer; crushed to death by his own prize stallions after they were stolen from him, purchased by his rival and set against him in one last, fatal race. She thought she had just an inkling of what poor Margameth must have felt as he died—not the fear, nor the pain, but the mute, ravenous outrage.

At the end of it, Kanediel rose and offered Annuweth his hand. "It has been a pleasure, Sandaros."

He turned and for the first time he saw her. His smile was broad and genuine; it made her feel all the guiltier that her own felt so forced in return.

He took her hands. "I hope to see you again, Lady Sandara," he said.

"It has been a pleasure," she said. "Karthtag-Kal was right about you; you are a good man."

Kanediel blinked. "High praise, coming from the prefect." He glanced slyly at his sister. "I'll take it where I can find it."

"Just don't let it go to your head," Camilline said, rolling her eyes.

The two of them departed. Shortly after, Karthtag-Kal followed them out the door, descending to the barracks to speak with one of his lieutenants.

Which left her and Annuweth alone in the villa.

She found him in the sparring room, dressed only in a loincloth, his back shiny with sweat as he went through his drills—high, low, back, counter. His blade like the head of a snake, darting in and out as he struck and parried the blows of an invisible adversary.

"Good swordplay," she remarked, and he jumped, wheeling to face her. "*And* good strategy," she grinned mirthlessly. "You'll be a captain

179

in no time, just like Kanediel said. The Valennos Maneuver. Very nice. Wonder where you got that from."

He frowned, staring at her. "Do we have a problem?"

"Did you tell Kanediel you learned that from me?"

"No."

"You just let him think you came up with it all on your own. Isn't that right?"

"What does it matter where I came up with it?" Annuweth asked, shaking his head. "It was just a game, Marilia. A friendly game after dinner."

"You weren't there to see how I beat Ilruyn. So, who told you?" she asked, taking a step into the room. "Come on; you can tell me. Was it Crescens? I doubt it was Ilruyn himself."

"What does it matter?"

"If it doesn't matter then you can tell me, can't you?"

"This is ridiculous." He turned away from her.

"What's ridiculous is that Kanediel thinks you came up with that trick all on your own. You? I bet you haven't even read all of Valennos' Histories."

"I have read them," he said tightly.

"Oh? And how long did that take you?"

He spun about, his teeth bared. "It was Petrea, all right?" he spat. "There? Are you satisfied?"

Marilia drew back. For just a moment, her fury was swallowed by confusion. "Petrea? You barely even know her."

"That's not true. We know each other very well, for your information. Guess she doesn't tell you everything."

Something about the way he said it sent a chill through her. Dimly, as if through a fog, she recalled Petrea's words as she described her first kiss. *He was younger than me...very handsome...and of course a fine little warrior, I take only the best.*

"You're lying," she breathed. She had thought she knew the measure of her rage. Now she discovered that, like the depths of the sea, it held hidden currents still waiting to be explored.

"I came here to practice," he said coldly. "Do we have a problem?"

"The problem is that I could beat you at Sharavayn while I was drunk on rice-wine," she snapped. "And all the special tutors in the world won't change that." She saw pain on his face. Not enough.

"You think you'd make a better captain than me?" he demanded. "Is that it?"

"Yes. That is it."

"Because you know some fancy tricks in a game? Because Karthtag-Kal taught you a few moves with a sword? You're not a knight, Marilia. What you are is ridiculous." He made a face, his eyes squinting, his mouth screwed up into a frown of concentration. A wicked imitation of her own. "Have you seen yourself? Have you heard the noises you make when you practice? You sound like a painted lady."

"Take it back."

"Make me." He snatched a wicker-wood sword from the rack against the wall. "You want to be a knight? Defend your honor." He tossed it to her and she caught it by the handle, feeling the soft texture of the cloth binding against her palms.

She looked at him—really looked at him, as if seeing him for the first time. He had grown significantly in the past two years. He was of a height with her, but broader in the shoulders. She saw the muscles in his arms and his bare chest tense as he brought the practice sword up to guard. She felt a tremor of apprehension crawl down her spine.

181

She angled her own sword up before her, taking several more steps towards him, until she stood just a few paces away. "Take it back," she said again, her voice low and even.

"No."

She lunged at him, sword chopping down, and she hit nothing but air as he turned aside. His return strike was blinding in its swiftness. She threw her arms up, her sword at an angle, Karthtag-Kal's lessons ringing in her ears—*water, be like water*—and she still felt the shock of the impact rattle through her arms.

She side-stepped quickly and cut at his neck, just as she'd been taught. She missed again, but barely. She followed it with a lunge at his chest but his practice sword swept down and across, driving the point of her sword towards the mats on the floor. His return to guard—a quick turn of the wrist—sent his sword up into her face. She stumbled back, her ears ringing, her head throbbing from the force of the blow.

Annuweth twirled his sword end over end, a needless flourish. An image came to her—Castaval, spinning his practice sword in his hands as he stood over Annuweth's huddled, broken body. "Yield," Annuweth said.

She ran at him again, shifting her grip on her sword. *Deceive your enemy,* she thought, Urian's maxims springing to mind.

She faked a stab at his face, swinging around and chopping at his side instead. But he wasn't fooled; he caught her sword squarely on his own and followed the parry with a short jab. The tip of his sword caught her in the ribs and she fell back, winded. The second blow had come harder than the first; just as she'd thrown away her own inhibitions, so Annuweth had parted with his. Except for the fact that the swords in their hands were wicker-wood, not aeder, this might as well have been a duel to the death.

She sprang at him, finesse forgotten, wanting nothing more than to wipe the smug look from his face, to send him scurrying away, to knock him down, make him hurt. He responded in kind; their swords crashed together until her palms began to go numb.

Sweat dripped into her eyes. Her breath came in ragged gasps. Still he stood before her, calm, confident, untouched. It was like being the white king in a doomed game of Capture the Emperor. Everywhere she went, everything she tried...

Blocked.

As her strength began to wane and one of her blows went wide, he slipped around her and drove his sword across the small of her back.

She wheeled about, lashing out with both hands. Parried. And even as she felt her wooden sword scrape against his, she realized her mistake; she had overextended, an error Karthtag-Kal would have shaken his head at. She was powerless to stop him as he side-stepped and brought his sword in low against the side of her knee. Her leg buckled. She went down on one knee, and his sword cut across in a blur, knocking hers from her aching fingers. She stared up at him with eyes stinging with sweat. The tip of his sword brushed against her chin. There was no pity in his eyes, and it struck her how far they had come from that moment when they'd lain together, hand-in-hand, in the cabin of Karthtag-Kal's galley.

"Yield," he said again.

Her skull pounded. It felt as if the blood in her head had turned to molten wax.

Never, she thought. She made a grab at his sword, missing as he jerked it away. Relentless, she tried to regain her footing. And in that instant, as the muscles of Annuweth's forearms tensed, as his fingers tightened around the hilt of his sword, she saw that he would not let her.

He stepped in and the hilt of his sword, gripped in both hands, slammed into her gut, just below the line of her ribcage. All breath left her. It felt as if she had been hollowed out, as if a hand had reached inside, scooped everything out and set it to one side, to be returned later. She fell onto her back, wheezing, shivering as he stood over her.

"Are you done?" he asked, coldly.

"And how many more hours have you trained than I have?" she shot back, resisting the urge to curl up and be sick. The pain spread through her like a stain; she felt its grip in her groin, in her back against her spine, in her lungs.

"Several hundred, probably." He nodded his head at where her hand clutched her bruised waist. "Stings, doesn't it?"

She bared her teeth. "You know he still likes me better than you."

He flinched as if struck. Maybe she hadn't been able to touch him with her sword, but it pleased her to know she could still wound him with her words. She thought for a moment he might strike her again. She saw in his eyes that he wanted to. But he didn't. Instead, he kicked her sword away to the far corner of the room and replaced his own on the training rack.

"Feel free to try again, when you're ready," he said, and left her there on the floor, sliding the door closed behind him.

She stumbled back to her room, her body aching. With shaking hands, she shuttered the windows against the last, wound-red light of the setting sun and lay there in the dark, hidden from the world. She glared at her reflection in the mirror, disgusted at her own frailty, at the body that had betrayed her. She seized it and turned the midnight-stone surface flat against the dresser.

After a time, she heard the steady rhythm of Karthtag-Kal's footsteps in the hallway outside. She grimaced, aware of the bruise that was forming on her brow, along with the other, unseen bruises on her side, her leg, her back; Annuweth had held nothing back. In the dim light, she hoped, her father would not notice. There would be questions asked tomorrow, surely, but by then she could have some excuse ready-made.

"Come in," she said when he knocked.

Karthtag-Kal entered the room. He seated himself on the cushion by her desk. "I was hoping we could talk," he said.

"We are talking, father."

"True enough." He chuckled. She didn't. "There are others, of course," he said. "Magistrate Crathes' boy, for instance. Even Victaryn Livenneth. I could arrange meetings with them, if you like. But as I said before, I thought that on Svartennos…"

"I would be happier."

"Yes. In a perfect world, Svartennos would be a little closer to Ulvannis…but I lived for years alone in this villa before you and your brother came to Ulvannis and I expect I'll survive after you're gone."

As she looked at him, she realized that perhaps she wasn't the only one who was troubled by the prospect of her marriage. She could see old sadness in his eyes, a sadness that had been locked away for a long time, a loneliness that had carved its traces into Karthtag-Kal's rough face.

She'd been angry with him since the day she'd battled Ilruyn in the royal gardens; now, at last, she felt most of what was left of that anger drain away. She knew he was telling the truth; he'd always been telling the truth. He *did* want her to be happy.

185

When Petrea's friends had talked of the men they hoped to someday marry, they had described a similar feeling of excitement when they looked on those boys—a sensation like being tickled by lightning. Marilia felt none of that when she looked upon Kanediel. But that didn't mean she didn't know what it was; she'd felt it before, in the sunlit garden of Claria's villa and now she had felt it again, during her ride across the fields outside Ulvannis.

She feared that searching for it in a husband would be nothing but a waste of everyone's time.

Karthtag-Kal had promised her that Kanediel was the best Svartennos had to offer. He was kind, he was patient. *If I don't marry him, what then?*

She could find a husband in Ulvannis. She'd be close to Karthtag-Kal. Their occasional games of Sharavayn might continue, in secret; she sensed that his resolve on that point was softening.

She'd also be close to Annuweth. She'd get to watch him rise the ranks of the Order of Jade—on to the Emperor's Dragonknights; maybe, if he studied hard at it, captain within a couple years. Quite possibly prefect within a decade, once Karthtag-Kal stepped down. He'd never climb to the top of Ilruyn's Sharavayn club, but he'd land himself among their ranks, at least. He *could* climb to the top of the tournament field—she'd just seen firsthand how good he was with a sword. She'd watch him rise and rise, his glory burning bright as the golden sun while her own faded into the night.

No. No, I won't do that.

"I'll marry Kanediel Paetos, father."

"Are you sure?"

She didn't feel sure. Not at all. What she felt was an all too familiar flutter in her belly. An unease that was the precursor to fear.

186

She closed her eyes.

She pictured Annuweth standing over her, the tip of his wooden sword against her throat as she knelt, bruised and hobbled, at his feet.

And she knew that whatever it was she sought, she would not find it in Ulvannis.

"Yes," she told Karthtag-Kal, "I'm sure."

Chapter Fifteen

Svartennos marked the easternmost border of the empire. The largest island of Navessea, it sat between the Bay of Dane to the south and the Sea of the Lost to the north.

Compared with the rest of the empire, its position was a perilous one, and always had been. The island was beset with many dangers. Earthquakes were frequent; though the Mountain Gods that watched over Svartennos had succeeded in trapping Shuvakain, the Pale One, below the earth, he was not happy in his chains and made frequent attempts to break free. When he did, the houses and castles of the island trembled, and waves hammered against the shores

Crabs the size of small horses roamed the island's beaches (which were few; most of the island was ringed in steep, craggy cliffs). Though the efforts of Svartennos' warriors had done much to thin their ranks over the years, still there were enough that it was a brave or foolhardy soul that ventured into the sea for a swim. Stay too close to the land, and a crab's claws might shred your flesh to ribbons. Venture too far into the depths, and a prowling razorfish wouldn't even leave ribbons behind.

And the natural perils were not the only ones.

In the old days, Svartennos' enemies had been many. From the south came roaming bandits from Tyrace. From the north came Valdruk slavers. Once, years ago, the slavers from Valdruk conquered Svartennos and made its people their chattel, until Svartana, the daughter of the old king, rose up and cast them out. *Never again*, was the mantra the people of Svartennos lived by. Never again would they fall prey to their enemies, never again would they be shamed or humbled or left at a tyrant's mercy.

Like the hammer of a smith's forge beating heated aeder crystal into shape, the dangers of the island only served to make its people stronger. The knights and lords whose task it was to keep the island safe gave themselves to their task with unflinching resolve. They stripped themselves of the finery that they saw as a mark of the mainlanders' weakness; their Council of Elders went so far as to set limits on the amount of silk, gold and midnight stone any man or woman could possess. The one luxury they did not limit was aeder, which the mountains in the north of the island were rich with. The people of Svartennos fashioned it into swords, spears, and arrowheads, and with it they brought death to any enemy that dared to sail along their coasts or land on their shores.

When they turned fifteen, the sons and the daughters of knights were taken into the mountains, where, beneath the watchful gaze of an assembly of Elders and the island's guardian gods, they trained. By the time the island joined itself to the empire of Navessea, the knights of Svartennos had already won a reputation as some of the best warriors in the world.

What struck Marilia most as the island appeared in the distance was the sense of vast age it imparted. Its twin mountains, Phelkos and Aphexia, had risen ever taller with the passing of time. Now they towered to the sky, their peaks ringed in clouds like the heads of a newly-acclaimed emperor. In their stones they carried the weight of ages, a constant reminder of an older time, a time before senates and empire, when kings and Horselords battled each other for the fate of a vale, a river, a forest. If Navessea was the future and the warring city-states to the north were the past, Svartennos was the proverbial giant with one foot on each side of the river. Sacrifices were made to Viveos, Shavennya, Yalaeda and the rest of the imperial gods even while the people of the island sent their best and wisest to join the Elders of Mount Phelkos, a group of holy men and women who devoted themselves to the Twin Mountains that had been the gods of the island for longer than anyone could remember.

Marilia watched as the island slowly filled the horizon. Hills of rolling yellow-green grass stretched ahead as far as the eye could see. Herds of yoba roamed the fields, their calls echoing mournfully out across the water. Farmers with broad-rimmed wicker hats raised their heads to watch the ship's approach.

Much of the southern coast was dominated by tall cliffs, a natural defense against pirates and other enemies from the sea. Their pilot steered the galley into a gap between two bluffs where a harbor had been built. Ships bearing the sigil of Espeleos—a green banner with three gold spears—bobbed at anchor.

"Almost there. Just three days' ride to Svartennos City," Karthtag-Kal said, coming to stand beside her at the rail. "Are you all right?"

She looked at Karthtag-Kal. Considered telling him of the dreams that haunted her nights—dreams of One-Eye's rough, blood-red fingers, of drowning, of painted ladies with ash for eyes. They had begun not long after she'd first spoken the words—*I'll do it, father. I'll marry Kanediel Paetos*—and had only grown more frequent in the months since.

In the end, she only nodded. "I'm fine," she said. He patted her on the shoulder.

"You'll be all right," he promised her, though she couldn't help but think it sounded as though he was trying to convince himself, too.

"You'll be all right, my daughter."

He seemed to sense she wanted space; he moved off to join her brother on the other side of the deck. It had been several months since her duel with Annuweth in the armory of Karthtag-Kal's villa. The weeks had passed in a blur, over before she could begin to mark their passing. In all that time, the two had hardly shared more than a few words. Now, in a matter of days, he would sail back to Ulvannis and fade out of her life.

Isn't this what you wanted? she asked herself. *Isn't this exactly one of the reasons you decided to go to Svartennos in the first place?*

She looked down at the sea, feeling that familiar churning in her stomach. She could still picture him staring down at her, glimpsed through the stinging sweat that ran into her eyes, her body throbbing with pain, his wooden sword at her throat. *Unforgivable.*

But somehow, despite all that had happened, it still felt wrong to leave things as they stood, to let him sail away without at least trying to mend what had been broken between them.

She took a step towards him. She realized she had no idea what to say, where to even start.

You could start by apologizing, the voice in her head suggested. But the problem with that idea was that he had hurt her more than she had hurt him. He was the one who had demanded the duel and struck the first blow. Who had stolen her strategy to impress her husband.

Her desire to put things right warred with her pride. In the end, pride won. She stayed where she was on her side of the deck. The ship slid into the harbor; the gangplank was lowered. Annuweth swept past her with hardly a glance.

Kanediel, Camilline, and Ben Espeleos were waiting for them on the shore. Kanediel gently took her hand, helping her down from the gangplank. Ben was less reserved. His smile swallowed his face as he spread his arms. "Welcome to Svartennos. Land of heroes. Quite a sight, eh?"

They rode north to Svartennos City. Though it was called a city, after the vast streets of Ulvannis, it seemed more like a village. It was maybe a tenth of the capitol's size. The houses were built of aged, yellowed stone, with sloped roofs gleaming with tiles of lava-stone. Windows shuttered with vellum panels glowed invitingly in the evening as they drew near.

They passed the crumbled remains of a half-built wall. Annuweth remarked upon it.

"After the days of the Valdruk, one of our princes tried to build a wall to protect this city," Kanediel explained. "He didn't get very far before the earth heaved, destroying much of his work. The Elders decided it was a sign from the gods—the wall was not meant to be. It would make the people of Svartennos weak, would steal the special quality that made them the world's best warriors. *The walls of Svartennos City are its ships and the swords of its sons*, they said."

"I wonder if a real wall wouldn't be more effective," Annuweth said.

"No one has really threatened the island since it joined itself to Navessea, so I suppose there's not much need," Kanediel answered. "Even if there were, it would be hard to convince the Elders to let it be built. Change does not come easily to Svartennos."

Marilia sat on a cushion as servants fussed at her hair. They had drawn it up into a strange sort of bun atop her head—two tightly wound curls bound together with a golden thread. It was some kind of

Svartennos marriage custom; Catarina had said something about it at dinner last night but Marilia hadn't really paid attention.

There was a full-length midnight stone mirror in front of her, and she stared at it because there was nothing else to stare at. A hard-faced, nervous girl stared back at her. She grimaced as she felt a tug at the side of her head.

"My lady looks very beautiful," the servant girl said. She was plump, curly-haired, with a bright smile. On another occasion, Marilia might have found her good cheer endearing.

Marilia smiled weakly. "Thank you." *Gracious,* she thought, but she did not feel beautiful. Nor had she felt beautiful yesterday, when she'd been forced to stand, near-naked, before four Elders of the island (all women, thank the gods), who had assessed her physical fitness to determine whether she was worthy to serve as Kanediel's wife.

Karthtag-Kal had assured her it was a mere formality, something that all young nobles of Svartennos had to go through before the men earned the right to their swords or the women to their habithra sashes. That hadn't really made it any less miserable, or terrifying.

Behind the opaque vellum panels of the wall behind her she could see the shadows of men and women moving about—setting the table for the wedding feast out in the castle courtyard. She would have to walk between those tables, down the length of the courtyard to where Kanediel Paetos would be waiting for her beside the white statue of Sothia. The mere thought made her feel ill, as ill as she had been standing on the deck of a galley for the first time.

The servant girl had apparently finished what she was doing to Marilia's hair. She left, and Marilia was alone…for a few seconds, at least. Then she heard the scrape of the door sliding open. She opened her eyes. Her stomach swooped yet again; it was Camilline.

"You look fine today," Camilline said, kneeling before Marilia, her dress folding around her; she made the movement look effortlessly graceful.

"Thank you. So do you."

"By this evening we will be sisters. Camilline and Marilia Paetia."

The name sounded strange to her. It didn't roll smoothly off the tongue the way the name *Sandara* did.

"Still nervous?" Camilline asked.

She nodded. She hoped, at least, that Kanediel wouldn't be able to tell.

"It's nothing to be ashamed of."

"I know it is a great honor to wed Lord Kanediel..."

"A scary thing is scary no matter how great an honor it is," Camilline said. "There's nothing quite as frightening to the human heart as the unknown."

"Akeleos of Svartennos," Marilia said, remembering. "The son of Queen Svartana. He wrote that last part."

"You know your famous Svartennan writers. That's lucky for you. I don't think I could have let you marry my brother otherwise. We might have had to call the whole thing off." A pause. Camilline tilted her head to one side, studying Marilia's face. "I'm only joking—you know that, right?"

"Oh. Right."

"You *are* nervous. Have you tried talking to Lady Catarina?"

"No. Why?"

"She told me when she got married, she was terrified. All those eyes, staring at her. You know, my mother always used to say that in times like that, it helps to try imagining them naked."

"Naked?" Marilia's eyes widened.

"The guests, I mean. To make yourself feel less nervous."

"I…I'm not sure that's really helpful…"

Camilline pursed her lips. "I suppose not, come to think of it. That advice is real horseshit, isn't it?"

Marilia coughed.

"Sorry for the language. All this time around Ben has ruined me for proper company. I just don't see how imagining a horde of naked men surrounding you is supposed to make you feel better. Besides, there are a good many lords and ladies on this island I'd rather not ever see naked, even in my imagination." Marilia smiled despite herself.

"If you want some advice that's not horse-shit, just remember it's only Kanediel," Camilline said. "I love my brother, and I'd never let him hear me say it, but when all's said and done I've seen Danish pastries more frightening than he is. And one of those would be more likely to do you harm, too." She grimaced and put a hand on her stomach.

"Thank you," Marilia said.

Camilline squeezed her hand. "I'll see you soon," she said, and left.

The servants returned. They hovered over her, adding a few finishing touches to her face. Then they left again. The screen door closed behind them. It was considered ill-luck for a man, especially the husband, to lay eyes on the bride on the day of her marriage before the moment she stepped out onto the wedding path. That meant Marilia was left alone, watching the shadows move about outside, the noise muffled by the walls of thick paper that enclosed her like a kwammakin's cocoon. She waited there until Catarina came to escort her to her new husband.

"Lady Espelea," Marilia said, getting to her feet. She bowed her head. It was a great honor, for the daughter of the emperor and the wife of the prince to be the one to present her to Kanediel.

"You can call me Catarina. And I will call you Marilia, if that suits you."

"Yes, Catarina."

"It's almost time." From out in the courtyard came the sound of a reed flute playing. Marilia took Catarina's hand.

It took a moment for Marilia to work past the dryness in her throat. "Forgive me, my lady, but...the Lady Camilline told me that...you were frightened, too? At your wedding?"

"Oh, yes. I was terrified of all of it." Catarina gave a rueful nod, remembering. "I thought Svartennos a strange and wild place. I was sure I'd be a terrible disappointment to my husband. You have to understand—I was always a quiet girl. I had spots, too, and even the make-up couldn't completely hide them, though the handmaidens did their best. I knew that men of Svartennos usually married their own kind, and they only made exceptions in rare cases, if the woman in question was from strong blood, if she was *fit*. I never really thought I was. And then there was my husband—well, you've seen him, you know what he's like. I thought I'd be completely...how to explain? Swallowed up by him. I was sure I'd disappoint him. I was no woman of Svartennos."

"He's very…memorable."

"Memorable." Catarina smiled knowingly. "That's one way to say it. He was everything I wasn't—confident, handsome, experienced. And he didn't care what anyone thought of him. Still doesn't, really."

"Experienced?" Marilia caught sight of herself in the mirror, realized she was chewing her lip. She made herself stop.

"With women," Catarina said in an undertone. "I'd already heard talk of Ben Espeleos before I ever set foot on this island. How he was a man with no fear. How he once killed his own uncle in a duel. How he'd wrestled a dremmakin. How he'd out-swam a razorfish, and been with many women. *I wonder,* I heard a man say once, *whether Espeleos has stabbed more men with his sword or women with his...*well, you know."

Marilia felt her cheeks flush as she looked down at her hands. That vein was showing again. She tugged at the cuff of her sleeve, pulling it down to hide her wrist. But that only caused the other sleeve to ride up, baring her left forearm. She frowned, perplexed. "And now?"

"Now? Now I have a loving husband and a beautiful young daughter. He can be difficult sometimes, and wild. But he loves me. The first time we spoke I hardly knew what to say. But he didn't seem to care. He asked me questions, lots of questions, about my parents, the capitol, my little brother Rufyllys. I even told him about the paintings I'd done, and talked about the artists I liked, and he was kind enough to pretend to be interested. I think you'll find Kanediel to be easier to handle."

"Will it..." Marilia hesitated. "Will it hurt?"

"A little," Catarina said candidly. "But you'll be all right."

It's only Kanediel Paetos, at least, she tried to tell herself. *Not Ben Espeleos. He's not legendary, or fierce, he's just ordinary.*

She heard the voice of the priest. She turned to face the opaque wall, gathering herself. She felt Catarina's fingers tighten momentarily around her own before they stepped out together into the courtyard

Karthtag-Kal's voice was in her head. *Don't chew your lip. Don't move your fingers. Certainly don't bite your nails.*

The hem of her black gown trailed behind her as she followed a pathway of wooden planks set across a bed of white pebbles. On either side of the path, wildflowers had been scattered; their petals drifted with the wind.

The statue of The Lady of Four Arms was directly ahead. Beside it stood a Mountain Priest of Svartennos, his aged face as deeply lined as the cliffs that marked the island's shores; a priest of an old god beneath the statue of a new goddess, a perfect example, she thought, of the incongruous nature of Svartennos.

At the statue's base, waiting for her, was Kanediel.

She saw Annuweth and Karthtag-Kal standing to one side, watching her. Karthtag-Kal's weathered face creased as he smiled at her. She almost smiled back, then remembered she was supposed to be composed. She measured her steps, making sure they were small and graceful, as Nelvinna had shown her.

She stopped in front of Kanediel. She let go of Catarina's hand and took his instead; Catarina melted back into the watching crowd.

"Do you take this woman, Marilia Sandara, to be your lady wife?" the Mountain Priest asked.

"Yes," said Kanediel.

"Do you take this man, Kanediel Paetos, to be your lord husband?"

"Yes," Marilia said, and was relieved at how firm her voice sounded.

"Here in the shadow of our guardians, Phelkos and Aphexia, I see this man and woman joined. Behold them."

"Behold," the crowd answered.

"So it goes," the priest said.

Kanediel reached back to the golden ribbon that bound her hair and untied it with a deft motion of his fingers. Her hair cascaded down across the back of her neck. He broke the ribbon in half and handed one end to her. They turned as one to face the statue. In front, the priest was lighting a brazier of draleen oil with a candle.

The flames crackled to life, hungry and bright. "Go ahead, my lady," Kanediel said with a gentle nod. "You first."

She cast her half of the ribbon into the fire, watched as it curled in on itself as if it had been wounded, blackening in an instant. It was a morbid image; it hardly seemed suitable for marriage.

Kanediel cast his ribbon in after hers. He took her hand in his. They turned as one to face the crowd.

"Behold them," the priest said again.

"Behold," the crowd answered.

By the gates of the castle, a small group of minstrels began a Mountain Song. According to the old legends of Svartennos, the notes of such songs were what bound Shuvakain, the Pale One, beneath the earth. The song was not beautiful in the same way that the songs she had heard in the Jade Keep were beautiful; its beauty was of the same sort as that of the island itself—rough and unadorned. Each instrument was meant to mimic the sounds of the mountains themselves; the light, reedy notes of the flutes were the wind, and the low rumble of the drums was the sound of falling stone.

Kanediel turned to face her. The intensity in his eyes made her feel light-headed. She forced herself to hold his gaze. He leaned in and kissed her on the lips.

She thought back to the other, earlier kiss she had shared with Petrea. In the moment the princess had kissed her, her mind had come undone, her thoughts scattering into little flecks of color. She had wanted nothing except that Petrea keep on kissing her.

She waited to feel something like that now. But all she felt was the dry touch of Kanediel's lips, the rough prickle of his skin against hers, the uncertain touch of his fingers against the back of her head. Then, as quickly as it had begun, the kiss was over, and they were stepping down to join the crowd.

The next few hours passed in a blur. Gifts were exchanged; Karthtag-Kal presented Kanediel with a fine blue aeder sword forged by the best smith in Ulvannis. Kanediel presented Marilia with a finely-woven habithra sash that she bound around her waist—blue and white with two crossed swords in the center, just like the banner of his house.

She wandered among the guests; men and women toucher her arm, again and again, congratulating her. *But I did nothing*, she thought, blankly. *All this was Karthtag-Kal. He found me my husband. All I did was exist.*

For the first time, Marilia met her aunt, the Lady Dartimaea, and her cousin, Aerael Dartimaos, who each took her hand and expressed their delight to finally meet her in person (she couldn't help but think that neither of them looked very delighted).

She did her best to eat, staring down at the glazed berries Ben's servants had heaped on her plate, separating them into piles with her fork.

Annuweth had teased her about that habit once. *Which army will be winning today, the arandon berries or the heart-berries?* She felt a lump form in her throat as she looked at him.

It's not too late to make amends, the voice in her head whispered.

When the sun had fallen and the meal ended, she got to her feet and made her way over to him.

He spoke before she could. "Congratulations, sister." He took a deep breath, and, to her surprise, bowed his head. "I'm sorry for what I said in the armory." There was nothing but sincerity in his voice. "And I'm sorry for striking you. It…it wasn't how a knight should act. And I am ashamed of it."

If there was anything left of the fury he'd shown in their fight, he hid it well. Maybe there wasn't. Maybe the fury had been forgotten when he'd become a knight. She wasn't worth his anger now. Before, she'd been a threat, a rival for Karthtag-Kal's affections. Now she was just some Svartennan lord's wife, and he was a knight of the Order of Jade, one who had passed his Trials with distinction, who had subsequently proved himself such a prodigy that he'd been made one of the emperor's personal protectors—a Dragonknight.

I'm sorry too...sorry for the things I said in the armory. That was what she'd meant to say when she'd approached him, but the words died in her throat. All she said instead was "thank you."

What might have been minutes of hours later, Kanediel took her arm. He guided her away from the crowd, into the castle, up the stairs into the room Ben and Catarina's servants had prepared for them.

A rich blue and white carpet covered most of the floor. A cage of chicayas was perched atop the dresser, singing a song that sounded like the one that had played at her wedding feast. There were pots of white sand with sticks of incense laid out beside them on the dressers. She lit a couple. When she closed her eyes and breathed in the smoke it was almost like being back in Karthtag-Kal's shrine.

But she wasn't. Karthtag-Kal's shrine was far away, across an ocean, part of another world and another life.

"Marilia." Her heart lurched. Kanediel was standing just behind her; she could feel his warmth against her back.

It has to happen sooner or later. What is wrong with you? All the other women do it. Just get on with it.

He turned her to face him and she backed away from him until she

201

was at the foot of the bed. The room was dark except for the glow of a couple of candles in yellow-white paper lanterns. He reached out and took her wrists, easing her hands out of the pockets of her dress. His thumb traveled over the bump of the vein in her wrist and she bit her lip.

"My lord husband…Kanediel," she said, forcing a smile. She felt as though she was turning to water beneath his gaze.

"Marilia. You are beautiful," he said, untying the silk sash at her waist, easing her dress off one shoulder, then the other. He let go of her hands, reaching up to touch her bare skin.

"Thank you. That's kind of you to say." She stood naked in the candlelight. She felt like a child again. It took everything she had to stand there, open before him.

He stripped off his robes. She stared at him and felt blood pounding in her head. She closed her eyes. When she opened them again he was still there.

"I'm sorry, Kanediel," she said. "I…I hope I don't offend you. I just…I'm no good at this."

"It's not so complicated," he said, gently but firmly pushing her down onto the bed. His hands traveled up her legs, making the hairs rise along her skin. He found her knees and slowly eased her legs apart. He gave her a faint smile.

For a moment she was not Marilia Paetia, lady of Svartennos, but Marilia, the painted lady's daughter. For a moment, she was back in Oba'al's pillow house, pale silk fluttering all around, One-Eye's bulk looming above her like a mountain, his rough lips pressed against hers.

No. I am here in Castle Paettios. I am here with Kanediel, my husband, who cares for me. I am the daughter of Karthtag-Kal, and I will not be afraid.

202

His hands found hers. Their fingers twined together.

She felt a sudden spark of pain that snaked upwards from between her legs, climbing her like a vine climbing a wall. She gasped, her breath stirring the ends of her hair. Her grip tightened on his hand.

"Marilia."

"Kanediel?"

"Look into my eyes. Please." She realized she had been staring at one of the paper lanterns.

"Right. Sorry." She forced herself to look into his eyes as he moved above her; she felt she owed him that much. His hips moved faster. Her muscles were hard as corded ropes.

He asked, "am I hurting you?"

"No," she lied, and while she wasn't sure he believed her, she was relieved he did not press the point.

She could feel her hands trembling at her sides. *Get a hold of yourself,* she thought. *You're the prefect's daughter. You've hurt worse before. He's been nothing but kind and gentle with you.*

But her breath was coming too fast, and her heart was running wild inside her.

She stared up at the ceiling. The chicayas in the cage atop the dresser stared down at her, and if there was anything close to pity in those black eyes, she couldn't see it. For a moment it seemed that she split apart; she was the chicaya, looking down at a naked girl lying beneath her husband, the red stain of her blood darkening the sheets between her legs.

Dizzy, she closed her eyes. When she opened them, she was back on the bed; she was herself again. *It's done,* she thought. She lay there on the bed, feeling the softness of the blankets against her back, feeling the hairs of Kanediel's chest tickle her breasts. His hands shuddered in hers. He remained motionless above her for a moment, then quietly pulled away.

She exhaled slowly. At her sides, her hands were still shaking on the bed.

He stroked her face. "Marilia," he said.

She smiled weakly. "That was…" she didn't know what, exactly.

"It wasn't very painful, was it?"

"I'm all right," she said. The pain had faded to a quiet ache that had settled somewhere above her groin.

Kanediel closed his eyes, rolling over to lie beside her. She lay there with his arm around her, intensely aware of each breath. She tightened her hands into fists until the trembling stopped.

Above her the candles in the paper lanterns burned themselves out.

CHAPTER SIXTEEN

Marilia Sandara of Ulvannis became Marilia Paetia of Svartennos. The Elders of the island need not have worried; though she had been raised beyond the island's shores, Camilline soon made a proper Svartennan lady of her.

Like the rest of the island, Marilia's life in Castle Paettios—Kanediel's home, about twenty miles north-east of Svartennos City—was a mixture of the Navessean (she continued with the needlework and water-script she'd used to do at Karthtag-Kal's villa) and of something a little older and wilder. She wore the dresses she'd worn back in the capitol, but more frequently, she wore the training garb of Svartennos: a light tunic and leggings beneath a skirt that, by the standards of Ulvannis, was scandalously short, ending just above her knees. They were the sort of garments that allowed for ease of movement—running on foot and, more importantly, galloping on horseback. Camilline taught Marilia how to ride like a true Svartennan lady. Camilline showed her other things, too—the games that Svartennan men and women played to keep their bodies strong, how to hunt with bow and arrow from horseback, where the best rivers and hills were to be found.

Throughout Marilia's first four months on the island, letters continued to arrive from the mainland—long, effusive ones from Karthtag-Kal and shorter ones full of basic pleasantries from Annuweth. Through the letters, she learned of her brother's swift rise.

Annuweth had been considered for the post of Captain of the

Dragonknights.

Annuweth had passed his Captain's Trials.

Annuweth had been appointed—the youngest Captain in the history of the Order.

She wrote back, her letters brief as Karthtag-Kal's were long, different words but always the same message—*Kanediel is well. The island is well. I am well. Everything is well.*

She tried to be happy for her brother. But with each letter, she felt a cold, familiar ache in the pit of her stomach. It was a feeling that was hard to shake; it lingered with her the day after she learned of Annuweth's promotion, when Camilline led her out into the wilds of Svartennos, insisting that she knew a place that would make for a wonderful water-script painting.

Together they climbed until they came to the top of a bluff overlooking a plain and a glimmering pool of water. They sat there, feasting on rice-cakes, their legs dangling into the air, watching a herd of wild yoba as they roamed through the grass. Camilline laughed, her cheeks flushed dark with the exertion of the climb. But Marilia did not share her laughter; she stared down at the pool, lost in thought.

"How can you be frowning on a day like this?" Camilline asked.

"Sometimes I feel…" Marilia paused, searching for the right words. "Sometimes I feel as if I don't really *do* anything."

Camilline snorted. "You just climbed a small mountain. Is that not something?"

"Yes. I mean, it is. I just meant…I don't know what I meant." She gave a sigh of vexation. "We do things, but not like Kanediel; he manages the castle and the lands. Not like my brother."

"Is that what you're looking for?" Camilline raised an eyebrow. "Sweating in a training yard and squinting at…what is it exactly that captains squint at? Payroll papers? I'd take the mountains, myself."

"I suppose you're right."

"You should enjoy this. When you have a couple of children chasing each other around the hem of your dress you will look back on these days fondly." Camilline finished off her rice cake and dropped the leaf it had been wrapped in off the edge of the cliff; the wind carried it down to the pool, where it spun on the surface of the water.

Marilia felt a shadow fall across her chest. She forced a smile.

The truth was that when it came to the bed-chamber, she knew she was a disappointment to Kanediel, though he did his best to hide it. She'd always known the first time would hurt, but she'd thought that it would get better after that. It hadn't; if anything, it was even worse. After a few weeks of infrequent and uncomfortable coupling, at Kanediel's urging, she'd gone and consulted his physick.

Marilia looked down at her body, a grimace twisting her lips. *One task*, she thought. *That's all you had, one task, and you couldn't even do that right.*

The physick told her that a dremmakin may have taken root inside her. He'd given her a sixty-day course of tonics designed to kill it that left her with the lingering sensation of mild nausea. The nausea was much preferable to the pain. She hoped that it would work.

It either will or it won't, she thought, *and there will either be less pain or more, but House Paetos needs an heir, either way. If you can hardly manage to lie with your husband, how will you fare when the time comes to bear a child?*

She shivered. She couldn't help but remember her mother's blood-red fingers. She'd heard physicks say such deaths ran, sometimes, from mother to daughter.

Will I go the same way?

It would be a while before she had to face that question; she and Kanediel had chosen to wait to try again until the following spring. According to Svartennan tradition, it was generally considered good fortune when a child was conceived during the rains of spring or the heat of summer (the time when Queen Svartana and her son had driven the Valdruk slavers from the island's shores), and not during the harvest season or the cooler winter that followed. One of the Elders had informed Kanediel that in his family's case, this was particularly true; a long line of House Paetos children born during the winter had suffered early deaths, the most recent of whom being the deceased sister of whom Kanediel and Camilline rarely spoke.

Still, Marilia knew how fast time could pass. Her road only led in one direction, and she was afraid of what waited at the end of it.

"Are you all right?" Camilline asked. "You got so quiet."

"Just enjoying the view," Marilia lied. She tried not to think of children, or the future. She turned her gaze to the field and watched the yoba run through the grass.

But she'd never been much good at hiding her feelings from Camilline.

Camilline scooted closer until their hips were touching, their feet dangling together off the edge of the cliff.

"You seem like you're searching for something."

"I don't know what I'm searching for," Marilia said. "Sometimes I think I wasn't meant to be a lady. I've never been terribly good at it."

Camilline was quiet for a while. "Did you ever hear the story of Prince Bariel? He's the one who built the old wall around Svartennos City."

"I think I did once. But I forgot."

Camilline grinned. "He *loved* that wall. It was his obsession. Big, hard thing it was…some say that maybe it was a bit of wishful thinking on Bariel's part. If you know what I mean."

Marilia felt her face warm. "I think…maybe I have an inkling."

"He spent years finding the stone to build the thing, cutting it from the sea cliffs, hauling it over the hills. He almost had it finished. And then one day the earth had a particularly strong shake and it all came crumbling down."

Marilia winced. "Too bad for Prince Bariel."

"My point, Marilia, is that the world can get on without us."

"I know it can."

"My father always kept himself well-occupied," Camilline said, stretching back and staring up at the sky. "To be honest, my mother isn't much different nowadays, but my father…well, he and Prince Bariel had a few things in common. The more papers he signed, the more judgments he pronounced, the happier I think he was. I think he had some idea that the greatness of his spirit could be measured scroll by scroll. As for me…as for my little sister, an ill girl who, as far as he was concerned, couldn't really *do* much of anything—well, as you can imagine, he never spared much thought for us at all."

Marilia glanced sideways at Camilline. Marilia had never asked what had become of their lost sister; she guessed if they'd wanted to speak of it, they would have. "I'm sorry about your sister."

Camilline grunted. "Wonderful. Dead sister talk. And here I was trying to make things *less* gloomy." She said the words lightly, playfully, but Marilia thought she saw a flash of real pain, however brief, cross Camilline's face.

Marilia grimaced. "Sorry."

"You're missing my point, Marilia. My father was wrong. My mother is wrong. I don't care if your brother is dining with the

209

emperor's council right now. You are here with me, sitting on top of a cliff, and it is a beautiful day, and I will not have you moping about. As the Lord Paetos' sister, I command you to cease this instant."

"I'm not moping." Marilia smiled despite herself.

"No. You're right." Camilline sprang to her feet and offered Marilia a hand to help her up. "You're jumping."

"Jumping?" Marilia glanced down at the pool of water, chewing her lip. "It's a long way down. Are you sure we won't…"?

"Die horribly?" Camilline suggested. "Would that count as 'doing something,' in your opinion?'"

"Not the sort of thing I had in mind."

"Don't worry, it's deep enough. I've done this before."

"Of course," Marilia said. She couldn't say she was surprised.

"Come on, I'll race you to the bottom."

Marilia stripped to her undergarments. Her long hours of training with a wicker-wood sword had left her with quick hands, and she was done before Camilline. She was pleased by the look of surprise on Camilline's face.

She stepped nimbly to the edge of the cliff. "See you down there, then," she said, and, before she could change her mind, she dove from the edge of the cliff. She saw that Camilline was right; in the moment between leaping and falling, there was no room in her for doubt or regret; there was only the fierce howl of the wind that filled her lungs. She hit the water and rose to the surface, blinking it out of her eyes, feeling as if a million tiny sparks were leaping across her skin. Camilline landed beside her.

They swam together in the clear water of the pool while the yoba roamed around them; the sound of the beasts' cries mixed with the sound of the wind reminded Marilia of the Mountain Song that had been played at her wedding. When at last they'd had their fill of swimming, they dried off, and, their arms and legs aching pleasantly, made their way back towards Castle Paettios as the sun began to set.

Once they were inside, Marilia started towards her room, but before she had gone three paces Camilline came up behind her and slipped a hand over her eyes.

"What are you doing?" Marilia asked, startled.

"There's something I want to show you."

"What is it?"

"You'll see. Follow me."

Camilline led her down a hallway, then another. Marilia could feel the softness of carpets and the smooth surface of polished wood beneath her feet. She could feel her heart beating in her chest, as fast as it had been when she'd sprung from the cliff.

At last they stopped. "All right," Camilline said. "You can look now."

She did and her breath caught. She was standing atop a terrace at the very top of Castle Paettios, staring out across the farmers' fields. Directly ahead, in the gap between two hills, a red wheel of fire danced beneath the clouds. The light of the setting sun was reflected in the water of the milk-yam fields. Down below, the farmers of Svartennos were packing up their tools and making ready to head home for the night.

"It's like your painting; see?" Camilline said quietly, her hand tightening around Marilia's. "The one that's hanging in your room." One of several she'd brought with her from the prefect's villa—the one with Karthtag-Kal and Nelos Dartimaos, standing proudly atop a hill, raising their blood-red swords to the sky.

"It's beautiful," Marilia said in a hushed voice.

211

"It's yours."

Marilia felt Camilline's fingers tighten around hers. *It's ours*, she thought, but did not say.

They stood for a while on the balcony, the wind blowing past them, their hair streaming out behind them and mingling, until the sun went down, and the air grew cold, and—with a shiver—she turned and headed back inside.

Part III: War

CHAPTER SEVENTEEN

The story of Marilia's first war began when she was just a girl serving drinks in Oba'al's pillow house. It began with the death of Kanadrak.

After Karthtag-Kal slew the northern chieftain, his kingdom dissolved. All the many peoples who had been part of his great army drifted apart, and things in the north returned to a state much as they had been before his rise.

But all was not *quite* as it had been. Thousands of lives had been lost, and, inevitably, the balance of power had shifted. Daevium, once the greatest city of the north, had suffered mightily at Kanadrak's hands. Weary and shaken by the ravages of the warlord's army, it no longer had the strength or the will to match its old rival, Cardath.

Its vulnerability drew notice.

Aemyr-Kal, warlord of Western Cardath, former ally of Kanadrak, saw a chance to make his mark on the world—what better way than to burn the city of the cursed ship-builders to the ground? Daevium had insulted the people of Cardath for years; the Daevish stolen her holy places, had overrun her best land, had left her people to freeze and starve in the barren mountains, had even gone so far as to turn her sons and daughters into slaves, an indignity which could not be forgiven.

Now it was time for revenge.

Aemyr-Kal called his banners and marched on Daevium.

Many who had grown tired of peace found themselves drawn to this war like moths to a flame: mercenaries, pirates, bored nobles from the coastal cities looking for glory or plunder or simply a chance to use their swords.

One of these was Ben Espeleos, Prince of Svartennos.

Years before, during the days of Queen Svartana, Daevium had generously returned Svartennan heirlooms that had been plundered by the Valdruk slavers, so Svartennos owed Daevium a sort of debt. At least, this served as a sufficient excuse for Ben to launch his ships, even though Emperor Vergana had decided that Navessea would not take part in the northern conflict. In truth, for Ben Espeleos, any excuse would have been sufficient. He simply wanted to stab something.

He brought with him his foremost strategoi, including his cousin, Kanediel Paetos.

Who in turn brought Marilia.

It was considered ill luck for a newly-wed lord of Svartennos to be parted from his bride before she had even conceived, so Kanediel offered Marilia the chance to come with him. It was not exactly common for lords of Svartennos to bring their wives with them to war, but it was not unheard of, either, especially in cases such as theirs, where both lord and lady were young, in good health, and childless.

Marilia assured him that she was not averse to the idea; far from it. She was fit and strong, able to handle the voyage and the hardships of the road. Besides, she was curious to see the land where Karthtag-Kal had been born.

So Kanediel had brought her with him; and, since it was not fitting that a lady should be left without any sort of companion with whom to pass the time, Camilline joined them as well.

Though Marilia had read the stories of a thousand conflicts, reading and seeing were two different things. It was fascinating to watch an army at march—to see firsthand what she'd theretofore only gleaned from Karthtag-Kal's books. To experience all the minutiae of war, the complexity that even Sharavayn (the most complex game there was) could never hope to capture.

On the day before the fleet of Svartennos was to set sail, Marilia watched as Ben Espeleos climbed on a bluff overlooking the harbor, upon the mass of Svartennan ships assembled there.

"I am invincible," he proclaimed, standing on the very edge of the cliff, spreading his arms into the wind.

Maybe the gods heard his words, and maybe they wished to punish him for his pride, because that night a storm sprang up. The ships could not leave harbor; a few snapped free of their moorings and were shattered against the rocks.

The rain continued the day after, and the day after that, and on until the end of the week. All the while, across the sea, the war was unfolding.

Finally, two weeks after the rains had begun, they subsided, and at last the fleet of Svartennos set sail for Daevium. They made anchor three days later on the Island of Smoking Rocks, only to receive word that the delay had proved critical; Daevium was in dire straits. Her allies had been outmaneuvered and were now trapped beyond the mountains. Meanwhile, the Duchess of Daevium's personal army had suffered a brutal defeat and the forces of Aemyr-Kal had laid siege to the city itself.

Aemyr-Kal's besieging army had set up formidable defenses to prevent anyone from rescuing the city; to the east, a river provided a natural barrier against an attack, while to the west and south, the mountains did the same. All the bridges across the river had been destroyed; the only crossing was the shallows, and these were overlooked by a tall hill at the top of which perched a stockade wall lined with Aemyr-Kal's archers.

"An attack would risk great losses," Kanediel explained to Marilia, after returning from one of Ben's war councils. The two were sitting together in the shade of his tent, the last of the storm's rains drumming on the canvas overhead.

Marilia didn't need to be told; she understood all too well the peril of the situation.

"When I brought you with me, I assumed this campaign would be easy," Kanediel muttered. "I didn't count on the rains."

"What is Ben going to do?" she asked.

"He's not sure," Kanediel said. "Antiriel wants to turn around and sail home. Ben insists—and several of the other strategoi are with him on this—that it's a matter of honor. That we owe Daevium our aid. I'm not so sure." He chewed his lip. "They gave us aeder and some water-script paintings, heirlooms which rightfully belonged to us in the first place. Hundreds or even thousands of Svartennan lives seems an overly generous repayment."

"A little," she agreed.

"Ben's having another council in the morning," Kanediel said. "He said he'd take any suggestions then."

Marilia frowned. It was a puzzle, she saw—no different from the ones she'd struggled with under One-Eye's watchful gaze, or Karthtag-Kal's, except that this time, real lives hung in the balance.

The enormity of that fact almost took her breath away. *Don't think about that*, she told herself. *You can't, if you want to be of any use—it will overwhelm you. You have to take a step back. Pretend that it is just one of Karthtag-Kal's games. Assume there's an answer, and find it.*

"I think..." he began, tentatively, "I think I might have something."

The following day, Kanediel presented a plan to Ben Espeleos. The plan involved focusing on the river that barred access to Daevium from the east. Instead of trying to cross the shallows on foot—beneath the black rain of Aemyr-Kal's arrows—the Svartennans would begin constructing rafts along the shore of the river. They would make sure that Aemry-Kal learned of these rafts, but make it *appear* as if the rafts were meant to be a secret. Hopefully, Aemyr-Kal would take the bait; he would march the bulk of his forces to the south towards the river, believing the Svartennans meant to sail across.

Meanwhile, in the dead of night, a second, greater force of Svartennan ships would land to the east, marching by night through the mountain passes and attacking the siege lines around Daevium from the west—the opposite direction.

A deception within a deception. *Let your enemy believe he has seen your mind; upon finding one trick, he will not look for a second one.* Classic Emperor Urian.

It was not without risk, but Ben Espeleos had never been one to shy from risk.

The plan worked beyond Marilia's expectations. Afraid of the Svartennan army massing on the bank of the river, Aemyr-Kal pulled a large part of his forces east to deal with the threat—allowing a force of soldiers under the command of Ben himself to attack from the west, charging down out of the hills at first light and driving the confused and disorganized enemy before them. Within an hour, the western gate of Daevium was clear. The knights of the Duchess of Daevium sallied forth to join Ben, clearing away the siege lines to the south. Then they joined together to attack the greater forces of Aemyr-Kal's forces to the east.

The siege of Daevium was no more.

Through the end of the harvest season and the winter, Marilia traveled the northlands with Kanediel and Camilline as the armies of Svartennos and Daevium won skirmish after skirmish against the battered forces of Western Cardath until at last Aemyr-Kal himself sickened and died and his disappointed army scattered to the nine winds. The army of Svartennos returned to Daevium to celebrate and prepare to return home.

As the celebration began to die down and the moon rose in the sky, Marilia retreated from the stifling confines of the castle feast hall to the balcony outside the room she shared with Kanediel. Breathing deeply, she gazed out at the glow of the torchlight, at the darkness beyond, where the moonlight cut through the silver-white clouds that hugged the tips of the mountains and danced on the surface of the river. In that moment, it looked truly beautiful.

Kanediel found her there. He came and put a hand on her shoulder.

"It all began with that night in the tent," he said. "Your plan."

"Not just mine." Before presenting it to Ben, Kanediel had talked it over with her, and afterwards, the other strategoi had contributed to the strategy. Her idea was just one piece of a greater whole.

"Whatever you want to call it," he said. "It began with you. You were the spark behind it, at least." He tilted his head to one side, considering her. "You spoke as one who knows war."

"I know something of it," she admitted. "I learned from my father."

"You are a strange bride," he laughed.

"Strange?" she glanced at him uncertainly.

"I didn't mean it as an insult," he said. "It's just…you're not like other women."

"I don't know," she said. "I don't think I'm that different."

They stood together for a moment, watching the clouds pull back to reveal the full white face of the moon. The wind swept by, tickling Marilia's neck with her own hair. A warm wind, that carried the smell of flowers. Spring was here again.

She tried to think of something more to say. Even now, nearly a year into their marriage, the easy familiarity she'd found with Camilline eluded her when it came to her own husband, no matter how hard she looked for it. She felt as though there were a shell inside her as thick as a yoba's that she was powerless to break through. Though they ate together and rode together and slept together, Marilia felt that there was a something that lay just out of reach, like an evening firefly dancing just beyond the grasp of a child's fingers.

"It's spring again," she said, as a flower petal, blown by the wind, whisked past her face.

"Yes."

Her heart was beating fast, hammering inside her chest. She leaned in and kissed him, pressing her lips against his. He searched her eyes, surprised; it was the first time she had taken the first step. In his eyes, beneath his kindness and his quiet nature was the same hunger she'd seen on their first night together. She tried to match that look with one of her own.

She took his hand and led him inside. There he undressed her and laid her down upon the bed. They made love with the last fading sounds of the night's revelry echoing in their ears. As he entered her she let out a shaky breath.

Maybe whatever the physick had done had worked, or maybe it was only the passage of time, but it no longer hurt as much as it had those first few months. It wasn't the pleasure Catarina had described, and she thought that it never would be—not for her—but that was all right. She didn't need it to be.

This time, unlike those few others they had shared during the campaign, Kanediel did not pull away when the end came. He shivered in her arms.

He fell asleep quickly. She stayed awake awhile, her face where it lay in the thin sliver of moonlight. He had a peaceful look to him.

Once, upon drifting awake, she found him sitting beside her, watching her just as she was now watching him. She feigned sleep, studying him through the cracks beneath her eyelids. She saw such tenderness upon his face that it was like the sharp tug of an anchor-rope drawing taut inside her chest. It was the same way that he gazed at her sometimes when they made love—his eyes full of feeling.

She had always found it easier to close hers. Not tonight; this time she had kept them open, staring up at his face. She had heard the catch in his breath and known that she had surprised him, and that the surprise was a welcome one. She smiled faintly. She was glad she could give him that.

She fell asleep again to the feeling of his fingers running through her hair.

The following day, the army of Svartennos began the journey home.

Unfortunately, that homecoming was not to be what any of them had expected.

In fact, had Ben Espeleos known what was in store for him and his army upon their return to Svartennos, he never would have set sail for the northlands at all.

CHAPTER EIGHTEEN

Marilia awoke in the pre-dawn darkness with the vague understanding that something was wrong.

She threw back the thin silk sheet covering her and scrambled to her feet. She grabbed the chamber pot and ran out into the hall. Her stomach clenched as if it might turn over. But in the end the sickness passed. She swallowed, taking a deep breath as she leaned against the railing, gazing out at Svartennos Harbor and the sea beyond. They were staying in a boarding house near the water's edge, and the fresh salt air helped to steady her.

They had returned to Svartennos Harbor three days ago. Each day since their return, she had awoken to a similar feeling of unease; though she had left the deck of the galley, it seemed that her stomach had not yet realized it.

Perplexed, she had spoken with Catarina's physick the day before. He had informed her that such disturbances were not altogether uncommon...among women who were with child.

It *might* have been something else—the lingering effects of the sea voyage, some food that had turned her stomach.

It might have been...but in her heart she knew it was not. It had been six weeks since her last cycle, and now, at last, staring at the sea's stark endlessness, she felt the knowledge of her condition coalesce inside her.

What was strangest to her was the *shock* she felt at the realization, for there shouldn't have been any. This was inevitability, the fulfillment of an eternal promise that had been made before she'd ever crawled from her own mother's womb. Life creating life creating life.

She peeled up her night-dress, laying her hands upon the bare skin of her stomach. The hairs rose along the back of her neck. She stared at it as if she might see it swell before her eyes. But of course, nothing. It still looked and felt the same as it always had.

There was a time-keeper sitting on the railing nearby, smoke trailing from the smoldering stick of incense. Absently, she moved her fingers through it, watching it coil around them. She chewed her lip, thinking of the dark earth that had eagerly swallowed her mother's blood. She tried to push those thoughts away, to think of something else, but it was as impossible as trying to ignore the drip of water in an otherwise silent room. She looked doubtfully at her hips. They still seemed dangerously narrow.

The flame of the time-keeper continued its slow descent, burning itself down, leaving a feeble stain of ash on the white sand. Marilia had a sudden urge to blow it out, to stop the steady curling of charred wood. Instead she raised her arm above the flame until the sharp heat's touch against her forearm made her gasp.

She returned to her room, where Kanediel was still slumbering. As if he sensed her presence, he rolled over to face her, smacking his lips in his sleep.

She sat beside him, gazing upon his face.

He stirred awake, blinking. "Marilia?" He squinted at her. "Are you all right?"

She hadn't realized until that moment that she would not tell him.

She pictured what would happen if she did—his smile, the way he would embrace her, how they would tell Camilline, Catarina, and Ben, and they would all smile too, offering their congratulations, and Marilia would smile back, *oh yes, it's wonderful, just as we hoped.* She knew that all that was part of the inevitability; it would happen just as she'd pictured it, sooner or later.

Just not yet. Just not right now. After all, she told herself, she might as well wait until she was *completely* sure.

So she shook her head. "Nothing," she said, in answer to Kanediel's question. "I had a cramp in my leg and needed to walk it off." She lay back down beside him and pulled the blanket over them both.

Ben was in no hurry to return to Svartennos City. The island's southern coast was beautiful in late summer, and this year the weather was especially perfect, as if even the clouds and the wind were celebrating their triumphant return. Ben spent his time with his young daughter, Clariline, watching their pet dragon dive for fish along the coast, or riding with Kanediel, Marilia, Camilline, and Catarina along the coast, hunting the giant crabs that wandered the hills and beaches along the shore.

Ben's hunting dragons led the way, their keen noses sniffing out their prey as they scuttled through the grass, hugging the ground, their long, sinuous bodies carving a path for the horses to follow. When their party came upon one of the creatures, the riders would take turns loosing arrows at it from the saddle. The trick was in finding the places unprotected by the crabs' armor: the face, the legs, the sides beneath the rim of their shells. The dragons finished off the wounded with a strike to the throat.

Surprisingly, it was Catarina who turned out to be the best shot among them; twice she felled a beast with her first shot. Marilia's first arrow, on the other hand, went so wide off its mark that it went sailing off the edge of a cliff into the sea. Hot-faced, she handed her bow to Kanediel.

"It's all right," Catarina assured her. "I'll teach you."

On the sixth day, Ben and Catarina chose to stay behind with their daughter (who had caught a light cold) while Marilia, Kanediel, and Camilline rode alone into the plains.

At first it seemed as though it would be a day like any other. It was only on the way back that they realized something was wrong.

Camilline saw it first; she had ridden ahead, as she so often did. She halted abruptly, shading her eyes and pointing into the distance. "Look."

Marilia followed her finger. Somewhere beyond the hills to the south, gray smoke was rising. It was a shade like liquid midnight-stone, supple as the body of an eel. A reddish glow like a counter-point to the greater glow of the sun hung like a stain of spilled wine over the southern portion of the sky.

Somewhere to the south, something—something large—was burning.

"The harbor," Marilia breathed.

"Pirates?" Kanediel asked, his voice tense.

Camilline was already galloping ahead; Marilia and Kanediel followed not far behind.

As they drew nearer to the source of the fire, the extent of the destruction became apparent. Glowing cinders came to them on the wind like flame-seared moths, fading to gray as they fell. Marilia could hear the low notes of yoba-horns blowing—battle-horns, sounding a desperate retreat.

They crested a rise. There, below, lay Svartennos Harbor. The galleys were burning, the masts limned in flame, the contours of their hulls painted orange-red like the letters of a book illuminated by a scribe's hand. Some of the buildings on the outskirt of the town were burning, too. Dark shapes scurried below, some in the streets, more in the plain to the north—a great mass of people streaming away from the town. Out in the harbor, enemy warships circled like hunting birds toying with their wounded prey. Their sails were full, their oars turning the bay to white foam as they knifed the water. Their sails bore an insignia that Marilia recognized, one she had seen at several Solstice Festivals, waved above the sands of an arena before a tournament began: a gold silvakim on a field of black.

There are no silvakim in Navessea, she thought, with a feeling of dread.

Several men on horseback came thundering towards them—soldiers of the Svartennos light cavalry, dressed in vests made of draleen leather, with iron lances in their hands. The lead rider's face was bloodied. "My lord," he gasped. "They came without warning. The harbor is being overrun. It's a disaster."

"Who is it?" Kanediel asked. "Pirates? Valdruk slavers?"

"Not pirates, my lord," the man said gravely.

Marilia swallowed. Her throat was dry. "Tyrace," she answered for him. "Tyrace is attacking us."

CHAPTER NINETEEN

Of all the provinces in Navessea, there were two that had not been the spoils of conquest, two that had willingly placed themselves beneath the rule of the dragon emperors. One of them was Svartennos; the other was Dane.

Dane has once been the northern-most province of Tyrace, until hard times fell on the kingdom and the king, in an ill-judged effort to fill the coffers of his treasury, decided to more heavily tax the exports of midnight stone.

It was an edict that was felt keenly in Dane. Since the province was little more than mountains and desert, it depended on trade with Navessea for its livelihood. The relationship was simple; Dane sent aeder and midnight stone north, to provide the empire with weapons for its men and jewelry and mirrors for its women. Navessea sent grain south to help keep Dane's people fed.

The king's edict upset this balance, and before long Dane rebelled, tearing free of Tyrace and joining itself to Navessea. It was a slight that Tyrace had never truly forgiven. For ever after, Dane would remain a simmering point of contention between the two nations.

The tension finally came to a head when a particularly violent earthquake rocked Dane to its foundations. No one was spared; even the governor's villa collapsed, and one of the governor's daughters was smashed beneath a falling column. One of his best friends and closest advisers was simply swallowed by the earth; his body was never found.

Though Dane was a province of Navessea, there were many living there who still held to the religion of the Horse God. And, when the dust settled and roving eyes began to seek the cause of the gods' wrath, it was upon the heretics that the swords of those seeking retribution inevitably fell.

The blood of the Horse God's faithful ran thick in Dane. And in Tyrace, priests took to the streets, crying out to the king for justice.

Emperor Vergana did all he could to prevent a war. He sent emissaries to Tyrace (just as he had when Marilia was a child), and King Damar received them, playing along, pretending to listen—as if there was still a chance that he might be swayed.

But too many of King Damar's people had had their hearts inflamed by the words of the Horse Priests. The chance for peace was lost. Even as King Damar treated with Vergana's emissaries, he gathered his armies in secret.

The King of Tyrace was no fool. He knew that Navessea held a military advantage—its armies and its fleets were both more numerous than those of its neighbor. His plan was to negate that advantage by striking fast and hard, weakening Navessea with several quick, decisive blows. To the west, his ships pushed up towards Vaerennis. In the center, on land, his armies fortified the Neck of Dane.

And to the east, a fleet under the command of Tyrennis Nomeratsu landed on the southern coast of Svartennos.

"Where is Ben?" Kanediel asked.

The messenger shook his head. "I don't know, my lord. He sent me to warn you. Last I saw he was rallying the harbor-master's men, trying to stop the meat-eaters from landing. I don't think he realized what was happening at first—the first of the ships that came into the harbor had blank sails. He must have thought it was the Valdruk."

"Same as I did." Kanediel cursed. He looked down at the harbor, where the galleys were burning.

"The Tyracians wouldn't burn the ships; they'd want to capture them," Kanediel said. "Ben or the harbor-master must have ordered them burned. And they would not do that unless..." He trailed off. *Unless the ships were doomed to fall into the hands of the enemy,* Marilia thought.

Unless they didn't think they could win.

Kanediel gnawed his cheek, his fingers tightening on his reins.

"He also said to give you this," the messenger said, and held up Ben Espeleos' signet ring. The center was of midnight stone, etched with the Espeleos family crest of three rising spears. "So that you could command in his absence. In case...well, in case he didn't make it back."

Kanediel took the ring, staring at it with a dazed expression on his face. "He said to give this...to *me*?"

"I suppose he appreciated your help during the northern campaign, my lord."

"My help...oh, by the gods." Kanediel laughed harshly.

"We should go," Camilline said quietly. "We should head north while we still can."

Kanediel shook his head. "Camilline, my cousin is down there somewhere. The Prince of Svartennos."

"I count four light cavalry, two knights—not wearing armor—and you. What are you going to do to change the tide of the battle, brother?" Her voice rose sharply. "The harbor is lost. Ben will have to find us. He put you in command; he wanted you to get away. If you go back now..."

"Fine. Enough. We will take the north road," Kanediel said bitterly. He wheeled his horse about and galloped away from the harbor with the rest in tow.

They passed a long line of refugees fleeing north. Marilia saw children with tear-streaked faces, men with shadowed eyes who kept casting glances back over their shoulders. Women who clung to each other and to their husbands. All of them packed so tightly they might have been a hive of kwammakin. Some rode yoba; a few of the lumbering beasts had so many perched atop their shells that they were struggling to move, their knees bowed and their feet trailing along the ground. Others had carts that bounced and swayed on the dirt road. Most were on foot. They stared hopefully at Kanediel's party as it passed by. When it became clear he had no help to offer them, their expressions turned dark.

"The lords of Svartennos are sworn to protect the people!" one woman yelled. "That's the pact! So it goes!"

Kanediel's head swiveled so quickly that Marilia heard his neck crack. His eyes scanned the crowd, looking for whomever had spoken.

"Running away," the woman went on. "Coward. Oppel." She used the name for those who had violated the Oppulate Law, a restriction on how much wealth the lords and ladies of Svartennos could own. It was used as a term of derision for the weak and timid.

The hands of Ben's knights crept to their swords. The woman sensed she had gone too far; fear lit up her face. Kanediel shook his head. "Leave her alone," he said. "Come on; we must reach the village of Redonda." He rode on, his jaw clenched tight.

If the Tyracians sent cavalry ahead to attack the column, there was no way these villagers, on foot, would be able to outrun them. They would be cut down like animals. But there was nothing Kanediel could do to protect them, either. Their fate was in the hands of their ancestors.

The woman began to weep. Her limbs shook; heavy tears carved their paths across her face.

Marilia bowed her head and followed her husband.

They left the woman behind; they passed on up the road until the sounds of the horns in the harbor faded and the only sign of the battle raging to the south was the smoke-stain on the underbellies of the clouds like the gray of rot on a maimed limb.

Then, as they passed the head of the column, they heard the cry of a familiar voice. "Kanediel!"

It was Catarina. She rode with her young daughter atop a white horse, her personal bodyguard, Septakim, a gaunt and grim figure at her side.

Kanediel drew his horse up alongside her. "Thank goodness you're safe," he said. "What about Ben?"

Catarina shook her head. "He ran down to the harbor when he heard the horns blowing," she said, sounding shaken. "He would not wait. He told me to take our daughter and get out of the town. He said we should make for Redonda."

"Well, he is a fierce fighter," Kanediel said with a strained smile that tried to be encouraging but failed. "He might have made it out. We may see him yet, my lady."

"I hope so."

The sun was setting by the time they reached Redonda. They stopped inside the village headman's house. Catarina retired to the village shrine to pray while Kanediel seated himself at the headman's table.

There was no mistaking the meaning of the signet ring. Despite his confidence, Ben must have known that there was a chance he would not return from the harbor. He had chosen to leave his oldest and favorite cousin in charge of the defense of the island.

"You said you recognized the banner out there," Kanediel said. "Whose was it?"

"Tyrennis Nomeratsu," Marilia replied. "He has lands north-east of Tyracium."

"I know the name."

"You do?"

"Yes; the gold silvakim. Of course. I should have remembered." He shook his head, a muscle twitching in his cheek. "He's no friend to Svartennos. A few years ago, Ben's younger brother went chasing a group of pirates who had been raiding our shores. He followed them onto the edge of Nomeratsu's lands, and instead of granting our men safe passage to hunt them down..." Kanediel sighed wearily, shook his head, pressing a hand to his brow. "It doesn't matter. What do you know of the man?"

"Not much," Marilia admitted helplessly. "I only...I recognized his banner from the tournaments." She wished she had more to offer.

Kanediel gave a brief nod. "I see." He turned to the village headman, who was standing nearby, wringing his hands anxiously. "Where are your chicayas trained to fly?" Kanediel asked. The headman rattled off several villages. Kanediel nodded. "I will need to send messages to all of them, and have those messages sent on from there to every lord and lady on the island. Bring me wax, paper and ink."

He wrote, stamping each letter with Ben's ring, pausing only to flex the sore muscles of his right hand or to run his hands through his hair. Marilia hung by his side, chewing her lip until it smarted. She read over his shoulder, catching snatches of text.

To Lord Antiriel of Dromolokin, I bid you muster what forces you can and proceed with all haste to Svartennos City. Svartennos has been attacked by an army of Tyrace, numbers as yet unknown...

To Lady Dartimaea of the Southern Valley, I warn you that we are under attack by the army of Tyrace. They have burned Svartennos Harbor and will make their way north soon. I command you to send your strategos along with what knights you have to Svartennos City...

To the Elders of Svartennos City, I write to inform you that Svartennos Harbor has come under attack by a great host of Tyracians. Prince Espeleos was last seen in the harbor, managing the defense and buying time for the retreat. He has left me in command in his stead. The ring I bear will serve as proof of this claim.

Kanediel leaned back in his seat, rubbing his eyes. He seemed to remember for the first time that Marilia was there.

"What are you still doing here?" he asked.

She blinked. "I... I thought..."

"What did you think?"

"That I should stay. I thought you might have need of me."

"Need of you? Why should I have need of you?" he asked sharply.

"I mean...I thought I could help."

"I don't need my wife's help. I'm trying to manage a war. It's hard enough without you standing there, peering over my shoulder. Go keep Catarina company in the shrine."

"My lord husband." Stiffly, Marilia turned and strode from the room.

She went to the shrine. It was filled by now with many of the village folk—all hoping that the gods would spare their village from the Tyracian army, and that their ancestors would protect them from Tyracian swords and spears—as well as some of the early arrivals from

Svartennos Harbor…those lucky enough to have owned horses. The rest were still out there on the road, in the dark.

Some lit candles and called out to their ancestors; others scattered offerings into the bowls arrayed around the pit of white sand. Still others hummed the song of the mountains quietly to themselves. Catarina and Camilline knelt among the candles, their heads bowed in silent prayer. Marilia took her place beside them.

It wasn't long before the headman arrived to fetch them. "My Lady Espelea. News from the south."

Catarina's eyes snapped open. "My husband?"

"A couple of light cavalry escaped the battle in the harbor, my lady. They are under the command of your brother-by-marriage. Zeviel Espeleos."

Marilia heard Camilline's sharp intake of breath.

Catarina's knees cracked as she rose to her feet. "Does Zev have word of the prince?"

"Yes, my lady. He is in my home now."

Had Zev Espeleos been the brother of any other man, he might have seemed more impressive; his curse was that he was born to the same mother as Ben. He was tall, while Ben was taller; broad of shoulder, while Ben was broader. Handsome, but Ben was handsomer.

Whether this inferiority had bred resentment in Zev which had driven him apart from Ben or whether the cause of his estrangement was owed to some other source Marilia was not entirely sure. What she had gathered, from her time in Svartennos City and on campaign with Kanediel, was that Zev Espeleos was, as the old saying went, the white yoba of the family—the outcast. He had been there during the northern campaign and during the celebration after, but always at a distance, hovering about the edges of the proceedings like a moth not quite daring to try for an open window.

One thing Marilia did notice—as Zev entered the headman's house, the look on Kanediel's face suggested that he would have gladly thrown him back to the Tyracians.

Zev did have word of his brother, but the word was grim.

"It was madness in there," he said. "Madness. They took us by surprise—that's the only reason they were able to do so well. Ben tried to hold them back; when he saw them climbing on our ships, such a rage took him. I tried to fight my way back to him, of course. I was calling out for him—*Ben! Brother!* I must have cut down ten, no, a dozen of them trying to reach him, but I saw that it was no use. They had him surrounded. I think they took him alive, my lady, if it's any consolation."

"You cut down a dozen men?" Camilline interrupted. "Just by yourself?"

"That's what I said, isn't it?" Zev said sharply. "Maybe it was ten. I wasn't keeping count. I was more concerned with helping my brother." He sounded rather like a dissembling child trying to convince his teacher that he had finished all the studies he'd been assigned.

"That was very impressive of you," Camilline said in a flat voice that might have been sarcastic or might not.

Catarina sat without blinking. Marilia offered the Lady of Svartennos her hand. Catarina squeezed it so hard that Marilia gasped.

"But you didn't help him, did you? You ran and left him." Catarina's voice was like the snap of a whip.

Zev's lips pressed together into a thin line. "The harbor was lost," he said. "I had to leave. But…" he held up a fist, a note of forced determination in his voice. "It was the element of surprise that defeated us, my lady. Once we gather more men, once we prepare, things will go differently. Even as it was, we must have killed a few thousand of them."

"It's a wonder they have any left," Camilline muttered.

"It's easy to see they're weaker than we are, my lady; the heretics lack our training—our men are worth five of theirs." He broke off; no one seemed to be listening to him.

All the life seemed to leave Catarina. She wrapped her arms across her chest as if seized by a sudden chill. "Thank you," she said. "I think I need to be alone with my daughter now."

"Of course," Zev said. "Of course. Only natural. Yes."

Catarina got to her feet. She walked from the room, head held high, knees lifting proudly, using the same step that Nelvinna had taught Marilia; even now, despite everything, the woman's grace could not be diminished. She slid the door shut behind her.

The lanterns guttered. In the silence Marilia could hear wet wax sizzling. Kanediel looked as if he had turned to wood. He stood with his spine stiff, his shoulders squared, as if he feared to relax his posture for even a moment lest the heavy weight that had fallen on his shoulders crush him to the ground.

For a long moment no one spoke. Zev fidgeted, making a show of adjusting the collar of his robes and scratching an itch on the side of his neck that Marilia was fairly sure wasn't really there. "Well," he said at last. "We'll have to mobilize our forces. The headman told me you've been sending out letters, cousin."

"Yes," Kanediel agreed.

"That was good of you. Once the army is assembled, I'll make these Tyracians regret landing on this island."

"Cousin," Kanediel said. He held up his hand; Ben's signet ring glinted in the fire-light. "I received this from your brother. One of his riders brought it to me."

Zev stared at the ring. His tongue flicked out against his dry lips like a snake testing the air for a scent. "Ben's ring."

"Yes. He put me in command of the army."

Zev frowned, as if Kanediel were speaking a dialect that he could almost comprehend, but not quite. "Well," he said slowly. "As to that. I was in the harbor with him during the battle. He must have feared I wouldn't make it out—as I very nearly didn't." He gave a rueful laugh. "I'm sure if he knew I would escape, he would have put me in command. The brother comes before the cousin; that's the proper way of doing things."

"Apologies, my lord, but the rider that came to me specifically said Prince Espeleos was giving the ring to me," Kanediel said, respectfully...but firmly. "I must honor my prince's command. He wished for me to lead Svartennos' armies."

"Now, I don't see how you can know that for certain," Zev said. "It's only a ring, not a prince's edict. It's not as though he wrote you a letter and poured his heart out." His tone was a little less cordial this time.

"When a prince gives a man his signet ring during a time of war, it means one thing," Kanediel said, refusing to back down. "And the words of the rider who bore it to me were clear."

"Do we really have time for this right now?" Camilline interrupted. "The Tyracians are marching on us; there are more letters that need to be written. The longer we sit here arguing, the less time we have to prepare."

"Of course," Zev said, nodding. "Of course, letters. You've already been managing things here, cousin, so you should keep on with that. Your sister is right; this is not the time. We can discuss this further when we reach Svartennos City." He held his eyes on Kanediel a moment longer than was natural. He had backed down for but a moment, but Marilia knew this quarrel was not over.

"As you like," Kanediel said, looking Zev in the eye, matching him stare-for-stare. "Now if you'll excuse me, I must see to those letters."

Marilia walked with Camilline to the village shrine. Evening had fallen. The sky was violet-red, and the stalks of grass were lit up with a bloody color, as if they had been dipped in the gory waters of Svartennos Harbor. Candles glowed in the windows of the houses. Tattered banners bearing the lyrics of the Mountain Songs fluttered over the entrance to the shrine, stirred by the wind.

"What is it between Zev and Kanediel?" Marilia asked.

"You noticed?"

"How could I not notice? Every time he draws near, you and my husband look as if a dremmakin just crawled out of the ground. Whenever I speak his name, Kanediel gets quiet. He and Zev detest each other."

"There's a lot in Zev to detest."

"Are you going to tell me?"

"All right. You want to know? Let me tell you a story." Camilline crossed her arms over her chest. "It's about my little sister. Her name was...well, what her name was doesn't matter. She was a beautiful girl, and kind, but she wasn't right in the head. You know Svartennos has no place for children who are sickly or ill-made; if the Elders had caught it when she was still an infant, she would have been left in the Wailing

238

Marsh for the Harvesters to bear away, but it was not until she grew older that her illness became clear. The official story was that the dremmakin had cursed our mother while she was with child, that her habithra failed, that they entered her and stole away part of the child's spirit. Our parents insisted she was just born that way; there was nothing that anyone could have done. But I think we all had our doubts. I mean, if she was so...wrong in the head...when she was born, shouldn't the Elders have been able to catch it? That's what they do, after all. So maybe there was something else. Another reason she was...the way she was." Camilline's voice cracked.

"What do you mean?" Marilia asked.

"When she was an infant, Kanediel used to like to hold her. One day, when he was holding her, he tripped and dropped her on her head. We'll never know if that was why...maybe it wasn't, and even if it was, it wasn't his fault. But all the same...he blames himself, you see. He thinks he was responsible."

"I'm so sorry."

"So are we all."

"I don't understand. What does this have to do with Zev?"

"Our cousin always liked to play tricks on her. To make her do things...it was easy to make her do things." Camilline was speaking in a rush, not looking at Marilia, not looking at anywhere, unless it was at the clouds. Her fingers tugged at a loose strand of a hair as if she were ringing a bell. Marilia found herself staring at those fingers, like a child hypnotized by a rhovanna's magic trick. "One day, he took it too far. There was this beehive behind the castle stables that no one had bothered to clear away. He convinced her it was empty, that there was honey inside. I suppose he thought she'd just suffer a few stings, and he and his friends would get a few laughs. It's only bees, right? They're

239

small, the worst they can do is make you hurt a little. Or maybe not."

Camilline's fingers pulled faster, faster, and Marilia was reminded of the way she dug her heels into her horse's sides, galloping faster, faster, as if she could outrun a ghoul that was always at her back.

"Zev killed her, to put it simply," Camilline said. "It took hours; I can still remember the way she screamed. And though there was some *fuss* about it afterwards, it wasn't that much; no Elders got involved, no sanctions were made, because Zev was the prince's brother, and my sister was just an idiot girl."

Marilia put a hand on Camilline's shoulder and felt it tremble. "I could have stopped it," Camilline whispered. "I was there when it happened. I saw everything, Marilia. Everything. I told Zev to stop but I should have done more. I should have run for Mother or Father. I should have grabbed my sister's hand and taken her away. I should have done something."

"Camilline…"

Camilline put up a hand. "If you were thinking about telling me that I can't blame myself, or that it wasn't my fault, or any of the other things people always feel obliged to say when things like this happen, don't—I've heard it all before. I suppose it's all true; I was just a little girl. I know that. But knowing and feeling aren't always the same thing."

"I'm sorry. I had no idea."

"Yes, well," Camilline said, still not looking Marilia in the eye. "It's not something we like to talk about."

CHAPTER TWENTY

It took them nearly two more days of fast riding to reach Svartennos City. Though by now his eyes were ringed with dark circles—the result of too little sleep, too many cares—Kanediel went straight to the great hall.

He fell into a cushion at the end of Ben Espeleos' table, holding his head in his hands.

Marilia started for the staircase, meaning to head up towards the quarters that had been prepared for her on the castle's second floor, when Kanediel called out to her. "I'm sorry for before," he said. "I spoke harshly; I was unfair to you."

She paused. "I understand."

He motioned to a cushion beside him. "Sit with me."

She went and sat beside him, laying her hands on the smooth, polished surface of the table, tracing her fingers over the pattern of dyed wood—two cherry-blossom trees in bloom, their branches intertwined. For a while neither of them said a word.

Above, through a screen that had been drawn up across a gap in the ceiling to keep out the marsh-gnats, she could see the sky. It was blue-gray like the autumn sea. An occasional gleam of sunlight broke from a gap in the clouds, striking the surface of Ben Espeleos' table, catching the vellum panels along the walls. When that happened, the room felt almost welcoming—the panels glowed with warm light, and the shadows at the edges of the room did not seem so dark. But the glimpses of light were always brief; the clouds from the south rolled on, endless as the Tyracian army, snuffing them out one after another.

Kanediel cleared his throat. "The truth is this," he said. "The Tyracians will be at this city in anywhere between four and six days, if the scouts' reports are true. We have four thousand men here, and more are being marshaled, but it's not enough. Vergana must be mustering reinforcements back on the mainland, but they will not arrive in time. And from what I've been hearing the army of Tyrace is...rather large." His voice broke on the final word.

"How large is it?"

"Larger than Aemyr-Kal's. Fifteen thousand men, if the scouts are right."

Marilia swallowed.

"If they reach us here, they'll...we..."

"You're thinking of evacuating the city," Marilia said, understanding.

Kanediel refused to look her in the eye. He seemed to have become fascinated by one of his fingernails, which had cracked. He picked at it. "This city has never been conquered. It was built after the Valdruk were driven out, and it has never been taken. Never. Do you understand what that means?" He raised his shadowed eyes to look at her. "I'd rather not be the one who lets it fall."

"It will take time for the northern lords to gather their forces and march them to meet us," Marilia said. "If we pull back farther north, it will give them the time they need. And they'll have less far to march."

Kanediel spread his palms face-up on the table. He studied them the way a man might study a battle-map. "It's the pride of Svartennos I hold in my hands," he said quietly. "Two hundred years."

"If you pulled north, you could also meet the Tyracians on better ground," Marilia said, thinking. Trying to recall her rides through

242

Svartennos' hills, the maps she'd seen of the island, the books she'd read in Karthtag-Kal's and Kanediel's libraries. "Maybe..." she paused.

"Maybe?" Kanediel prompted her.

"Chrysathamere Pass," Marilia said. "It's by far the quickest path to the northern part of the island. In the pass, there are marshlands to the west and mountains to the east—the ground is difficult enough that it would help protect a defending army from being outflanked. It might help negate their advantage."

In theory, the Tyracians could always march around the pass, or pull back to their ships and sail around to one of the landings farther north—but taking the longer way would give Vergana's reinforcements time to arrive. It was far more likely that the Tyracians, who held the advantage of superior numbers, would choose to meet the Svartennan army inside the pass and attempt to claim a quick and decisive victory.

Kanediel nodded. "Yes. I was thinking just that. Chrysathamere Pass."

As she looked at him, Marilia felt her chest swell with an ache that she couldn't explain. She put her arm around his shoulders.

"After all," Kanediel said, "the city can be rebuilt. It's been rebuilt before. My chief concern is with the people. I have to think of the people..."

"Of course."

His hand found hers. "I'm glad to have you with me," he said. "Truly, I am."

"I know," she said softly. "I can let you work...I mean, I can go. If you like."

"No, that's all right," Kanediel said. "I think...I think it would be fine if you stayed."

They worked together, side by side, for the better part of two hours.

For some reason, she was reminded of that night in the galley with Annuweth, out on the river, heading north towards Navessea. Though the dark outside was pressing in, for the moment, at least, they were beyond its reach, wrapped in the golden glow of the lanterns, a circle of light that pushed away the gloom of the sky beyond their windows. She felt the warmth of the flames as she leaned close over the table, reading over one of Kanediel's letters. His arm touched hers as he reached for a fresh pot of ink, and she felt the warmth of his skin, too.

The second hour was just drawing to a close when Zev Espeleos entered.

"It's time, cousin," he said. "I should be in command of the army."

"That was not our prince's wish," Kanediel said flatly.

"Are you really going to play this game?" Zev asked, seating himself on a cushion at the side of the table. "I suppose I shall have to speak to the Council of Elders. We will see whose claim they back."

A muscle moved in Kanediel's jaw. The threat had touched a nerve. Marilia laid a steadying hand on his arm. "And what would you do, if you were in command and not I?" Kanediel asked. "Please; I would hear your wisdom."

"I would do as my brother would have done. I will take our army, march it south and..."

"Forgive me, but I think I misheard you. You said you would have marched south, as your brother would have done."

"Yes."

"Your brother, being a skilled commander, would not march south. He would march north and find defensible ground on which to meet the Tyracian army."

"You don't know him as I do. You think Ben Espeleos would *retreat?*" Zev scoffed.

"I think Prince Espeleos likes battle, and he is good at it. Being good at it, yes, he would retreat, to fight them on his terms."

"My brother has faith in the strength of our gods and our people," Zev said. "I think he would trust in that strength, and not abandon our greatest city, the home of our princes and the Elder Council, to the heretic scum. Is that what you mean to do?" His lips drew back to show his teeth.

"I mean to save Svartennos' people."

"You mean to run like an oppel. That is *not* what my brother would do." Zev got to his feet. "Listen to me, cousin; step down."

"Your brother's ring..."

"Enough about that ring!" Zev shouted. "I am Ben Espeleos' brother; you understand? His brother, and you are his cousin. The brother comes before the cousin. It is a simple concept; yet I should not be surprised you struggle to understand it. It seems a lack of wit runs in your line."

Marilia saw disaster looming. "My lord," she began, but it was too late. She wouldn't have known what to say, in any case. Kanediel was on his feet, too, and angrier than she had ever seen him. The gentle, mild expression he so often wore had been wiped away. His hate shone naked and bright as a freshly-cut aeder blade.

"Your brother wanted me in command, my lord, and we both know it. I know you mean well, cousin, but I think you'll find Tyrennis Nomeratsu to be harder to outwit than a little girl with a wounded head. I will not step down and let this island fall to the Tyracians—because that is exactly what would happen with you in command. To be honest, cousin, if one of my horse's shits could don armor and grip a sword, I would sooner have that pile of muck as my commander than you. If you wish to bring this to the Elders, then by all means, let us go together, now."

Silence. Marilia looked from one to the other with her mouth half open. Her heart was hammering in her chest.

"As I said; let's go." Kanediel started for the door. A tremor ran through Zev's hands. All at once, he moved, his arm jerking like the hand of a rhovannon's toy. The sound of his sword drawing was like the slithering of a snake in the sand.

"Draw," Zev said.

Kanediel stiffened and froze in the doorway.

"You dare to speak to me in such a manner! I am your prince's brother! I don't care if you are my cousin. Draw, may the dremmakin take you. Draw if you have honor."

"My lord Zev, no..." Marilia began, but she might as well have been a cushion, a lamp, part of the scenery, for all the heed they paid her. She reached to touch him, and he shoved her aside. She fell back upon the cushion she'd been seated on.

Kanediel turned to face Zev. As he drew his sword there was a look of inevitability about him, as if he had known for some time that the course of his life would bring him to this moment—as if he was a mariner whose course had been charted long before.

"I have honor," he said. "Far more than you. Don't you dare touch my *fucking wife*."

Zev attacked, his blade flashing with terrifying speed. Aeder flickered, blue against blue. Marilia watched, helpless, as Zev drove Kanediel out the doors of the dining hall, down a hallway, and out into a garden courtyard. Men and women turned to stare. Some knights made as if to interfere, but Zev's voice brought them up short.

"A duel!" he cried. "Stand aside!"

"A duel," Kanediel echoed, a confirmation.

246

A duel was a sacred thing, to be witnessed by the gods themselves. It could not be interfered with; a challenge, once accepted, had to be followed through. Marilia—like all the others—could do nothing but stand and watch. And pray.

Spirits of the ancestors, help him. Give him strength. Give him strength.

The courtyard was a garden in the classic Svartennos style; few flowers, but many leafy plants which grew on a bed of dark sand, while to one side, a pool of murky water lay nestled amongst tall ferns. The sound of chicayas singing in the reeds mingled with the ragged breathing of the combatants.

Camilline appeared, drawn by the scraping of the ae der blades. She pulled up short beside Marilia. The two women held hands. Marilia saw Camilline's lips moving—her own silent prayer.

Zev was bleeding from a gash in his upper thigh, Kanediel from a cut on his left arm. Both were breathing hard.

Zev lunged. Kanediel slipped aside, his blade slapping down across Zev's. His return strike nearly took off Zev's head. Zev leaped back and his foot slipped on a pebble. Kanediel bore down on him. Their blades ground together. Their teeth were bared; they flecked each other's faces with spit. Zev gave ground, falling back towards the wall of the castle. His rear leg buckled.

"Yield!" Kanediel growled. "Yield!"

"You yield!" Zev yelled back. He tensed his muscles and threw Kanediel back.

Marilia's eyes burned hot, but she didn't dare to blink.

The two grappled together and fell sideways into the pool of water. Kanediel vanished beneath the surface. Zev slashed down at the water and Marilia's heart seemed to stop. But then Kanediel exploded out of the water to Zev's left, a slash grazing Zev's forearm as he dodged back towards the ferns.

And at last, Marilia could bear it no more; she blinked.

A couple of chicayas, startled from their roost by Kanediel's presence, exploded out of the plants, flashing in a blur of white wings past Kanediel's head. He blinked, too. Zev's sword cut across the space between them, and bright spots of crimson appeared on the leaves of the plants.

Marilia yelled, but the only sound she heard was that of the chicayas, carrying their song up into the wind, into the sky. Camilline screamed.

Kanediel fell, the sword that had been Karthtag-Kal's wedding gift landing on the ground behind him. Zev stood over him with eyes gone wide as he saw what he had done.

It was as though two giant, invisible hands had seized either side of Marilia's head and begun to squeeze. Everything narrowed until all she saw was her husband's fallen body, directly ahead of her. She ran to him.

"I..." Zev took a faltering step back, the tip of his sword lowering until it touched the ground. "I..."

Kanediel's lips moved but no sound came forth. Blood welled up, gathering in the center of his chest, sliding down either side, leaving marks like tear-tracks across his ribcage. Camilline was weeping. "He's still alive," she said. "He's still alive. We can help him..."

Zev found his voice. "Physick! Get a damned physick!"

Numbly, Marilia let go of Kanediel and rose to her feet. Servants lifted him up onto a stretcher, bearing him back inside the castle. Marilia's ears were filled with a strange ringing. She wheeled on Zev.

"Look what you've done!" she screamed. "We don't need the

Tyracians—you've done their killing for them. You're more a friend to them than you are to Svartennos."

She could tell she had stung him. It wasn't enough. He deserved to be cut down where he stood. She could have done it—she had been trained by Karthtag-Kal, and Zev was hurt and tired.

Her eyes fell on Kanediel's sword. For a moment she saw Zev on his knees at her feet, her sword slashing across to take off his head, feeling the shock of the impact tingling down her arms...

By the spirits, how *good* that would feel.

But she lost her chance; Zev reached down and picked up the sword.

She wheeled away from him, her hands clenched so tight her nails stabbed like needles into her palms.

"My lady, I am sorry," Zev said. "I didn't mean..."

"To kill him? *You* called for a duel."

"He's not dead."

"And if he lives, it will be in spite of you."

Zev fell silent. He turned away from her, staring at Kanediel's blood. It was spreading slowly across the surface of the pond. There seemed to be far too much of it.

Marilia made her way inside the castle. She followed the sound of Kanediel's groans and found him in a small room at the end of a hallway on the first floor. Camilline knelt on a cushion by the side of his bed. A physick toiled over him. The scent of candles was thick in the air.

Come back to me, she prayed. *Spirits of the dead, help him.*

But the pain in her chest was worse than before; her heart seemed to be stabbing her someplace just behind her collarbone. So far, all the prayers of the last few days had gone unanswered. Those of the harbor-folk, their homes now ash. Those of the villagers, slaughtered on the road. Those of Catarina for a husband who had never come home to her. Now it was Marilia's turn to try, but her hopes weren't high.

It seemed the gods had turned their eyes from Svartennos.

CHAPTER TWENTY-ONE

"I was hoping to discuss the defense of Svartennos," Marilia said to Zev. She had come to see him out of desperation, even though she loathed him, and now was standing near him in the same dining hall where he had quarreled with Kanediel not long before.

Zev sat stiffly on his cushion. "My lady, I am very sorry for your husband, but you should not be here. Go to him."

She took a deep breath to stop herself from screaming. "I hate being away from his side. But I wanted to speak with you. I know you mentioned taking the army south earlier. But I had the thought that..."

"Why are we discussing this?" Zev asked. "I am in command of the army, and I will make sure that it is led properly. You do not need to concern yourself with this."

"I only wanted to say..."

"Maybe Kanediel was in the habit of listening to war counsel from you, but I am not. You forget yourself, my lady." Zev's hand made a slicing motion in the air. It had an air of finality to it, like the killing stroke of a sword.

Her chest tight, Marilia got to her feet. "My lord. Chrysathamere Pass." She threw the words out in the desperate hope that he would grasp their significance.

She had a feeling he would not.

His face darkened. "Go," he said.

She went back to Kanediel and knelt on the floor beside her husband's bed. The air was heavy with candle-smoke and the scent of blood. On a nightstand, the crushed remains of herbs were strewn beside a puddle of spilled tea that was slowly drying, leaving a stain on the wood.

The physick held a fresh cup of tea laced with salvia—for the pain—to Kanediel's lips. He coughed, his muscles tightening.

"How is he?"

The physick's face was grave. "He is...not well, my lady."

"Can he live?"

"If the gods help him. I suppose…it's possible." From the way he said it, she had a feeling it might not be.

She wished she were like Almaria the Blessed, who had healed Neravos' lethal wound with her tears after his duel with Mollagora, the dremmakin king. Then she realized that wouldn't have helped; despite the ache in her chest, her eyes were dry.

She hadn't cried properly in a long time. *Tears are the weapons of those who have no others,* she had heard Karthtag-Kal tell her brother back when they first came to Ulvannis.

She had heard those words and adopted them as her own, though they hadn't been meant for her. It had paid off—though her eyes had turned glassy with pain once when her father's sword had struck her, she had not wept, and she had seen the respect in his eyes and been glad.

She wished she would cry now, though. She forced her eyes open, staring at Kanediel without blinking until they burned like fire and she could stare no more.

Kanediel moaned quietly as the needle entered his flesh, first on one side of the wound, then the other, the thread pulling taut, drawing the severed flaps of skin back together. "You don't need to watch this, lady," the physick said.

252

She looked at him blankly. "I'll stay," she said. "Where else would I go?"

"As you wish."

She stared at Kanediel in a daze. His wound grinned up at her, a red, taunting smile.

"I brought more prayer candles," Camilline said. Together, they set the red candles up in a pot of white sand and lit them.

Kanediel's fingers were limp in Marilia's hand. She knelt on the floor-mats, her knees beginning to ache.

"I've done what I can for him," the physick said at last, stepping back. "I will come again when a few hours have passed." He left; she and Camilline stayed.

As evening fell, Kanediel stirred. The salvia that the physick had given him earlier in the day was wearing off. His eyelids fluttered. He looked incredibly weak, his lips chapped, his eyes sunken.

On an impulse, Marilia leaned over the bed and kissed him full on the lips, holding his head gently between her palms. At last the tears came, welling up in her eyes. It was a relief to discover that they were there inside her, waiting. She kissed him harder and the water fell onto his cheeks.

"Who...?"

"It's your wife," she said. "Marilia."

Kanediel's eyelids opened a fraction. "M... Marilia? Oh." And for a moment his eyes focused on her. "You have been...a good wife."

"That's not true."

"Of course it is..."

She felt herself tremble. She opened her mouth to answer him, to deny it again, but he shook his head. "No. Don't. I won't hear it."

She looked down at her hands. "You honor me, Kanediel," she said.

253

"I love you," he said. His eyes closed and he drifted off again.

"He was always good to me," Marilia said quietly to Camilline. "He was. Even when I…I'm not sure I deserved it."

An hour passed. More; Marilia lost track. She felt her knees aching beneath her. The pain was sweet. It climbed her like a creeping vine, tightening its grip with each passing moment, a ribbon of fire around her skin.

"You should get a cushion," Camilline said. "You'll hurt yourself."

"I'm all right," Marilia said.

"I can bring one."

"It doesn't matter."

Camilline shook her head. "Fine."

The evening drew on. A few times Marilia caught her head falling forward and she shook herself awake. She nearly pressed her bare wrist against one of the candles, knowing the sting would keep her alert— only remembering at the last moment that Camilline was in the room. Instead she slipped the physick's needle (which he had left on the table) into her hand and jabbed its point into the flesh of her thigh. The pain brought her back to herself. Her legs had gone almost numb beneath her.

"You look terrible," Camilline said.

"I'm all right," she said again. Her mouth felt thick, as if someone had stuffed it full of silk.

"Why are you doing this?" Camilline's voice rose. "What exactly are you trying to prove? That you love him the most? And ruining your knees somehow shows that?" Marilia said nothing, but she felt heat rise to her face. "Well, let me tell you—you don't love him the most, all right? He was my brother before he was ever anything to you." Camilline got to her feet. "I'm bringing you a damned cushion."

Marilia hung her head. "I'm sorry," she said. Camilline grunted and left. "I'm sorry," she said again, this time to Kanediel.

Camilline returned, tossing a cushion at Marilia's feet. When Marilia uncoiled her legs to get up, pain shot through her so fiercely that she gasped and nearly fell. She had to bite down on her hand as she bent her legs to take her seat on the cushion Camilline had brought her. "You were right," she said. "I know he's your brother. I'm sorry."

"I'm sorry, too," Camilline said. "Sorry I yelled at you. It's not you I'm angry at." Her face hardened. "It's that piece of shit. That dremmakin-spawned, meat-eating, yoba-fucking piece of *shit*. To think of him leading the army of Svartennos." Her lip curled. "Did you know he's seen battle before? I'm not talking about the war in the northlands—before that. He was once sent to chase down a group of pirates that had been raiding the coast."

"Kanediel started to tell me. What happened?"

"Well, he chased them, sure enough. All the way across the sea and into Tyrennis Nomeratsu's lands. He kept chasing them, even though Nomeratsu warned him to turn back, and he got his pirates in the end. He also got himself captured and more than three hundred men of Svartennos killed because he didn't know when to stop. It took almost a year to arrange his ransom. That's the kind of man he is. That's the kind of idiot that killed my brother."

"He's not dead," Marilia said. The words sounded hollow.

"No, but he will be, no matter how much I pray or how much you bruise your knees or how many times you stab yourself with that needle—yes, I saw. Even if we drain the sea of draleen and turn all their wax to candles. We both know it. It shouldn't be like this, it shouldn't be him. Of all people, it shouldn't be him..." Camilline swallowed. Her voice was choked. "He always blamed himself for what happened with our sister, but doesn't that say something? That his worst crime was an accident? Of all of us—mother, father...me...and the rest of our family, he alone was never cruel to her. He was always good—he was the best of us."

"I hate Zev," Marilia said. "I wish he was dead." She wasn't sure who she hated more; him or Tyrennis Nomeratsu.

It took Kanediel another hour to die. When the last breath left his lungs Camilline closed her eyes and did not open them for a long time. A tear squeezed its way between her eyelids and left a shining streak across her face. Marilia stared at her husband's body until the servants came and covered it with a shroud and bore it away. It seemed incredible to her that only that morning he had been alive and issuing commands.

"You should lead the army, not Zev," Camilline said, opening her eyes.

Marilia stared at her. "What?"

"You've read all the strategy books. You're brilliant; my brother once told me he thought so. I remember what you did in the war in the north."

"I've never led anyone," Marilia said. Her heart skipped in her chest.

"Well, I think you'd probably do a better job of it than Zev."

"Well, thank you."

"Don't *thank* me!" Camilline's brows narrowed. "I'm not here to flatter you. I'm being serious."

"The lords of Svartennos would never follow a woman into battle."

"They would if the Elders backed you. Every time there's a war like this, they test girls and women, you know—to see if they might be Chrysathamere Reborn."

256

Dimly, she recalled her first meeting with Ben Espeleos; it must have been six or seven years ago now. A magic trick, an exchange of stories, and that song—*everyone on Svartennos believes that prophecy.*

"Catarina could make you an introduction," Camilline was saying. "If the Elders said the gods had chosen you, the lords, even Zev, would have to listen. And who do you think the men would rather follow— Zev, the pirate-chaser, or the Lady Chrysathamere? It would give them hope."

Marilia stared down at her hands. *"Hope is worth a thousand swords, and an army that lacks it is halfway to the pyres,"* she muttered, quoting emperor Urian. Then she shook her head. "But I'm not Svartana Reborn." Still, even as she spoke, a shiver ran down her spine. It was a feeling not unlike the moment she had laid her lips upon Petrea's.

"How do you know?"

"Wouldn't the gods have sent me...a sign, or something?"

"Think about it," said Camilline. "Who would the gods of Svartennos want to lead their army? A kin-killer, or you?"

"What if I fail?"

Her heart seemed to have taken off, like a horse given its head. She felt the beats hammering inside her and for a moment it seemed as if it might burst, filling the hollow cavity of her chest with the heat of her own blood. She could hear Karthtag-Kal's voice in her head. *You have the mind of a commander.*

"I don't know. Maybe it's mad," Camilline said, sounding deflated.

Karthtag-Kal's voice continued to speak in her head. *Our lives are not planned for us, girl. We are put on this earth where we are as the dice come out.* What if, this one time, the dice came out right? What if Karthtag-Kal was wrong?

Hadn't she used to wish that he was wrong?

She stared at the empty bed where Kanediel had been. *A good wife,* he had called her, but she hadn't been. She hadn't been able to give back to him in equal measure what he had given her. And even at the end, as he'd lain unconscious beside her, the two of them alone in the room, she hadn't found the courage to say what she'd wanted to.

To say sorry for not loving him as he deserved.

Sorry for trembling at his touch.

Sorry most of all for how she used to close her eyes when he kissed her and pretend he was Camilline instead.

Now he was gone, but maybe she could still give him something; she could carry on his last purpose—defending the island against those who would destroy it.

Maybe she was meant to.

Of course, if she failed, she would be shamed, hated for the rest of her life by the people of Svartennos for pretending to be someone she wasn't—assuming they didn't simply kill her. She knew the story of what had once become of a Svartana impostor.

She took a deep breath. "I'm afraid," she admitted.

"It's all right," said Camilline. "Maybe we should just forget I said anything. I'll be the first to admit I may not be thinking clearly."

"No," Marilia said. "I think...I think maybe you have a point."

Camilline studied Marilia's face as they sat together for a long moment. "What are you thinking?"

"About something I once heard my father say."

"What did he say?"

"He said we all must do what we can for the good of the empire. We must do our duty." She took a deep breath. "If you have the chance to help, and the power to help...then don't you have to try?" She chewed her lip until the skin broke and she tasted her own blood on her tongue.

"My brother would have said yes."

"Then I'll do it," Marilia said. "I'll go to the Elders."

Although the princes of Svartennos had command of the island's armies and its lords watched over the castles and marshaled men into battle, it was the Elders who made the laws that all, even the princes, had to obey. Their voice was the voice of the gods. Even the most unruly princes and princesses of Svartennos dared not go against the Elders' laws, for they, like all the other men and women of Svartennos, feared the Elders' greatest weapon—the power of denouncement, by which they could cast a wayward Svartennan from the grace of the gods and condemn their spirit to the cruelty of the dremmakin.

The Elders were the sons and daughters of lords and ladies; widowers who had grown too old for war, and widows who could no longer bear children. They chose their own members, through a rigorous test of the Four Virtues—wit, knowledge, faith, and courage.

On the slopes of the twin mountains, Phelkos and Aphexia, grew a special kind of plant, with dark purple leaves in the shape of a ghoul's tongue. The Elders—when they were not writing laws, providing blessings to Svartennos' warriors, or dealing out judgments—partook of this plant. Through it, they were gifted visions of the gods' will. For any other besides an appointed Elder to consume the rare plant was a crime punishable by both denouncement and death.

Councils of Elders were to be found in every part on the island, but the Great Council—the one above all the others—was in Svartennos City.

It was to this Council that Marilia went now, accompanied by

259

Catarina.

"Wait here," Catarina said. She slipped into the Elders' room,
leaving Marilia standing in the hallway, her fingers twisting together as
she listened to the low murmur of voices through the door. At last the
door rasped open. Catarina stepped out and gave Marilia a brief,
encouraging nod.

"They'll see you."

"Thank you," Marilia said.

"I have made you an introduction with the Elders, but the rest is out
of my hands. They will hear you out, and then they will make their
decision." Catarina briefly took Marilia's hand in her own and gave a
reassuring squeeze. "Camilline believes in you. So do I." Then she was
past, and Marilia stepped alone into the Elders' room.

They faced her, a silent semi-circle of twelve aged men and women,
all clad in the same loose-fitting, formless white robes. They were
seated on cushions ringed around a low table. On the ceiling, golden
lanterns flickered, making the water-script paintings on the walls seem
to move. She glanced at them; they were passages unknown, from the
Mountain Song, not the Book of the Gods.

A man spoke. His eyes were piercing—green flecked with gold, not
unlike Annuweth's. They reminded her of sunlight in spring grass. His
face was weathered; the pale line of an old scar traced its path across
his brow. "Marilia Paetia," he said. "Allow me to offer you our
condolences. We have learned of Lord Paetos' fate."

"Thank you, Elders," she said. Though he alone had spoken, she
knew that it was proper to address them all.

"I am Patos, the Voice for this Council. I am only the first among equals; if you wish us to support your claim, you will need to win over ten of us. No fewer will suffice; we take Svartana claimants very seriously."

"I understand, Elders."

He frowned. "Normally, we would not awaken in the middle of the night, but out of respect for the Lady Catarina and consideration of the urgency of this island's peril, I asked my brothers and sisters to join us here. The Lady Catarina has informed us that you believe yourself to be the answer to the prophecy concerning Queen Svartana. This is so?"

"It is, Elders." Her throat felt dry.

Their eyes were like a wave, threatening to knock her from her feet. She stared back, trying her best to appear undaunted.

"You believe the spirit of our lady rests inside you? Did she come to you in a vision?"

Marilia hesitated, then shook her head. "No," she said. "But I still believe I carry her spirit within me."

"And why do you hold this belief?"

"I... I believe there are signs, Elders."

"What signs?"

"I am the daughter of Nelos Dartimaos and Karthtag-Kal Sandaros," she said. "Two men who fought to save Svartennos when it was in peril. I carry Dartimaos' blood and Karthtag-Kal's teachings inside me. From a young age, I always sensed that I was different. I have always had an affinity for strategy. I have studied the books of war. I have defeated Karthtag-Kal and Prince Ilruyn at the Sharavayn table; I have aided the army of Svartennos during its war to the north." Her voice was growing stronger with each word. When she looked at it like that, all laid out so plainly, it was enough to make her believe. So many little things all coming together—all leading to this. "I helped advise Kanediel Paetos and Ben Espeleos. I helped to devise a plan that allowed us to rescue Daevium before it fell to Aemyr-Kal's siege."

"Interesting," said Patos, lacing his fingers together. His face was unreadable. "Of course, some of this cannot be proven—given that Kanediel Paetos and Prince Espeleos are not with us—and those parts that can cannot be proven in any kind of timely fashion. So we are left with only your word for these signs."

She swallowed. "Most of all, I believe this, Elders," she said. "I believe that I can lead the army of Svartennos to victory. I believe that between Zev and I..."

"Ah, yes, Zeviel Espeleos." One of the other Elders spoke for the first time—an old woman, with hair as pale and thin as sea-mist and a voice that sounded like wind rocking through a thicket of wicker-wood stalks. "Do not worry; we know much of Zeviel...the man responsible for the death of your husband. You hate him, do you not?"

"I do not hate him," Marilia lied.

"Forgive me for saying so, but you must understand that your motives for coming to us appear...questionable."

Marilia bowed her head humbly. "I came to you because I believe that I can help Svartennos. I came because I believed it was my duty to come."

"You believe it is your duty to lead the armies in defense of Svartennos?" Patos asked.

"I do," she answered.

"And where would you lead them?"

She hesitated again. She knew that everything would depend on the next few moments. They were all watching her, keenly, with the same care a tournament judge might watch the flurry of a final, decisive exchange. What they were looking for, what they were waiting to hear,

she could only guess. So she did the only thing she could think to do—
she told the truth. "I would lead them north to Chrysathamere Pass."

"Because it bears the name of the flower that was Queen Svartana's
banner?" Patos asked, raising an eyebrow.

"No. Because it is defensible. I have ridden through the pass, and I
know that there is marshland to the west and mountains to the east. The
Tyracians would have to march uphill to reach us, and the narrowness
of the valley would work against them. It is much more defensible than
the land to the south of this city."

There was a long pause. Patos leaned back on his cushion, lips
pursed thoughtfully. Before they had been Elders, the men in this room
had been knights or lords; some of them must have led men on the
battlefield. Some of them would, she hoped, recognize the sense in her
suggestion.

"You would leave this city to be burned to the ground?" A third
Elder, a skeletal man with heavy-lidded eyes, asked her.

"I would try to protect Svartennos' people," Marilia replied. "The
city can be rebuilt, as long as enough still live to rebuild it."

"I will be straight-forward with you," Patos said. "Years ago, when
Kanadrak menaced this island, there were others like you. Some had
been put up to it by their husbands, their fathers, their mothers. Some
were consumed with hysteria. Some had a dream, and took its meaning
too far. For sometimes dreams are only dreams, lady, and it is a fine art
telling the difference. All these girls wanted me to let them stand beside
Prince Espeleos and Prefect Dartimaos as they commanded the
empire's forces. We considered their claims, and we decided that all of
them were false. I do not doubt that before this war with Tyrace is over
there will be many more. Do you understand?"

"I think so."

"And you are still here. You still wish to be tested?"

She looked into his eyes. She saw doubt in them. But that was a familiar thing; it was the same doubt she had seen in Karthtag-Kal's eyes when she'd first faced him across the board of Capture the Emperor, and the same she'd later seen in Ilruyn's. It was the kind of look she had always enjoyed wiping away, watching it crawl from sight like a grave-beetle cowed by the light of the sun.

And suddenly the idea of returning to the room, to weep beside Camilline, to burn her husband's body and then be sent off to who knew where, to wait and light candles while Zev led them all to ruin— Zev, the man who had killed Kanediel, and Kanediel and Camilline's sister, who had waved her away as if she were nothing—seemed so hateful that she would have done anything at all to avoid it.

"Yes," she said. "I wish to be tested."

"Then let us begin."

First, they tested her knowledge of the history of Svartennos and its gods. She had learned much from Karthtag-Kal's books and stories, still more from Kanediel and Camilline. She knew which chicayas to put in which lantern at which time of year, so that the wind would carry them to the Twin Mountains and their music would please the gods. She knew the names of the verses of the Mountain Song; she knew the names of the great prophecies that the first lawmaker had brought to Svartennos long before. There were a few questions she could not answer; she felt her ears grow hot and her stomach twist as if an anchor's hook had lodged there. But she refused to stop; she pressed on.

Next, they asked her about battle strategy. They questioned her

264

about the war with Kanadrak, about maneuvers made by Dartimaos or Vergana, about the battles of Emperor Urian and Svartennos' struggles with the Valdruk pirates.

"What would you do if..."

"How could a commander avoid defeat when..."

"Which of these courses seems most prudent to you? Why?"

They sat her in front of a table of Sharavayn pieces. They made her play against Patos and three others. She defeated the first three. By the time she came to Patos she was exhausted. The long hours kneeling beside Kanediel, the ride to Svartennos City, the hour answering questions while the Elders' eyes fixed on her...she had been worn down. Her head spun, and there was a buzzing in her ears like the sound of flies. She imagined a swarm of them, dark and glittering, crawling through the cavity of her skull.

She still managed to win, though with only two pieces left; the final exchange came down to a toss of the dice.

"Rise," Patos said. He handed her a sword of wicker-wood. She stared at it.

"Strength of mind is only one part," he said. "For time uncounted, the princes of Svartennos have led their armies from the front. It is assumed that our Svartana Reborn will do the same." A man entered the far side of the room. He was thin, and a little shabby looking, with cheekbones that seemed like two knives attempting to gouge holes in the flesh of his face. But he moved with a grace that she recognized; a grace that Karthtag-Kal and Annuweth both possessed.

He was Septakim, Catarina's personal bodyguard, and a member of the Order of Jade's Dragonknights. He was supposed to be one of the best swordsmen on the island. She recalled that he had been one of the final four in that tournament all those years ago when Karthtag-Kal had

265

defeated Ben Espeleos and then refused to fight Andreas.

"Septakim will test your swordsmanship," Patos said. "Return to us when you have changed."

Marilia made her way into an adjoining room. She stripped off her dress. It took longer than usual; her hands were unsteady.

The princes of Svartennos lead from the front. Of course; how had she not realized? Her head had been so full of stratagems and her heart so full of grief and fear and hope that she had not stopped to consider that the commanders of Svartennos, unlike those from the rest of Navessea, were in the habit of charging headlong into battle alongside their men.

And then, like a kick in the stomach, she thought of the child.

Five more days had passed, and still she had not bled. If she rode to battle, she would be risking not just her life but that of Kanediel's unborn child, too.

For the first time since she had gone to Catarina, doubt entered her.

She stood there naked, feeling sweat prickle on the small of her back, staring at the wicker-wood sword. The trembling in her hands grew stronger; she closed her eyes, feeling dizzy. But child or no child, she was here, in this room, the twelve greatest Elders of the island and Catarina's Dragonknight waiting for her outside. She had come too far to turn back.

The Fates had given her a gift, a mind that had outwitted Karthtag-Kal's. It came from the blood and spirit of Dartimaos; and as surely as she knew that, she knew that blood was meant for something; meant, as Camilline had said, for this.

No matter what, she could not stop now. Infants died all the time, many before they were ever born. Yes, if she were killed or hurt, Kanediel's child would die.

But if she turned back and thousands of Svartennans died because of her…

Kanediel's child was in the hands of the gods and the spirits, she thought. Just as they all were.

She dressed in simple training clothes, the sort women of Svartennos wore when they ran or grappled with each other. They left most of her skin bare; she felt her stomach twist again as she walked back into the room before all those eyes. She was highly conscious of the smallness of her breasts, the un-ladylike breadth of her shoulders, the vein in her wrist.

She stared at Septakim. He stared back, inscrutable.

She wished Karthtag-Kal had given her more lessons before she'd left Ulvannis.

"Begin," Patos said.

She lunged at him, driven by a heat that had settled in her breast, as if a smaller version of the sun were trapped there. She attacked him with all the cunning and strength that she had, remembering Karthtag-Kal's lessons, remembering the games she had played with Annuweth in the streets of Tyrace.

And it was not enough.

He dodged back, turning aside her first several blows. He pressed into her, and though she tried to break away and set herself against him, he was too strong, too relentless. He was always there. In the end, he swept her legs out from under her and rapped his wooden sword against her throat.

She climbed back to her feet, winded.

"That will do," said Patos, and Septakim bowed and left without saying a word.

Again, she was sent to the adjoining room while the Elders deliberated. She re-dressed, her clothes sticking to her sweaty skin. When she returned to the Elders, her face still flushed with heat, Patos spoke to her.

"You did well," he said. "Very well. But one thing we cannot forget is that you were born in Tyrace, not Svartennos. And it seems to many of us that Svartana Reborn would be a woman native to our island."

She felt sick, as if she had just swallowed a rancid oil. "The blood of Nelos..." she began, but he held up his hand.

"Thank you, Lady Paetia," he said. "You have shown courage in coming before us. Your knowledge and your cleverness are undeniable. Yet we cannot at this time give you our endorsement. I am afraid our decision is final. You may go."

CHAPTER TWENTY-TWO

Marilia lay in the warm water, her hands floating at her side like two lilies. The water had made the tips of her fingers wrinkle. Wearily, she turned one hand over, staring at the puckered skin as if it belonged to someone else.

The room was dark, a single oil lamp swinging overhead. The sky outside was dark gray and the light that came in through the window was like the foggy endlessness of a dream. She could barely see her legs beneath the water, two faint dark shapes like a kraken's arms against the blackness of the water.

Camilline sat beside her in the water, hair damp with the coiling steam. Red-eyed as Marilia herself was. They had burned Kanediel earlier that morning.

In an hour the army would march—south, to a battle Marilia doubted they could win.

"I just wanted to do something," Marilia said. "I just wanted to help."

"Maybe it wasn't meant to be," Camilline said. She laid a hand on Marilia's shoulder.

"It just made so much sense. It... I saw it all coming together..."

"Saw what coming together?"

"Different things. Signs. I really started to think you might be right." She trailed off into silence. "The waiting is the worst."

"It's the burden we ladies bear," said Camilline.

"We wait and sit and light candles and tell ourselves it matters,"

Marilia said bitterly.

Camilline's voice was soft. "I like to think it matters."

"You're right. Sorry." *We all like to think so.*

They sat for a while, sweating in the steam until it seemed that the water was their skin, their skin the water, and there was no space between. Marilia was glad, at least, that Camilline was with her. Gladder than she could say. She wished this moment could go on and on; that she could forget the war waiting beyond the castle walls, forget Kanediel, forget Zev and what he was about to do. But the sun crept up; the water turned cold. At last, reluctant, Marilia sighed and rose from the bath. "Well," she said in an empty voice. "I suppose we had better go down and see them off."

They dressed and made their way down into the courtyard. The knights of Svartennos were arrayed there inside the courtyard, the footmen beyond the low wall that enclosed it. The strategoi stood on the porch by the castle gates, with Zev at their head.

The Elders gave their blessing while the minstrels struck up the Mountain Song. Then Zev stepped forward to make his announcement. Marilia stared at him, wishing she could simply burn him away, that he were a stick of incense her gaze had the power to set ablaze.

Here it comes, she thought. *The words that will doom us all.* She hoped at least that Camilline and Catarina would be spared. They had suffered enough and deserved better than to die for Zev's stubborn pride.

Zev cleared his throat. She waited for him to speak, but he did not. The knights stood still, only the quick movement of their eyes betraying their confusion; the Elders waited on their cushions, bright-eyed and expectant. Still Zev was silent.

Patos cleared his throat. "My lord commander..." he began.

"Prepare to evacuate the city," Zev said. "We march north for Chrysathamere Pass."

Marilia's heart missed a beat.

A murmur swept through the crowd; Lady Dartimaea gave a wail of dismay—her lands lay close to Svartennos City, and a march north meant leaving them open to the Tyracians. Lord Konos blinked quickly, as if a quick gust of wind had just thrown sand into his eyes.

But Marilia saw the ghost of a smile light up the faces of several other strategoi. Relief that was plain to see.

She and Camilline exchanged a quick, disbelieving glance.

It seemed that Zeviel Espeleos could see reason after all.

The army marched north. Three thousand knights at the head. Five thousand footmen behind. The people of the city trailed after, carts loaded with their possessions wearing ruts in the earth. The clouds rolled in, fog hiding the peaks of Svartennos' twin mountains. The sky felt heavy, as if a giant's thumbs were slowly pressing down upon them, trying to blot out the island. Plates of yoba-shell shone with a dull light like an old blister.

Some looked behind. Some looked ahead. In their eyes was hope and fear and the pain of loss fresh and bright as newly-spilled blood.

Somewhere in the distance, the army of the Tyracians, nearly fifteen thousand strong, followed them.

Marilia rode beside Camilline. She knew she looked a mess. Her eyes were puffy and red, her lip cracked in a few places where she had bit it too hard, her hair tangled. She didn't care.

So much had happened so fast— learning she was with child, the beginning of the war, the loss of Kanediel, the shock of failure as the priest turned her down, the fear that they would march south, the second shock as Zev changed his mind. Her spirit had been battered and hurled about and now crouched somewhere, hunched like a traveler in the middle of a gale, waiting for the winds to pass. She had gone numb. *Come what may*, she thought. *It's out of my hands now.*

On the evening of the third day of their march, a scout came with word that the Tyracians had burned Redonda and were in the process of ransacking Svartennos City.

They made camp between the mountains, Phelkos and Aphexia, at the top of a slope covered with blue flowers. Marilia spent most of that day resting in her tent, too exhausted to move, to think, to do anything at all.

By the afternoon, some measure of her strength had returned. She mounted her horse—the one that had been a gift from Kanediel—and rode with Camilline through the camp and around the valley, taking in the sights—the marsh to the west, the defile that ran around the back of the camp, the foothills of Mount Aphexia to the east. Camilline rode fast, as if she was trying to outrun the memory of Kanediel's death.

At the end of the day they dined with Catarina. They spoke little; each of them was locked inside the cage of their own private grief.

"I have heard things from some of the strategoi and their men," Catarina said at length. "Zev has barred himself inside his tent. He has not emerged since this morning. They say he sits there, staring over maps and reports from the scouts, that he will hardly speak to anyone." She sighed. "I fear he is out of his depth. He never was a match for Ben, even if he always wished to be. Even if he'd never admit it. I fear...I fear he is too proud to accept help from another man, even if he wants to."

Marilia frowned. She stirred her food around on her plate without taking a bite. Her mind, which had been half-asleep since her meeting with the Elders, ground slowly back to life, like the rusty chains of a castle gate being drawn upward.

"What about from a spirit?"

She struggled through the night and into the light of morning. Pacing her tent, chewing her lip until it was raw and swollen, lighting blue candles until the pot of white sand in her tent was covered in their melted remains.

She pleaded with the gods and the spirits. "Please, help me. I don't know what to do…"

Time spun like a wheel passing her by; through the gap at the top of the tent-flap she watched the sky turn black, then gray again as dawn came. The sun hung above the camp with a pale, wan light. The smothering clouds were like a thick piece of vellum the gods had lit a weak candle behind.

And finally, with Camilline's hand in hers, as Svartennos City burned in the distance, she finally found what she was looking for. An idea that might actually work.

A strategy that might save them.

She found Zev in his tent.

"Forgive me, my lady, but I do not have time to speak to you," he said. "I am planning for a battle."

He looked much like Kanediel had after the weight of command had fallen on his shoulders, except worse. His back was hunched as if to ward off a blow.

"That's why I've come," Marilia said softly. "Last night, as I was sleeping, Queen Svartana came to me in a dream. I still feel her spirit inside me."

He turned to face her. In the tent's dim light, she could barely see his sunken eyes—it looked as though someone had punched two holes through his face. "Is that so? And what does that mean, exactly? That you're Chrysathamere Reborn? Why haven't you gone to the Elders, then?"

"You don't understand," Marilia said. She took a step closer. "I'm not trying to usurp your command. That was part of what Svartana showed me—you *are* meant to lead this army. I was wrong, and Kanediel was wrong." The words hurt her; she felt as if she might be sick. She felt as if hot cinders were clawing at the inside of her throat, choking her. But she kept on, because she had to. Because it was what was required; it was what Karthtag-Kal would have said was her duty. "All I am meant to do is to tell you what Svartana showed me. A vision of the battle."

"A vision?" Zev repeated. "What vision?"

Closing her eyes to still the sickness inside, she told him.

Chapter Twenty-Three

The Tyracians filled the valley to the south. Their banners, showing the gold silvakim on a black field flapped in the wind.

Marilia and Camilline rested their horses atop a tall hill at the northern end of the valley, overlooking the field. From there, they could see everything—the army of Svartennos arrayed across the plain, with Zev and his best knights on horseback on the eastern flank to the left, and a thick wall of shield-men in the center.

A white flag of truce was raised on the opposite end of the field, and a number of horsemen broke from the Tyracians' ranks and made their way out into the space between the two hosts. Marilia's hands clenched tight on her reins as she watched them come; one of those men was probably the Tyrennis himself.

"They're not going to make a truce," Camilline said, shaking her head. "They have no need to; they've got the bigger army. Besides, Svartennans never surrender."

"No," Marilia agreed. "But they have to go through the formalities, all the same." Her toes curled and un-curled restlessly. Doubts crept up on her like serpents rearing their heads out of the weeds. Yesterday evening, her plans had seemed sound. But war was not like a river; it did not follow the course that was planned for it, but went as it would, wild as the sea's waves.

But even the sea's waves have patterns, if you know how to read them. Who had written that? It was one of the lesser-known writers in Karthtag-Kal's library. It must have been a sign of her nervousness that she couldn't remember.

What if the Zev changed his mind at the last second? What if the Tyracians had a cunning plan of their own? What if the men lost heart and broke ranks and…?

She jumped as she felt Camilline's fingers around her hand. She looked over at the other woman.

"You did what you could. It's in the hands of the gods now," Camilline said.

Zev and a couple of his knights rode to meet the Tyracians. Words were exchanged; no doubt the Tyracians demanding the surrender of the island. Before long, just as Marilia and Camilline had known they would, the Tyracians rode back the way they had come, and the yoba-shell horns were sounded, signaling the start of the battle.

Marilia stared across the field towards the fifteen thousand men who were coming to kill her.

At her side Camilline let out a long sigh. "That is a lot of soldiers," she said.

"Yes," Marilia agreed faintly. "A good many."

On the flanks, Tyracian cavalry thundered over the hills, the whinnying of the horses muffled by the thin layer of fog that hung, shroud-like, across the valley. From this distance, the sound of their hooves sounded like the rumble of an approaching storm. In the center, the infantry continued their slow, steady advance, shields locked together, feet shuffling, trampling the blue chrysathamere flowers, leaving a trail of bruised and broken petals to mark their passage.

Archers loosed arrows. The wind was with the men of Svartennos, and they had the advantage of height, as well; their arrows traveled farther. Some found their marks, and Tyracian shield-men fell and vanished, swallowed by the sea of their own army. Most of the missiles caught in the thick wall of yoba-shell shields.

Camilline shivered, wrapping her arms around herself. Marilia stared at the plain, barely blinking, until her eyes began to water.

As the shield-men advanced, the cavalry came together on either flank. Marilia could hear screams, the sound of the knights' armor rattling.

Marilia thought she knew what Tyrennis Nomeratsu intended. His formation was familiar, basic—one she had seen a hundred times in Karthtag-Kal's books of strategy: the shield-men in the center, the front rank composed of better-armored knights in yoba-shell plates, the back ranks drawn from the commoners' levies, armored only in vests of toughened draleen hide. Cavalry on the flanks, a reserve force of the strongest knights held back so that they might sally forth in a final, decisive strike after weariness had taken its toll on the enemy.

It was a sound strategy, one she had predicted. The Tyrennis had the larger army; he had no need for innovation. His cavalry would try to outflank the Navessean shield-men; if that could not be done, he would simply overwhelm them, hammering them head-on until their lines broke.

When that happened, the battle would end. The killing would not stop—that would go on for at least another hour more—but it would no longer be a battle but a slaughter. For every ten men that fell upon the battlefield, eight of them were slain after their army's lines broke.

To counteract his numerical disadvantage, Zev had put all his best knights to the east, leaving only light cavalry to defend the right flank.

A fatal move, Zev had said to her the night before, his brows furrowed in doubt. *If we leave one flank so poorly guarded, the Tyracians will ride right over us.* He sighed. *My lady, I am sure you believe that Queen Svartana came to you in your dreams, but...* he shrugged. *During times of danger women...and men...see all manner of things. Dremmakin in the fog...the faces of gods in the clouds...the voices of spirits in the rain. Not every vision is real.*

Just hear me out, she begged him. *Then you can decide if this vision was real or not.*

Zev would have been right, ordinarily; under most circumstances, light cavalry would have had no chance against a charge of armored Tyracian knights, no matter how brave they were. But Zev had not considered the land itself; on the right flank, the ground was thick and marshy, and the hill beyond the marshland was steep. The hill was guarded by a triple wall of shield-men, and its peak was lined with Svartennos' best archers.

As Marilia watched, the Svartennan light cavalry on the right flank began to break and flee; they were no match for the Tyracian knights. The Tyracians followed eagerly, drawn by the prospect of an easy victory. Their excitement turned to alarm as their horses floundered in thick mud, as black shafts loosed from the hill above found their marks. Weighed down by their heavy armor, the Tyracians slowed. The Svartennan shield wall closed upon them. Blades thrust, and men went toppling from their saddles.

A knight on horseback at full gallop would always defeat a single man on foot; but a disorganized company of knights trapped in bog-water facing a tightly-formed shield wall was a different matter entirely.

All the while, the archers continued to rain their darts from above.

Seize the high ground where possible, for it offers an advantage in nearly any battle. The words of Governor Sullyn, Volume II, Section Twelve of his Battlefield Tactics.

Though the Tyracian knights were encased head-to-foot in their yoba-shell plates, their horses were not; and even the knights' thick plates of armor had gaps. Although most of the arrows splashed harmlessly into the swamp, some found their marks in man or animal.

"They're beating them!" Camilline exclaimed. "Our shield-men are beating them."

"For now. But it won't last."

Zev had known this, as well. *Forgive me, my lady, but...even with the land on our side, the plan will not work. The footmen and archers may hold out for a time, but sooner or later they will fall without knights to defend them. Peasants can only stand against that many Tyracian knights so long. They won't last forever.*

Marilia stood her ground. *They don't need to hold forever*, she said to him. *Only long enough.*

The Svartennan light cavalry continued their retreat, slipping through a gap in the lines of footmen and disappearing from sight. *But not from the battle.* Marilia's heart beat faster. She turned her eyes to the other side of the battlefield, where Zev's knights were dancing with the Tyracians.

They moved with their enemy like a lord and his lady stepping in time. When the Tyracian knights galloped right, Zev's knights went with them. When they wheeled left, Zev's knights were there. When the Tyracians attempted to charge, the front ranks of Zev's knights fought them off while the rest spun away, refusing to fully commit to the fray. They moved with all the dexterity and skill she would expect from knights of Svartennos—men who had trained for this since they were boys, born on an island whose two most prized possessions were horses and aeder. Theirs was a difficult part to play, and one that might have gone badly in the hands of a lesser force of men. But the Svartennan knights were equal to their task. The back ranks held back even as their brothers in the front struggled and died before them. They knew their purpose, and would not be shaken from it.

They were waiting.

"This is it, isn't it?" Camilline asked.

Marilia nodded; she found that now that the moment had come, she could not speak. *Any moment now…* she thought.

Camilline's fingers found hers once again. Marilia squeezed hard, not taking her gaze from the field. She refused to blink. The wind picked up pace, plucking tears from the corners of her eyes and sending them streaking across her cheeks. She counted each breath as it passed between her lips: *one, two, three...*

"Where are they?" Camilline whispered.

What if something had delayed them? What if she'd misjudged the time this maneuver would take? She said a silent prayer.

Please…Viveos, Sothia, Neravos, anyone who's listening…

Nelos Dartimaos, give us your strength.

"Look!" Camilline pointed.

And Marilia saw them.

The light cavalry that had fled the bog had not left the battlefield; instead, they had made their way behind the Svartennan lines to where a gorge ran along the back of the hill where Marilia and Camilline were standing. They followed that gorge west, riding fast in their light armor. Many of them would die this day; but they were loyal sons of Svartennos. They were ready to die if it meant the battle could be won. If it meant their home could be saved.

The light cavalry exploded up out of the gorge at a full gallop at the same moment that the Svartennan knights banked hard to the east; when the Tyracian knights moved to pursue, they left themselves exposed. The light cavalry bore down on them hard, taking the Tyracians completely by surprise. In moments, the enemy cavalry was enveloped.

Which left Zev's knights free to charge at a diagonal straight across the center of the battlefield directly for the Tyracian reserve.

And, more crucially, directly for Tyrennis Nomeratsu.

The Horselord hung towards the very back of the field, defended by his best knights and a triple wall of shield-men. It was a formidable array.

But against the downhill charge of almost three thousand of Svartennos' best knights, they had no chance.

Camilline stood up in the saddle; a cry burst from her lips. Her eyes were shining, the same as Zev's had been last night. *Thank you*, Marilia thought. *Oh, gods, thank you. It worked.*

Tyrennis Nomeratsu saw the danger. Marilia watched his men scurry about, trying to brace themselves, to prepare for the charge. But she could tell even from this distance that they were going to be too late.

The battlefield was a curious thing, both like and unlike the figures in a game of Sharavayn. In the game all was order, each piece part of a pattern. Here, things were different; men running about, clusters of soldiers breaking away from the fighting—retreating, re-positioning to attack again. Straight ahead parts of the Svartennan main line threatened to buckle; farther along, it was parts of the Tyracian line that were faltering. Groups of horsemen wheeled about on the left flank, hacking at each other. On the right arrows rose and fell in black clouds like clumps of marsh gnats, rattling off armor, picking off pieces of the squares of men. If you looked at any one part of it, it seemed like chaos. It was only from up here, atop the highest point of the hill, as

281

you took it all in, that you could find the order in it.

And in that moment, the order was beautiful.

Zev's charge smashed through the Tyracian reserve. Down below, the thunder of the hooves, the rattle of the swords and armor, and of course the screams must have been deafening. From where Marilia stood on the other side of the battlefield, the charge appeared to be near-silent. As she watched the Tyracians scatter, she was reminded of watching a hive of newborn kwammakin emptying before an incoming flood, watching the dark shapes spinning as they were swept away, kicking their legs, all in silence; whatever screams they might have made too small for anyone watching to hear.

Swords painted the blue chrysathamere flowers red, and horses' hooves broke their petals and crushed them into mud. On the other side of the field, the black and gold Tyracian banner wavered. The silvakim writhed in the air. For a second the banner seemed to steady itself; then it fell, plunging from sight, lost beneath the tide of cavalry like a ship's mast surrendering to the waves.

Sometime later a messenger summoned Marilia to the edge of the battlefield. There, in the shade of a gnarled tree, Zeviel Espeleos lay sorely wounded. A bearded, gaunt-faced knight stood over him, his brow furrowed with concern. He stepped up to meet her as she drew near.

Zev waved a hand. "Thank you, Captain Aexiel," he said. "Let me speak with the Lady Paetia...the Lady Sandara."

The knight Aexiel backed away. His eyes met Marilia's for a brief moment. In them, she saw a look she'd seen before in the eyes of Kanediel's physick. *He is...not well, my lady.*

And he truly was not; Zev's face was taut with pain. A vein bulged in his neck, another in the center of his forehead. His lips were bloodless. But his teeth were bared in a fierce grin of triumph. "I got him," he gasped as she drew near. She noticed that the council of Elders was there, too, waiting nearby in grave silence. They, the physicks, and the knights drew back in deference as Zev waved Marilia forward.

"I captured Tyrennis Nomeratsu," Zev said. "We dragged him back here after Captain Aexiel cut off his hand. Now our knights are finishing off his reserve." Next they would make for the western flank; the Tyracian cavalry there would be trapped. "Ah, the look on that bastard's face when I cut my way through to him...I suppose he thought I'd never manage it. That was what defeated him—his over-confidence." Zev coughed, and blood flecked his chest. It made a pattern like the stroke of a painter's brush. "I'm afraid I got myself hurt rather badly," he said. And though he did his best to appear composed in front of his men, she saw his fear, a spasm that crossed his face. "My own fault; I got carried away. I tried for the Tyracian banner. Didn't make it."

He must have thought he was his brother, Marilia thought.

Zev gave a nod to the bearded knight. "Aexiel carried me back. Good of him, but too late, I fear."

She stared at him—this man who had been her enemy. Though his passing didn't really fill her with sorrow, she realized that she didn't feel much pleasure, either. As she looked upon him, she felt that for the first time, she was seeing him for what he really was; a scared young man who'd tried to be Ben Espeleos but couldn't quite figure out how. She remembered one of the oddities she'd once seen in the Ulvannis arena—a mountain tiger with all its fur shaved away; underneath, the body of the predator had been pale and wrinkled and awkward. It had been hard to watch; she'd felt, somehow, that she ought to turn her eyes away. She felt the same way now. "My lord..."

Zev held up a hand. "I will die with dignity," he said. "I am a son of the princes of Svartennos...Zeviel of the house Espeleos. A proud house. A *proud* house."

"Yes, my lord."

"That's why I called you here. I wanted to tell you...tell you I'm sorry for your husband...my cousin. And I thank you, lady, for your vision."

"I only offered you what Queen Svartana showed me."

"As you say. I'll give her my thanks to her as well, when I meet her." He took a deep breath. Marilia could hear something wet bubble in his chest. "I told the Elders what you did," he said. "How you helped me...how together we...wove the plan that destroyed the Tyracian army."

That wasn't quite how Marilia remembered it, but she didn't correct him; it would have been improper to argue with a dying man in front of his own men.

"I owed you that much," Zev went on. "Now my debts are paid." He stiffened; his hands clutched at the grass, tearing up a clump of it.

A rider, a battlefield messenger, came thundering past them. He was on his way to the back of the lines where a company of Svartennan knights was held in reserve, ready to swoop down upon whichever part of the battlefield needed them most. He pulled up short as Zev called to him.

"Rider! What news?"

"My lord." The rider's eyes widened as he saw the truth of Zev's condition.

"What *news*, I said?"

"I...I was on my way to the reserve, my lord. It's the right flank...they're beginning to break. The Tyracians are too many. Strategos Laekos sent word to the knights on the left, asking them to lend aid, but I fear they are already too fully engaged."

"The right flank?" Zev repeated blankly. "Breaking? *Now*? Those dremmakin-spawned bastards."

"I... I'm afraid so, my lord." The rider hung his head. "Strategos Dartimaos...he managed to rally them for a while, but I've heard he's wounded, or dead, I don't know..."

On the right flank where the bog lay, the horses, superior arms, and numbers of the Tyracians were taking their toll. It seemed that even the proud sons of Svartennos had a breaking point. Half their ships were burned; their prince was in chains; their greatest city reduced to embers. Their army and their fate, so far as they knew, rested in the hands of a man who had lost the only true battle he'd ever been a part of. And, despite the devastating blow it had been dealt, the Tyracian army was still strong.

"They can't break now," Aexiel said, looking anguished. "Tyrennis Nomeratsu is captured and crippled. We're *winning*!"

"The men on the far right are facing towards the west, to prevent the Tyracian knights outflanking them," the rider said. "They could not see Tyrennis Nomeratsu's banner fall. All they can see, sir, is that they are being overwhelmed. They are losing heart."

"Then we must give it back to them." Zev managed to raise one hand. He beckoned to Marilia. Uncertain, she stepped forward.

"Promise me something," he said, his eyes searching her face. "Promise me that when the history of this day is written, the name Zeviel Espeleos will not be forgotten. Promise me they'll sing of my charge."

285

Marilia stared at him blankly. She didn't understand why he would ask such a thing of her, why he thought it was something in her power to give. She simply nodded.

"Promise me. Swear it. On the spirits of your ancestors, of your father, swear it."

"I swear it. By the spirits of my ancestors, I will make sure everyone will remember what happened today," Marilia said.

"And my name," Zev insisted.

She almost turned away; this was asking too much of her, after what he'd done. But he was dying, and in pain, and no matter how much she had hated him, she couldn't find it in herself to deny a dying man. "Why would they forget? You're the one who lead them to victory."

"The first victory, yes. But now we need a second."

He offered Marilia what she at first thought was his hand; then she realized it was a sword...Kanediel's sword, which Zev had claimed after his victory in the duel.

Her eyes widened. She looked to the Elders. They looked back at her. Patos bowed his head towards her; a sign of deference, or acknowledgment, or perhaps apology. "In light of Zeviel Espeleos' account of your vision, we no longer have doubt," he said.

She opened her mouth, but no words came.

"Hurry on," Zev said, his voice growing weaker. He lay back, staring at the sky. "You have to lead them now. We will not speak again. Farewell, Lady Chrysathamere."

CHAPTER TWENTY-FOUR

The armor they found for her was too large, though it had belonged to a small man. It rubbed awkwardly against her shoulders.

She bound her breasts back with a strip of leather. They gave her a woolen tunic and thin linen leggings to wear. Next came a leather jacket. Lastly a coat of yoba-shell plates bound with cord, which one of Zev's knights lowered over her head.

The press of the armor on her body was too heavy. She felt crushed between the weight of all those plates. Each movement was an effort. She took a deep breath, closing her eyes as her heart fluttered like a trapped moth beating itself to death against her ribs.

The mount Kanediel had given her shortly after their wedding was meant for rides over Svartennos' hills, for hunting or racing—not for charging into battle. She had traded it out for a big roan stallion that twitched nervously underneath her as she took her seat and slipped her helmet on.

She realized then just how mad this all was; the sensible thing to do would be to jump down off the horse and tell the gathered knights that this was all a mistake. She couldn't charge into battle. This was all as absurd as a badly-written rhovannon's play, and it would end, as so many of those did, in a nasty death.

I could stand at the top of the hill; I could direct the captains, tell them where to go. I could wave a flag about, if need be, if that would lift men's hearts. But this…this is too much. This will never work. Zeviel Espeleos just died in this battle; Tyrennis Nomeratsu lost his hand. Ben

Espeleos was captured.

What chance do I have?

"I'll be right beside you," Septakim said. "Every step of the way. I'll keep you safe. How do you feel, my lady?"

"I feel...I feel all right," she lied, wishing he hadn't asked. Things were at least a little better than they had been on the ground. Her arms still felt like she was moving them through thick, muddy water, but she no longer had to worry about her legs; her horse would do her running for her, so long as she managed to stay in the saddle.

"Well, then. Shall we?" Aexiel asked, hands tightening on the reins.

Hurry on, Zev had said to her. He'd said it while dying; he must have been terrified. It was a marvel that he'd had the presence of mind to say anything to her at all. Despite his many faults—and they were many—Zeviel Espeleos had died a warrior's death; he had put aside his fear and done what he'd thought he had to.

How could she do any less?

She nodded at Aexiel. "Let's go."

Behind her were almost three hundred knights of Svartennos—all those who had been kept in reserve, as well as the men who had accompanied the wounded Zev back to the Elders. It wasn't much. It wasn't enough to turn the tide of the battle—or it shouldn't have been. But, as Emperor Urian had known, hope could sometimes work wonders.

Maybe it could work one now.

She raised Kanediel's sword in the air.

She tried to remember Karthtag-Kal's lessons, but it had been more than three years since she'd last held a wooden sword, and besides, he'd never taught her anything about fighting from horseback. So many of his lessons—*move like water, fight with your feet first, let them lead your strikes*—came to little now that she was perched in a saddle. Even those lessons he had given her had been at least two years ago. She found herself wishing she hadn't humiliated Ilruyn back in the royal gardens, wishing Karthtag-Kal hadn't been so quick to put an end to her training—every day of practice, every hour, might be the difference now between life and death.

Her throat felt very tight, and for a second, she was seized with the fear that now, at this key moment, nothing would come out but a squeak like a dying animal.

Then she heard a voice, and realized it was hers. It was, to her amazement and relief, strong and clear. "Knights of Svartennos!" she cried. "To me! For your homes, for your Elders, for the gods!" *For Kanediel*, she thought. She would finish what he'd started, or she would die trying.

They took up a cry. "Chrysathamere! Chrysathamere!"

As she kicked her heels into her horse's flanks, as she felt the animal stir into motion beneath her, she felt as though she were reading an account of an old battle in one of Karthtag-Kal's library books. *Then, with Zeviel Espeleos, the commander of Svartennos' army, mortally wounded, his cousin's wife, Marilia Paetia, took it upon herself to marshal the reserve for the purpose of bringing aid to the right flank...* but it wasn't really her in that story, and she wasn't really here charging at the head of three hundred men. And since it wasn't really *her* here, since she was only watching it, she could handle things properly; she knew exactly what such a scene demanded. Hadn't she read about enough of them while studying for her games of Sharavayn?

She raised her sword above her head and howled. Her men were yelling, too, spurring their horses to a gallop, the shield-men passing in a blur to their left, the gorge on their right as they sped behind the line of battle towards the right flank. They crested the top of the hill; they began their descent down the other side, a lethal, unstoppable wedge.

The shield wall on the right flank wasn't breaking, as Zev's rider had said; it had already broken. And the Tyracians were cutting through its remnants like a razorfish through water, men on foot stabbing with their short-swords, knights on horseback slashing down with their long dueling blades. The Svartennans fleeing up the slope paused as they heard the cry of Marilia's knights. Men with hollowed eyes turned, seeking the source of the shout that had gone up, that grew louder with each passing breath. "Chrysathamere! Chrysathamere!" And the spark that had nearly gone out in their eyes began to burn again.

The cries of her men echoed in Marilia's ears. Her horse rocked beneath her. She clenched her fingers hard around the hilt of Kanediel's sword. Her eyes were fixed on the enemy ahead. She watched as on one of the Tyracian knights cut down with his curved blade, as a fine red mist erupted from where it landed. But for the color it might almost have been sea foam, the sort that had tickled her cheeks and dampened her hair during her galley voyage with Annuweth and Karthtag-Kal.

In a few moments, though, those blades were going to be swinging at her.

You don't have to defeat them, she reminded herself. *Just hold them long enough for the rest of the knights to take them from behind.*

Just long enough.

Not so hard a task.

But as her center of gravity tilted inexorably forwards, as her horse barreled down the hill towards the company of Tyracian knights, she felt her fear, until then held at bay by the golden splendor of the moment, hit her with all the chill force of a storm-wave. A fist seemed to be repeatedly slamming her in the stomach. She fought the urge to vomit over the neck of her horse, for what would become of her glorious charge then?

Back on the hill there had been order; now she had descended too close, and everything became chaos. It was like staring at a water-script painting from a hand's breadth away, so close you could see each individual, imperfect thread in the fabric, each brush-stroke—the dashes of color, but not their meaning, not their whole. There were so many swords, all aimed for her and her men, and all that was needed was *one* to make her meat, to reduce her to something no different from the thousands of other pieces of meat lying on the field already, nothing to make her Chrysathamere, nothing even to make her Marilia except her lifeless face, if even that was left to her.

The only thing that kept her from breaking down completely was the knowledge that if she died right now, in the next few seconds, at least she'd made it this far. She'd become something bigger than she'd ever believed possible. And that was something.

"Chrysathamere!" Her men screamed, the shield-men and archers trapped and embattled at the foot of the slope taking up the cry as they rallied, fighting back with a fervor that stopped the Tyracians in their tracks. Those who had been fleeing swung about as Marilia yelled at them.

"Form ranks! Shield wall! Turn about, and have no fear!"

She hoped that their fear was nothing like her own. If it was, they were all dead already.

"Oh, fuck," she whispered, and of all the thoughts she might have had in that final moment, the last thought that entered her head before she closed with the Tyracian knights was what would Karthtag-Kal have thought of such language?

At the last moment, Septakim gave a nod, and he, Aexiel, and

291

several of the other knights dug in their heels, pulling ahead of her, forming a wall around her so that she was no longer at the head of the charge. But she still felt the shock as the two forces collided: a feeling like having her head plunged beneath the waters of a choppy sea. All around was white noise. She saw Septakim hacking left and right with his sword, saw Aexiel wrench a man from the saddle and split his helmet as he tried to rise—she blinked in shock as she felt the heat of the blood on her face. Beside her, a knight of Svartennos fell from his saddle with a spear through his head. She caught a glimpse of his jaw hanging slackly off one side of his face before he was gone and a Tyracian knight was there in his place.

She wheeled her horse about and swung her sword as Karthtag-Kal had taught her. She had never fought on horse-back before, so she missed terribly; instead of cutting the man's throat, she left a scratch across his cuirass. His return blow bent one of her shoulder-plates inward and sent a cold ache through her left arm. He raised his sword again, but the movement left his under-arm exposed; the point of Septakim's sword plunged eagerly for the gap and was out again before Marilia could even register what had happened. The man coughed blood into her face and died.

"Chrysathamere!" Septakim yelled, spinning and laying all about him with his sword, carving a circle of protection around her.

"Svartennos!" she yelled, because she felt she ought to say something. "Svartennos!"

A Tyracian knight came at her on foot, trying to stab her or drag her from the saddle, she wasn't sure which. She slashed down with her sword and he was too slow to raise his shield. She felt the jolt of impact all the way up her arm. When she lifted the sword again the entire blade was stained red. She squeezed the handle of her sword until she thought it might fuse with her skin.

Septakim was struck hard with the slash of a sword. It came out of nowhere, slamming into his side with enough force to send him toppling from the saddle with a grunt.

Another Tyracian knight came for her through the gap where he had been. He cut at the side of her head and she made an angle with her sword—water, something about water, Karthtag-Kal had said—feeling his blade slide off. His horse stumbled in the mud and their two steeds came up alongside each other. He grabbed for her, his hand finding her shoulder.

Which is not good, which is not good at all...

She tried to pull away. They both lost their seats and went toppling into the marsh, and it was his good fortune that he landed on top.

The weight of his body landing atop her drove the air from her lungs. He drew his short-sword and stabbed; she twisted her head to one side and felt it skate off the side of her helmet. She smashed a fistful of mud into his face and he choked and jerked back, blinded. She hit him hard with her fist and managed to roll on top of him. They grappled together. Somewhere along the way he lost his sword.

She struck at him with her fists, and then remembered her own short-sword. They'd belted one to her waist, just as they did with all the other knights. She reached for it—a mistake. As her hand went for her waist, his hands found either side of her head and he flipped her under him.

She tasted bog-water. She felt the rough leather of his gauntlet against her nose, the back of her head sinking into the slimy mud of the river-bottom. There was grit in her eyes, in her mouth; she tasted the battle on her tongue; thick, rough, with a rich, coppery layer throughout.

She heard feet splashing all around her. All she saw was brown, flickers of sunlight. She felt panic, a heat in her belly like a fire burning. She screamed and kicked, but the man on top of her was too strong.

Then at last one of her flailing hands found something hard—the hilt of his short-sword!—and she stabbed up. The blade took him in the neck, between his helmet and his breastplate. She felt his grip slacken. She surfaced. Water mixed with his blood cascaded from her helmet into her eyes and she rubbed it away with trembling fingers.

A horse knocked into her and she lost her footing again. A hoof kicked her in the side, and she felt it through her armor. As she rose again the thrust of a short-sword caught her in the abdomen. She doubled over, the plates of her armor bent inward. It was a deep, breathless pain that felt as if her ribs had turned to splintered glass. If the blade has been fine aeder, a knight's weapon, it might have gone clean through. But her enemy was only a Tyracian shield-man, his blade the clouded amethyst color of cheap crystal.

He stabbed again, and purely on instinct she snapped her short-sword up, driving the point of his blade wide. She went down on her knee and lunged for his groin where the armor was weak. In Karthtag-Kal's hall, unencumbered, dressed in nothing but her under-clothes, she might have landed the blow. Here, she stumbled, weighed down by her water-logged armor, and hit nothing but the center of her enemy's shield. Her thrust left her over-balanced, down on one knee in the mud. She had no shield of her own to block his return strike.

The man's head exploded as a sword burst through it from behind. A second later a hand was beneath her arm, hoisting her to her feet. Septakim's hand.

"Well, that was a close one," he said.

"Force the heretic bastards back!" Aexiel yelled. Svartennan knights closed around them, forming a protective bulwark as Septakim helped Marilia into an empty saddle and mounted his own horse beside her.

"Are you well, my lady?" he asked.

She laughed, so loudly that her horse started beneath her. Her sides shook, making her wounded belly throb. She could hardly breathe. Turning her face from him, she vomited a mixture of bile and filthy water all over the body of the knight she had recently killed.

"As well as all that?" Septakim grunted. "Excellent. We'll have the Tyracians running in no time."

"This leading from the front thing..." she said, spitting the last of her sickness out of her mouth. "Someone should really do away with it."

She hadn't meant it as a jest, but Septakim laughed heartily. "A fine wit you have, my lady. Excellent. Just stay close to me."

"That's what I'm trying to do," she muttered, but he didn't hear her; he was busy warding off the slash of a bloody Tyracian sword. He jerked on the reins, his horse slipping sideways so that his opponent's next cut missed completely. Before the over-balanced Tyracian could right himself, Septakim's sword had carved a chunk out of the side of his neck.

"I'm going to die." Marilia had thought she'd only said the words in her head, but she must have said them out loud, because Septakim turned to her.

"Not today, my lady," he said.

"What do you mean?"

"Look," he said, and smiled. "Zev's knights have arrived from the east. Our reinforcements are here. The Tyracians are retreating."

"Retreating..."

"My lady," Septakim said, putting his hand on her shoulder. "We've won."

Though the Elders had acclaimed her, and Zev had given her his blessing, most of the strategoi still did not yet know that Queen Svartana's spirit walked among them. That meant she didn't have the authority to give them orders, not yet, so she trusted in them to know their work and complete the rout of the Tyracians. She could not have ridden with them any further in any case. The battle had already taken all her strength.

She was still shaking when she returned to her tent. Camilline was waiting there. Camilline stared as Marilia collapsed into a folding chair, still wearing the dented, bloody armor she'd fought in. Outside, the sounds of battle could still be heard—the Svartennans pursuing the retreating Tyracian host, cutting them down.

Someone sent a servant to her. He helped her out of her armor. She was so exhausted that she took no notice of his gaze upon her nearly-naked body. A handmaiden brought her a bucket of water and she rinsed herself, the blood and grime of the battle falling away. She shivered.

"Are you all right?" Camilline asked.

"I don't know."

"It's over. We beat them." Camilline put her arms around Marilia and Marilia held her close, sobbing without even knowing why, burying her face in Camilline's hair.

CHAPTER TWENTY-FIVE

By the time she emerged from her tent an hour later, the news of her victory had spread through the camp. The warriors of Svartennos knew that the wife of Kanediel Paetos had received a vision from Queen Svartana that had tipped the battle in their favor; and later, when the battle turned ill, that she herself had ridden with the reserve to throw back the Tyracians on the right flank. She had received the blessing of the Elders.

And so, when she stepped into the light, the cries of the army washed over her. "Chrysathamere!" they yelled. "Lady Sandara!" Someone cried, and soon enough they were chanting that, too.

Marilia stood there. She felt as if she had slipped into a dream. As if she were made of smoke, a spirit walking among them—or maybe they were the spirits, and she the only one that was fully real.

She took a few steps forward, away from the tent. She was back in her dress, black fringed with light blue, and she could feel the grass tickling her ankles as she walked.

They continued to cheer for her.

Gravely, Patos and two of the other Elders approached. In his hand Patos carried a furled banner. He handed it to her. Two servants trailed behind. They laid a thick wooden chest on the ground before her feet. Inside was armor—yoba-shell plates painted blue, the color of the flowers in the valley. The color of the Paetos flag. The armor was smaller than the suit she had worn to battle; it was the same armor that had been worn by Queen Svartana. It would serve until a new suit could be fashioned, one that was all her own.

A wind sprang up, pulling the clouds back like a curtain being drawn aside to let in the sun. It whipped her hair about her face. It caught the banner in her hand, unfurling it, the great blue flower standing proud above the plain. Marilia felt her chest grow tight. She couldn't breathe.

The banner snapped in the wind, a sound like distant lightning. Tears filled her eyes. The wind found them, too, tearing them from her and hurling them away into the air.

She was keenly aware of being alive, aware of each breath as it entered her lungs, aware of the cool touch of the air against her face as a light rain began to fall, washing away the dust and blood on the field. She could smell the damp grass and the damp earth beneath it. The little blue flowers in the field shone with light. She felt that somewhere above beyond the clouds someone—Nelos Dartimaos, perhaps—was watching her.

Catarina appeared at her side. Gently, she touched Marilia's shoulder. Marilia found her voice.

She knew what was expected; Patos had already been by her tent to tell her. *Prepare a few words for the men.* Strange that she could think of a plan to defeat fifteen thousand Tyracian warriors, but this simple task had proved to be beyond her. But Camilline had rescued her; Camilline had told her what to say, and now she said it.

"They came and threatened our homes, our land, our gods. They believed that because they had more men, they were stronger than us. Thousands of men, thousands of waves from across the sea, came to drown this island. But our strength is in our swords and our spears. In the gods' fire, filling our hearts. In this land that bore us, the mountains that stand above us, the ground beneath our feet. We are Svartennos, and we will not be defeated!"

The roar made her ears ring.

Patos spoke. "By the power vested in us by the gods, we, the Council of Elders, do recognize this woman, Marilia Sandara, formerly Marilia Paetia, blood of Nelos Dartimaos, daughter of Karthtag-Kal Sandaros, to be the Lady Chrysathamere. In her spirit we see the spirit of our Queen Svartana."

Then a new voice spoke, a young voice; a presence so small and slight that Marilia hadn't even realized she was there. It was Clariline, the daughter of Ben and Catarina; her mother stood behind, a gentle, reassuring hand on her daughter's shoulder. "Since Zeviel Espeleos is dead and Kanediel Espeleos is dead and my father, the Prince of Svartennos, is missing and has named no one to command his army, custom states that the strategoi must choose a new leader from among themselves. In the name of my father, Beniel Espeleos, who we wish could be with us today, I ask you, lords and strategoi of Svartennos, to choose this woman, to swear to her until this war is over or my father returned to us."

The strategoi stepped forward and drew their swords. Marilia could feel each beat of her heart as it pounded in her chest, faster and faster like the drum of a galley moving to the attack. *This isn't real. This isn't possible.* Yet another part of her felt that it was more than possible—it was inevitable. It was what her whole life had led her towards. It was what Karthtag-Kal had prepared her for.

Laekos, the strategos in service to Lady Siria, was the first to swear. He laid his sword across his palms. "In the name of Phelkos and Aphexia, I swear to follow this woman, Marilia Sandara, into battle. I take her as my commander for this war to come. I pledge my sword to her service."

"So it goes," Patos said, acknowledging the oath.

So begun, it could not be stopped; the moment gathered momentum like a stone speeding down a mountainside.

One by one they came before her. Leondos, a huge warrior with a beard thick and bristling as the spine of a Danish boar and a scar upon his brow. Antiriel, a thick-faced man with a missing eye. Konos, hair streaked with white, nearly old enough to be an Elder. Aerael, Marilia's cousin, the son of Lady Dartimaea, hardly more than a boy, with a handsome face and short-cropped hair. They spoke the words and Patos answered them.

"So it goes."

"So it goes."

"So it goes."

When the last of the strategoi had come and offered her their swords, Patos raised his hand. They knelt before her, strategoi, captains, sergeants and simple soldiers alike.

And so it went.

Part IV: Chrysathamere

CHAPTER TWENTY-SIX

"Thank you for the speech," Marilia said. "I couldn't have done it without you. I couldn't have done any of it."

Camilline shrugged. "Somehow, I feel like that's complete horse-shit, but it's generous horse-shit. I suppose I'll take it."

They were back in the tent they had been sharing since they'd left Svartennos City. Tomorrow, they would begin their march south, back to the ruins the Tyracians had left behind—to rebuild, and to await the arrival of Vergana's fleet.

Outside, four of Kanediel's household knights—*Marilia's* knights, now—stood guard. Camilline was the lady of House Paetos now; since she had no husband, it was up to her to choose a strategos to lead her soldiers, and she had chosen Marilia. While the entire army lay under Marilia's command, only the knights of House Paetos were hers *directly*.

The two of them sat together at the supper table, spoons scraping against soup-bowls, and it was all Marilia could do to sit still. Her feet shifted restlessly on the floor of the tent.

Her life was moving so fast. Outside the tent, banners with the chrysathamere flower were being woven. Men were singing of the battle of the valley, of the final charge. They were singing of *her*. When she and Camilline were quiet, Marilia could almost make out the words. The thought of being the woman in those songs, hour after hour, day after day, left her dizzy.

"They loved it," Marilia said. "Your words, Camilline. I think we can win. Not just this battle, but the whole war. When I stood there...I know it sounds mad, but...I think I felt something. Just for a moment...it's hard to explain..."

"The spirit of Queen Svartana, I suppose." Camilline smiled faintly. She looked down at her soup, slurped down another spoonful. "Well," she said, "you certainly looked very good up there. Svartana Reborn...yes, I could see it."

"It was you who gave me the idea to try it in the first place. You convinced me to go to the Elders." Marilia reached out and took Camilline's hands. "I didn't think it could work at first, but you were right, Camilline. You were right all along."

Without warning, Camilline pulled her hands back out of reach. "Well, you seem very pleased," she said sharply. "If I didn't already know, I'd never guess that your husband died less than a week ago."

Marilia drew back. Camilline might as well have struck her in the stomach; she felt much as she had when the Tyracian's short-sword had hit her there, denting the plates of her armor.

"I didn't...I didn't mean..."

"What? Did you forget?" Camilline's crooked grin was a harsh, slanted mockery of the smile she usually wore.

"Of course not. I just meant..."

"I know what you meant." Camilline's face was hard. "Do you know something terrible?" she tried to keep her voice even, but it cracked on the last word. "We won; we defeated the Tyracians, we saved the island and thousands of lives. And it turns out you're Svartana Reborn after all. It's all gone so well, hasn't it? Better than we could have hoped for. But a part of me wishes I could take back time, go back to that moment when we were hunting crabs outside Svartennos Harbor. When Kanediel was still alive."

303

"I wish it, too," Marilia said.

"Do you really?"

Hurt, Marilia stared down at her soup bowl. "Of course," she said. "I loved Kanediel."

She *had* loved him, though not in the way she'd wanted to. She wished he were still alive to see Svartennos safe.

But there's a part of you that likes being Lady Chrysathamere more than you ever liked being Lady Paetia, isn't there? If you could trade all this that you have now—this glory, this freedom*—for Kanediel's life…would you?*

Yes, she thought. *Of course I would.*

She wanted to believe it was true.

They ate for a while without speaking, with only the slurping of soup and the clattering of wood on wood to break the silence between them.

Marilia found that she couldn't bear it; of all the things that had changed, her bond with Camilline was the one she needed to put back as it had been—the constant, the spur of rock among the ocean waves.

"Come with me," she blurted suddenly.

"Where?" Camilline asked, raising one eyebrow. "To war?"

"We did it before."

"That time we had my brother and my cousin with us. And that war was not half as dangerous as this one."

"But still."

"You won't need me."

"I will. I don't want to be alone."

"You won't be alone. You'll have the entire army of Svartennos, and Emperor Vergana's fleet with you. He's sending his brother-by-marriage, Livenneth, isn't that right?"

304

"You know what I mean," Marilia said.

Camilline shook her head. "You don't need me, Marilia. The Tyracian fleet is still between us and Dane, remember? That means a sea battle, most likely, as you were telling me just this morning. What would I do on a warship?"

"You could join me afterwards. You could come to us in Dane after we break their fleet and…"

"And do what? I could do more here; I could help rebuild what the Tyracians burned down. I could finally find the time to mourn my brother."

Marilia had no answer to that. All she could say was "I want you by my side."

How could she say what she really meant? That she needed this— needed moments like the one she'd shared in the bath with Camilline before the march from Svartennos City. Like the ride outside Ulvannis, or the many moments they'd shared together during the flight north from Svartennos Harbor. Needed the sight of Camilline's smile, the warmth of her skin, the real, human closeness of her.

She had a sudden urge to reach out and take Camilline's hands again. She wasn't sure what stopped her. She looked into Camilline's eyes and willed the other woman to understand what she felt without the need for words.

But Camilline broke the stare. "You don't need me. You'll do fine on your own." She finished her soup with a slurp and set her bowl aside. "Come; let's light some candles for the dead and go to bed."

The following morning, Marilia awoke to a sudden pain in her abdomen. She sat up in the darkness of her tent, her breath catching. It was an ache like the tug of a rrope somewhere deep in her groin; she felt it all the way through her body, as though the Tyracian short-sword that had struck her three days before had managed to pierce her after all.

She started to get up, and felt a familiar wetness against her thighs. The blood had not yet begun to dry on her skin.

What she saw in the thin strip of moonlight was barely larger than the tip of her thumb. She didn't look too closely; she didn't think she could bear to. With trembling hands, she wrapped it in a strip of linen, carried it outside, and buried it in the grass.

She returned to her cot in the tent, letting out a shaky breath, staring up at the ceiling. She felt sick. She pulled the covers up to her chin with shaking fingers.

Whether it was because of the terror of the last few days or the rigor of the battle or the blows she had taken, or none of those reasons at all, she didn't know. Kanediel's physick could probably tell her, but that would mean informing him that she had been with child in the first place, and she had no intention of doing that. This was one secret she would share with no one else. She supposed that meant she would never know for sure what it was that had cut short the life growing inside her. Maybe it was better that way.

One thing she *could* be certain of: Kanediel's line would end with him. His spirit would have no children to guide or lend strength to. He would have to content himself with nephews, nieces, cousins, friends. All because she had charged into battle. Because she had decided to become the Lady Chrysathamere.

And she knew that was tragic—those were the words that would be used, if she were to tell anyone of what she had lost: a tragedy, a terrible, *tragic* accident.

She would tell herself it was a sacrifice, a price she'd paid for Svartennos' salvation. One life lost so that thousands could be saved. If she hadn't made that charge, she couldn't begin to guess how many might have died.

And while all of that might be true, she knew also that a part of her that had once witnessed her mother's final, blood-soaked breaths didn't feel as if this was a tragedy, or a sacrifice, but a *relief*.

Maybe Camilline was right to stay behind, after all, she thought. *Maybe she looked at me and knew me better than I know myself.*

She brought her hands to her chin and held them there until the shaking stopped.

"I'm sorry, Kanediel," she whispered. "I'm so sorry."

CHAPTER TWENTY-SEVEN

Marilia entered the prisoner's tent and found Tyrennis Nomeratsu chained by his ankle to a stake. He was lying on a cot, the stump where his right hand had been swathed in bandages. He raised his head as she entered, dressed now in the armor that had been Queen Svartana's.

He had lost a good deal of blood. His face looked gaunt and haggard, and his movements were slow, like those of man twice his age. Though someone had been in to wash him, it had been a lackluster effort; there were still clumps of dried mud in the hairs of his black beard.

He squinted at her blearily. "Who in the name of all the ghouls are you? Does Svartennos send its women to fight us now?"

"Only one," she said.

"Even without my hand, if I weren't chained to this bed, I would slaughter you."

"I doubt it." She regarded him coldly. She searched herself for pity and found none; this was the man who had burned the harbor and Svartennos City, and whose knights had run down helpless villagers as they fled north. The scouts' reports had already come back; the fields and roads to the south were dark with blood. He was the man whose attack had left Camilline without a brother. Maybe it wasn't fair to put the blame for that death on him; but she wasn't feeling particularly fair just then. "I imagine that hurts, my lord." She nodded towards his missing hand.

He looked as if he was considering denying it; then he shrugged.

308

"Yes," he said. "It hurts."

She knelt on the grass before him, the plates of her armor creaking as she took her position. Tyrennis Nomeratsu was too valuable a prisoner to harm, especially when they didn't know what prisoners of their own the Tyracians had taken. The benefit of having noble blood was that if you were captured on the battlefield, the customs of war dictated that you be kept alive and unharmed. If you were a commoner, on the other hand, surrender all too often turned out to be just a desperate roll of the dice.

The customs of war also dictated that men like Tyrennis Nomeratsu not be compelled to betray their homelands under torture; but while she would not cause him any further harm, neither was she obligated to do all in her power to ease his pain. "You have suffered a great deal," she said. "I imagine you'd prefer the rest of your stay here be comfortable. I mean to leave Lord Konos in charge of this island when I march, and he is an honorable man. I know he would see to it that you are treated well. However, you and your men have caught us unprepared. Our supplies are scattered, and we do not have enough even for all our own. We must reserve our best comforts for those that most merit them."

"I have no patience for veiled words. Not now. Let me see if I understand correctly...you won't torture me—you wouldn't sink that far—but you will allow me to suffer, deny me the best medicines unless I betray Tyrace's secrets? To tell you how many men lie ahead, how many ships? Where we have struck along your empire's coasts? The movements of our forces? No, my lady; I have nothing to tell you."

"You misunderstand. I am not here to compel you to betray Tyrace," Marilia said. "I am here on behalf of my friend, the prince's wife. I am here to ask you—does Prince Espeleos still live? And if he does, I would like to offer you the chance to trade yourself for him."

"Ah, yes, Espeleos…the mad-man at the docks. We have him. But you want to trade a one-handed man for *him*—your prince, one of your greatest warriors? I would not make such a deal, not even to save myself, even if I had the power—which I don't. Prince Espeleos will have been shipped back to Tyrace, to join the other noble prisoners we have taken, and his fate is in our king's hands, not mine. If any trade is to be made, it will not be for me, believe me."

Marilia nodded; she had feared as much. "Can you not at least tell me how he fares?" she asked. "Was he wounded? One commander to another…"

"One commander to another…" Nomeratsu repeated, running his tongue across the inside of his teeth. His eyes darkened. He leaned in towards her, coming as close as he could, his chain rattling. "You are no commander," he hissed. "No matter what madness drove the Svartennans to dress you in a knight's armor. No matter what priest or Horselord or fool magistrate you had to fuck to convince them all to follow you."

He was a broken, spiteful wreck of a man, and his words were nothing more than his last, feeble attempt to hurt her. She knew that; but even so, she felt her anger rise, heat coiling about her throat. And that angered her even more; that this man still had the power to offend her.

She rose to her feet. "I made a mistake coming here, I see."

"You have made many mistakes. You are a child playing with sticks, and it's all fun until you get hurt; then you will cry, long and loud."

"I was one of you once," Marilia said, her voice cold. "I grew up in Tyracium. My mother was a painted lady from the South Quarter." The look on his face was one of dawning horror. She savored it. She didn't bother to hide her smile. "That's me; Marilia, the bastard, a painted lady's daughter. I'm the one who defeated you today. I wanted you to know that."

She was grateful for the chain that bound him to his cot, for she did not doubt that had it not been there, he would have tried to kill her.

After a moment, though, the rage left his features; a lean, dark look appeared in his eye, as if a cord had been pulled, curtains drawing in to cut off the light. She was impressed, despite herself, by the display of self-mastery.

"Let me tell *you* something, Lady Sandara—that is your name, isn't it? The king of Tyrace gave me command of this landing force because he favored me, but if I am going to be honest with us both—just between you and I—I was not the most deserving of the honor. When all is said and done, there are commanders in Tyrace whose minds are keener than mine. Well; one of those commanders waits for you now, out there across the sea. His name is Tyrennis Castaval. Still young, but such a prodigy."

At the sound of the name she felt something inside her open, a crack into a closet she'd thought long since closed. Suddenly, the air in the tent seemed too close and too cold. She kept her face carefully blank; she would not let this man see her fear.

"He is the one who slaughtered the Kangrits at the age of seventeen; he is the rising star who has never been beaten. Hardly more than a boy, still, but men already say he's another Neravos. He will break you, girl. Today you got lucky; you will not get lucky again."

The Tyracians continued to flee south. Many were caught by bands of pursuing Svartennan knights and cut down. Some made it back to their ships and cast off back for Tyrace, where they would regroup and prepare to meet Emperor Vergana's army.

The Tyracians had lost the element of surprise; their chance to conquer Svartennos and gain an early advantage had been squandered. But rumor had it they were faring better in the west. And the war was far from won. Though not as large or as wealthy as Navessea, Tyrace was a strong, proud kingdom, and it would not be easily defeated.

Marilia's army followed, a long ribbon of men in polished armor, glittering like the undulating scales of a serpent as they made their way back to the land that had been stolen from them.

When the Chroniclers of Yalaeda wrote the story of this war, when it was added beside the others in Karthtag-Kal's library, her name would be in there, right alongside the likes of Moroweth Vergana, Nelos Dartimaos and Karthtag-Kal. Even if she died tomorrow, the Battle of Chrysathamere Pass would bear mentioning, as would her part in it.

She had seized something that could not be taken away.

But the people of Svartennos had named her Chrysathamere, and she meant not to disappoint them. She meant to seize more.

She tried not to let Tyrennis Nomeratsu's words rattle her. They were an empty boast, she told herself, a feeble threat from a man with no other weapons left to him. They meant nothing; Nomeratsu had fallen, and Castaval would follow just the same. She was the Lady Chrysathamere—surely a match for him.

But when she closed her eyes, she could still picture him, even after all those years—the haughty hook of his nose, his narrow chin and small, sharp eyes, narrowed in anger. The sound of his stick as it hammered at her brother's back. His voice, scornful and cruel. *You're not a prefect's daughter. You're dirt.*

312

Don't forget it.

They marched for seven hours a day, stopping to rest once around midday to eat. That hour, and the hours between the moment they stopped to make camp and the moment the sun went down, were filled with the logistics of command—appointments to be made, quarrels between strategoi to manage, reports to listen to, letters to read from other parts of the empire regarding the movements of the Tyracians and the Navessean legions.

The Elders took it upon themselves to determine what would become of those whose homes had been burned, as well as planning the reconstruction of Redonda and Svartennos City. But even with that weight off her shoulders, Marilia had more than enough to occupy her.

By the time the sun had gone down Marilia's eyes burned, and her head ached as if Tyreesha had just taken her pestle to the top of her skull. But that was not the end of her day.

Half an hour after sundown during the first day of the march, Marilia called Septakim to an empty tent she had set up near her own. Her met her there, raising one eyebrow as he looked around. Besides a rack with a couple of blunted aeder swords and the bare grass on the ground, it was empty.

"What's this?" he asked.

"Did Catarina not tell you why you were to come here?"

"All she said was she wanted me to assist you."

Marilia was dressed in full armor. Awkwardly, she moved towards him, handing him a blunted sword—purple aeder, the poorest kind, with a false edge that could not cut flesh.

"I need to learn how to fight in armor," she told him. "I expect I may have to do it again at some point. And with a shield." And on horseback, too, but she figured that could wait. One step at a time. First she'd learn to walk, then she could worry about how to ride.

"Well, you couldn't do much worse than last time. My lady."

She frowned. "Do you speak to the Lady Catarina that way?"

"I do. She is accustomed to it by now." He bowed his head. "Forgive me, my lady. I only meant to say that you are bound to improve. Take heart. I must ask—why me? I'm the Lady Catarina's knight, and you have...how many of your own? House Paetos is a proud house; I'd guess a thousand, at the very least."

"You are one of the Dragonknights. Only the best swordsmen can hold such a post. I need one of the best swordsmen to teach me. And the Lady Catarina told me your father was a sword instructor. And... because you were there beside me. You saved my life."

"You flatter me, and I don't deserve it. I'm not proud of that performance in the bog. I almost let you die."

"But you didn't."

Septakim pursed his lips. "My father was a sword instructor, it's true...among many other things, most not fit for the ears of ladies. Fortunately for me and unfortunately for your training, I am not sure I inherited much from him besides my name—I'm no teacher. But I suppose I would be game to try."

"Let's do it, then." She handed him one of the blunted dueling swords.

Septakim hefted it, looking bemused. "I never would have thought that my life would lead me to this—beating ladies. That was more of my father's past-time."

"Well, you seemed quite skilled at it when we met before the Elders."

"I was just following their orders. It wasn't personal. Patos was a tournament champion himself once. If I'd held back, he would have known."

"I want you to make it so that next time, if you don't hold back, you'll end up on yours."

He grinned. "Well put, my lady." He held his sword out before him, studying her across the dim confines of the tent. "You move well," he said.

"My father used to teach me," she said. "A little." Karthtag-Kal's lessons in the prefect's villa seemed painfully inadequate now.

"Well, you're taller than most women," Septakim said. "If our last match was anything to go by, you've got some strength to you, too. I might be able to make at least half a warrior of you yet." He beckoned to her. "Let's begin."

She took a deep breath, a firm hold on her sword, and lunged at him.

He finished her in three moves, his sword neatly sliding off hers, twisting like a snake in mid-air so that the point touched her throat. Had it been sharp, it would have had her bleeding out in seconds.

"Could we maybe start a little slower?"

This time he stepped in close. She managed to get a lock on his blade, briefly, but he simply flicked his wrists and sent the top of his sword past her guard, striking her lightly on the top of the head and then drawing down for a cut that would have most likely claimed her nose.

"When our blades are touching," Septakim said, "you can feel me start to move—the pressure against your blade will change. When that happens, you move with it, with me, or you'll get hit."

They trained for an hour. By the end of it, even though he tried to be gentler than he had before the Elders, she was bruised in at least five places and gasping for breath.

Septakim grunted. "You have true mettle, my lady."

"We'll do it again, tomorrow, with shields," Marilia said. "And we'll do it the day after that, and the one after that, until I've learned."

And so they did—an hour and a half each evening. When they were finished, Marilia fell into her bedroll at long last and was asleep almost as soon as she lay down.

On the evening of the third day of their march they reached Svartennos City. Marilia felt a lump form in her throat. The grass around the city was streaked with flakes of ash. The city itself was a ruin; the proud castle in which she had married Kanediel was nothing more than a skeleton, shattered timbers jutting like the broken ribs of a carcass mauled by a pack of ghouls. The garden where Kanediel had fallen was so coated in ash that it looked like a sculpture made of pale sand, something a child of remarkable skill might craft on the edge of a beach. Everything was the same gray-white color—the flowers, the ferns, the grass—except the surface of the pond, a blank, dull mirror. The chicayas had gone silent.

They rode farther south, hoping to escape the ashy ruins of the city, and came upon an even worse sight.

The road to the south was clogged with bodies. The Tyracian soldiers had left them where they'd died. As the horses approached, the dead shed their black cloaks; clouds of flies alighted into the air. The smell was like a fetid breath come straight from a fissure in the earth, from the throat of Shuvakain the Cursed. Marilia heard the gravers gagging as they dragged the bodies away to be burned.

Marilia passed a hand over her eyes; she urged her horse away from the road. She could not escape the smell of death, but she could at least put some distance between it and her.

"So many lost so fast," Catarina said, shaking her head.

Though the common people of the south had lost the most, even the strategoi had suffered; Lady Dartimaea's lands were ash, two of her nephews claimed at the harbor. Lord Antiriel's eldest son had died at the pass, and his youngest had lost his leg. Zeviel was no more. Kanediel was gone. And this was only the beginning.

The soldiers cursed loudly, their cries of fury ringing through the hills. Their eyes turned southward, where, somewhere beyond the hills and the ruined harbor, lay the wide expanse of the Bay of Dane and beyond, the enemy that had done this to them.

"The people of Svartennos want revenge," Catarina said quietly.

"And you?" Marilia asked.

"I want my husband back. And I want all this to be over. Revenge is a man's game." She sighed. "How goes your training with Septakim?"

"It goes well," Marilia lied. She was improving, but she still felt clumsy in her armor.

"Take him with you when you go south. I have plenty of protectors here."

"Thank you, Catarina."

"No. Thank *you*," Catarina said. "For giving us hope."

Later that day, the Vergana's fleet finally arrived, galleys drawing up onto the beach where, less than three weeks before, the army of Tyrace had landed.

Marilia met their leaders on the plain overlooking the harbor. It seemed like a lifetime ago that she, Kanediel, and Camilline had stood there and watched the Tyracian attack, witnessed the black smoke curl into the sky.

Livenneth rode atop a fine black charger. To his right was Prince

Ilruyn.

"Marilia Sandara," Ilruyn said. "I must say, I didn't think I'd see this day." He raised his eyebrows. "Though perhaps I should have, considering your skill at the Sharavayn table."

She had no idea what to say to that. She tried to read his expression—was it respect? Resentment? Amusement? "My prince. We are glad you've come," was all that she came up with.

"Yes. It's time to turn this war around," Livenneth said. "I see you've already started with that. I read the letter you left for me in the harbor—your victory in the pass. Congratulations. It was well-fought."

"Very impressive," Ilruyn agreed.

"Here is how things stand," Livenneth said. "When they attacked Svartennos, the Tyracians also landed on the coast of Dane, north of the castles in the Neck. They wiped out Dane's ships. Now they have surrounded the Neck on both sides. If the Neck falls, the Tyracians will be able march their army north between the mountains and run amok in Dane. Emperor Vergana is marching south to reinforce the Neck, but there is no telling if he will arrive in time. That is where we come in." He jerked his head down towards the harbor, at the galleys that were massed there. "We will take two days to resupply, then make our way south towards the Bay of Dane. The Tyracian fleet still stands in our way, but we have the greater numbers, and our sailors are more skilled on the water. I think we will have the victory." His smile was fierce. "Make whatever preparations you need. Oh; and I have brought you a gift, Lady Sandara."

He urged his horse to one side, and another horseman, clad in green armor, rode forward through the gap. He pulled off his helmet and smiled at her.

"Hello, sister."

The intervening time had changed him, just a little; he was broader, fully filled-out, his jaw sharper, his hair longer, nearly down to his shoulders.

"Annuweth," she breathed.

"I know it's been some time since you've seen each other," said Livenneth. "I'll leave you to get re-acquainted."

The thick clouds that had blanketed the sky of Svartennos finally drew back; the evening was warm and clear. The chicayas sung in the grass; the men of Navessea sang around their campfires. Marilia's tent rested at the top of a tall slope—a slope where, not so very long ago, she, Camilline, Catarina, and Kanediel had gone hunting for giant crabs. At the base of the slope the harbor's waters glittered, red-gold like liquid fire.

She sat with Annuweth just outside the tent, her guards a respectful distance away. She was grateful to just sit here in a dress, her empty armor lying in the tent behind her, grateful to spread out on the linen blanket and curl her toes in the grass.

All along the hill, the men of Svartennos were singing the praises of the heroes of the Battle of the Pass. She heard Zev's name shouted, saw cups of spiced kraken wine and jala juice raised into the air in toast. Just as he had begged her, no one had forgotten the part he'd played in the battle.

She heard Aexiel's name—men were calling him the Hero of the Charge, Captain Hand-Taker—followed by a brief account of how he'd bested Tyrennis Nomeratsu and pulled Zev back from the fray so that he could die with dignity.

Then came Kanediel's turn; how he had mustered the host. It was unfair that Zev's part in the song should be longer, louder—but he had led the charge, and bold charges always made for a better verse than the letter-writing and logistics. She tried not to let herself feel bitter.

Finally, she heard her own name, and, the way thunder follows lightning, the word *chrysathamere*. She had heard it many times by now; it still sent a shiver down her back.

"Well," Annuweth said, taking a drink of jala juice and setting the cup beside him on the grass. "This was not what I expected. You, in command of Svartennos' army. You've done well for yourself, sister."

"As have you," she said. But she knew her feats now eclipsed his. "The youngest Captain of the Dragonknights in the history of Navessea...congratulations." It was for that reason that he had come; Emperor Vergana had given her brother command over a small company of the Order's knights who would watch over Ilruyn and Livenneth during the coming battles.

"Seemed an incredible feat at the time," he said. "Now, though...tell me, how did you manage this?"

She told him everything: Kanediel's death, her quarrel with Zev, the meeting with the Elders, her plan, the charge. "And afterwards, there was no real commander, so instead of choosing one among themselves, they all...chose me."

"Incredible." Annuweth shook his head and looked down into the recesses of his cup. "But then, you always were clever."

"I never said I was sorry...for the things I said in the armory," Marilia said, feeling her face grow warm at the memory.

"Well. I suppose you didn't."

"I'm saying it now. I'm sorry, Annuweth. I was frightened, and sad about Petrea leaving, and I let it get to my head." She wanted things straight between them. She wanted it to be as the gods or the Fates had clearly meant it to be—she and he together against their old homeland, the land that had nearly swallowed their lives. Just as it had been that day they'd fled together from the pillow house. "I'm glad you're back," Marilia said. "Together we can beat them."

"Let us hope."

"Do you remember that day we cursed Castaval? Do you remember..."

"I never forget," Annuweth said tightly.

"Of course. I only meant...it seemed so impossible back then, but now...here we are." She looked out across the starlit waters of the bay. "And there he is," she whispered. "Just out there, almost within reach. The past week has been full of impossible things. Maybe we can have just one more. Maybe a couple of bastards from a pillow house can show Tyrennis Castaval that we're more than dirt, after all."

"I'll drink to that," Annuweth said, raising his cup to touch hers. They drank together; he his jala juice, she the simple tea the Svartennans favored.

Between a gap in two tall hills to the west was the setting sun, its light slanting orange towards them, making Marilia's shadow spread out beside her. The two sat side by side, staring up at the sun-lined clouds. One cloud caught Marilia's eye as it approached from over the water, a vast, fiery shape that might have been the House of White Sands itself.

"It reminds me of the Tower," Annuweth said. "Remember how we used to look up at it from the river? How we used to imagine what was up there?"

"I remember."

"Do you ever miss it?" he asked. "I mean, I know everything is better now, but sometimes...does a part of you miss it? Back before

Mother died, before One-Eye and all the rest of it? That time?"

"You mean the pillow house?"

"Well...yes, I suppose. Do you ever wish you could go back? Just for a moment?"

Marilia frowned. She felt a small shiver tickle the base of her neck, like a breath. "No," she said. "Not really."

He looked away. "Well. I suppose you're right."

For a long while neither of them said a word. A heavy wind caught the tower and blew it apart into threads of white like the hairs of a dragon's beard.

"Good fortune in the Bay, my lady," Strategos Konos said to her the following morning. "I will have the supply ships ready before two days are out, I promise."

Livenneth's fleet would travel light and fast; only war ships would sail into the Bay of Dane, loaded with only enough supplies to see them through the three-day journey to the Tyracian fleet and another three days after that. Once the fleet was defeated and the way to Dane was cleared, the rest of the supplies—horses, food, medicine, spare armor and weapons—would follow.

Marilia nodded, touching her knuckles to his. "Thank you, my lord. May the spirits watch over you."

"May they watch over us all."

Marilia made her way down the hill towards the beach and the charred remains of the harbor. When she reached the bottom of the slope, she handed her horse off to Camilline. "Keep her safe for me," she said.

"I will," Camilline promised.

The two embraced.

"I'll do what I can to put this island back together while you're gone," Camilline said.

Marilia started down towards the beach. She had only gone a few steps when she heard a voice call her name.

"Marilia!"

She turned and saw Livenneth. He jerked his head sideways towards a small grove of long-neck trees. "I thought we could have a word."

"Of course, my lord," she said. She hesitated, glancing back at Camilline. Camilline's brows were furrowed; she gave a helpless shrug, apparently as perplexed as Marilia herself was.

She followed Livenneth into the shade of the trees.

"Well…I never expected to find myself in this position," Livenneth said ruefully. "I won't pretend I don't have some misgivings… Ilruyn and I have been speaking, and we've come to a decision. I'll be passing the word on, but I wanted you to hear it first."

She searched his face, feeling a prickle of unease. He couldn't, she thought, mean to leave her behind—could he? The Svartennans had chosen her; they had lifted their swords and sworn to follow her. They were a proud people, and their strategoi could be touchy; how would they take to a move by the emperor's general to remove their chosen commander?

Ilruyn and I have been speaking… She pictured Ilruyn's face, that day she had bested him at the Sharavayn table. The flush in his cheeks, the tight strain of his smile. Would he have tried to convince Livenneth to leave her behind, to pay her back for that humiliation? She wouldn't put it past him; she was sure he was just as proud as the rest of his family, and she wouldn't be surprised if he knew how to carry a grudge

323

every bit as bitterly as his adoptive sister.

Her unease coalesced into something stronger, more furious. "My lord…"

"The emperor put me in command of this fleet. Obviously, Ilruyn is my second. I hope to all the gods we'll both make it through, but if by some cruel stroke of fate we do not, I must give thought to who will follow us in the chain of command; it's my duty as general. The Governor of Neravenne is my third, but as to my fourth…well, there I had a choice." He frowned, looking at her. "You're not experienced, but neither is Surennis' new commander. Andreas *is*, but…he's also not a true lord of Navessea, and never will be. He's a Tyracian noble's son, and he was once an enemy of the empire. Even though some may have forgotten it, I haven't, and won't. What you did here at the pass was a sound military feat, equal to the best stratagems of my career. I can admit that. Now, I don't know if the gods speak to you or not, but whoever does seems to know their business. I'd like to name you third lieutenant of this army."

Speechless, Marilia stared at him. That was not what she'd expected; not at all. "I…Prince Ilruyn…" she began.

"…supports my decision," Livenneth said firmly.

Another shock. She felt her face grow warm, felt a twinge of guilt in her stomach. It seemed she'd been wrong about him.

"I…I would be honored, my lord."

"Good, then." He gave her a crisp smile. "Let's get to it."

Dazed, Marilia walked down to the beach, where Svartennos' surviving galleys had been gathered. One ship, larger than the rest, had a black sail with a blue chrysathamere flower in its center.

"*Svartana's Revenge*, it's called," Septakim told her. "It's yours."

Taking a deep breath, she turned her eyes to the Bay of Dane and

324

the war to come.

CHAPTER TWENTY-EIGHT

"That's a lot of ships," Septakim said.

Marilia, standing just behind him on the bucking prow of the galley, had to agree.

Ahead of them, the Tyracian fleet stretched out across the Bay of Dane, sails bearing the red horse of Tyrace glaring at them across the choppy green waves.

"How many, do you think?" Marilia asked.

"More than a hundred, certainly," he answered, surveying the fleet arrayed before them.

"We have more," Marilia said. She ran through the tally in her head. *Forty three-deck galleys from Svartennos and five four-deck flagships, forty three-deck ships from Antarenne, twenty from Osurris, thirty from Surennis, forty from Neravenne...*

"Yes," Septakim agreed reassuringly. "We have more."

She felt her stomach lurching. Part of it was being on a ship again, and part of it was fear.

She'd played hundreds of games of Sharavayn with Karthtag-Kal, and all of them had one thing in common—no ships. Yes, she'd read about many of Navessea's naval battles while going through Karthtag-Kal's books of strategy—how could she not? —but she hadn't dwelled as much on them, because they were of less use to her.

Now she wished she'd studied them more.

Though, then again, it might not have mattered. It wasn't as though she could do much besides relay the most basic of orders to the other ships under her command by means of the navigator on her stern.

This was Livenneth's show; her place was, for the most part, to listen to the horns from his flagship and pass those commands on to her men. If all went to plan, she wouldn't need to display any tactical brilliance.

Livenneth is a match for Tyrennis Castaval, she told herself. *He's one of Svartennos' most seasoned naval commanders. This will be easy.*

But she couldn't shake the memory of Tyrennis Nomeratsu's knowing smile.

She scanned the wall of ships to either side. She and her Svartennan ships lay at the center-left of Livenneth's formation; to her right were the galleys from Surennis, then Neravenne, and to her left the white razorfish of Antarenne flew from the top of the galleys' masts—forty three-deck ships and one five-deck flagship under the command of the Graver, who, apparently, had managed to work his way up the ranks to become the Governor of Antarenne's commander.

Directly in the center, at the head of it all, lay the twenty galleys from the imperial port of Osurris, including Livenneth's massive flagship, *Destroyer*. His eyes lingered there. There, beneath the green dragon on a field of black, her brother stood with the emperor's brother-by-marriage and adopted son. If she squinted, she could just make them out.

She wished Livenneth hadn't been quite so brave, so Svartennan in spirit; she wished Annuweth hadn't been at the very front. But there was nothing she could do about it now. She'd already lit candles for her brother the night before they set sail; she'd lit candles for them all. She hadn't been the only one; after the campfires had burned out, while the army slept, the Elders of Svartennos had delved into their stores and combined their own prayer candles with what Livenneth had brought with him from Ulvannis; together, they had covered the hillside overlooking the harbor with a thousand flickering points of light.

Now the spirits waited above in the House of White Sands, looking down. Watching, and, supposedly, helping, though Marilia had yet to feel any great surge of strength or clarity, no matter how many red or blue candles they'd melted.

The sky was a patchwork of gray and blue. Salt spray, torn from the tips of the choppy waves by the galleys' prows, whipped around them, spattering the deck, making Marilia squint as it peppered her cheeks. She shifted her weight, rolling her shoulders. The armor she wore was a little uncomfortable. It was not the new suit that had been crafted for her; that was back on Svartennos, with the rest of the supplies. For now, she wore instead a lighter, special kind of armor designed for combat at sea; the knots that fastened the plates together were designed to be pulled apart quickly to allow the wearer to shed the plates and escape drowning.

Of course, it also meant that the plates were less effective at their primary purpose, less likely to save you from a killing blow. A fact about which she was less than happy.

Ahead, the galleys of the enemy fleet drew closer. Or, rather, the Navessean fleet drew closer to them. The Tyracians were waiting, letting the Navesseans approach, *Destroyer* leading the way into the Bay of Dane.

Six deep, staccato notes echoed through the fleet, making the timbers of the deck tremble under her feet; the signal came from Livenneth's flagship.

"Battle speed!" Septakim cried. He had seen sea battles before, had captained his own ship in a battle against Valdruk pirates before joining the Order of Jade, so she had given him command *Svartana's Revenge*.

The drummer picked up the beat. The oars began to move faster. The long iron spike at the prow made ripples through the water.

Marilia took a firm grip on the hilt of her sword. The Tyracian ships loomed closer. How close? Two hundred strides? Three hundred? The oars creaked, the drum boomed. The sea sped past, gray sunlight flickering off the tips of the little green waves. She looked over the rail and saw the dark green surface of the sea, impenetrable, like a carved face of midnight stone. She remembered the stories of the dark castle that lay beneath the waves, where the king of the dremmakin hunted spirits for sport in his chariot drawn by razorfish. She shivered, thinking she might be sick.

Spirits protect me. Svartana protect me.

Livenneth's plan was simple—they had more ships than the Tyracians, so they would charge, and fight, and win.

As Laekos Valennos had once written, sometimes the simplest plans were the most effective.

Though, on the other hand, Karthtag-Kal had always thought Laekos Valennos had always been a little too glib for his taste.

Behind Marilia stood thirty-nine knights of Svartennos. They lined the top deck of her flagship, stern and silent, wood creaking under them, the sail snapping overhead. Bows were slung over their shoulders, quivers of arrows with green feathers across their backs. Dueling swords were belted at their left hips, short-swords at their right.

"Ready bows," she said, unnecessarily; her men were already doing so. Another horn-blast came from *Destroyer*, the notes faster this time, more urgent.

Septakim gave a deafening shout. "Ramming speed!"

The drum below-deck beat faster, and the oars moved in a blur, water droplets whisking away behind them in the wind. *Boomboomboomboomboom...* The fleet surged ahead like a chariot leaping from the starting gate.

A man is never so alive as when faced with death. It was an expression from the work of Emperor Urian, and for the first time in her life, Marilia found that she disagreed with him.

"Perhaps my lady would be safer at the stern," Septakim advised.

Perhaps, she thought. It was certainly preferable to the prow. She made her way to the back of the galley, Septakim following alongside her, stopping near the galley's catapult. An iron brazier was set nearby, to kindle the balls of pitch that would be loaded into the weapon's arm; Marilia felt its heat against her back, welcome after the chill of the sea's spray. Her ship's navigator stood atop the cabin, a series of colored flags tucked into his belt. Right now, he was waving the green flags. Imperial green—the color of conquest. The signal to attack. He spared her a brief glance, and she gave him what she hoped was an encouraging nod.

She crouched behind the galley's railing, her hand griping it for support. "Prepare arrows!" she yelled. She watched a Tyracian galley draw nearer, nearer...a hundred paces away, fewer...she knew you were supposed to wait until the other galley was close, because the rolling of the waves made it harder to aim.

"Now, my lady," Septakim breathed.

"Loose!"

Arrows hissed back and forth between the galleys. Some splashed into the sea, some thudded into the galleys' wooden railings, and some found their marks. One from the Tyracian galley narrowly missed her hand where she held the railing.

"Catapult!" Septakim yelled.

Wood groaned as the arm of the catapult sprang to life. Its missile went blazing out, hissing as it arced overhead, leaving a trail of fire across the sky. Water came splashing over the railing as another ball of pitch, loosed by the enemy, landed not far from their ship.

"Ready ballistae!" she yelled, raising her hand.

That was her galley's most important weapon; there were eight of them in total, four along each side of the ship, loaded with fearsome iron spikes with ropes attached; once an enemy ship was struck, it could be reeled in and boarded. Marilia pointed to one of the closest Tyracian galleys.

Before she could give the order to loose, an Antarenne galley came out of nowhere and struck her target from the other side with enough force to send the men on the deck flying like so many tumbling dice. Marilia swallowed and lowered her hand.

The battle was joined; balls of pitch and bolts the size of young trees were flying in all directions. She heard the creak and snap of the ballistae, the twang of bowstrings, and a tremendous crash as two galleys collided head on, wood splintering, decks heaving, men toppling into the Bay.

A ball of pitch, aimed for *Svartana's Revenge,* whipped past, barely missing the cabin at the stern. It slammed into the mast of a smaller galley following close behind, bouncing across the deck, causing men to scream and dive out of the way.

Septakim was squinting into the foam, seeking the Tyracian ship that had attacked them. He pointed. "Right! Hard right! Take down that ship!"

To the right, the Tyracian galley had snared a Navessean with its grappling hooks and was reeling it in. Or maybe it was the other way around.

Ponderously, *Svartana's Revenge* began to turn. The Tyracian ship ahead of them saw them coming, and it tried to move—too late. The prow of *Svartana's Revenge* caught it in the side, driving in deep. Marilia felt the shudder of breaking wood through the deck beneath her feet; it made her teeth chatter. She lost her feet and went sprawling onto the deck.

"Pull back! Pull back!" Septakim's voice. She was very glad to have him with her.

Water rushed into the wounded ship, and men scrambled to tug free of their armor. As *Svartana's Revenge* pulled away, Marilia's archers scrambled to the railing, raking the listing deck of the Tyracian four-decker with arrows. The angle was good; the arrows found their marks, and the struggling men on the deck died by the dozen.

Then the oarsmen came scrambling half-naked up the stairs. These were no knights, not even the professionals that manned the oars of the Navessean galleys. They were peasants and fishermen, conscripted into the king of Tyrace's navy. They didn't even have iron weapons to defend themselves.

The archers turned their arrows on them. Most of them died before they reached the deck, clogging the stairs, leaving those behind to crawl their way through the bodies of their companions only to die the same. She heard the screams of those still trapped below the deck, fading piecemeal as the water came in, like a shrine full of candles burning out one by one after a long night.

Marilia's chest tightened as she watched the doomed ship slide beneath the waves until only the water-logged top deck and mast remained above, like a marker for a grave. Men thrashed their way through the water.

She saw a red blur out of the corner of her eye; moving swiftly beneath the waves. She recalled Ben Espeleos' story a second before the water parted in an explosion of white teeth. She caught a brief glimpse of a scaled, red-brown hide, three rows of jagged teeth, a baleful yellow eye like a sick, dust-clogged sun.

One of the Tyracian men was snatched clear out of the water. He screamed, shrill and loud. The monster shook him like a hound toying with a bone and he simply fell apart, his head and shoulders landing atop the galley's submerged deck with a sound like a Tyracian butcher striking a flank of meat. The rest of him remained in the monster's jaws and was dragged away beneath the waves.

The sickness that Marilia had long held at bay struck her and she vomited over the rail, hoping that in the commotion of the fray, no one had seen her.

How long the battle went, she could not say. It all passed in a blur, witnessed through a veil of the red-white foam that exploded from the prows of their ships.

The next thing she knew, a hand was clapping her hard on the back, nearly making her vomit a second time. Septakim's shout was deafening right beside her ear. "Look, lady. We've won again! They're fleeing!" He pointed straight ahead, where, through a gap in the massed ships, she had a clear view of the bay ahead of them.

Just as he said, the Tyracian ships were beginning to turn, fleeing back towards the mouth of the River Ob and the safety of their homeland's shores.

"Thank the gods," she muttered, wiping sea-water out of her eyes. "Get me off this cursed deck. I'm not made for ships."

A mighty blast came from *Destroyer*, a signal that was clear and unequivocal—full speed ahead.

The few Tyracian ships that had been unable to break away, those that had remained behind to slow the Navessean advance, were quickly swallowed by Livenneth's fleet. They fell quickly, taken by boarding parties, their numbers added to the Navessean lines.

For the first time, the air was absent the sound of screams. All that could be heard was the heavy breathing of the men, the creaking of the oars, the waves, the wind. Marilia returned to the prow. *Destroyer* led the charge, with the galleys from Osurris and Surennis not far behind. Marilia's ship began to lag; several of her oars had been snapped during the melee. That was all right with her; she was happy to leave the mopping up of the Tyracian fleet to the others. She'd had her fill of naval combat.

And then, in a move so graceful and sudden that it must have been carefully rehearsed, the retreating Tyracian fleet parted to each side, clearing a space in the center. Through that open space a line of galleys came charging towards them.

Septakim frowned. "By the ghouls...that was quite well done. Must have been planned."

"They mean to delay us," Marilia said, chewing her lip. "To give the rest of their ships time to make shore so they can try to escape to the mouth of the river, or the cover of their harbor at Tyr Phalai to the east."

"Well, if that's their delaying force, I don't think much of it," Septakim said. "It's only a single line; we'll cut right through them in a matter of minutes."

Livenneth seemed to have the same idea; a moment later, Marilia heard the signal to move to ramming speed.

Then a horn blew from one of the Neravenne galleys to their right.

In order to avoid confusion, the horn-blowing was supposed to be limited to *Destroyer*, except in a case of urgency. That's what this was, Marilia realized: a warning. She turned to look.

On the Navesseans' right flank, a line of galleys was emerging, seemingly, straight out of the rock of the shoreline, fanning out as it entered the bay. But that was impossible. She blinked, squinting against the spray, looking closer.

What had appeared to be another stretch of unbroken coast was actually a hidden cove. From out of that cove the warships came. The masts bore a pennant showing a sack of gold coins. Not a subtle design, perhaps, but telling in its simplicity.

"Mercenaries," she breathed. "Mercenaries from the eastern lands."

"Valdruk scum," Septakim hissed between his teeth.

Ahead, the thin line of Tyracian galleys spread out to block the way forward. Behind that line, the ships that had before been fleeing began to swing back around. The maneuver was admirable for its grace and suddenness. It might have been even beautiful, if the implications hadn't been so devastating.

Septakim's voice was faint. "Well," he said. "Yes indeed. That was quite...expertly done."

Marilia recalled Tyrennis Nomeratsu's words to her back in the tent: *he is the rising star who has never been beaten. He will break you, girl.*

She closed her eyes, feeling sick. It was like watching a rhovannon in a play die in slow-motion, each movement exaggerated, each second extended so that the anguish of the scene could be not merely felt, but explored, examined.

"What do we do?" she said. "What do we do?"

But there was no time to do anything; to the left lay a stretch of shallows, coral-studded rocks poking from the waves like the teeth of a gigantic razorfish. There would be no escape that way. Now the Tyracians completed the circle; with the sound of wood shattering, they closed upon the Navessean fleet from the front, right, and rear.

Chapter Twenty-Nine

Like kwammakin burrowing through wood, the Tyracian fleet ate its way through the edges of Livenneth's formation. Though Marilia couldn't see it—couldn't see anything except the ships to either side—she could smell it: the acrid stench of smoke, making her eyes itch and sting, scratching like the claws of a wicked spirit at the back of her throat.

And she could hear it—a chorus of screams drawing closer with each passing second.

She turned her eyes to the sky. She was crying, whether from the smoke or from the anguish of the moment, she couldn't tell. Tendrils of smoke from the north, the south, the west met above her, coiling around each other like a pack of baby dragons at play. Bit by bit, the darker gray of the smoke swallowed the lighter gray of the sky as an early twilight descended.

Spirits of our fathers and mothers protect us. Give us strength; give us the clarity to find a way out.

But no clarity came. Tyrennis Castaval had done to her what she had done to the Tyracians back in the pass—seized a victory against grim odds.

"Svartana," she whispered. "Help us."

"Look, lady! Look!" Septakim pointed.

Marilia's head snapped around.

A horn blew to their right; a signal. On the stern of the closest Antarenne galleys, Andreas' navigators were waving blue flags—

follow.

She would learn later what had happened.

Livenneth, faced with certain defeat, showed his true mettle at last: the man who had routed Kanadrak's ships, the conqueror of pirates who had so impressed Emperor Vergana that he had been given command of the Eastern Fleet.

He rallied his three-deckers around his flagship, creating a deadly wedge with which he drove straight into the heart of the Tyracian lines. It was a maneuver that cost him dearly; of the twenty ships from Osurris, only three made it through.

All the while they fought, his men cried out one mantra, again and again: "protect the emperor!"

Livenneth himself stood at the prow, waving his green aeder sword above his head—a color that only the Order of Jade or the imperial family was permitted to wear.

The Tyracians took the bait.

Faced with the prospect of the emperor of Navessea so close, just within reach, the Tyracian fleet lost its discipline; eager for the glory that would come with such a catch, the closest galleys broke off to pursue *Destroyer*. In so doing, they left a gap in their formation.

What came after was elementary; Andreas spied the gap and he sent his best, swiftest galleys into it, widening it so the rest of his ships could slip through and turn upon the Tyracian formation from the rear.

Like a strand of silk threading the eye of a needle, Marilia and the fleet of Svartennos followed him through.

That was when she saw *Destroyer*.

It was a marvel that Livenneth's flagship still stood un-captured;

only the incredible fortitude and swordsmanship of Annuweth's knights had kept the Tyracians at bay so far. Even so, the ship was failing fast, beset by three Tyracian galleys, which were perched around her like grave beetles squatting on the dying body of a desert animal; men swarmed onto her deck, eager as flies.

Marilia didn't hesitate. Her navigator waved his flags; her ships charged to the rescue.

Maybe Svartana helped her after all—maybe the cool wind that enveloped her ship from behind, that skipped its way down the staircase to the cramped hold where the oarsmen labored and swept across the deck to touch the side of Marilia's face like a parent's comforting palm—maybe that was the spirit of Svartana, lending them speed, filling them with fire.

They slammed into the closest Tyracian three-decker at full tilt and it was hurled away like a stray die sent bouncing across a tavern table—crippled, sinking.

"Save your general!" she yelled, but what she was really thinking was: *save Annuweth.*

Her men lowered boarding ramps; moments later she was on Destroyer's deck, eyes scanning the crowd, searching...

Livenneth was dead at the prow, a short-sword buried deep in his armpit. Ilruyn was struggling in the grip of two Tyracian knights as they hauled him away towards one of the waiting galleys. Annuweth was on his knees, his back against the railing, grappling with one of his enemies, doing his best to stop the bigger, stronger Tyracian from forcing the point of a short-sword into his throat.

It looked like he was failing.

"Get my brother!" she yelled to her knights, and she and they stumbled their way across the heaving deck to Annuweth's side. Her men seized the Tyracian from behind, drew back his head, cut his throat, and tossed his body over the railing into the sea for the razorfish.

Marilia offered Annuweth her hand, pulling him back to his feet.

"We have to go!" she yelled at him.

Annuweth's face was a mask of anguish. "Ilruyn!" he cried. "I can't leave him!"

Ilruyn's legs kicked in the air; his face contorted in fury, his eyes bulging like those of a fish as the Tyracians pulled him from his feet and dragged him back to the railing. There were ten Tyracian knights between him and them.

"You can't reach him!"

"He is my commander!" Annuweth said, throwing off her hand as she reached for him. "I am sworn to protect him! I am sworn..."

A pair of Tyracian knights came blundering into them, forcing them apart. Marilia hit the galley's railing hard enough that she dropped her sword.

She found herself face-to-face with a young, bearded man with a captain's sash around his upper arm and a scar through his bottom lip through which she could see the gleam of his teeth. Something tugged at her memory; she realized, with a sudden shock, that this was Oberal, Castaval's companion, the one who had held her and forced her to watch while the tyrennis' son beat her brother. He had changed over the years, but she knew his face all the same.

He swung his sword at her face, and she dodged, her back coming up against the railing. His second swing left a long scratch across the side of her breastplate as she slipped away; his sword gouged a chunk out of the wood next to her. She caught his third blow with her forearms, her yoba-shell gauntlets stopping the blade. He pressed into her; she smelled his breath. It tasted of blood and salt.

340

The deck lurched; the world shifted under her. She cried out and heard Oberal's own wail of dismay. The clouds wheeled overhead and suddenly she was free-falling, the dark wall of the sea rushing up to meet her.

The water hit her like a fist. The shock of impact tore the breath from her lungs. She strained, fighting the weight of her armor; felt her fingers brush wood—a broken piece of an oar.

She lunged for it, kicking with everything she had. The wood was slick and her fingers in her water-laden gloves were clumsy. She lost her grip, and the waters of the Bay of Dane swallowed her.

The first thing she noticed was the absence of sound. Above her, the water trapped the sun's light and turned it into a pin-wheel of white spears that faded as she sank deeper, like a flower closing its petals before the onset of night. Somewhere below her lay the castle of the dremmakin. They were waiting for her.

She panicked. She kicked wildly into the darkness, feeling the cold climbing up her legs, settling insider her chest. She was blind, breathless, like a worm burrowing through wet earth. She was a helpless girl, back in One-Eye's arms, the sound of the rain echoing in her ears, loud as thunder.

Swim, she thought. *You know how to swim. You've done it before.* But her armor was dragging her down.

Then take it off.

She passed to a place beyond panic, a place she had reached before during her games with One-Eye and Karthtag-Kal.

She drew her short-sword. First went her belt, then her gauntlets, one after the other. She fumbled with the straps of her armor. The cords were tough, heavy with salt water. The tip of the sword nicked her cheek as she sawed, desperately. She managed to cut one cord through.

341

Another. A third. That was all this was—one problem solved and on to another, like a game of Capture the Emperor you played one move at a time until you blinked and realized that you'd reached the end; all the problems were solved.

At last her cuirass fell away. She let the short-sword follow it into the depths; she would swim faster without a blade in her hand.

Her lungs were red with pain. She kicked her way up, up, her legs straining. *You can make it,* she told herself. She remembered diving towards the bottom of the River Tyr at Nyreese's urging, remembered feeling her way along the mossy stone, her fingers brushing the rough metal of the grate in Tyracium's wall. This was just like that (legs kicking, lungs aching), but in reverse; pushing her way up, instead of down.

But, a voice inside her said, *you never did make it to the bottom of the River Tyr.*

Her head spun. She felt as if something, or several somethings inside her would surely burst.

And then her head broke the surface. She sucked in air and salt water all at once, choking, thrashing blindly until her hands found the broken oar.

Oberal was only a few yards away, clinging to a piece of driftwood of his own. He blinked water from his eyes and stared at her, as if amazed to find that a woman had sprouted from the sea beside him.

"Do I fucking know you?" he asked.

"Just stay away."

"Heretic bitch."

He let go of the driftwood and started towards her. He was bigger, and heavier, and she knew that when he reached her she would have a serious problem.

And then he vanished. He was taken suddenly, in one fierce tug from below; like a farmer ripping a milk-yam out of the earth, but in reverse.

A moment later he reappeared. The razorfish that had seized him showered her with water as it leaped from the sea. Oberal was clutched between its jaws, the fish's teeth locked tight around his waist. His arms flailed, beating at its jutting jaw; he might as well have tried to punch the side of a mountain. The razorfish's teeth pressed slowly together; Oberal's armor crumpled like paper. His mouth opened wide and out of it came blood and water and pieces of things she couldn't identify, didn't want to see. She turned and kicked for the ship.

When she looked back over her shoulder, she saw that the razorfish had turned towards her. Its yellow eye was fixed on her; its rusty-red hide made a hump out of the water as it sped closer. It opened its mouth wide, and three rows of teeth as long as knives grinned at her. She opened her own mouth to scream.

A ballista bolt hissed over her head and buried itself deep in the monster's open maw. The fish choked, shuddered, died. Its spasms turned the sea around her to a seething cauldron; Marilia nearly lost her grip on the oar.

"Marilia!"

Annuweth was there above her, standing on the deck of *Svartana's Revenge* beside the ballista. He tossed her a rope. With numb, quivering fingers, she took it.

He hauled her up onto the deck. She fell against him, completely spent, shivering as the water pooled around them, as Septakim barked orders to the helmsman and the galley began to turn towards the south.

Annuweth handed something to her. Dazed, she took it, staring at the piece of blue crystal and trying to figure out what it was.

343

"Your sword," Annuweth said. "I...I found it for you. You dropped it on the deck before you went over the side."

"Oh." She dropped it into her scabbard, then realized her scabbard was gone; her belt had come undone and followed the rest of her armor down the halls of the dremmakin. Her sword landed point-first in the deck of the ship and stuck there. "Thank you."

"You should keep low, my lady," Septakim called to her. "Your armor is gone. One arrow and you're finished."

She seated herself on the deck, leaning her back against the railing of the galley. Annuweth sat next to her. A light had gone out in his eyes; they looked as cold and lifeless as the ash spread across the surface of the sea. "They're gone," he whispered. "All the Dragonknights who sailed with me. They took Ilruyn. They killed Livenneth. I couldn't stop any of it."

Ribbons of flame cut pieces out of the gray sky overhead. *Destroyer* blazed behind them; some brave soldier had kicked over the fire-pot before throwing himself off the deck, deciding it was better to let the ship sink than to leave it for the Tyracians. Sparks and flakes of ash—the remains of their ships—swept by on the wind, light as spirits, brushing across their armor, landing in their hair. "You tried," she said, taking his hand. "It wasn't your fault."

"I failed. I was sworn to protect them, and I failed. I should have done more."

"You couldn't have stayed. The Tyracians would have killed you."

"It was my duty," he said weakly.

"Your duty is to keep fighting," she said. "That's what Karthtag-Kal would say. There's more yet to come. That way this wasn't for nothing."

"I suppose you're right."

She offered him her fist. After a moment, he tapped his knuckles against hers. But it was a light touch, one she barely felt. The touch of a man who wasn't sure he really meant it.

Though Livenneth's gambit had allowed most of the galleys of Antarenne and Svartennos to slip Castaval's noose and attack the Tyracian fleet from behind, it was not enough to change the tide of the battle. The Tyracians soon regrouped and, having finished destroying the fleets of Surennis and Neravenne, came for Marilia and her allies.

The surviving Navesseans did the only thing they could. They fled—across the Bay and on south into the mouth of the River Ob.

There they found a defensible position, a spot where, to proceed forward, the Tyracian fleet would have to open itself to attack from two sides.

The Tyracian fleet drew up before them and paused, like a great bird of prey considering whether it was worth it to attack the angry serpent it found before it. Marilia held her breath.

Tyrennis Castaval knew the river's twists and turns; after all, its waters were named for one of his forefathers. He knew the danger that lay ahead, and he judged it too great; the Tyracians did not attack. They stayed where they were, the two fleets facing each other across a space the width of the Great Plain that lay to the south of Ulvannis.

"We did it!" Septakim said, touching Marilia's shoulder. "We survived."

Marilia said nothing. Yes, they had survived. But they were outnumbered, trapped in a hostile land with little food. And they had paid heavily for their escape.

Almost all the ships of Surennis, Osurris, and Neravenne were gone, and ten Svartennan galleys had disappeared beneath the waves or been dragged off by Tyrennis Castaval's men.

Though the Navesseans had added several captured Tyracian galleys to their ranks, there was no denying that the balance of power had shifted; of all the ships that had sailed with Livenneth into the Bay of Dane, only a third were left.

The very river that had been their salvation could easily become their tomb; just as the Tyracians could not advance, neither could the Navesseans escape, not with Castaval's ships blocking the river's mouth.

At the moment, Castaval clearly believed he lacked the numbers to attempt a decisive attack up-river. But his numbers would soon grow. The Tyrennis would haul the Navessean galleys he had captured back to the harbor at Tyr Phalai, where he would repair them and fill them with Tyracian knights. It would take at most a week.

Then the Tyracians would return, and there was nothing Marilia or her allies could do to stop them.

The game she and Castaval were playing had entered its final stage.

CHAPTER THIRTY

The heat rolled in, a dry desert wind from the east that caked the furled sails of the galleys with sand. It caught in the seams of Marilia's armor, chafed her skin and made her eyes water.

The ships of the Navessean fleet bobbed at anchor, formed up in battle-lines, awaiting the attack that might come at any time.

Marilia felt a second heat inside her, a stronger counter-point to the fire of the sun and wind. It was a wet heat like bubbling stone. Fear.

She sat alone on a hill overlooking the riverbank, exhausted, her hair coarse and matted with salt water. The bank was made of golden, rolling dunes, with patches of grass growing in the distance, scraggly like a boy's beard. Gulls nested in the grass and thronged by the water's edge.

One of the birds landed on a rock nearby, cocking its head to one side as it stared at her. It reminded her of the way Ilruyn had cocked his head to one side before their game of Sharavayn—calculating scrutiny with a touch of mockery. *Tell me, little girl, what will you do now?* She grabbed a stone and flung it at the bird, missing by a wide margin. She was reaching for another when Septakim found her.

"They are ready, my lady."

They—her strategoi and the lieutenants of Antarenne. Though there wasn't much any of them could do to escape, they could at least try to find a way to make the best of what the Fates had given them.

Marilia climbed to her feet. The gull gave her one last cold look before it flapped away, alighting on the top her flagship's mast and streaking the chrysathamere flower sail with its droppings.

Marilia glared at the bird. She felt a sudden rush of fury. She gave a motion to a nearby knight, who lifted his bow and brought it down with a single shot.

That made her feel somewhat better, at least.

She followed Septakim down the slope to where a makeshift command tent had been set up on the bank—nothing more than a sail draped across two gnarled trees.

As she went, she caught sight of Andreas, making his way down from the deck of one of the beached Antarenne galleys. The commander walked with a weary stoop to his shoulders. The sockets of his eyes and his short, spiky hair were coated with a fine layer of dust.

Marilia paused, considering him. She had not forgotten Karthtag-Kal's warning. *He has no honor.* She had heard ill rumors of him over the years; he wasn't the sort of man who was a prime target for gossip among Petrea's circle of young ladies, but every now and then he came up.

On the other hand, he was—by birth and history—*different* from the other nobles in Ulvannis. And she knew only too well that the rumors told about the *different* were not always true.

In any case, he was one of the only allies she had left. The Tyracians were enough to deal with; they could not afford to quarrel among themselves, too.

"Lord Andreas."

He turned to face her, raising one hand to shield his eyes from the sunlight. "Lady Paetia...or I suppose it's Lady Sandara again, now."

She stopped before him. The man who had killed her father. The man Annuweth used to talk of killing someday.

Perhaps she ought to have hated him. But the wrong Andreas had done her was only an abstraction—the kind of wrong that, admittedly, was elemental enough that to speak it sent a shiver down the spine. *He killed my father.* But her father had never been more to her than an idea. She could conceptualize the injury Andreas had done her, but that was not enough to stir her heart, not right now. She was weary and uncertain; there was only so much hate she could manage, and she needed it for Tyrennis Castaval.

"I wanted to thank you," she said. "For what you did back in the Bay. It was you who found the way through the Tyracian lines."

Andreas studied her for a long while in silence. What he was thinking, she could only guess. "I merely saw an opportunity and seized it," he said at last.

"You saw an opportunity others might have missed, and seized a moment others might have let slip by."

Andreas inclined his head; a gesture of deference. "If we are speaking of snatching victories from the jaws of defeat, then we cannot forget yours. I heard what happened in Chrysathamere Pass."

"Thank you, my lord." She took a deep breath. "It seems we'll be working together in the days to come."

"That's one way to put it. You are in command here, are you not? Livenneth named you his third lieutenant."

"I was as surprised as anyone. I know you have more experience…"

"Yet Livenneth chose you, all the same. You may have been surprised. I wasn't. Tell me, Lady Sandara, what did you wish to discuss?"

"I would not have there be any…any bitterness between us. I know that you and my father are not friends…"

Andreas laughed. "Not friends? I thought they did not mince words on Svartennos. For years, the prefect and I have been like young krakens, biting pieces out of each other, each doing his best to devour the other. At every turn, he has done his best to block my advancement; the only reason I am where I am is that I've always had a peculiar talent for amassing gold, and with enough time and enough gold, many doors will open." He leaned in closer. "Everything I am now, I am despite Karthtag-Kal's best efforts."

"My lord, I merely wished to..."

Andreas held up a hand to forestall her. "However," he continued, "you are not the prefect. And that is important, my lady. You came to me, in good faith, with an offer of peace, it seems."

"That was my intention."

"It was nobly done. A chance to start from a blank page...even though I killed your father." He spoke the words bluntly, as if he was testing her. She felt her breath catch for a moment, but she did not flinch.

"You did," she agreed.

"It was never personal," he said. "We were at war." They made their way across the dunes of the riverbank, the sand swirling around their ankles, the gulls circling overhead, the span of their wings casting brief, flickering shadows like half-forgotten memories across the path ahead. "Now we are at war again," Andreas said. "And *that* is what matters, Lady Sandara. Even if I detested you, we are both commanders, and we have our enemy. The only one that matters." He gestured towards the massed Tyracian ships in the distance. "I can't think of a single reason why we cannot work together, can you?"

"No," she agreed. "I suppose not."

He offered her his closed fist; a warrior's offer. She closed her own and touched it against his.

"Good," Andreas said. "Now that that's settled, let's go and figure out how to get out of this with both our lives."

The first order of business was to send out several chicayas to the north, where Lord Konos was waiting with the rest of the Svartennan army. It took a full hour to write the nine coded messages that contained all the details of their predicament.

As Marilia watched the insects take wing, she knew that many of them would not make the journey; Tyracian hunting birds would take down some, and the weather itself was always a danger, especially over waters as changeable as those of the Bay of Dane.

She had to hope that at least one would get through.

Next, she, Andreas, and the strategoi of Svartennos and captains of Antarenne assigned foraging parties to scour the surrounding land for desperately-needed supplies.

"Allow me to recommend my man, Captain Aexiel," Lord Leondos offered. "He is a skilled rider and one of my best fighters. More importantly, men will follow him into danger without fear. They have faith in the man who cut off Tyrennis Nomeratsu's hand."

So Aexiel, Captain Hand-Taker, was sent to the farthest villages within riding distance, with orders to take what the Navessean army needed from the Tyracian villagers (the lives of the Navessean soldiers had to come first; that was a practical reality of war) but to spare any Tyracian civilians they found from rape or slaughter, and to leave the villages un-burned. Marilia gave the same orders to all the men under her command.

Aexiel raised his brows at that last part—as did Leondos—but he rode off without comment the following morning. He returned just before sun-down with enough supplies to delay hunger a little longer.

That was enough to lift the men's spirits...but only momentarily.

On the second day of their entrapment, scouts reported that enemies were massing to the east. It appeared that the Tyracians had won a tribe of Kangrits to their side, several thousand strong.

Yet the Navesseans could do nothing to escape, because if they moved from their defensible position, Tyrennis Castaval's galleys would descend upon them, a battle that no one believed they could win.

Time was running out.

During the second night on the river, the campfires burned hot, and the men's voices were loud—a gesture of defiance against the long, cold dark of the Tyracian sands. They sang the same songs they'd sung on the hill overlooking the Bay of Svartennos: songs that told of how Zev had struck down the Tyracian banner, of how Aexiel had carried him back, killing twenty men single-handedly along the way, of Marilia's charge, how she had cut her way through to the heart of the Tyracians unafraid, driving the enemy before her.

But that wasn't right, Marilia thought; the songs were lies, embellishments. It hadn't been Zev who had cut down the Tyracian banner, but rather one of the knights under his command. She doubted Aexiel had truly killed twenty men, however good a swordsman Leondos claimed he was. And she herself had fallen from her horse before she'd made it fifty feet into the Tyracian lines, where she'd been dragged scared and shivering from the bog by Septakim.

They trusted in their Lady Chrysathamere to save them, but she was just as lost as they were.

She felt a chill fall over her; she made her way inside the cabin of her flagship and closed the windows to drown out the sound of the voices.

The third night, the songs were quieter, the voices hoarser. The fourth, they were softer still. It was as if Tyrace were a great, black leech that had curled itself around the throat of her army and was slowly tightening its coils, draining it of blood.

On the fifth night, she couldn't hear the songs at all.

It was that night that she received a coded message from the imperial army via a single chicaya that had slipped the Tyracian blockade, sent from the north-west. It was a short message, all that could be fit on the strip of cloth bound around the insect's leg.

No Navessean ships available to reach you in next week. No naval forces able to lend aid. Deep regrets. Spirits watch over you.

Karthtag-Kal, Prefect

When Marilia had stood before her army after the Battle of Chrysathamere Pass, she had felt as if she were made of aeder crystal. As she looked over the stern of her galley at the men huddled on the decks of the ships and the campfires along the shore, she could not help but feel that she was only glass, and that the first cracks had been made. *Doubt is the commander's first and final enemy*, Emperor Urian had written; and now doubt was here, sending its dark fingers throughout her army.

Septakim told her that rumors were beginning to make the rounds in the camp. Some men continued to take heart from the prophecy; they believed that because Lady Chrysathamere was with them, they could not fail. But others had begun to whisper darker thoughts: what did the prophecy say, exactly? That when Svartennos stood in peril, a woman would arise to save it: Svartana Reborn. But Svartennos wasn't really in peril any longer, was it? Maybe the prophecy had already been fulfilled; maybe Marilia had been meant to win the Battle in the Pass, and no more. Maybe her command of the army, the Battle in the Bay, everything that had happened since the pass was outside the prophecy's scope. What if it all came down to this—the Elders had made a mistake?

Make a speech, Septakim urged her. *Go down among them, give them hope. Strike the doubts down now, early, before they can take root and grow.* But Camilline had written Marilia's last speech for her; how could Marilia find the words to lift her men's spirits now? How could she promise them that deliverance was on the way when she didn't even know if it was true?

She did her best; she went before them and told them that the gods were with them—that the gods had tested Neravos, too, for thirty long days and nights, before they'd lifted him from the dremmakins' pits. She told them not to lose faith. Compared to the fire she'd lit back in Chrysathamere Pass, the words sounded weak and hollow. The sort of empty platitudes any newly-robed priest plucked off the street might have thought to say. She only hoped they couldn't see that she was just as afraid as they were.

Some of the strategoi began to talk of attacking the Tyracians, of forcing a way through before Tyrennis Castaval's reinforcements arrived. Tempers frayed; voices were raised. In the sweltering heat of the Tyracian sun, Lord Antiriel and strategos Laekos almost came to blows.

That afternoon, Marilia found Annuweth in the cabin of *Svartana's Revenge*. She sat with him by the narrow window, looking out at the distant Tyracian ships.

"I don't know what to do," she admitted. "Antiriel says we should attack them; he's afraid our men will lose heart if we delay any longer. He says the Kangrits could be here by tomorrow at the earliest. But

Laekos says we should try to face them here. He says we're not strong enough, that if we attack, they'll destroy us."

"It all comes down to guessing," Annuweth said. "You know as much as Antiriel, who knows as much as Laekos, who knows as much as me. Whatever you do, or don't do, there's no reason in it. It'll all come down to chance."

She nodded. "Do you think the gods will help us?" she asked. "They were supposed to be on our side, weren't they? That's what everyone says. I mean, I know they're not going to just sweep the Tyracians away…they don't work like that, they have to work through us…but do you think it's true? The Tyracians have their candles, too, and their shrines to their own ancestors. What if someone's helping them, too?"

"That's not the kind of thing I'd expect to hear from Svartana Reborn," Annuweth said. "All the Tyracians' ancestors are out walking the black sands. Isn't that right? They can't help anyone from there."

"Do you really think that's so?"

He shrugged. "So the priests tell us."

He had a wall up, a wall that had been there ever since he had first come to her on Svartennos. It had grown taller and more impenetrable after Ilruyn was captured and his Dragonknights died. She wanted to rip it down; she needed the real Annuweth back now. She had seen him weak and afraid, which meant that he, in turn, was someone before whom she could afford to let herself be afraid, just for one moment. If the strategoi saw her doubts, her control would start to unravel. She touched his arm, forcing him to look at her, to meet her eyes. "'Weth…please."

"You really want to know what I think, Marilia? I think that there's no way that Mother is with the dremmakin at the bottom of the sea.

355

And if she is, then the gods have got it wrong. I think that if Castaval had finished me off when we were in Tyrace, I wouldn't have gone down to Mollagora's Hall, either. It wouldn't have been fair. So I suppose what I'm saying is…yes, on the whole, the gods are on Navessea's side…I believe that much…but the Tyracians aren't as alone as our priests pretend. Some of the Tyracians' ancestors are up there with ours, giving them courage and strength. I want to think that somehow, our ancestors' spirits will see us through this, but to be honest I'm not sure. I suppose we'll have to wait and see."

She nodded; she couldn't disagree with any of that.

The sun was going down; its orange light was a cat's eye nestled between the peaks of the mountains of Dane to the north-west.

"If we die…" she said, and swallowed. "If we die, what do you think it's like? The House of White Sands?"

"Sandy, I suppose."

"'Weth, I'm serious."

He sighed. "Why do you want to talk about this now?"

"When else?"

"Fair enough. Well…Princess Petrea, of all people, once told me it was actually an enormous garden. The wind is the sound of beautiful music. Petrea always liked gardens and singing, though, so I suppose it makes sense…"

"Did Petrea really tell you that?" Marilia remembered Petrea's grinning face, her tinkling laugh. The thought of that laugh now seemed so out of place, so distant. Marilia found herself wishing Petrea were here; the princess had always seemed so invincible. Somehow Marilia thought, Petrea would have found a way to skip right past the Tyracian ships, all the way across the water, back to Svartennos.

"What about you?" Annuweth asked. "What do you think of?"

Marilia closed her eyes. The words came from deep inside her. "Someplace warm," she said. "Some place warm, and bright, with the sound of the wind, and that feeling when you first wake from a dream to find the sun is shining."

She opened her eyes to find that Annuewth was staring at her, with a look on his face that she hadn't seen before.

"That was...very beautiful," he said.

The sun vanished behind the mountains, plunging the fleet into shadow. One thing was certain; there would be no attack today.

"Until tomorrow, I suppose," Marilia said, and rose. She made her way back to her own cabin and crawled into bed.

She did not sleep that night. She spent her time thinking. By the end of the second hour, she had decided to attack just after dawn. By the end of the fourth, she was convinced an attack was madness. By the end of the fifth, she was so tired that attacking the Tyracians seemed tempting yet again.

The gods decided for her.

She awoke to the sound of shouting. She sprang from her cot, staggered onto the deck, blinking, rubbing sleep and dust from her eyes.

What she saw she did not at first dare to believe; ahead, the river was open. At its end, at the place where the river met the Bay there was a mass of red-brown sails, as if a range of bloody mountains had sprouted overnight from beneath the sea. The ships were sailing north-east, their oars rising and falling at a swift, steady pace to the beat of a distant, unheard drum.

The Tyracian fleet was leaving.

Before the Battle of Chrysathamere Pass, Kanediel Paetos had sent a plea for aid to Daevium.

Daevium finally responded.

While the crippled Navessean fleet lay trapped, one of the northern city's best commanders sailed to Svartennos. There, Lord Konos, having received one of Marilia's chicayas with its coded message, furnished the Daevish with the knowledge they needed—the details of the Tyracian and Navessean movements, the tale of Livenneth's failed attack.

Disguised as mercenary ships from the Valdruk Isles, the fleet of Daevium sailed east, threading its way through the small islands of Tyrace's eastern coast—a path less traveled, and less watched. They made their way not towards Castaval's fleet (which would have had ample time to see them coming and prepare for them) but to the harbor of Tyr Phalai, where the captured Navessean galleys lay at anchor, still under repairs. Still helpless.

Castaval had left a contingent of warships to protect the harbor— but not enough to defend against the entire fleet of Daevium, which, though nowhere near as strong as the fleets of either Tyrace or Navessea, was still a force to be reckoned with. By the time the Tyracians realized the danger descending upon them it was almost too late.

That was where Tyrennis Castaval's fleet had disappeared to the morning Marilia opened her disbelieving eyes and blinked out at the empty mouth of the River Ob; they had sailed away to reinforce Tyr Phalai.

But the wind turned against them; they would arrive too late.

Once again, the tide of the war had turned. Caught between the remnants of Livenneth's fleet and that of Daevium (its numbers bolstered by forty newly re-captured and mostly-repaired Navessean warships) Tyrennis Castaval's fleet turned tail and fled to the safety of the harbor in the Neck of Dane.

Daevish transport ships bearing fresh supplies, horses, and over three thousand Svartennan knights landed at the mouth of the River Ob.

Marilia's army was free at last.

Marilia turned her eyes to the heavens and whispered a heartfelt *thank you* to whoever was listening.

She had been given a second chance.

She made her way down to the water's edge to meet the first ships as they landed. She blinked; at first, she thought the sunlight sparkling off the waves was playing tricks on her eyes. But no—there could be no mistaking the woman making her way towards her at the front of a small company of knights in the telltale blue armor that Marilia herself wore. She was dressed in the same garb that she used for training and riding—a light tunic and leggings beneath a skirt ending just above her knees. It was the garb of someone ready for hard travel; the garb of someone who meant to stay.

Marilia was at a loss for words. "I thought…you said…"

"When I heard what happened to the fleet, I couldn't sleep," Camilline said. "I would stay up into the night, wondering…not knowing. What was it you said? The waiting is the worst." She took a deep breath. "I already lost my brother…and my sister. I don't want to lose you, too. I'm not sure what use I'll be, but I'll do what I can."

"I wasn't sure I'd ever see you again," Marilia said, giving voice to the fear she never would have dared admit to any of her strategoi.

"Well, you have. Looks like your story's not over yet, Lady Chrysathamere." Camilline frowned, curious. "How do you mean to end it?"

Marilia glanced back up the beach, to where men were hauling supplies off the ships, setting up a proper camp away from the sand, where the ground was firmer. A green and gold tent rose into being, larger than the others, its shape familiar; she had only ever seen it from the outside, during the struggle against Aemyr-Kal. It was Ben Espeleos' command tent—now, for the moment, hers.

"I'm not sure," she said quietly. "But I suppose we're about to find out."

CHAPTER THIRTY-ONE

Marilia, Andreas, the lieutenants of Antarenne and the strategoi of Svartennos gathered inside the command tent. Beyond the tent's walls, the men of Svartennos and their allies from Daevium continued unloading supplies; hammers pounded tent-pegs into the baked earth, supply carts rattled by, their wheels bouncing on the uneven terrain; horses whinnied and men shouted commands. A strong sea wind made sand patter against the walls of the tent. Marilia did her best to ignore all of it, narrowing her focus as she had during all those games with Karthtag-Kal, until the noise of the camp faded to a muted murmur no more distracting than the drumming of rain.

To her left was Leondos, the most experienced and respected of her strategoi; then Antiriel, Aerael, Laekos, and a young cousin of Ben Espeleos who—with Ben captured and Kanediel and Zev dead—had become the default leader of House Espeleos' forces. On the other side of the table Andreas stood with his four lieutenants, a reserved bunch who seemed content to let their commander do the talking for them. They hovered behind him, quiet and inconspicuous—or at least, as inconspicuous as they could be given that one of them (Dorokim, she recalled his name was) was about the size of a small mountain.

A map of the surrounding lands was spread across a table before them. The map represented the sum of the knowledge accumulated by Navessean visitors—merchants; renouncers who had risked their lives to enter Tyracian lands and attempt to wean the people of Tyrace from the heretical cult of the Horse God; ambassadors; those who had traded

361

with the tribes of the Kangrits and Tigrits that roamed Tyrace's eastern border. It wasn't perfect cartography, but it was a lot more than the Tyracians had had to work with when they had landed on Svartennos.

The scouts who Marilia had sent out on patrol had made their own additions to the map—a mountain here, a small peasant village there. The twisting ribbon of the River Tyr bisected the map, running from Tyr Phalai down into the south-west, to Tyracium.

Somewhere in those painted rivers and mountains and black circles that were cities lay, perhaps, the answer to the war.

Which, truth be told, was not going very well.

Andreas shook his head. "The Governor of Dane always was a fool."

In addition to supplies, the ships from Daevium had brought tidings of the situation in Dane. Seeing the Neck on the verge of falling to the Tyracian forces, the governor had decided not to wait for Emperor Vergana's reinforcements. He had led a mad, valiant charge against the Tyracian lines in an attempt to save his homeland.

And he had failed spectacularly.

The Neck was lost, and the Tyracians had pushed north into Dane's heartland. Now Dane City itself was surrounded by the Tyracian army.

The Order of Jade had been driven back; how many were dead was hard to say.

And rumor had it that Emperor Vergana himself had fallen gravely ill; though this might just have been the fearful campfire talk of a few shaken soldiers.

"We sailed with Livenneth to save the Neck of Dane," Leondos said, running a hand through his dark beard. "And we failed. The Neck of Dane has fallen; half of Dane has fallen. The question is what we do now."

"Question? Is there really any question?" Aerael Dartimaos was all twitching, nervous energy as he stood in the corner of the tent, rubbing his fingers together, stroking his chin, shifting his weight from one leg to the other. "We sail north and try to break the siege of Dane City."

"It seems to me," Antiriel said, leaning over the map, "that if we do that, we are conceding the initiative to the Tyracians."

Aerael frowned. "Conceding the initiative?"

"Right now," Marilia explained, "we have a rare opportunity. Tyrennis Nomeratsu's army has been destroyed; the remnants of Tyrennis Castaval's fleet have been driven off. We have a chance to strike into Tyrace's lands—there is almost no one to resist us. If we turn back for Dane, Tyrace will call up its reserves, muster fresh armies, and we will lose that chance."

"So where would we strike?" Aerael asked, making a sweeping motion with his hand. "Try to capture Tyr Phalai?"

"Or perhaps the Tyracian mining lands," Antiriel said, drawing a finger across the surface of the map. "They would be a valuable prize if they could be taken."

"They would," Leondos agreed, "But there are mountains blocking our path, with Tyrennis Nomeratsu's castle, and presumably, a substantial number of men guarding the pass."

"If we move too far into Tyrace, if we commit to a long siege, we risk being surrounded and cut off," Andreas said. "No help is coming to us from Navessea, not in the near future. The Kangrits are marching on us from the east; I would imagine that Tyrennis Castaval will pull forces from the Neck as well, so we may find ourselves facing enemies on two fronts."

The strategoi raised their eyes to regard Andreas. Marilia saw a flicker of distaste cross Leondos' features, and Aerael's eyes narrowed;

they had scant love for the man who'd killed Nelos Dartimaos. Still, there was no denying the sense of what Andreas had said.

"You've been quite quiet, Lady Chrysathamere," said Aerael. "Has Svartana imparted you with any wisdom?" The way he said it wasn't quite a challenge, but it wasn't quite *not* a challenge, either. She had the impression that Aerael was not very fond of her, either.

"Let me think," she said, meeting his gaze evenly. She looked down at the map. And she *did* think—harder, perhaps, than she had ever thought in her life.

She traced the paths of the Rivers Tyr and Ob, gazed upon the small black marks that represented Tyrace's castles and cities. One in particular seemed to call to her; a mark slightly bigger than the rest, staring up at her like the black cavity of a missing eye. A threat, but also a promise.

And she let herself fall back into that darkness; a current that took her back years, to when she was just a little girl swimming in the waters of the River Tyr.

And at last she saw it, sliding together; the last piece she hadn't even known was missing, fitting into place like the final beam of a house being laid to rest. Now at last she understood the picture in its entirety, and she felt her heart swell.

She placed her finger on the map. "What if we could take Tyracium?"

The place where the king's tower stood, where the Temple of the Horse God looked out across the sacred river. It was more than just Tyrace's greatest city; it was her heart, her holy place.

The question had been rhetorical; she knew exactly what would happen if they could take Tyracium, as did all the others.

If they could take it, it would end the war.

"My lady, Tyracium cannot be captured," strategos Laekos said. "According to all the reports, their walls are very strong. They have..."

"Cliffs to the north to cut off the approach there, the river Tyr guarding their western wall, and thick gates with towers overlooking them. I know. I have been there, after all. But what if it could be taken?"

"How?" asked Aerael, looking doubtful.

She told them her plan.

For a while no one spoke. Doubts and hopes crowded the air of the tent until there was scarcely room to breathe.

"I like it." To her surprise, it was Andreas who spoke first. He was nodding, slowly, a light filling his eyes—not all at once, but piece-meal, the way the rising sun traveled down a mountainside. "It's bold. I rather think...it's the sort of thing Nelos Dartimaos would have done. The glory if we succeed..."

"Bring the war to Tyrace's heart," Antiriel said, and his mouth slowly lifted into a grim smile. "Take it to their homes. Yes...we would pay them back for Svartennos City, and more."

Laekos agreed; Leondos shrugged; even Aerael nodded.

"It's decided, then," she said.

She stared at the mark on the map, the place where she had spent the first ten years of her life. Once the city had seemed so big—a shadow the size of a mountain. But now she saw it for what it truly was.

She knew the gesture was a bit melodramatic; Karthtag-Kal probably would have rolled his eyes at it. But she couldn't help herself. She bent over the table and laid her finger upon the little black circle. "Tomorrow, we march on Tyracium."

"Tomorrow, we march on Tyracium," Andreas said as they left the tent, coming to stand beside her. He was staring out towards the river—towards the south where it curved through a couple of dusty foothills and out of sight. "Indeed. There is one more thing you should consider."

"And what is that?"

"Your plan will take us inside Tyracium's outer walls. But it would be better if we could take the keep as well—the Tower of Tyrace. That is where the king's family resides. Without them in our hands, we have only half a victory."

Marilia nodded, chewing the corner of her lip. "True. I was considering that."

They spoke strategy, standing together on the bank of the river beneath the shade of a crooked palm tree. The shadows of the leaves on the ground moved with the wind; they looked like the curved blades of dueling swords. In the end, they came up with an idea that Marilia was at least moderately confident would work.

"I meant what I said back in the tent, you know," Andreas said. "Your plan—it is the sort of thing Prefect Dartimaos would have done."

"You sound like you admire him," Marilia said, surprised.

"I did...I do," Andreas answered.

"Why?"

Andreas chewed his lip, considering the question. "I suppose because...he was everything I ever wanted to be. The son of a disgraced house who built himself back up from the bottom, who saved his name, who built a story that outlived his body. That is all I have been trying to do for twenty years, since the day my father died and left me his legacy—the Scorpion Company."

The face Andreas wore was like the surface of a pond on a windless day; placid, amenable, so much so as to be almost forgettable. Marilia realized now that it was not his true face; for the first time, the calm surface pulled back, and she saw a glimpse of the person underneath. There was a look of need in his eyes that reminded her of a man crawling from the chill of a desert night towards the light of a campfire that continued to shift with the sands, always just out of reach.

"Well, it seems you have done well," Marilia said. "Now you are a commander of Antarenne."

"It has been a journey." His teeth tugged pensively at his lower lip. "When I was a child, of course, before the one-eyed king banished my family, I was a Tyracian noble. Then, in the years after, I was nothing—a disgraced scion of a lost house, the bane of my own family. A northman who didn't even speak the language. And the *unfairness* of it—I felt it deeply. There were the spirits of great, brilliant ancestors behind me. I felt that I was capable of more…that they *expected* more…but I was trapped in my place, a prisoner of fate."

Marilia swallowed; the last thing she'd expected was to feel any sort of kinship with the man she'd spent a good many childhood hours fantasizing about murdering. But an image came to her, unbidden—herself, staring down at her river-stones after her mother had scattered them across the dusty flagstones of Oba'al's courtyard, her eyes stinging with tears. *The daughters of painted ladies become painted ladies…*

"You'd be surprised by many great men begin that way…humbly, I mean," Andreas said. "Even Aryn, the first and finest of Navessea's emperors. There's something powerful in the mixture—a mighty spirit trapped in a lowly cage. But I suppose I don't need to tell you that." He turned his gaze to her. "Maybe it's because we start so low that we are

367

always compelled to reach for more...to quote old Emperor Urian, *to rage, to burn, to see how wide a mark we can make, and never to stop.*"

"Maybe," she answered, thinking of the feeling that had filled her as she stood at the top of Chrysathamere Pass and listened to her men cheer for her. *This, at last, means something. This, at last, means that I have lived, that I walked and fought and mattered; if life is a game of Sharavayn, then I am not a piece. I am one of the players.*

"Farewell for now, Lady Sandara." Andreas made his way along the beach to his tent. Marilia stood there for a long while, listening to the whisper of the river's current.

She sent a coded letter to Emperor Vergana, requesting that he sanction her attack on Tyracium. She didn't dare put the details of her plan down, even in code—but she assured him that there was a chance of taking the city, if they moved quickly. She didn't wait for a reply; time was slipping away from them, the Kangrits advancing from the east, Castaval's forces from the north-west. If they were going to succeed, they had to act quickly. She had to trust that Emperor Vergana would understand.

They set to packing their supplies, loading men and animals onto the galleys for the voyage up the river. Men, and animals, and... women. Among the other supplies that the ships from Daevium had carried with them were over two hundred painted ladies from Svartennos.

They had been present during the northern campaign against Aemyr-Kal as well, hanging towards the back of the camp, far from Marilia's sight. Technically, they were Svartennan comfort women, somewhat different from painted ladies. They lived in special houses set up by the Elders of Svartennos and were only to be enjoyed by men on or immediately after campaign, not by merchants or village-folk during peace-time. Kanediel had explained to her that there was a certain honor to the profession. Instead of trading the act of pillowing for gold from those they lay with, they traded it for a life of respect, and to better the lives of their fathers, mothers, brothers, and sisters, who were all provided for by the Elders. When not on campaign they spent their time learning water-script painting, needlework, and the history and music of Svartennos.

So, they weren't quite the same thing as painted ladies, but they were similar enough that Marilia felt a touch of irritation as she watched them ascend the galleys' gangplanks.

"Truly, a pressing necessity," she said dryly.

Laekos, passing nearby, overheard her. "Svartennan comfort women have been part of every large campaign since the time of Queen Svartana and before," he said. "You disapprove?"

For some reason—even though she knew it didn't entirely make sense—she couldn't shake the feeling that the comfort women of Svartennos were in some way a personal affront to her. But she simply shrugged. "If the warriors of Svartennos believe that they are as essential as grain and wood and armor, then by all means, let us make room for them on our galleys."

Annuweth finally emerged that day as they were finishing their preparations, looking drawn, as if he had just finished battling an illness. With his company of Dragonknights dead, he had no one to command, so she put him in charge of a company of House Paetos's knights, naming him captain. He took to his new role with a zeal she had not expected, immediately offering to lead a scouting party up-river; he took one of their fastest galleys and sped away out of sight. He returned near the end of the day and informed her that there was a small Tyracian village two days' sail ahead that was quickly emptying in anticipation of the Navessean army's arrival. It would be a good place to land and unload the galleys in preparation for the march that would take them to Tyracium.

Marilia would have liked to speak with her brother more, but Annuweth was distant. He threw himself into task after task, managing his company of knights with an efficiency that was the envy of House Paetos's other captains. Between the demands on her time and his ferocious commitment to his new command, the two of them barely had a moment to exchange more than ten words at a time during the first day's journey.

"Give him time," Camilline urged her. "He has to make peace with the fact that his men died when he thought it was his duty to save them." Her face clouded with sympathy. "I know a little of what that's like. Your brother probably feels like he's Neravos wrestling with his own personal dremmakin king right now."

"If he would just talk to me…"

"Well, he won't. From what you've told me, he's pretty prideful. And a little stubborn. Sort of like someone else I know."

"Prideful?" Marilia scoffed.

"Only about the things that really matter to you." Camilline grinned. "I've never seen anyone take a friendly game of Capture the Emperor so seriously." Her tone sobered. "Time heals the spirit—isn't that what your favorite stoic philosopher says? I think it's true."

"He also says that regret can turn a man's heart. That it's like a poison, and if you don't draw it out, it turns people into razorfish, biting at whatever's in sight."

"I guess I should have known better than to try quoting stoics at you. You've read all those grim old men much more thoroughly than I have."

"They're not so grim."

"No offense, but I'm not sure you're the best judge of that."

"So you think I'm prideful *and* grim." Marilia furrowed her brows. "Remind me why you're my friend, again?"

"Look, Marilia; you've got enough to worry about. If anyone's going to help your brother, it's not going to be the sister who keeps succeeding at all the things he's not. That's just how it is. Tell me—do you really think we can reach Tyracium in less than two weeks?"

They would; Annuweth's scouts had reported that the river-side village they'd found was only eight days' march from the Tyracian capitol, if they moved quickly.

After that it all came down to whether or not Marilia's plan would work.

But she was convinced that it would. Ever since the gods had given her that first chance back on Svartennos she had beaten every challenge that had been thrown her way. Her plan had won them the Battle of the Pass; her actions in Daevium had secured the alliance that had saved their fleet.

This plan, she believed, would succeed, too.

When doubt finally came, it concerned another matter entirely.

After her supper, Marilia remained sitting before the table with her war-map for a long while. She stared until she could see the black dot of Tyracium even when she closed her eyes, seared across her vision like the lone fire of a lighthouse on a clouded night.

The excitement of the day's planning, the hectic furor of the preparations, had begun to subside ever so slightly. Now, for the first time, she was able to consider the full implications of what she was about to do.

She frowned, troubled. Antiriel's words drifted through her head. *Bring the war to Tyrace's heart. Take it to their homes.*

Pay them back for Svartennos City, and more.

She remembered the ash Svartennos City had become, remembered the smoke above the harbor, the haunted eyes of the doomed villagers in their long, pathetic line. She remembered the ruined bodies she had discovered on the march back from Chrysathamere Pass.

She knew that taking Tyracium was the right thing—it was what was meant for her. It could be no accident that she had been born within its walls; the Fates had put her there so that she could learn how to conquer it. Her attack on Tyracium would end the war, force King Damar to sue for peace, and in so doing, it would save thousands—maybe tens of thousands—of lives.

But when she closed her eyes, she remembered the face of the woman who had shouted after Kanediel as he rode away. She remembered the sound of that woman weeping.

She remembered the bodies on the road, the blankets of flies shooting up into the sky like a black silk shawl ripped away by the wind.

Somewhere inside Tyracium's walls were her childhood friends—Nyreese, Damar, Saleema and all the rest, who had never had their own Karthtag-Kal to rescue them.

Septakim poked his head into her tent, clearing his throat. "Is it time for your lesson, my lady?" he was holding two practice-swords in his hands.

She didn't answer. "You were there when Moroweth Vergana brought the war home to Kanadrak," she said. "Weren't you?"

"I was, my lady." Septakim let the tent flap fall back into place. He frowned, looking puzzled, wondering, perhaps, where this was going.

"And what happened?"

Septakim's voice was quiet. "It was not the sort of thing you might find in Emperor Urian's books, my lady."

Or, if so, just mentioned in a single line: *and they passed into the city, and there were many spoils, and the men of the imperial army were taken by great excitement.*

"I forgot, my lady...are there still some you know inside Tyracium's walls?"

Marilia chewed her lip. "I will address my army tomorrow," she said. "Please let the strategoi know."

"My lady...what exactly do you mean to do?"

"I mean to give orders to my men. There will be no burning of homes or killing of innocents. No pillowing with Tyracian women—no raping. From now until Tyracium falls."

Septakim took a deep breath.

"What, Septakim?" She turned about to look at him. "Is there something you want to say?"

"In my experience...on long campaigns, men grow restless."

"They will find gold and glory aplenty when we take the Tower of Tyrace. That will be enough to satisfy them."

Still Septakim looked hesitant.

Marilia felt a sudden surge of irritation. His reluctance, his failure to understand, galled her. "Tell me, then, what would you have me do? Order the deaths of fishermen and yam-farmers?"

"No, not necessarily deaths, my lady...but to placate some of the common-folk...you might consider..."

"What? Stealing the bread from the mouths of their children? Or did you mean the rape of craftsmen's wives?"

"Well...they are not noble women," Septakim said. "Their honor is not so dear that..."

"*No*, Septakim."

"...But regardless, that wasn't what I was going to suggest. No; I was merely thinking of Tyrace's painted ladies."

"Tyracian painted ladies," Marilia shook her head. "Do you really think they are just going to wait around in their villages for us to come and claim them?"

"Most will not, I imagine. But there will be some along our path. Certainly, some inside Tyracium, when it falls. Those willing to sleep with the enemy, who put gold above gods."

"I don't understand; our men have their *comfort women*, remember? Why do they need Tyracian painted ladies?"

Septakim spread his arms in a helpless shrug.

"No; I ask you honestly. Why?"

"Some prefer Tyracian women. Why do knights dice each other for a taste of the Tyracian jala fruits when the arandon berries of Svartennos are just as sweet?"

"How poetic," she said coldly.

"Thank you."

"No."

"No?"

"No. No Tyracian painted ladies."

"Well, I doubt the men will much like *that*."

"I was nearly one of them once, Septakim, before Karthtag-Kal found me."

"That is just my point, my lady. You were once of Tyrace. And our knights and shield-men, they have forgotten it; to them you are only Lady Chrysathamere, the woman who saved Svartennos. Don't let them remember anything else."

She'd had enough of his doubts, enough of his little frowns and grimaces. She rose from her chair, standing before him in her armor. "They will do this, Septakim; they will follow my commands. The strategoi, the knights, the shield-men...all. Do you know why? Because they *believe*. They believe in what we are doing. They believe in Queen Svartana. Most of all, they believe in me. Last night when I walked through the camp, men knelt before me. Some of my knights even begged me to whisper to them what the gods have planned for us. They still sing of our charge in the pass."

"Yes, my lady, I know your men love you."

"Then what is the problem?"

"Love has its limits. I hate to be a pessimist, but it's my nature; and, being a pessimist, I can tell you that hate is a thing somewhat stronger. And after all the heretics did to us..." he made a face. "There is a lot to hate."

She said nothing.

"Pillowing helps to cool men's passions," Septakim said. "Just out of curiosity, my lady...are you going to order the men of Antarenne to refrain from painted ladies, too? Or ask Lord Andreas to order them?" He gave her a pointed look. "Because it won't be the Lady Chrysathamere asking them; just a strange Svartennan commander, their general purely by an accident of fate, taking away one of their few meager comforts on a hard campaign."

She felt a deep ache somewhere in her skull. "Fine." She held up a hand to stop him talking. "Fine; they can lie with painted ladies...if they pay them. But only if they're of age. And only if the painted ladies are not harmed. Is that enough for you?"

"I think it is...wise, my lady."

She grunted, annoyed, feeling as if somehow, by forcing this concession, he'd claimed some small victory over her. "I feel tired tonight, Septakim. No lesson, I think."

He made for the entrance of the tent. She couldn't help but call to him as he reached for it.

"You're wrong, you know," she said. "About hate being stronger."

"Spoken like a woman," Septakim said, his mouth twitching.

Marilia felt her anger rise. "You forget yourself, sir."

Septakim's smile vanished. "Apologies. I speak only of my experiences. Of what I have seen. Of the way things have been."

"The way things have been," Marilia repeated. "But has there ever been a bastard girl from a pillow house in command of the army of Svartennos? Things aren't as they have always been, Septakim. And they won't be. Remember that."

CHAPTER THIRTY-TWO

"Forgive me for disturbing you, my lord. I would ask a favor," Marilia said, facing Andreas across the dim confines of his tent. Outside, the last orange smear of evening glazed the sky like a fine dust of pollen.

She had caught the commander preparing to sleep. But she had to do this now, to have his answer, so that she could sleep herself, untroubled.

"A favor?" Andreas repeated.

She told him. "Please," she said. "You were once one of them, too."

"I see," Andreas said. "Years ago, during Kanadrak's war, I fought alongside men I could not control—or, rather, men I was too unsure of myself and too weak to dare try to control. My brave captains of the Scorpion Company." His mouth formed into a hard line. "Your father the prefect may have mentioned their deeds to you, perhaps."

"He mentioned...rumors."

"Of course he did. Well, the captains who were responsible are long dead now, but I have never forgotten what I saw that day. And I can tell you..." he took a slow breath. "Yours is the better path. But I must warn you...your men will be harder to control than mine. My knights of Antarenne lost some brothers in the Battle of the Bay, but yours...they have seen their homes burned, their prince taken. They have lost far more, and I would guess their anger burns hotter."

"I will take care of my men, my lord," Marilia said firmly. "All I ask is that you keep yours in check. If you help me, I will be in your

377

debt."

Andreas nodded. "I will do my part. That I can promise you. As you said, Tyrace was once my home, too."

"Thank you, my lord."

Andreas held up a hand. "One favor deserves another. I have my price."

"And what is that?"

"Only this." Andreas caught her eyes and held them with his own. "The next time you see the prefect, please tell him that I do have at least some honor left. Tell him that it's time to stop pulling strings and raising his walls in my path. Climbing over them has been diverting on occasion, but it's also tiring, and I'd like to save my energy for our next duel."

The following morning, just after sunrise, after she had bathed herself and applied shadow to her eyes, she made her way out onto the top of the hill overlooking the camp. Her men gathered below her, the strategoi at the front.

They had paused in their morning routine—in taking down tents, putting out campfires, packing up supplies—because runners had gone through the camp with the news that the Lady Chrysathamere wished to address the army.

Marilia wished she was taller, at least as tall as the lords who served under her. She took a steadying breath to bolster her voice. Her eyes scanned the sea of faces below her and found Annuweth, who stood with his company of knights near the front of the crowd. Her gaze lingered there for a moment, and on Camilline, Andreas, and Septakim, drawing strength from the knowledge that they, at least,

378

would not only understand what she was doing but support it as well.

Even if she yelled, there was no way all her men would hear her. That was why there were other criers, spaced at intervals throughout the company, to carry her words through the rest of the camp.

Silence fell as they waited for her to speak.

It was a speech that she had spent the last several hours before sleep preparing—with Camilline's help. She supposed that the speech was the best it could be; Camilline had a way with words, and could fashion a phrase into a weapon as lean and precise as a master-crafted sword.

Even so, facing down that crowd, the words that had seemed so potent when she'd spoken them alone to Camilline the night before felt meager now in the light of day, like a child's shadow-monster that shriveled to nothing with the rising of the sun.

"Men of Svartennos!" she called out. "A week ago, the enemy stood upon our doorstep. Now we stand upon his! What better proof that the gods are on our side?"

A great cheer went up. That was comforting.

"There is more yet to come," she said. "The gods have promised a way to the greatest victory of all! I believe Tyracium will fall before us!" Though the army must have guessed her goal by now, she had shared the full extent of her plan with only a select few—the top captains of Antarenne, her own strategoi, Camilline, Andreas, Septakim and Annuweth. It was safer that way; the more that new of her intentions, the easier it would be for the secret to fall into the hands of their enemy. She saw the men below exchanging quick, excited glances; their Lady Chrysathamere was confirming now what most had suspected.

Marilia filled her lungs with air, drew herself up straight and waited for the sea wind to die down so that her voice would carry as far as possible. "The gods now seek to test us, just like they did to Neravan Vergana, just as they did to Akeleos of Svartennos when they sent a traitor into the midst of his great army. They want us to prove that we are worthy of their favor. They ask us to put aside the instinct of revenge and to walk Almaria's path of mercy."

More glances, this time of confusion. Marilia's mouth was dry; she licked her lips, tasting sea salt and the thick grit of the desert. She saw the great depth of emotion in the eyes of her men, a warmth like the glow in a shrine—sunlight through aeder crystal. She was about to put a chill on that warmth, and it hurt her. But she knew she was right.

"The warriors of Tyrace have done us great wrong; I, who lost my husband, know that as well as anyone. But this is what must be—what the gods ask of us in return for our victory. We must kill only those with swords in their hands. We must rape no women, light no fires, harm no peasants or city-folk who know nothing of war. In this way, we prove ourselves *better* than they are. And in this way, we will win their souls from the lies of the Horse God."

The silence that greeted her this time was not as warm or eager as the last one had been. A mutter swept through the crowd, gradually growing stronger, like the murmuring of a spring brook swelling after a heavy fall of rain. Antiriel looked as if the ground had opened under him; Aerael's mouth had come open. Even grizzled Leondos looked doubtful, his lips tightly pursed.

"This is what the spirit of Queen Svartana has told me," Marilia declared. "This is what is asked of us. This is the path, and if we follow it, the reward will be great."

Laekos, strategos to Lady Siria, spoke first. "The Lady Chrysathamere shows us the way," he declared loudly. "She led us to victory once; I believe she will do it again."

Marilia gave him a nod of gratitude. "Tomorrow, we leave our ships and begin our final march," she said; she knew she had to go out on a high note. "We are the sword, the saviors of Navessea," she announced. "The Battle of Chrysathamere Pass was only the beginning."

There were cheers again. But they seemed strained and thin, like rice-wine mixed with too much water.

She found that she did not want to stand upon that hill a moment longer; she did not want to look upon the faces of her men and see what was missing there, to mark the absence of what had been there before.

She made her way down the hill towards the gangplank of *Svartana's Revenge*. Camilline's knights of House Paetos—the group her men had come to call the Flower Company—fell into step around her.

"It was well done," Annuweth said when they were back aboard the galley. "I was going to mention it to you…but it looks like you already thought of it."

"I don't think a lot of the men much liked it," she said, chewing her lip.

"My main concern is the men of Antarenne," Annuweth said in an undertone. "If they start looting, it might be hard to keep the men of Svartennos from following. In fact, I'd been meaning to speak to you about him…"

"I already spoke with Lord Andreas. He promised to keep the men of Antarenne in line…"

"Wait. You've been meeting with the Graver?" Annuweth frowned.

"With Lord Andreas. Yes. I spoke with him in his tent, and he said…"

"Whatever he said, whatever he promised…" Annuweth spat over the rail of the shop. "He's the one you should watch most of all."

"He's from Tyrace, the same as we are, in case you've forgotten," Marilia said. "He understands."

"Understands? You really think he gives a horse's shit about the people of Tyrace?" Annuweth snorted. "You should get rid of him."

"Get rid of him? Just like that? He's a lord of Navessea, not a marsh-gnat you can just swat away."

"And you're in command of this army, aren't you? Livenneth put you in charge. Until the Emperor decides otherwise, you can do what you like here. You *could* send him away."

"Away where?"

"It's war; I'm sure you can think of a reason. Head off a Tyracian army—defend the supply lines—scout the western front—create a diversion—I don't know, you're the military master-mind."

"It would be an insult, 'Weth."

"It's sweet the way you care so much about his feelings."

"He saved our lives in the Bay. He helped us come up with a strategy to take the Tower. If I send him away now, I'll create another enemy, and for what?"

"Did you ever stop to think that maybe a man who lost his head over a bone bracelet is being a little a little *too* helpful? Not to put too fine a point on it, sister, but you haven't always been the best judge of character."

"And what is that supposed to mean?"

He looked away. "Forget it."

"No; tell me."

"Well…remember One-Eye?"

If he'd sought to wound her, he'd succeeded. "This is just about the fact the Graver killed our father, isn't it?" she asked sharply. "I'm sorry, 'Weth, but there are bigger things happening right now than our childhood vendetta."

Annuweth's brows drew together; a storm seemed to be gathering between them, a pressure building. "Don't talk down to me," he said in a voice that was tight as a drawn bowstring.

She glared at him and he glared back. She tried to smother her anger, to keep in mind what Camilline had said—*he's probably wrestling with his own personal dremmakin king right now*—but it was a struggle. Whether or not she would have won that struggle, she would never learn, because as she opened her mouth to speak; there came a call from below.

"Lady Sandara!"

It was strategos Antiriel. He stood at the base of the gangplank, looking up at her, his jaw set, a decidedly grim expression on his face. "Could I have a word?"

She would have rather said *no,* but it didn't seem polite, so she took a deep breath and nodded. "Of course."

He made his way up the gangplank. He glanced around, at Annuweth, at Septakim and the other knights of the Flower Company who stood nearby. "Alone?" he said meaningfully.

Marilia nodded. "Annuweth, I need to speak with Lord Antiriel."

Annuweth moved away to stand with the other knights by the prow of the ship; they left a space for she and Antiriel to talk, unheard, by the cabin at the stern.

"What is it, my lord?" Marilia asked, though of course she knew what it was.

Antiriel spoke in an urgent undertone. "I wonder if you might, perhaps, have misinterpreted the dreams Queen Svartana showed you," he said, appearing to choose his words carefully. His hands twisted together; a mark of distress. "I know we all swore to follow you, and no one questions the things you have done for us, least of all I. But before we sailed from Svartennos I—and many others—swore an oath: to revenge the wrongs done to us, the fires they brought to our shores. To stamp out the heresy of the Tyracians' false king. My lady, let me remind you, when Tyrennis Nomeratsu came to our lands, *he* did not show mercy."

"True, Lord Antiriel. But Tyrennis Nomeratsu is our prisoner now, his right hand gone. His army is gone, too; his men lie dead on the fields of Svartennos." She tried to offer him more; she gave him what she hoped was a fierce, knowing smile. "And we will have our revenge. Our revenge will be the humiliation we deal the Tyracian king when we bring Tyrace to her knees."

"I simply find it difficult to understand that the gods, *our* gods, would wish us to simply...forget about Svartennos City, burned to cinders? About our sons..." his voice broke and he coughed, clearing his throat and waving a hand through the air as if to suggest that it was merely the dust which had aggravated his lungs. "...our sons, taken from us by that treacherous attack..."

"I will never forget," Marilia promised, her voice softening. "But we are talking about simple craftsmen, weaving-women, villagers and city-folk who wouldn't know how to use a sword even if they had one to swing. They have done us no harm."

"No harm?" He repeated, incredulous. "These are people who worship the Horse God of Tyrace. Each time they pray to their false dead king, they let the dremmakin into their hearts. Each time the dremmakin claim a spirit, King Mollagora grows stronger. And the stronger the dremmakin king grows, the more injuries his ghouls cause." He raised a finger with each point. "Sickness. Famine. Tremors of the earth. Storms of the sea. Curses and dark dreams. All that misery.

What greater harm could the Tyracians do?"

Marilia stared at him, unsure what to say.

"They worship their own dead king, my lady. Men worshiping kings...making offerings to their own kind...that is the very arrogance that brought the dremmakin to their doom in the first place. As long as that heresy is allowed to survive, the world will never be made whole. Kill the meat-eaters now or kill them later, but some day they must fall. Everyone knows it."

"What if they can be changed? They can be won over."

"Do you really believe that?" Antiriel asked, raising his brows. "The city-folk of Tyracium may not have sailed to our shores and spilled our blood, my lady, but make no mistake. They would kill us all if they had the chance. If you lay naked and unarmed before them with only your pleas for mercy to protect you, those craftsmen and weaving-ladies and city-folk would happily rape you, beat you, carve out your heart and tear your body limb from limb."

Marilia had a brief mental image of an enraged crowd, of flying rocks, of men dying around her as Karthtag-Kal carved a path to the docks. She felt the hairs rise along her arms. She knew that what Antiriel said was almost certainly true.

"All the same," she said evenly, "I must follow the will of the gods. I can't ignore what I was shown."

"What you were shown," Antiriel repeated. "Indeed, lady; but are you *sure*?" And there it was, spoken more openly than she had expected. The challenge rested between them, something dangerous, like an untrained silvakim that neither wanted to reach out and touch. He had dared to voice aloud what others might only think.

"There can be no doubt," Marilia answered, hearing how brittle her own voice sounded and hating it.

Antiriel bowed his head. "Until this evening, then, Lady Chrysathamere," he said, referring to the time when she and her strategoi would convene in the command tent. He sounded none too pleased.

"Until this evening, Lord Antiriel," she agreed. "May the spirits protect you and the gods watch over you," she added, an insufficient attempt to smooth the waters between them.

Antiriel merely grunted and turned away.

They sailed south, banking for the night in the mostly-abandoned village that Annuweth had found the day before.

Not all the townsfolk had left; some of the very old and the very young and the ill had been left behind. Just as she had instructed, neither the Svartennans nor the men of Antarenne harmed a single Tyracian villager. Instead, for the time being, the Tyracians were herded into the town's common buildings, the doors barred, grim-faced Svartennan knights standing guard outside. The houses and fishing boats were searched for supplies.

As a group of Tyracian girls—they might have been between the ages of eight and twelve—were herded into the buildings where they would be kept under guard, they stared up at Marilia in awe. It seemed almost incredible to her that she had once been one of them; now she passed over all, a strange armored shape astride a coal-black horse. Not one of them dared hold her gaze for more than a second.

The next day they turned off the river and began their trek overland, winding their way between the dunes and foothills of Tyrace. It took six and a half days of marching to reach Tyracium. It was mid-afternoon when they arrived at the city's walls. The movement of the Navessean army had raised a great cloud of dust, and the sun was diffuse and yellow as it shone through, like the eye of a man struck with fever. In the distance, the formidable walls of Tyracium cut a square out of the orange of the sky. The Tower loomed over all, the shaft of a spear raised in challenge.

As she caught sight of it, Marilia felt her breath stop. Before, she had pictured her trajectory as a climb, bottom to top, foothill towards the summit. But for a brief, trembling moment it seemed to her that it was instead a circle, and she stood again at the apex where she had begun.

She set up camp around the city, setting her men to work digging trenches and sharpening wooden stakes to prevent an attack from behind. Others she set to work digging a different sort of trench, a labor that would require at least a week's work. She made sure to keep her tents carefully positioned around the excavation area so that the Tyracians would not see it and guess what she intended.

The following day the city sent a man to treat with her. He came at her request; he came because it was part of her plan.

They met him in an open space between the walls and the camp. On both sides, archers readied their bows, prepared in case the negotiation should take a turn for the bloody. Yet no one expected it to; killing during a parley was the lowest and most dishonorable form of conduct, reserved for oath-breakers and dremmakin-spawn.

Marilia approached with Annuweth and three of House Paetos's knights; the Tyracian emissary was accompanied by four protectors of his own.

"I am Tyrennis Bastet of House Saleth," the emissary announced. "Emissary of her grace, the Queen Dibella of Tyrace. Commander of her royal guard."

"I am Marilia Sandara, commander of the army of Svartennos, lieutenant of the imperial army of Navessea," Marilia said. The emissary blinked, doing a double-take. He appeared horrified.

"My...lady," he said slowly.

"I am here on behalf of the gods you insult with your false idols," Marilia said. "They have shown me that your city will soon fall before us."

Bastet composed himself, drawing himself up in his saddle. "My lady, our walls are strong. If you try to scale them, we will be ready. If you try to undermine them, our men will be ready with trenches of their own. If you try to break through our gates, we will rain the gods' wrath on your heads. Tyrennis Castaval knows you are here. Within a few weeks you will find the forces of Tyrace all around you."

"My lord—Tyrennis," she said to Bastet, with a vague, dramatic gesture of the hand, "all your armies are grass before the spring storm. Whatever aid you seek will not arrive in time to help you. Before you reply, consider this; Tyrennis Nomeratsu also thought himself above us, untouchable. He thought his numbers would give him the power to conquer Svartennos. Now he is missing his sword-hand, and I am here. Even your famous Tyrennis Castaval could not stop me."

"Why did you request this parlay, my lady?" Bastet asked, shaking his head.

"I called you here so that I could ask you to advise your queen to surrender the city. If she does this, anyone who wishes will be allowed to pass through the gates unharmed. I swear it by the many gods, and I am not a liar."

"My, lady, I think we both know that is not going to happen."

"You have no chance. The gods have shown me your city will fall. They showed me in a dream, my lord. We will break your gates; we will swarm over your walls." Her eyes were wide and unblinking. She hoped she looked at least a little mad.

Bastet raised an eyebrow. He could not hide his amusement. "Well, my lady. We will see."

"You will fall before me, Bastet of House Saleth. I am the reaper of the north, the flower whose thorns bring death. I am Marilia Sandara, Chrysathamere Reborn."

"I think this parlay is at an end; we have nothing more to say to each other." Bastet did not bother to hide his contempt. He wheeled his horse around.

Let him think me mad, Marilia thought. *Let him think me an arrogant fool who just got lucky once. An easy foe to defeat.* It pained her to watch him ride away, smirking, to know how little he must think of her, but she took comfort in the knowledge that, if all went to plan, it was he who would soon be proved the fool.

If he thought she meant to smash the city's gates and storm over its walls, maybe his men would be less likely to notice when she finally did make her entrance through other means entirely.

"Did you say it? All of it?" Camilline asked Marilia when she was back inside the camp.

"I did. I was kind of worried it was a little much. *The flower whose thorns bring death?*"

"Well, I think it's brilliant. Brilliantly tasteless. Just the sort of thing an inexperienced young woman with her head swollen from a recent, lucky victory would say."

"I suppose." Marilia chewed her lip, glancing back the way she'd come. *The plan will work,* she told herself. Why wouldn't it? All the strategoi agreed it was clever. Still, standing here, facing down the walls of the second-greatest city in the known world, it was hard not to feel a little nervous.

Camilline sensed her anxiety. "Come on," she said, putting a hand on Marilia's shoulder. "You look like you need a ride. It will clear your head."

Marilia and Camilline mounted up. Annuweth and four other knights of the Flower Company went with them. Even though a scouting force under Aexiel had recently scoured the area and assured her there were no enemies within riding distance, it was always better to be safe.

They rode without speaking; the howling of the wind would have made speech difficult, in any case. It cut eddies through the sparse grass and across the surface of the sand beneath, tracing patterns with the deftness of a master water-script painter's brush. It was swift enough to banish at least some of the sun's blistering heat, and for that Marilia was grateful.

They followed the line of the hills north and west away from the camp, up towards a series of bluffs where the grass began to thin. Their hooves crunched on gravel; small lizards scuttled for cover as they passed. Ahead, red rock cliffs rose up to embrace the afternoon sun, throwing welcome shade out towards them.

Camilline raised a hand to shield her eyes, squinting. "Is that…a house?"

Ahead, a cave was set into the sheer red stone of the cliffs. Built across the entrance of the cave was a canvas curtain to keep out the wind. In front of the curtain, planted in the soil beneath the shade of the cliff wall, was a crop of jala trees, purple-red fruits glistening on their branches.

"Some Tyracians live in caves in the sides of cliffs like these," Marilia explained. It was something One-Eye had told her, long ago.

"They make their living growing and selling jala fruits."

Camilline wiped some dust from her brow, shifting in the saddle; the back of her neck glistened with sweat. "A jala suit sounds pretty appealing right now, actually. Think they'd sell to us?"

"I think we can afford a few fruits," Marilia grinned.

They dismounted, tethering their horses to one of the trees, making their way on foot towards the entrance. As she pulled aside the soiled curtain, Marilia's grin froze and then faded. From somewhere in the depths of the darkened room came the sound of weeping.

It took her eyes a few seconds to adjust to the light. When they did, she saw four figures. The first was a man, who lay unconscious on his back on a cot against the far wall, his chest rising and falling shallowly, his face swathed in makeshift bandages.

Hugging the far wall of the dwelling was a young woman in her early twenties. She was weeping; the source of the sound Marilia had heard upon entering the dwelling. Her eyes were swollen, and she looked at Marilia and her knights with the kind of pure terror Marilia had once seen in a yoba in the moments between the cut of the knife across its throat and the time it took its ichor to bleed out. As Marilia took another step forward, the young woman turned and fled behind a second curtain.

It was the look on the other girl's face that haunted her, though.

She must have been Marilia's own age, or close to it. She lay on her side on a cot tucked against the far wall beside her father and stared blankly at Marilia and her knights. Although Marilia marked a flicker of fear on her face; it was nothing but a feeble stir. It seemed as if shutters had snapped shut across the girl's eyes.

The fourth figure, a woman in a worn and tattered dress, rose from her place by the girl's bedside. She gave an anguished wail that sent

Marilia stumbling back a pace. She moved to intercept them, limping with each step.

"No. Please, lord, no. I'm begging ye." She went down on her knees. Her voice carried the thick accent of rural Tyrace; it was worn and harsh, the sound of a sword being dragged across gravel. "My girls've suffered enough, by all the gods. No more, my lord. Please."

The woman had been beautiful once; Marilia could tell that much even through the swelling on her cheeks and the mottled bruises that marred her brow. Age and the harshness of the sun and wind and the injuries she had sustained had weathered her.

Marilia held up her hands. "We mean you no harm," she said.

The Tyracian woman blinked, her head jerking back in shock. "Ye're a woman."

"Yes."

"By the gods. Ye're *that* woman. The one we heard tell of in the market. The woman Horselord."

"Yes."

"They took everything there was, already. There's nothing left, I can swear to it. Please, don't hurt us no more."

"I told you, we mean no harm. We only came to trade…who took everything? What happened?" Marilia was afraid she didn't want to know the answer. Or rather, afraid that she already did.

"What happened? Ye can ask that?" The woman began to cry, her shoulders shaking, her tears cutting a path through the coat of dust on her cheeks. "They were knights like you, with swords, dressed all in dark red. They took our food…beat my husband when he tried to stop them. They hurt my daughters. They all took turns and when I tried to stop them…" she gestured at her battered face.

"You're hurt," Camilline said, her brow furrowed. "You need a

392

physick."

"There innit no physick would see us, lady. They're all in Tyracium."

"We can have one sent," Marilia said.

The woman swallowed, choking back another sob. She looked at Marilia doubtfully, as if she were something unaccountable; a mirage that might disappear—or transform into something terrible. "Thank you, lady. It would be a kindness."

Marilia turned away, her stomach lurching, squeezing her eyes shut until the illness passed. She motioned Annuweth and the other knights away.

"My lady..." one of the knights hesitated. "You wish us to leave you alone with...?"

"They're just jala farmers," Marilia snapped. "Do you really think I'm in danger?"

"Do as she says," Annuweth said.

The knights retreated beyond the curtain. Marilia faced the Tyracian woman, her heart pounding in her chest. She was afraid to look into the woman's eyes; frightened of the judgment she might see there. It frightened her almost as much as her charge down Chrysathamere Pass.

She fought to keep her voice steady. "The man who was leading them...was he tall? With a short beard?" She asked, even though she didn't really want to know the answer.

"Yes," the Tyracian woman whispered. "They called him Aexiel."

The words were like a punch to the gut. She had put Aexiel in charge of scouting the area—who better to brave the Tyracian wilds than the heroic knight who had cut off Tyrennis Nomeratsu's hand and carried Zeviel Espeleos back from the fray?

She had trusted him.

It was a mistake that had shattered this family.

"That piece of shit," Camilline cursed.

Marilia looked past the Tyracian woman, turning her gaze towards the girl on the cot. She wanted more than anything to turn away, to run from the cave, to climb back on her horse and ride away as far and as fast as she could. Instead, she forced herself to walk to the girl's side and kneel. The Tyracian girl watched her with those same empty eyes. She stirred feebly; her lips were bloodless. There was something wrong with her, something that went beyond the horror Aexiel's men had inflicted. When Marilia reached to take her hand, she saw what it was—the girl's forearms were swathed in bandages.

"What happened?" she asked quietly.

It was the mother who answered. "She did it herself, lady. With a kitchen knife—before I stopped her."

Marilia swallowed. She looked into the other woman's eyes. They were like a tunnel, carrying her into the past. For a moment, she was a little girl again, standing in the dark warmth of Oba'al's quarters. Listening to the drumming of the rain.

The dry air clawed her throat; it took Marilia a moment to find her voice. "I am so sorry," she whispered. "I never meant this to happen. I swear. What's your name?"

For a moment, Marilia thought the girl would not answer. Then—"Sylveetha."

"You have to live, Sylveetha. Promise me."

The girl said nothing.

"It's not you who deserves to be punished, all right?" Marilia's voice shook.

"There's a ghoul in me," the girl breathed. "The spirits won't speak to me anymore."

"That's not true. Please, Sylveetha. The spirits are with you. They're watching over you right now. They want you to live, all right?"

Sylveetha closed her eyes. After a few seconds, she nodded.

"I'll make you a promise, too," Marilia said. "I swear by the spirits that the ones who did this to you and your family will pay."

She stumbled away from the cave entrance and climbed back into the saddle.

She felt as if someone had lit a fire in her skull; it was as if she and the sand she walked on and the dry air she breathed were all one and the same; as if her spirit were a stick of incense someone had lit, the flame burning through her, and now she was drawing down to her last, smoldering remains.

"Aexiel," she spat the name as if it was poison.

"Aexiel," Annuweth heard the name and cursed. "Damn it. Of course it had to be *him*."

"He'll *pay*."

Her anger grew hotter with each beat of her horse's hooves, each lungful of desert air.

Marilia had given them the impossible; she had saved Svartennos, and if her plan worked, she would have delivered Tyracium itself. And in return, she had asked only one favor—an act of mercy of which even a child should have been capable.

Aexiel Hand-Taker. Captain Aexiel, the Hero of the Charge. Except he was no hero, after all; a hero wouldn't have done what he did. He wasn't even worthy to be called a knight.

She remembered what it had felt like watching her brother fold under the blows of Tyrennis Castaval's wooden sword. The breathtaking ease with which he'd been willing to beat Annuweth into the dirt, to destroy both their lives—as if they were nothing, because to him they were. Just two bastard children sprung from a painted lady.

Aexiel was, it turned out, just another Castaval. What were the lives of Tyracian peasants to a hero of Svartennos?

"Marilia…what are you going to do?" Annuweth's voice, from beside her.

"I don't know. What does it matter? He deserves anything…to die, even. He's *done* with this army."

"Marilia, just be careful…he's a war hero."

"I don't care who he is."

"The men will care."

"And who gives one piss what they think?" Camilline said hotly. "He disobeyed a direct order, didn't he?"

"All I'm saying…"

Marilia wheeled on him, turning so quickly in the saddle that she felt a stab of pain in her hip. "What *are* you suggesting, exactly? That I just forget this?" She couldn't; she had given her oath to the girl in the cave.

"No. Of course not. I'm just saying you should wait. Don't just ride up and confront him, not like this. We should think it through."

Marilia was finding it hard to think. The image of the Tyracian girl's dead eyes was seared into her mind's eye; when she closed her eyes, she could see them staring back at her, like two flat chips of midnight stone.

"Just leave her be," Camilline said tersely. "You don't understand, Annuweth."

"On the contrary," Annuweth said defensively. "I *do* understand—I understand what we're up against. Just the army of Tyrace's most dangerous tyrennis and a bunch of angry strategoi who are starting to question the word of a bastard girl from Tyrace who says she hears voices from the gods. Do *you* understand, Camilline?"

Marilia squeezed her eyes shut, the grit caught beneath her eyelids making them burn. Though she hated to admit it, she knew that Annuweth was right; she couldn't face Aexiel now. She wasn't ready.

Control at all times. One of Neravan Vergana's maxims. *Don't make a spectacle.* One of Karthtag-Kal's. When she faced him, she had to be in control—the general she was, not the girl that she had been.

"Enough," she said, as Camilline opened her mouth to argue. "He's right, Camilline. We won't go to him now. We'll find the physick first."

She spurred her horse ahead, faster, the wind tearing at her ears, drowning out whatever else Annuweth might have said. *Camilline always tried to outrun her horrors, her dark memories. Very well, then; let's see if it works.* Faster, faster, speeding down a final hill towards the edge of the camp. She tugged on the reins, slowing her horse's mad gallop, breathing deep to slow the frantic pace of her heart.

Her breath caught in her chest as she saw the colors of the tents— scarlet and gold. Leondos' colors.

Captain Aexiel...he's Leondos' man.

She jerked on the reins again, trying to turn her horse away, to come at the camp from a different angle.

That was when she saw them.

There were six of them in a circle near the edge of the camp, lounging in the shade of a tent. A blanket was spread on the grass between them. On the blanket was a feast fit for a hot desert day—at least two dozen freshly-picked jala fruits. The stems of those they'd already eaten lay scattered on the earth; the knights' lips were still stained purple with their juice.

They were eating what they had stolen from the Tyracian family, and they were *laughing*.

Marilia's chest went cold.

Annuweth saw them, too. "Marilia…" he said.

She swung down from the saddle; heard the muted thumps as her knights hit the ground behind her. A river was roaring in her ears; whatever control she'd imposed was gone. She couldn't have stopped even if she'd wanted to.

Whatever jest had just been told must have been especially amusing; the smile still hovered on Aexiel's purpled lips as she approached, clasping his right hand to his left shoulder in a crisp salute. "Lady Chrysathamere."

When she spoke, her voice was raw, like an exposed wound. "I gave you simple orders. But even that was too much for you; you disobeyed me anyway. I guess the great Captain Aexiel, Hand-Taker, can do whatever he wants, take whatever he wants. Is that it?"

Aexiel blinked. He took a step back

"You and your men forced yourself on two Tyracian girls and beat their mother and father when they tried to stop you. Do you deny it?"

His eyes strayed briefly to the men around him. In his hesitation, Marilia found her confirmation—as if she'd needed one.

"You're not fit to be my captain," she spat. "You're not fit to be a knight."

One of Aexiel's men bristled; he rose to his feet. A couple others glowered at her. But she still had Annuweth and the knights of the Flower Company behind her, and Septakim was nearby; he had seen her enter the camp and come to take his place at her side.

"You weren't there, general," Aexiel's knight said churlishly. "Those heretic girls…they practically threw themselves on us."

Aexiel threw the man a warning glance. "Phraekos…"

"Really?" Marilia shook her head. "Lies now, on top of everything

398

else? Sixty lashes for all of you."

"Sixty lashes?" Aexiel's brows narrowed. Thirty lashes a man might bear and walk away, though they'd pain him; sixty and he'd have to crawl, or lean on his friends to carry him. "You'd shed your own men's blood on account of some meat-eater girls? You'd *flog* me?"

She met his eyes. What she saw there was like a mirror, reflecting the white heat of her own fury back at her, stronger than before.

Anger. Not shame; not guilt.

Which meant even now, he didn't regret what he'd done.

He only regretted that she'd caught him.

"No; not you, Captain. You get the Mark of Akeleos."

Aexiel drew back as if struck. From behind her, Marilia heard a sharp intake of breath.

The Mark of Akeleos—a mark that had been given to those Svartennans who turned on the son of Svartana to join Svartennos' Valdruk enemies—two cuts across the brow, angled to form a V. It was a mark of dishonor, one saved for those whose transgressions had put them beyond redemption.

As soon as she spoke the words, she felt a tremor, a premonition. Even lost in the depths of her anger as she was, she could recognize that she'd crossed a line; there was no crossing back. The hairs rose along the back of her neck. She saw the wrath on Aexiel's face—a wrath equal to her own—and understood that she had made a mistake. Annuweth had given a warning—but it was too late.

Aexiel would never let her humiliate him, not for lying with heretic girls. He was a knight of Svartennos, and if there was one thing he didn't lack for, it was pride.

She glanced around. A ring was beginning to form around them—curious onlookers drawn by the sound of raised voices, more arriving every second, gathering like razorfish around a shipwreck. Lured by the spectacle.

She tried to backpedal. "Or, if not the mark, some punishment befitting what you've done…"

"You wouldn't be here if not for me," Aexiel spat at her feet. "I was the one who carried Zeviel Espeleos back. If not for me, he never would have spoken to the Elders, and you'd be back on Svartennos lighting candles. Where you belong." His voice rose, loud enough for all to hear. "The rumors were right, I guess. You're no Chrysathamere Reborn. There's too much heretic blood in you." His hand went to the hilt of his sword. Two of his knights reached for theirs, as well, but he shook his head. Proud, defiant, the picture of Svartennan courage. "No; no one needs to die for me. I'll see you later in the House of White Sands. I challenge you, Marilia Sandara." He drew his sword.

"No knight may challenge his commander," Septakim shook his head. "You know that."

"Then I challenge you, Septakim of the Dragonknights. If you're man enough to stand for her."

His lips drawn into a thin line, Septakim stepped forward. "Captain Aexiel, you have disobeyed your general and now you have betrayed her authority. This isn't a duel. It's an execution. And I…I am very sorry it had to end this way."

Aexiel didn't answer; or, rather, he answered with his sword. A great leap bridged the distance between him and Septakim; Septakim's sword rasped against his as the Dragonknight drew it from its sheath, deflecting the cut. He crouched and went sideways, evading the second—Aexiel's blade lightly brushed the crest of his helmet. Marilia watched, paralyzed. It was the second time she'd had to watch two men duel to the death in front of her.

This isn't what I wanted. None of this was what I wanted.

Well, girl. She could almost picture Queen Svartana shaking her celestial head. *This is what you've got.*

Septakim twisted at the hips, his feet quick-stepping sideways to evade another blow. He moved with the same speed that had left her wheezing at the end of his wooden sword in the Elders' sparring ring; he was, after all, a Dragonknight. Septakim's blade flashed across, angled downwards, swift enough to cut the air, to make the sky bleed. Aexiel's head landed in the sand.

Marilia stared at it. She felt light-headed. She took a tottering step back. The knights and footmen standing nearby began to murmur, a ripple radiating out through the camp like the cracks in the ground left behind by an earthquake—and at the center, she and Aexiel. The murmurs grew louder.

Aexiel's knights looked murderous. Yet they obeyed their captain's final command; none drew swords or moved to stop her as—with numb, trembling fingers—she motioned her knights forward to take them into custody.

The ghoul inside her had fled, along with what was left of her rage. She tasted bile at the back of her mouth.

"I…" she said, feeling like she had to say something—they were all staring at her, wide-eyed. "He…" she could not find her voice; the dust had clogged her throat. *Speak, damn you. You have to say something.* "These men disobeyed a direct command. There is a penalty for mutiny—even for a man like Aexiel."

Septakim's voice, near her ear. "My lady. No need to stay. I'll handle things here. I'll bring these other men to the whipping post once this has died down."

Annuweth's arm touched her shoulder, guiding her away. Dazed, she followed him back towards her tent, her knights moving with her, forcing a path through the crowd.

The crowd began to shout as Marilia made her way back to the tent. Men pushed at each other; bared teeth flashed like daggers in the evening light.

Marilia heard curses, cries; the words *Chrysathamere* and *Aexiel* echoed through the camp, equally loud. Men of the Flower Company and men wearing Leondos' colors snarled at each other.

She made her way into her tent and collapsed on a cushion. Her hand was shaking so badly that she could barely take the cup of water that Camilline offered her. The clamor outside grew louder.

Her knights slipped outside; she, Annuweth and Camilline were alone.

"Well done," Annuweth snapped. "Right in the middle of the camp, where everyone could see. You even gave him the chance to make a little speech."

"That's not fair," Camilline said tersely.

Marilia dug her fingers into her scalp. *Stop*, she begged silently. *Please, just stop.* She didn't want to hear it now, not with the shouts of the men outside still echoing in her ears. She needed him on her side— couldn't he see that?

"Could it really have gone any worse?" he asked. "Because I'm trying to think of how, and I can't. I tried to stop you, but you couldn't *listen* to me, could you? No; you always know what's best."

"That wasn't what I meant to happen," Marilia said. Another tremor shook her hands as she looked down at the ground. "I made a mistake."

"Maybe you should leave," Camilline said, facing Annuweth.

"You think so?"

"She's your general, isn't she? Just because you're her brother doesn't give you the right…"

"And what about your *right?*" he shot back, almost yelling. "If she wants me to leave, she can tell me herself." He rounded on Marilia. "Or can't you? Tell me, sister, how do you think your army is going to go on believing all that nonsense about your visions, about you being chosen by the gods, if you let your dead husband's sister make your decisions for you?"

Marilia sprang to her feet. She glared at him, feeling as if daggers were jabbing into her lungs, her anger back, and so intensely that each breath was painful. "What is *wrong* with you?"

"Nothing. What's wrong with *you?* It's a wonder they've believed your little trick this long already."

"My little trick?" she repeated. "What does that mean?"

"What? Isn't that what this is? You told me how it went—you went to the Elders, failed some tests, told Zeviel Espeleos the gods sent you a vision, and next thing you know here we are." He squinted at her. "Unless…you can't possibly believe it, can you? By the spirits—you think you're actually Svartana Reborn?" He gave a hollow laugh.

What was left of her temper snapped. She hurled the cup of water against the wall of the tent, where it left a dark stain, like blood. Her heart was beating fast in her chest, each beat, each breath, sending a hot pain like splintered lightning through her ribs. "Doesn't it seem a strange coincidence to you that I should be born to two fathers who helped save Svartennos?" she demanded. "That I should be married to a man on the only island in the empire with a prophecy about a warrior-queen?"

"So what is this, then?" he spread his arms. "This war, all just one great game of Sharavayn? A chance the gods gave you to show the world how clever you are? Well, sister, you're not so clever today."

"Still cleverer than you," she spat, wanting to hurt him at least half as much as he'd hurt her. "I think now I understand. Remember what you said to me, all those years ago? Us against the world?" She raised her arms. "It was all right, it was *us against the world* so long as I knew my place. As long as you were on top, the *golden child* and I was just your shadow. But now all that's changed, and you can't stand it. I brought us to King Damar's doorstep. I beat Tyrennis Nomeratsu, I saved Daevium so that they could come rescue us in the Bay. What are you? Just a Dragonknight who lost his commander and his men."

He flinched as if she's struck him across the face. He reached up to his shoulder, where his captain's insignia was bound across his pauldron, a black banner with a blue flower in its center. He tugged at the knot; the sash unwound. He dropped it on the floor at her feet. "Best of fortune to you, Lady Chrysathamere," he said, and spat. He turned and walked towards the entrance.

She felt as if a hot fist were slowly squeezing its way up her throat. "Go, then!" she yelled. "I don't need you. I never did."

He pulled aside the tent flap. Outside, the sun set behind the walls of Tyracium. The sky turned suddenly dark, the light slipping away like a timid child hiding her face behind her hands.

Chapter Thirty-Three

For seven more days, the armies of Svartennos and Antarenne lay camped before the walls of Tyracium. The shovels worked night and day, tearing clumps out of the earth, carving a channel nearly as deep as a man was tall and almost a quarter-mile long.

To the northwest, Castaval's reinforcements from the Neck of Dane approached. To the east, the Kangrits finally arrived and set up camp, waiting for Castaval's forces to arrive so that they could close the circle and entrap the Navessean army from all sides.

The mood in the camp had changed. There were many who were still fervent believers, the Flower Company foremost among them; men who never wavered in their support for the woman who had won them the Pass and brought them this far. Those men still painted blue flowers on their pauldrons right beside the colors of their houses.

But others saw things differently. Lady Chrysathamere had executed Captain Aexiel. And all over two Tyracian girls—two heretics who may or may not have been painted ladies...when it came to heretics, the distinction hardly mattered. The way Tyracians were, could Aexiel even be blamed for not knowing the difference?

Rumors that had first surfaced days ago, when the army had lain trapped in the mouth of the River Ob, began to make the rounds again.

Maybe the prophecy was over. Maybe Chrysathamere Reborn's work was already done. She was not suited for this last part of the war; her heart was too soft when it came to the meat-eaters, of whose number, let it not be forgotten, she had once been a part.

There were other rumors, too. No one knew exactly where they came from. One person heard it from another, who heard it from another...

The rumors were these, in order of most credible to least:

That the heretics who had raised Lady Sandara as a child had somehow worked curses on her in an attempt to sabotage the Navessean army; they had perverted her spirit and turned her against her own people.

That Marilia had been seen making offerings to the Horse God in the privacy of her tent as well as to the proper gods of Navessea.

That it was Commander Andreas, and not Marilia, who had come up with the plan to take Tyracium, and she had merely taken the credit. He had allowed her to do this only because Marilia had threatened to send him away to Dane unless he cooperated with her.

And the most far-fetched of all, but not without some who gave it credence: that the true reason for Aexiel's punishment was that he and Marilia had been secret lovers, and when she had found him with another woman, she had lost her head...and then he had lost his.

When Marilia dined with the strategoi of Svartennos—talking of reports from the north and the state of the siege—she sensed something hard and bitter in their stares that hadn't been there before. Laekos still seemed sympathetic, but the others...the strategos of House Espeleos was unreadable. Aerael had always been cold. Antiriel had openly doubted her. Leondos...she had taken the life of his best captain.

Four days later, a report came to her, information that was both danger and opportunity; the digging had been delayed by rough terrain, and it appeared likely that Tyrennis Castaval's forces would reach their camp before they could take Tyracium.

To prevent this, Marilia's only recourse was to send out a large force of men to block Castaval at a nearby pass, to harry and slow his army long enough for her own to complete its work. She decided to send out Leondos' men.

"Some of the strategoi and captains may see that as an affront," Septakim warned. "Leondos is well-respected...a veteran of several campaigns against the Valdruk pirates and a hero of the war with Kanadrak."

"Exactly why he's the perfect choice. He's our best commander. He can handle Tyrennis Castaval."

"It's just that...things being as they are, if you send him away, it might be taken to mean that you no longer trust him."

"I *don't* trust him. Two captains from Antarenne overheard some of Leondos' muttering about me."

Septakim's brow furrowed. "Threats?"

"I don't know. They couldn't hear the words. Just rumors, maybe, but..."

"I have to doubt Leondos would act against you, my lady. He swore to follow you. He may be angry, but he's traditional Svartennan through and through...not the type to break an oath."

"Are you sure?" She ran her hand through her hair. "I'm not."

"Well...I suppose one can never be sure," Septakim acknowledged. "Like you yourself said—things aren't the way they have been."

"I'm sorry you had to kill Aexiel."

"Well. I'm a Dragonknight." He gave a helpless shrug. "These things happen."

"I'm not sending him away because I don't trust him, I'm sending him away because I need by best strategos to stop Castaval." It was, she thought, at least half-true.

The following day, Leondos marched away with three thousand

men behind him, more than a third of the Svartennan forces. Those left behind worked faster, digging from sun-rise to sun-down.

She couldn't help but feel that whether or not her suspicions about Leondos were true, she'd lost either way. The Tiger of Svartennos had always been a strong, steady, stalwart presence at her war council. A bastion of imperturbable strength even in the most turbulent times. Now, either he'd lost his faith in her, or she had lost hers in him, or both.

How could that be measured as anything but a defeat?

I shouldn't have confronted Aexiel, Marilia thought as she lay on her cot in her tent, struggling to fall asleep. *Annuweth was right; I could have found another way. I could have punished him and kept my oath without making him a martyr. If there was one thing he never deserved to be, it's a martyr.*

Camilline offered what comfort she could. Since Marilia was the only other woman in the army—besides the comfort women, whose pavilion was *not* a place suitable for Lady Paetia—Camilline shared Marilia's tent. Even though Marilia knew that Camilline was telling her what she wanted to hear, it did help to hear it. Camilline was the only one besides Marilia who had been with her when she'd spoken to Sylveetha inside the jala-farmers' cave, and so the only one who fully understood her.

"Aexiel was the one who insisted he had to die," Camilline pointed out. "What did *you* do, actually? If you stop and think about it? You wanted to mark him with dishonor. Well; as far as I can tell, you weren't really adding anything—just making more visible what was already there. He dishonored himself."

"He was right about one thing—he made me what I am, by rescuing Zev during the battle."

"All that would never have been necessary if the Elders had listened to you in the first place."

"What if I wasn't meant for this?" A sliver of doubt had entered her the moment Aexiel had died, and the wound it had made had festered and grown along with the rumors in the camp.

"Then you wouldn't standing be here right now. Go on, step outside; you could shoot an arrow and almost hit Tyracium's walls from here."

"All I know for certain is this—once they all loved me. Now they do not."

"Now *some* do not," Camilline corrected. "Most do, assuming Septakim's to be believed. And once the city falls...once you deliver them the *war*...the rest will come around. They will forget everything else."

On Svartennos, she'd pushed Camilline away. Now, at least, Camilline was back at her side.

But in return, she had lost Leondos.

She'd lost the love of a significant portion of her army.

She'd lost Annuweth.

And then, only one day after Leondos' departure, she lost Camilline, too. She entered her tent for supper to find the other woman on her feet, her face drawn, a letter clutched in her hand. As soon as she saw Camilline's face, she knew.

"Marilia...I'm sorry...it's my mother." Camilline tugged at her hair, the way she often did when she was upset. "She's sick. Some kind of fever. The physicks aren't sure if she'll make it."

"Oh, by the spirits. I'm so sorry, Camilline."

Camilline bit her lip. She looked anguished. "This isn't what I wanted—leaving now, of all times...but Marilia, she's the only close family I have left."

"You should go to her," Marilia said, hollowly. "Of course; you must." She reached out and took Camilline's hands. "Please, don't feel guilty," she said, telling Camilline the same thing Camilline had been telling her for the last several days. "I mean it. Not a trace. I'll be all right without you."

Inside, she felt like a galley in a storm, the last of its moorings cut away. What lay ahead was the gray embrace of a sea she didn't feel ready for. But she knew she couldn't let Camilline see that—it would only make her feel worse, and Camilline had suffered enough. She forced a smile. "I do know a thing or two about strategy, after all."

"Thanks for understanding," Camilline said, her voice thick with emotion.

They spent one last night together, sheltered from the cold of the desert beneath the awning of Marilia's tent, watching the canvas ripple in the wind. There was so much Marilia wanted to say, but once again, she was afraid to speak the words.

The following morning, Camilline made ready to set off; four knights of the Flower Company would accompany her back north. She had traveled light; packing didn't take long. When she was finished, her horse saddled outside, she faced Marilia just inside the entrance of the tent.

"I'll light candles for your mother," Marilia promised.

"I'll light them for you and all the rest here. But I'm sure you won't need it."

Marilia breathed in Camilline's warmth. Their faces were close enough that their breath met between them like two spirits embracing. Desperate as she felt, Marilia almost kissed Camilline's lips; instead, at the last moment, she turned her head and kissed Camilline's cheek instead.

Coward, she scolded herself. But after what had happened with Aexiel, her confidence had been deeply shaken; the sense of daring that had driven her to attack Tyracium was nowhere to be found.

"This isn't goodbye," Camilline assured her. "I'll see you soon, on Svartennos."

Wordlessly, Marilia nodded.

Camilline mounted her horse and rode away, casting one last, regretful glance over her shoulder.

Marilia shivered, wrapping her arms around herself despite the desert's heat. Even though she was still surrounded by thousands of Svartennans, all ready to fight at her command, she couldn't help but feel alone.

Two days later, the trench was ready.

Marilia spent the time following Camilline's departure planning the final attack, hunched over a map of the city. Looking forward was preferable to looking back.

Take the city, show them a victory, and you'll win their hearts back. Camilline's advice.

The plan was this:

Most of her army would fake a massive attack against Tyracium's western gate.

A smaller, secret force would be waiting in the dark not far from the River Gate. This force would be spearheaded by the Flower Company and the other knights of House Paetos—her best and most trusted—and would be accompanied by the soldiers of Antarenne. Once the gate was opened, they would pour in.

As for who would actually open the gate for them…

That would be a third, even smaller party that would enter the city before either of the others.

And she would lead it.

Septakim had assured her that she ought to be the first one inside the walls—it was melodramatic, sure, but armies loved those sorts of dramatic gestures. There was a reason the Chroniclers' tomes were filled with them.

Her eyes lingered on the map. In one of those streets, not too far from the river-gate lay the pillow house that had once been her prison and her home. She traced its place on the map with her finger.

She closed her eyes, taking a deep breath. She wasn't the naïve girl she knew some thought her; she knew that when Tyracium fell, more than just Tyracian soldiers would die. The slaughter could not be confined only to those with swords in their hands, no matter what speech she'd made atop the riverbank. She'd never fully thought it could. She hadn't been able to control Aexiel; it would be foolish to imagine she could control everyone else. Despite her best efforts, there would be some few men struck with blood frenzy who would disobey her; now, after her public reckoning with Aexiel, that number would be greater than it might have been. She had herself to blame for that.

There was nothing more she could do to protect the innocent than what she'd already done. But she could protect her friends.

"Septakim?"

"Yes, my lady?"

"Send some knights to this spot. Someone you can trust. Make sure no one enters or leaves."

"What's there, my lady?" Septakim squinted at the map.

"A pillow house."

"A pillow house?" He paused. She saw a look of understanding cross his face. "Yes, my lady. I'll make sure it's done."

Her preparations finished, she drifted off into an uneasy sleep. Her dreams were filled with hushed voices, with chicayas that sang softly in the dark, a sound like spring rain falling, whispering lies into the night.

CHAPTER THIRTY-FOUR

The night air was cool, a stark contrast to the heat of the long desert days. The sky was cloudless, and the light of the stars piercing; it was as if the heavens were a thick blanket riddled with arrow-holes, through which the eyes of the gods stared down.

Marilia wore a cloak over her armor, black as the sky, and had painted her face black with mud from the river. She knelt with a score of other men, similarly garbed and painted. Together they waited in the reeds that lined the bank of the River Tyr.

By the western gate, a cry went up. She could hear the trumpets blaring. Her men were launching their assault, a diversion to draw away the city's defenders.

She waited. The water of the River Tyr was black as ink in the moonlight except where it trapped the starlight and shone with a cold silver glow.

The minutes slipped by. She stretched one leg, then the other. Beside her, Septakim tapped his fingers restlessly against the pommel of his sword.

To the north, another horn blew. Antiriel's men had been discovered attempting to sneak over the wall. That, too, was part of the plan.

A deception within a deception. Let your enemy believe he has seen your mind; upon finding one trick, he will not look for a second one.

She waited a few minutes more, her heart slamming in her chest, aware that with each breath men of Navessea were dying beneath the city's walls. "Let's go," she said.

Up ahead, the walls of the city were a blackness that vied with the blackness of the night sky. The stars began to wink out one by one as the walls rose up, battlements like teeth gnawing pieces out of the heavens.

There were five main gates that led into Tyrace, and a few smaller postern gates. All of those were well-defended.

But there were two other breaks in the city's mighty stone walls that *weren't* being watched—two metal grates through which flowed the River Tyr.

Normally, these grates would be underwater, inaccessible to any sort of assault.

That was why Marilia's men had worked tirelessly, digging a trench that led to a low, flat desert valley a quarter-mile away. When this trench was connected to the River Tyr, the effect was immediate and inevitable; the river's waters poured down into the valley, creating a lake where before there had been none.

The river itself shrank, leaving those metal grates exposed.

Marilia had chosen the southern grate for the simple fact that it was closer to the Tower and farther from the northern wall, the place she had chosen for her false attack.

It also happened to be the one she knew better, the one she'd touched as a child.

And that felt right to her. It felt *destined*.

The river had gone down, but it was still up to her thighs. It slowed her; made her clumsy. It reminded her of how she'd felt the first time she'd put the armor on.

She moved as swiftly as she dared. The river-bed was littered with smooth, mossy stones. Several times she stumbled. Once, she would have fallen, but one of her knights threw out his arm to catch her.

Luckily, the noise of her movements was drowned by the clamor of the battle to the west.

Her eyes scanned the battlements, looking for the glint of metal, for any sign of movement. But this portion of the wall seemed all but deserted.

Ahead was the metal grate she remembered. It was as wide as three men and tall enough that it could be traversed at a low crouch. She could see the traces of moss where the water had been before it had gone down, a long mark like the gash of an assassin's blade across a doomed man's throat. She could smell the musty dampness of wet stone, rusting iron, mud.

The grate was caked with flaking rust, the iron knotted with bumps like the back of a diseased man. She stopped before it and stepped aside. Two men stepped forward, carrying a vial of the concoction known as Daevish acid—that potent mixture formed from the venom of kwammakin bile and liquid aeder which, while not able to eat clean through these thick metal bars the way it had eaten through Ben Espeleos' coin all those years ago, would at least serve to weaken them. Her soldiers applied it to the top of each of the grate's bars, just below the point where they joined the wall. The mixture hissed and frothed.

Next came the ram, a thick wooden beam suspended in the air just above the water level. The ram's wheels churned in the mud of the river bed. The men pushing it grunted and strained. It squelched slowly forward until it was hidden beneath the shadow of Tyracium's wall.

They waited. Minutes slipped by. Then came a great cry from the northern wall. "Chrysathamere!" And a few seconds later, a crash of wood and yoba-shell as the shafts of spears were slammed against shields—just as arranged.

It was during that crash that they swung the ram forward, the head smashing into the iron bars, bending them inward.

A second cry followed the first. "Chrysathamere!" There was a second clamor of spears and swords against shields, and a second time the ram swung.

Marilia's breath came fast. With each second that passed, she grew more and more afraid that someone atop the wall would see them. But it was pure darkness they stood in, shrouded in their cloaks so that the light of the moon and stars did not catch on their armor or their blades. The defenders of Tyracium had other cares to occupy them; though a few sentries passed atop the wall above, they did not crane their necks and peer into the darkness below.

The grate gave way on the fourth blow.

Marilia stepped into the breach. The generals of Svartennos, after all, led from the front.

No arrows fell upon her; no cries of alarm greeted her entrance. It was almost anticlimactic in its simplicity. One moment she was outside the wall, the next she was inside it. As easy as stepping through the open door of a house.

She strode into the city and her men followed her, silent as dragons hunting in the grass. Water dripped from their cloaks and ran down their skin. It sloshed in Marilia's boots. As she stepped from the river its clammy touch followed her. She shivered despite herself.

"To the river-gate," she said.

The Tyracians guarding the river-gate barely had time to react before Marilia's men were upon them.

Mouths fell open. She saw naked terror in the Tyracians' eyes. Dark, glimmering with river-water, she and her men might have been dremmakin from the bottom of the sea. They had become the nightmares that mothers warned their children of.

Somehow, it felt to her as though in crossing beneath the wall of Tyracium she had crossed, too, the line between waking and dreaming. The wind on her skin and the water running down her face was worlds away—the flashing of the aeder swords was like the distant flickering of lightning over the desert. All of it remote, all of it only half-real. As she lashed out with her sword and saw a guard crumple before her even that felt distant, as if she had merely watched someone else's hands swing the blade.

Another Tyracian came at her from the side—she was saved by Septakim's training. Her mind might have been blank, but her body knew what to do, movements practiced so often they were second-nature, as instinctual as jerking her hand back from a hot flame. She pivoted, stepping back, angling her blade to deflect, then quick-stepped sideways, amazed by her own speed, the fluidity of her movements. She was a far cry from the girl who had fallen beneath Annuweth's wooden sword years ago, or the woman who had struggled to keep her footing during the battle in the Pass. The Tyracian moved his blade to parry but a twist of her wrist sent the tip of her sword around his guard, into the gap between his helmet and his breastplate—through his throat. He died and she stepped over him, relieved that she hadn't frozen in the killing moment, struck by how unexpectedly straight-forward it had all been.

Most of the Tyracians died quickly, any sounds they made lost in the greater sound of the struggle to the north. Mouths were stifled behind damp gloves; throats were gashed with aeder blades. Tyracians suffocated on the smell of wet leather and the thick, coppery warmth of their own spilled blood.

Her men took the dead Tyracians' armor. Some stayed at the gate to open it for her army; some, led by Dorokim, Andreas' giant lieutenant, made their way towards the Tower.

Marilia walked among them, her helmet off, unarmed, her hands bound with thick leather cords. Dorokim had his hand on her shoulder, his sword against the back of her neck. His bulk crowded close behind her, his size part of the image she was painting—the Lady Chrysathamere, small and helpless, nothing more than a girl who had tried to mix herself with forces beyond her control or understanding and paid the price.

She and Andreas had chosen Dorokim because the man himself had once been Tyracian—his father had served Andreas' back when Andreas the Elder had still been a lord of Tyrace. He had the right look to his face, the right accent, and a knowledge of the city that would lend credence to the lies he was about to tell.

When she had first come up with this part of her plan, she'd envisioned Annuweth in the role. But she had not spoken to Annuweth since that evening on the River Ob, had not seen him since the day Aexiel died.

"Who goes there?" one of Queen Dibella's guards called from the walls of the Tower's keep.

Dorokim gave the answer that was required—he was Captain Saleem Sothoryn, and he had *her* with him, the bitch herself, Marilia Sandara, she'd got herself captured trying to climb over the walls near the arena three streets down from Aldavere's pillow house. She tried to hide in the bath-house, the one near where they do the big yoba parade for the Solstice Festival—you know the one. Look; see for yourself, it's her. Go bring the commander.

And when Dibella's commander, Bastet of House Saleth, arrived and peered down at them, what he saw was Marilia, the very same arrogant woman who had dared to insult him a week before, mud-spattered, humbled, weeping, hands bound, surrounded by twenty men wearing the red-brown armor of the Tyracian watch.

In his eagerness, he opened the gates, glad to be the one to present this prize to the queen. No doubt he was already picturing the glory and commendations that would surely follow.

What he did not know was that Marilia's tears weren't tears of sorrow; Karthtag-Kal had all but cured her of that kind of weeping.

They were tears of relief; of victory.

The knights of the Flower Company were some of the best in Marilia's army; from among them, she had selected twenty of the very best warriors. They had the element of surprise entirely on their side. Marilia's nod was the signal; they drew and struck as one, and each one found his man. Then they struck again. And though the Tyracians had numbers on their side, they were confused and uncoordinated. They were soft silk, and the aeder blade of Marilia's best knights cut right through them.

Her knights pulled the drawbridge open and jammed its chains; Marilia ran to the battlements with a yoba-shell horn in her hand and blew three sharp notes on it—the signal for her army.

By the time the Tyracians had re-organized themselves enough to pose a threat, it was too late. Marilia's men were already at the Tower's gates, pouring in.

The Tower of Tyrace, the tallest building in the known world, the house of kings and queens, was about to be hers.

Marilia stood atop the gatehouse, watching her men battle their way across the courtyard. Tyracians rushed from the Tower, bows in their hands; several of the first Navesseans through the gates staggered or fell. But the rest pressed on, and the Tyracians were overwhelmed, swept backwards by the crush of men and smashed against the walls of their own stronghold. When the sea of men parted, they lay slumped and broken. The pools of blood spread and met in the depressed center of the keep's courtyard, forming a lake as dark as the surface of the River Tyr.

"Bitch!" Bastet of House Saleth was lumbering along the battlements towards her, howling in fury. "Face me, bitch! You treacherous snake!"

Marilia stepped from the gatehouse onto the battlement. Their eyes met.

"Throw down your swords!" Marilia yelled at him. "Surrender!"

With a strangled cry, he rushed her. He didn't get more than five strides. As he passed the stairs leading up to the battlements Dorokim swept into him from the side, ramming him with one heavy shoulder with enough force to send him flying over the ramparts. She looked over the side and saw him lying in the street, his head at an unnatural angle, his legs still twitching.

One of Marilia's knights staggered to her side; in his hand he held what she at first thought was a long spear. Then she realized it was a flagpole. Furled around the tip was a black banner with a bright blue flower in the center.

With a stroke of his sword the knight cut away the Tyracian banner and planted Marilia's in its place.

The knights in the courtyard cheered.

And in the space of silence between cheers, when the voices died away, Marilia heard an answering sound, one that made the hairs on the back of her neck stand on end.

It was the sound of the city screaming.

There had been screams, of course, ever since Marilia had entered the city—the cries of men dying, the sounds of battle joined. But these cries were different. There were the cries of women on the air, and...

Children, she realized. Somewhere ahead in the dark, children were screaming.

It was what she'd feared to hear—but worse. She had heard the screams above the sounds of battle. That meant it wasn't the work of just a couple knights stricken with blood frenzy. It was something worse—something wide-spread.

A slaughter.

She quickened her pace. Her boots, still damp from her trek through the river, sloshed with each step; she'd never had time to change them.

She and her knights forged ahead into the city, battling their way up narrow streets. There were still many Tyracian soldiers in the city, and their progress was slow.

Some of the streets Marilia recognized. Here was where she had once played at knights with Annuweth, Nyreese, and Damar; here was where her mother had comforted her after she'd watched the silvakim-tamer have his face mauled by his own pet. Up ahead was the square where the festival of painted yoba was held every summer solstice.

On either side, the shadowed windows of the houses hung like mournful eyes, watching as this last act of the war played out.

She exited an alley and found herself in one of Tyracium's great plazas. Ahead, maybe a few blocks away, Oba'al's Hill rose ahead of her, the rough edges of the hill like a darker ribbon cut from the darkness of the night.

All around, men of Svartennos were kicking down the doors of houses. She could hear the sound of splintering wood from within, the cries of families, louder now.

"What is happening here?" Marilia demanded, grabbing the arm of a footman. She squinted, saw that the mark on his shoulder bore the sigil of House Espeleos, and that three swords were pained beside it—the mark of a sergeant. "I gave orders that there was to be no butchery!"

The sergeant turned to face her. She saw his eyes widen as he realized who it was. "My lady," he stammered. "I...we thought you were dead..." He seemed at a loss for words.

"Stop them," she commanded, grabbing him by the shoulders.

"Forgive me, my lady. I will try."

She was already racing past him; she couldn't wait. She would stop them herself.

A fountain showing the rearing Horse God of Tyrace was situated towards the eastern end of the square. She ran to it, climbing atop the winged horse, shouting to be heard. "Remember the gods' command!" she cried. "Do not kill the innocent!"

"My lady!" Septakim shouted a warning. "My lady, mind the windows!"

Out of the corner of her eye she saw it, poking from the upper window of one of the houses that ringed the square; the point of an arrow, glittering like the tip of a beetle's pincer. Her breath caught.

There was a flash, a sudden blur of movement. The arrow struck her in the side of the head, ringing against her helmet. She fell, and the dark cobblestones of the street rushed up to meet her.

CHAPTER THIRTY-FIVE

Everything was noise, confusion. She came to and found Septakim and the sergeant crouching beside her, huddling over her in the shadow of the winged horse. All around, the night echoed with the sounds of misery, a ghoul's chorus. She struggled to her feet, only to fall back against the statue, dizzy.

"My lady," Septakim said, "you're not well..."

She ignored him. She stumbled to the door of the nearest house. On the floor lay a man and a woman, or rather, what had once been a man and a woman. Their flesh lay in ragged ribbons like the silk streamers that hung from the rafters in the pillow house. The floor was soft with their blood.

Outside, a couple ran past, then another, then a child. The people of the city, fleeing whatever fate Marilia's avengers had in store for them.

"When the men saw you fall, they lost their minds," the sergeant said. "I couldn't stop them."

"Are they all pillaging?" she asked sharply.

"My lady, I do not know. Surely not all, but...many are."

"I want to know how this started," she said. "I want to know what is happening in this city."

He bowed his head. "I will send out men, my lady. To find out what's happening."

"Then do it. Now!"

She turned from him, ran ahead to the next street, even as Septakim shouted at her to slow, to take care. "Order!" she cried. "Fall to order!"

But her body finally failed her; her head was still spinning, the world tilting dizzyingly. Her voice had grown hoarse. It cracked and faded to silence.

Order is, at times, a fragile thing. All it takes is the first kiss of chaos and the plunge begins.

The men of Svartennos, hearing the sounds of looting—the moans of women, the wailing of children and the crashing of wood and metal as houses were torn apart—began to feel the trembling, feverish madness that comes with the sacking of a city. It was a madness Marilia had hoped she could restrain through the fire of her vision and the force of her will. Through the power of prophecy and legend. And for a time, she had succeeded.

But now, in the night, surrounded by the smell of blood and the promise of swift vengeance, the tide began to turn. In the night, when all men look alike, it is easy for a man to tell himself that he may pass unnoticed. That the eyes of the gods are closed. That the horrors one does in the dark will vanish like the memory of a dream with the coming of the morning's light.

Clouds swept in from the east and covered the stars. Marilia stepped into an empty space beyond the sight of the gods.

Ahead, a group of soldiers had formed a ring around a boy who might have been twelve or thirteen years old. They laughed as they struck him, lazy backhanded blows that sent him bouncing back and forth. The boy made a mewling sound as his face softened and altered, as his ruined nose dripped blood. His eyes crossed; he would have fallen if two men had not seized him under the arms, holding him upright as their comrades continued to take their turns, the joints of their armor catching on his soft skin.

"Stop!" Marilia started towards them, but the knights were already moving on, their work finished.

Something slammed into her, throwing her sideways into the wall of the alley. She stumbled, looking wildly around. She saw nothing at first; then she thought to look down.

A girl—perhaps the younger sister of the doomed boy—stood not three paces away. She might have been ten or eleven, with long, straight hair and large eyes that reflected the moon's pale silver. Those eyes were fixed now on Marilia. A trickle of blood ran from one side of the girl's nose, where she had slammed into Marilia's armor; a red stripe marked the middle of Marilia's breastplate.

Marilia stared back, open-mouthed. The girl turned and fled from her towards the plaza. Too late, Marilia found her voice.

"Wait!" she called.

One of her knights—perhaps one of the sergeant's messengers— came thundering out of an adjoining street. A slight tug on the reins, a small adjustment of his course, was all it took to put him in line with the running girl.

Marilia closed her eyes. It took only an instant, the amount of time it takes for an executioner's sword to fall. She heard a rush in her ears, like the sound a river speeding over the edge of a waterfall, and something within her broke with a final, irrevocable tug.

She opened her eyes.

The girl was on her back, staring up at the sky. She was breathing fast, and with each breath Marilia heard a muffled sound like wind passing through wet silk. Marilia knelt beside her.

"It hurts," she coughed, and Marilia, leaning close, felt blood tickle her cheek. "It hurts."

Marilia stared down at her. There were no words that would have mattered. She took the girl's hand. She reached for her short-sword—at least she could try to end the girl's suffering. Her fingers were shaking so badly it took her three tries to get them around the hilt. She knew, deep down, she didn't have it in her to make the thrust.

The ribbon of the Tyracian girl's blood slid across the flagstones and wrapped tenderly around her, like a mother gathering her child in her arms.

The girl's head had fallen to one side; one eye, still open, was tilted up towards Marilia. It seemed to Marilia that as she watched, the girl's eye slowly filmed over, like a window pane on a cold night as a layer of frost crawls over it.

No need for the sword, then.

Marilia rose to her feet. The men in the alleyway had taken heed of her presence. They had stopped and were watching her uncertainly.

"Have you forgotten what you promised?" she yelled at them. "Is this what you've come to? Killing *children*?" She pointed to the dead girl, to the dead boy. "This is what cowards do."

That gave them pause. They seemed to draw back from her, ashamed. But even as she spoke, the cries continued to echo from the surrounding streets. The men before her exchanged glances—working it out in their heads—the illogic that was obvious enough even simple Svartennan peasants could grasp it. Marilia had said that the gods would grant them victory if they showed mercy—yet what more victory could they give? Tyracium was already finished.

"If you are loyal—if you fight for Svartennos—then stop this now," Marilia said.

She felt herself shaking. She knew she looked a far cry from the woman who had raised Queen Svartana's banner above Chrysathamere Pass.

"My lady." It was the sergeant of House Espeleos. He had returned. "My lady, as you ordered, I sent out men…"

"And what have you learned?"

"The stories are confused. Some say it was Commander Andreas who began it, my lady. His men started killing, taking what they would…and when the men of Svartennos saw, they followed. They say Andreas' men even…encouraged them."

"Encouraged them how?"

"They spoke taunts—they said that the men of Svartennos had left it to the soldiers of Antarenne to avenge them because they had grown too soft, cowed by a girl. They threw taunts until the battle fever took hold."

Not to put too fine a point on it, sister, but you haven't always been the best judge of character.

She pressed a hand to her brow, feeling a deep ache between her eyes, like a spike burrowing through her skull.

Annuweth had seen him for what he was.

"And where is Commander Andreas now?" *I will find him. I will kill him.* A part of her knew the thought was mad—he was a commander of Navessea, the governor's right-hand man—but another part of her didn't care.

"No one seems to know."

But Marilia felt a sudden, icy fear in the pit of her stomach. Her eyes traveled upward, to the slope of the hill beyond the plaza.

"The pillow house," she breathed. Then she was yelling the words. "All men, to me!" She sprinted as fast as she could towards Oba'al's

Hill.

She found One-Eye halfway up the slope. His was one of many fallen bodies that lay strewn across her path. She might have gone right past him—but several of the knights who went with her had torches to light the way, and the glow of one of the torches fell upon his face. She saw his dead eye, white like the moon.

He was leaning against the wall of a house, his feet resting in a puddle of water. His captain's cloak was shredded behind him, ruined tatters of red-brown cloth. He raised his head as she approached.

"Go on, then," he said in a hoarse, rasping voice. "Finish it; I'm halfway there already." And she realized that the puddle he sat in was not water but blood—his own.

She removed her helmet and crouched beside him.

He tilted his head back, offering his throat to her. She was close enough now to see where he was wounded; the blood ran from beneath his right arm, trickling down his side, beading on the plates of his armor like a gory morning dew. He had been stabbed in the armpit where there were no plates to protect him.

"One-Eye," she said.

He frowned at the sound of her voice. "Haven't been called that in years."

"I'm going to get a physick here," she promised. "I'm going to…"

"A woman," he muttered, his eyelids fluttering as he struggled to keep his eyes open. "A bloody girl. Now there's a fucking thing." He squinted at her face. She heard a sharp intake of breath. "Well, I must be dreaming. Marilia…girl, is that you?"

Mutely, she nodded.

"By the spirits," he said. "By the spirits, that's something, that is. Stroke of luck." He reached out and touched her hand with shaking fingers. "I heard it was you...a woman named Marilia, they said, leading the army, and I couldn't believe...but it really is you. That prefect who took you...wise man. Hope he appreciated what he found."

Marilia stared down at the face of the man who had been her friend, her mentor, her betrayer, her enemy. His hair was thinner and grayer; his face had more lines, but it was him. Once it had seemed that she would be swallowed up by him like a drop of water vanishing in the desert sun. Now, instead, he had been swallowed up by her.

She felt tears fill her eyes. They rolled down her cheeks and landed in the pool of blood between One-Eye's legs, making the reflected moonlight ripple. The clouds pulled back, and One-Eye raised his head to face the stars.

"I always thought you'd make it," he said. "And how you have, girl. Conqueror of cities. By the gods." He coughed, a wet sound like the one Zev had made as he lay in the grass, his time running out. "I just wanted to say...I'm sorry. I never wanted to hurt you. Sometimes, when you want to believe something…when every part of you wants to believe it…you can talk yourself into anything. You can ignore the truth when it's right in front of your face. You were never meant for me. But sometimes…sometimes the truth's not as welcome as the lies we tell ourselves to fill its place." His head lolled so that his chin touched his chest before it jerked upright again. "I'm fading," he said. "I won't last. If it's not too much trouble...I want you to do it. I think that would be right."

She nodded; he let go of her hand. She reached down and drew her short-sword.

"Here, girl." One-Eye tilted his head up again, indicating the space at the bottom of his throat. "Strike down, towards the heart. Strike deep. Make it quick."

Marilia stood over him. She took a deep breath, gripping the short-sword with both hands. She touched the tip of the blade to the hollow of One-Eye's throat.

For a moment she lost herself; Tyracium fell away around her. There was no city, no watching circle of Svartennan knights, nothing but her and One-Eye, a breath away from the completion of a cycle that had begun before she could even remember.

It was like pushing through thick silk. She felt his heat against her hands, through her leather gloves, the jerking of his body through the blade that joined them. But only for a moment; it was quick, just as he had wanted.

Her movements were automatic; she felt as if she'd stabbed something inside herself, too. She cleaned the blade, replaced it in the sheath at her hip.

He had betrayed her, had wanted to rape her, had upended her world. But he had also brought her to Karthtag-Kal—had saved her from Oba'al's pillow house. She had thought his passing would be something complicated, a storm of conflicting emotions. In the end, she discovered it was something more basic, and that when it came to emotions, she could only find one to put a name to—grief. A sensation of loss that was primal: the feeling of a little girl lost in the dark, watching one more piece of her past torn suddenly away without purpose or reason, swallowed by the fabric of the night.

CHAPTER THIRTY-SIX

The bodies of the knights she'd sent to protect the pillow house were heaped in the street. The men of Antarenne would say that the Tyracians had done it, and there were none who could say otherwise, though the neatness of many of their wounds was such that it seemed they had been taken completely by surprise.

The pillow house was full of men—Andreas' men. From inside came the same sounds that had echoed in the city's streets.

The Antarenne soldiers lounging outside the pillow house's doors looked quite taken aback by the sight of Marilia bearing down on them, nearly two hundred blue-armored knights—hastily gathered from the surrounding block—crowding the street behind her.

"My lady." One of the men clambered to his feet, spear in hand.

"I'm here to speak with Commander Andreas," she said, and made no move to slow. If he tried to stop her, she would kill him. She knew that beyond a doubt. He must have seen it on her face, because he did not try to stop her.

The common room's tables had been pushed to the corners of the room. Chairs were over-turned; pieces of paper lanterns and silk streamers lay in red ruins on the floor, mingling with the red blood that was gathering there.

Tangled in the fallen silk were the bodies.

Oba'al's strongman, a hole in his guts, broken sword still in his hand.

Tyreesha, her throat cut from ear to ear.

Raquella, huddled in a corner, her gaze dead and empty.

Saleema, still alive but not for long, crawling towards the door to the courtyard, trailing blood behind her.

Damar, sprawled over a table, pinned there by the short-sword someone had driven through his back and out the center of his chest.

And the children. Two young girls and a young boy who Marilia did not know—children of the painted ladies, born after she and Annuweth had left with Karthtag-Kal.

In the place where the minstrels had once played, Nyreese was splayed across a table, weeping as an Antarenne man grabbed at her thighs, forcing them apart.

She felt as though she were falling a great distance. She felt as though she were falling all the distance that there was to fall, and that she might never stop. She felt her knees hit the floor, felt a steadying hand on her shoulder, the only thing keeping her upright.

Tyreesha, Saleema, Damar, Raquella...

"Marilia!" Nyreese screamed.

"Nyreese." *Raquella, Tyreesha, Saleema, Damar...* The two women stared at each other, the walls of time and distance crumbling down.

She found her feet again. The distance between her and Nyreese was gone and her hands were on the soldier from Antarenne and her gauntlet was in his face, knocking him to the floor, scattering his teeth across the carpet.

Nyreese was tugging at Marilia's sleeve, her eyes wild. "He took my daughter," she said, pleading. "Please, he took my daughter...their leader. He's got her. She's just a baby, please, I beg you..."

Swords were drawn; her own, and those of her men. Those of Andreas' men. And then *he* entered, gliding down the staircase, still wearing his blood-spattered armor. She looked at his handsome, ordinary face and saw something that had not been there before—how had she missed it? It was as if a window had opened up and through it, she could see the true workings of his soul. And what she saw was *sickness*, something misplaced, something gone away.

What was misplaced was the mask he'd worn before.

Behind the mask was the Graver.

The Graver spoke. "My lady. Please refrain from drawing your sword on my men."

She walked to him and spat at his feet. Around her, men tensed. She didn't care. "You have no honor."

"That is a serious accusation," the Graver warned. "Before you say anything you might regret, perhaps you would care to step away from these men? These are words best had in private."

She didn't move. "You lied, right there in your own tent, you promised me..."

"What did I promise you?"

"That you would control your men!"

"Did I? I recall no such promise. Were there any witnesses, or do we have only your word for this promise? How convenient."

"You planned this. Right from the beginning."

"Planned what, my lady? My men simply got carried away. By the spirits, it's only a Tyracian pillow house...or did these people mean something to you?" She looked into his eyes and saw the truth; he knew. He had always known. Somehow, he had learned her secret.

She was shaking. "Let them go."

"You don't give me orders, my lady."

"I am your general. Livenneth's third lieutenant. If you disobey me, the emperor will..."

"Will what? He'll lightly reprimand me, most likely. I've been lightly reprimanded before. I've survived. My lady, simply put, no one cares about a few painted ladies and their bastards. No one but you." The last trace of friendliness had vanished from the Graver's voice. His smile was chilling. "Look at you. You think you can order things as you like, that in the span of days you can turn the world on its head. You think you can play at war, reaping glory but keeping your hands clean. The *arrogance* of it." He shook his head. "Here's some truth for you, my lady. The only one who commands is Zantos, gatekeeper of the fields of death. If you find the price of your victory too dear, perhaps you should have stayed on Svartennos."

Draw and strike him, cut him down, cut off his head. Her hand was on the hilt of her sword. But his men were close, and his own hand was at his side, ready, waiting for her to make the first move. "Let them go," she said again.

"This place was found by my men. The spoils are theirs, by right of conquest. My lady, you are intruding."

"Let them go or you will regret it."

"Threats now? What...you'll set your men against mine? We will have war in the streets of Tyracium, Navessean against Navessean? Undo all we have accomplished? Hand the war to the Tyracians? I think not."

"You will pay for this," she promised.

"Lady Sandara, please. Even if you gave the order, do you really think your men would take up arms against their own side in defense of heretics? Once, maybe...*maybe*...but that time is past."

"It was *you*," she said. "The rumors in the camp...all those camp-fire stories, those *lies* Septakim warned me about. It wasn't Leondos' men who began them, after all."

"Lies? Who says they're lies? Besides, it's not quite that simple, my lady," the Graver said. "Of course, me and mine played our part in wounding your reputation. But we were hardly alone. I must at least give credit to our most valuable ally."

"Aerael Dartimaos?"

"No. You." He dipped his head at her. "Lady Sandara, you've done a fine job turning your army against you. Killing Aexiel...a grave mistake. I'd guess that if you ordered your men against me right now, if you tried to have me killed over a few painted ladies like you did poor Aexiel, maybe a third of your own side would turn on you."

All she could hear, all she could see was *red*, red blood, red paper lanterns, red heat radiating through her head and heart, and the pain of it was all-consuming.

"Let me tell you what will happen now," the Graver said. "My men will finish reaping the spoils of their well-earned victory. A few weeks after that, we will all sail back to Ulvannis, and you will cry to your father and the emperor about how I *betrayed* you, and the emperor will have a stern word for me...but that is all. The Governor of Antarenne is my friend, you see—one of many—and in the end Vergana and everyone else will forget about this."

And then, from up the stairs behind him, there came the sound of a baby crying. An anguished wail, a cry that echoed in the silence, a raw, animal lament for the death and waste of it all.

"That's right," the Graver said. "Your friend's daughter. Still alive. I haven't touched her. My captain Drathyn was thinking to throw her from the window upstairs. He's a man of morbid appetites, Drathyn."

"Give her back."

The Graver took a step closer, so that their faces were only inches apart, so that she could see her own reflection in the flat, vacant surface of his eyes. "You want to save her? Save her mother and the rest of these people? There's a way...one way. I'll fight you for them. If you win, if you beat me, my men will walk away right now and sheath their swords...they will be meek as yoba. *My* men, you see, are disciplined." He winked at her. He raised his voice. "This I swear, so all can hear me. If the Lady Chrysathamere defeats me, this place, these people, are hers. She is to be left alone, in peace. That's an *order*." He lifted his arms, looking around at the assembled soldiers of Svartennos and Antarenne before at last settling his gaze on her. "How about it, Lady Chrysathamere? You against me. What is there to fear? The gods are on your side, are they not? Queen Svartana's strength inside you? How could you not triumph? Draw your sword and challenge me."

Marilia knew that this was what he had wanted, all along; she saw it in his face. To kill her, to strike down the daughter of the prefect—to have, at last, his revenge.

Marilla looked up at him. Her hand was on her sword. Each beat of her heart throbbed in her head like a drum; in its beat she could hear the names of the dead and the wounded. *Damar, Saleema, Tyreesha, Raquella...*

Svartana, help me...

She searched inside herself for some remnant of what she had felt on the slope of Chrysathamere Pass. But there was only stillness; only silence. And with that silence, a weariness that bowed her shoulders and turned her limbs to stone.

Nyreese gave a great cry, struggling against the arms of the two men who were holding her. "Please! My daughter! *Please!*"

But though Marilia's hand was tight on the hilt of her sword, though she wanted nothing more than to shout the words—*I challenge you, Sethyron Andreas!*—her lips wouldn't open and her throat was so tight she could barely breathe.

Raquella, Tyreesha, Saleema, Damar, One-Eye...

She wanted to be the champion Nyreese needed, but she was so very afraid. She had seen the Graver fight. She had seen him battle his way to the top of the tournament lists that day he and Karthtag-Kal had ended up face-to-face upon the sand. And she knew she was no match for him.

"Coward," the Graver breathed. "Karthtag-Kal would have fought me." With a grimace of disappointment, he took a step back towards the staircase.

Nyreese was wailing, and Marilia couldn't face her, couldn't face any of them. She stared at the ground and wished the floorboards were the teeth of a razorfish, that they would open and swallow her up.

A voice rang out through the room, sharp and clear as a sword being drawn. "Andreas of Antarenne! I challenge you!"

For a moment she thought the voice was her own.

But it wasn't.

Annuweth stepped into the light. His green aeder sword was in his hand.

Nyreese turned her stricken face towards him, eyes bright with hope.

"What do you say, Graver?" Annuweth demanded. "The prefect's son against the scorpion butcher? Or are you afraid?"

The Graver's tongue ran across his teeth. "I accept."

The men pulled back; Annuweth and the Graver stepped out into the pillow house's courtyard. The torchlight cast them in a fiery glow. The Graver's gold sword and Annuweth's green were almost the same color—the color of flame.

The Graver's face twitched; his lips contorted strangely. Marilia realized he was holding back a smile. He believed he could win.

She believed it, too.

Annuweth's brows narrowed as he took a fighter's stance. Though he was tall now, nearly the same height as the Graver himself, he seemed somehow diminished, like a half-grown boy facing down a giant.

The presentiment came to her, sharp as a blade between the ribs: her brother was going to die.

It wasn't supposed to be like this. It wasn't supposed to be him alone. *Come back!* She wanted to call to Annuweth. He couldn't win; she couldn't have explained how she knew that, but the knowledge was irrefutable.

Us against the world, she thought numbly. And the Graver wasn't the world, not exactly, but he was a hateful piece of it, all its evils in miniature. It had to be both of them, or else the balance was off; it had to be the two twins of Nelos Dartimaos, together, against the monster that had killed him.

And then, suddenly, she realized that there was a way to make it so.

"Wait!" she stepped forward, past the ring of onlookers, into the courtyard. The Graver paused.

"Both of us," she said, taking her place beside Annuweth. "Both of us, at the same time."

One of the Graver's men scoffed. "Get out of the way, girl. That is a thing unheard of."

But Marilia ignored him. She never took her eyes off the Graver's face. "The children of the prefect, of Nelos Dartimaos, together. What do you think they would say if you killed us both? How much renown do you think you would win then?"

The Graver tilted his head to one side, considering. She saw two conflicting impulses warring within him, the battle played out in the tightening of his features, the movement of the muscles in his cheeks.

But this was the man who, as a boy, had poked out the eye of the King of Tyrace with a wooden sword. Who had kept fighting after his sword had broken and, because of it, had killed a captain of the Order of Jade and been banned from the tournament lists for years. Who had done both these things against the dictates of prudence, for the simple reason that he could not resist.

The Graver's face stilled. The decision made; for a man like the Graver, no decision at all.

...to rage, to burn, to see how wide a mark we can make, and never to stop. Never to stop.

"Very well, Marilia Sandara," he said. He took a fighter's stance, pointing his sword towards her. "Let us begin."

So they did.

CHAPTER THIRTY-SEVEN

The Graver exploded towards her, sword cutting towards her face—
water, be like water—and she angled her blade so that his scraped off
hers. He followed his first attack with a thrust that had her stumbling
backwards. She tripped on one of the roots of the gray tree; he might
have had her right then, in the opening exchange, if not for Annuweth,
who lunged in from the side, his sword scraping against the Graver's
upraised gauntlet.

By the gods, he's fast!

And now the Graver was distracted, deflecting another attack from
her brother, and she saw an opening, the gap of his armpit, the place
where One-Eye had been wounded. She thrust at it, remembering
Septakim's lessons (keep the point steady) but the opening closed, and
she hit only armor. His knee came up and hit her low in the belly, and it
was like being kicked by a horse; all the air went out of her. He pushed
her back and she fell, her head slamming against the trunk of the gray
tree.

She heard Andreas' men whoop, hers groan. She scrabbled on the
ground, groping in the dust for her sword. Everything seemed to be
tilting, falling. Annuweth and the Graver were standing on a steep slope
as the world moved under them, threatening to spill them out into the
dark sea of the night sky.

Annuweth came in high with a blow at the Graver's head that the
Graver accepted against the side of his helmet; his sword hand punched
forward, the hilt of his weapon catching Annuweth's helmet beneath the

chin and snapping the strap that held it in place, lifting it clean off his head. The cross-guard of the Graver's sword left a deep gash below Annuweth's lower lip; she saw his blood spatter the dirt.

Get up, get up...

Marilia levered herself onto her feet. The Graver had cut Annuweth again, a gash on his upper-right arm between two plates of his armor. His blood dripped off his elbow as he took the prime guard, blade angled defensively before him.

Marilia hurried to his side as the world straightened again.

He looked at her, spitting blood from his mouth.

She straightened fully, her guts un-clenching with a feeling like ripping parchment.

He gave her the briefest nod.

"Together," she said.

They came at the Graver in tandem, driving him back towards the doorway to Oba'al's private quarters. It was just like they were back on the banks of the River Tyr, pressing Damar, his size and strength and age counting for nothing against them, because they were the twins of Nelos Dartimaos—two who moved as one. When Marilia went low, Annuweth went high. When she went high, he went low. When he thrust, she slashed—rattling bows off the Graver's armor until her sword slid up and through and cut into his shoulder as, at the same moment, the point of Annuweth's blade pierced the meat of his thigh.

A low murmur rose among the watching crowd.

They drove him through the door, all the way to Oba'al's bed until there was nowhere left for him to run, until the backs of his legs came up against the bedframe.

But rather than stumble or falter, the Graver simply rolled backwards over the bed. He accepted a blow from Annuweth, a cut that left a dent in his armor and must have badly bruised the flesh beneath; he sprang to the right, hurling a cage of chicayas at Annuweth's face. It smashed and the insects went everywhere, carrying their mournful song to the rafters. For a moment, in the blur of wings, Marilia lost sight of her enemy.

The twins' momentum had broken. The Graver saw his chance and he seized it.

He stepped in close, his blade locking with Annuweth's. His foot hooked Annuweth's ankle and he tripped him to the ground.

Marilia stepped around and came at him from the side, but she tripped on something—Oba'al's corpse—and it cost her a moment; once again the opening she'd sought was closed as the Graver's arm came down, batting her sword away. He gripped his sword halfway down the length of the blade and swept her next cut aside and down. She realized she'd erred, she'd forgotten Septakim's lesson, something about feeling the pressure of the blades changing, she couldn't recall, and it didn't matter because it was too late, she was wide open and he stepped in and rammed his sword into her chest and since he was holding the blade close to the tip it had the full force of his strength behind it and it went through her armor and into *her*.

She dropped her sword and grabbed the blade, straining against it. The Graver shoved her back against the wall. She was caught, pinned. When she looked down, she saw the red of her own blood running down the length of his sword. She heard the cries of her knights, Nyreese's piercing wail of despair.

It hurt. It made her want to cry.

The Graver looked into her eyes and moved one hand to the pommel of his sword. All he had to do was push and the blade that was in her flesh would go deeper, into her guts, and she would be dead.

But a flicker of movement and the sound of footsteps made him turn.

"Dremmakin take you!" Annuweth yelled.

In his eagerness for the kill, the Graver had left his side undefended, and Annuweth lunged for it. With the same impressive skill he'd displayed before, the Graver swept an arm across, his gauntlet striking the blade and forcing it aside.

But Annuweth knew his game. He knew the Graver's uncanny speed and he'd planned for it. He kept coming, following the dueling sword with his short-sword, which caught the Graver between two plates of armor and dug in deep.

The Graver stumbled back. In so doing, he let go of his sword. Marilia slumped to her knees, tugging the gold blade from her, taking a breath, another, waiting to hear the wet rattle Zev had made, or One-Eye...but nothing. Just pain, but pain was nothing new to her; it was something she could deal with.

She got to her feet, unsteady, leaning on the wall, and moved to help her brother.

She was too slow.

She watched as the Graver brought his head back. She saw the shine of spit on the man's lips. With terrible force, he brought his forehead snapping forward into Annuweth's face. Annuweth's eyes crossed; blood sprang from both nostrils. He let go of his short-sword.

No!

And the Graver took hold of it and tugged it free—

No, no, no...

And he stabbed it at Annuweth's face.

Somehow, her brother sensed it coming and threw up a hand to stop it. The short-sword glanced off his gauntlet and raked across the right side of the face, gashing his cheek, splitting his ear so that the lobe fell away from the side of his head and landed on the floor...

The Graver's second thrust landed squarely in Annuweth's chest.

NO!

Annuweth fell without a cry, landing on his back on Oba'al's bed, the blood running through the gaps between his fingers. His eyes were wide. From between his lips came a halting, wheezing sound, a sound that reminded Marilia of the girl dying in the city square.

He closed his eyes.

Marilia forgot the pain of her wound, the ache in her stomach where the Graver's blade had pierced her. She hurled himself at him, sword leading the way, and what she was seeing wasn't even him, it was moments she had almost forgotten,

It was she and Annuweth, standing up to their knees in the waters of the River Tyr, mud sailing through the air as they battled the children from a rival pillow house, grinning from ear to ear

Her first blow caught the Graver in the side of the head as he tried to turn away and knocked his helmet off—

It was she and Annuweth hunched over a table in the pillow house's common room with the dice clattering between them, she and Annuweth on the ship speeding away to Navessea, holding hands and listening to the wood of the cabin creak and groan...

Her second blow, aimed for the crown of his head, came down on his shoulder, bending one of his pauldrons inward, leaving a visible dent

It was, most of all, Annuweth lying beside her in the dark of Tyreesha's kitchen, whispering his promise to her, a promise that had never died.

Us against the world.

445

The Graver had nowhere left to dodge as her third blow came down atop his head, through his skull, down to the base of his neck, ending his life in a bright spray of blood.

At least, that was what she meant to happen.

But his arm got in the way again; he threw up his short-sword to parry and her blue aeder sword, the one that Karthtag-Kal had given to Kanediel as a wedding gift, the one Zeviel Espeleos had given to her, broke halfway down the blade.

She stared at it, dumbfounded.

The Graver shifted his weight. His right fist shot forward, filling her vision, smashing into in the face.

She went flying backwards, through the trellised wooden door that led to Oba'al's balcony, her head coming to rest against the railing that looked out over the steep drop of Oba'al's Hill. Pieces of broken wood landed all around her. Her cheek burned; the Graver's gauntlet had caught on her skin, her soft flesh parting easily for the yoba-shell, no contest. Now her blood was running down her face, its heat and the sting of her torn flesh the only thing keeping her from blacking out completely.

The Graver stalked towards her. He was limping, leaning on the door-frame for support. Blood dripped from his wounds, marking his passage. His breathing was ragged, labored. But still he came for her.

She'd dropped the broken end of her dueling sword, but she still had her short-sword; she drew and thrust. He caught her by the wrist and twisted, kept twisting as she felt the bones in her arm straining against one another.

What frightened her most was the look of equanimity on his face—as though he were disassembling an old cart. Her fingers fell open; the look on his face changed; she heard a sharp intake of breath, a deep

446

sigh.

The pain nearly brought her to her knees. Sobbing, she struck at his face with her other hand, but he blocked with an upraised arm. His knee found her stomach, then found it again. She spat bile all over his boots.

He shoved her and she landed on her back, right where she'd been before.

He could have killed her easily then—drawn his short-sword and brought it down upon her from on high. She had no chance of stopping it. But something made him hesitate.

Instead, he knelt over her. His hands closed around her throat.

He bent her head back, and she caught a glimpse of the city she had conquered. The morning sun was rising, the sky changing from night to day. She saw the sun brightening the tops of the buildings, turning them gold like the tips of prayer-candles. She saw the night's clouds racing across the sky like chariots speeding off down a track, eager to be somewhere, anywhere else.

Blood pounded in her forehead. She clawed at the Graver's hand, trying to break his grip. She might as well have tried to wrestle open a dragon's jaws.

Over the Graver's shoulder, she could see Annuweth lying where he had fallen. He could not help her.

Now, at last, she truly stood alone.

She cast around her for a weapon. A shard of jagged wood, a piece of Oba'al's broken door, lay not far away. She strained to reach it and the tips of her fingers just barely brushed it. It was too far away.

The Graver's hands tightened on her throat. There was no air, nothing but a dry, empty gasp as she sucked at the dawn. A pressure built inside her skull until she thought she couldn't take it anymore. She was sure that her head would burst, scattering her thoughts across the

447

balcony like the ichor of a slaughtered yoba, a sacrifice on the altar of Tyracium.

She reached for the Graver's face, but he turned his head aside, blocked her with his arms; she could find no purchase there. Her vision was darkening fast, a tunnel narrowing and at the end of it was him, his joyful eyes and nothing else.

Then her wandering fingers found the hole in his armor that Annuweth's short-sword had made, the opening her brother had left her. She pushed them in, through the gap in the yoba-shell plates, into him, and she felt his grip slacken, just for a moment.

Long enough to get her fingers around the shard of broken wood and jam it up towards his face.

She'd been aiming for his eye but, with her vision clouded in darkness, she missed. It caught him in the cheek instead, driving through at an angle so that the wooden point pricked the roof of his mouth. The Graver jerked his head back, releasing her, and she breathed in, the air hot and red in her lungs, as sweet a feeling as she had ever known.

She rolled sideways, curled her legs back, and kicked with everything she had.

Her feet connected with the Graver's face.

His eyes went somewhere else. He staggered back into the balcony railing; it was a delicate trellis, meant for show, not to support the weight of an armored warrior. It cracked, and broke, and the Graver fell, over the edge and down Oba'al's Hill.

He fell a long way.

Marilia rose to her feet. Her voice was hoarse, but in the absolute

silence that had fallen over the pillow house's courtyard, it carried far
enough.

"If you are a soldier of Svartennos, help my brother. If you are a
soldier of Antarenne, get out of here, now."

And they did. Andreas' men left, and Nyreese ran upstairs, weeping,
to find her daughter. She returned with the baby girl clutched to her
chest, babbling her thanks, dripping tears across the pillow house's
bloodied floor.

All the while, Marilia forced herself to remain standing, victorious,
imperious, until the last of Antarenne's soldiers had trickled out the
pillow house's door. Septakim, his eyes shining, marveling as he gazed
upon her, closed and barred it behind them.

Then Marilia's legs gave way; she fell. The last thing she saw
several knights of the Flower Company rushing forward to catch her.

All around her, she could hear the chicayas singing, the rustling of
the silk drapes in Oba'al's bedroom as the wind touched them, as they
swung back and forth. She closed her eyes and let go.

CHAPTER THIRTY-EIGHT

By midday the whole city knew of Marilia's astonishing victory. Everyone had heard the story—the Graver, the blademaster of seven tournaments in the city of Ulvannis and five in the city of Antarenne, the man who had killed Nelos Dartimaos, one of Navessea's greatest warriors—defeated by a girl. No, not by a girl; by Marilia Sandara, who had been Lady Chrysathamere, and now, in the eyes of all those who had begun to lose faith, was again. For how could such an unlikely victory be anything but a sign from the gods?

The Graver had attacked a pillow house and harmed the Tyracians inside it; the Lady Chrysathamere had ordered him to stop. The Graver had refused. Now she stood victorious and his body was scarred and battered by his tumble down Oba'al's Hill—he had been borne away by his men, screaming, three ribs cracked and his right arm and left leg out of joint. The soldiers of Antarenne had carried him to a galley and sent him off up the river. Whether he would survive was anyone's guess. The rest of his army had soon followed him; they did not dare to stay and face the wrath of Marilia's men.

There the matter stood—over, done, as clear as anything could be. Marilia triumphant, once again.

Doubts vanished like dew shrinking from the morning sun.

There could be no question—she really was Svartana Reborn, and all who had betrayed and denied her had been gravely wrong.

All attacks on the people of Tyrace stopped as men waited, anxiously, to see what would happen next.

Marilia's men offered to move her to the Tower, or at least, to a Tyracian villa, but she refused; she told them Oba'al's pillow house would be her home until she had recovered from her injuries and until Annuweth (who could not be moved safely) had recovered from his— or perished. A couple strategoi grumbled that it didn't seem proper for the Lady Chrysathamere to remain in the company of heretic painted ladies. She told them flatly that she didn't care; she was staying, and that was the end of it.

There, down the hall from the surviving painted ladies, she rested in the room she had once shared with her brother and mother, too weary to move, while physicks attended her. Annuweth slept in the room next door.

All day, soldiers thronged on the steps outside the pillow house. Many were those who had taken part in the looting and raping of the night before, come to ask her forgiveness. Among them was Antiriel, though she noticed her cousin Aerael failed to make an appearance. He would claim that he had stayed true to his orders, that it was merely some of his captains who had disobeyed, and she had no sure way to prove him a liar, though she knew in her heart that he was.

Septakim organized a guard outside the pillow house. All those who came to see the Lady Chrysathamere were disappointed; she kept inside, the doors closed. She saw no one. No one, that was, except for her physicks, a few guards—chosen from among those who had been with her in the courtyard when she'd confronted the Graver—and of course Annuweth, who lay near death in the room next door.

They were the only ones she cared to see.

Reports came—the names of many of the sergeants and the numbers of the companies that had disobeyed her.

There were more than a hundred of them—over a third of the

451

companies that had stormed Tyracium's walls. And those were only the ones she knew about.

They were men of Svartennos, tradition-bound, and she was their commander. And so, on the fifth day after her duel, when she was strong enough to walk, she made her way out to the balcony overlooking the hill and the square below—the same balcony where she had nearly been choked to death at the Graver's hands.

She knew what came next—what Svartennan tradition demanded. One man from each company would be chosen at random. The mark of Akeleos would be placed on his brow—the traditional punishment for such a grave insubordination, one that had nearly led to the death of their general and the general's only brother. Only she had the power to commute the sentence.

But she was not feeling merciful.

Even Antiriel's name was put in the lot. He was lucky enough not to be chosen.

Grim-faced, some weeping, the doomed chosen drew their daggers. Blades sparkled like tears in the sun. Their blood watered the streets of Tyracium. These were men who, less than two months ago, had cheered her name as she raised the hallowed banner of Svartana over the field of her first victory. Now they crept away in shame. Some would end their lives at a dagger's point in the hours or days to come. Others would light candles and beg the gods for redemption. They would live on to try to regain their honor or die in the attempt.

One looked back as he walked from the place of his mutilation. "Forgive us, Lady Chrysathamere!" he cried out to her.

But she felt none of the weakness she had after Aexiel's death; her heart was hardened, calloused by the deaths of those she had loved.

She walked back inside the pillow house without a word or a

backwards glance.

She lit prayer candles for Annuweth in her room. The smoke coiled in her lungs. She left the candles burning and limped painfully to her brother's side. He lay with his chest salved and bandaged. On his chin, the gash the Graver's cross-guard had left had hardened into a thick, crusted scab. Worse was the right side of his face, still bandaged. Her eyes strayed to the place where the bottom half of his right ear had been.

The sockets of both eyes were purple, and the skin of his face had an ugly yellow tinge. He opened his eyes a crack, but she wasn't sure if he was really seeing her, or if could hear her. "I couldn't have done it without you," she said. "You saved me." She pulled up a cushion and sat beside him, holding his hand. She stayed with him until sleep found her and the physicks came to carry her back to her own room.

Annuweth had been lucky. Had the Graver's blow been only a finger's breadth to the side, it would have punctured his lung, and he would have choked to death on his own blood. Had it been any deeper, it would have found his heart. Instead he lingered on, locked in a second, private battle with death.

As Marilia sat beside him the following day, she composed a letter to Camilline.

I hope your mother is well. As I promised, I lit a candle for her every day since you departed. I pray she recovers; if she does not, then I know she will find her way to your brother's side in the House of White Sands, and I know that both of them will look down with pride on the new Lady of House Paetos. They could ask for no one better.

Tyracium has fallen. I hope the war may soon be over; my strategoi believe that King Damar will sue for peace. But the price has been high.

Her hand feverishly traced marks across the parchment. She told Camilline of the terrible things she had witnessed, of her army's betrayal, of the sacking of the city, of the pillow house's fall. *Now they cheer for me again. They want me to come out, but I can't bring myself to face them. I'm surrounded by thousands of Svartennos' men, but I feel alone. I wish you were here.*

On the fourth day after the battle with the Graver, one of the knights of the Flower Company poked his head into her room and told her that Nyreese was there to see her.

Until that moment, Nyreese had remained closeted within her room in the silk hallway with her daughter and her sister, Raquella. Neither of them had spoken a word to anyone else. They and two other painted ladies were the only survivors of the Graver's massacre.

Marilia rose and limped to the doorway.

The blood and dirt had been washed off Nyreese, and her face was free of tears. She looked much more like the Nyreese Marilia remembered; the same narrow, angled cheeks, the same slanted cat's eyes, the same small, impish lips that reminded her of Petrea's.

The two women each stopped moving at the same time, neither quite ready to make the final steps to close the distance between them. Nyreese stared at Marilia as if she couldn't quite fathom what she was seeing. Somehow, Marilia felt her face grow warm under that stare, as if she were a child who had been caught playing at knights when she was supposed to be doing chores.

"Conqueror of cities," Nyreese said. "Flower of Death—did you know that's what they've started calling you?"

Marilia flinched. "I never meant for...what happened...to happen."

Nyreese's expression did not soften. "I know. I wanted to say thank you for saving me, my sister. My daughter."

"I couldn't save the others." She wanted Nyreese to tell her it was all right, there was nothing she could have done, that it wasn't her fault. But Nyreese's eyes were closed to her. It wasn't going to be that easy.

"No," Nyreese said. "I guess not."

Marilia looked away.

Nyreese's voice softened, just a little. "Is Annuweth all right?"

"He is..." Marilia didn't know what he was. "He is still healing." She hoped.

"I hope he recovers soon."

"I hope...I hope you and your family fare well," Marilia said. The words sounded empty to her, a hollow nothing when measured against the blood, fire, and pain the Graver had brought them.

"I got the gold you left for us," Nyreese said. "Two whole orets. Enough to set us up nice and easy. Not bad, as blood prices go."

"Not a blood price," Marilia said, wincing at the term. "It was a gift for a friend."

"I have a gift for you, too. Seems only fair. I'm not some sort of lady or general or whatever it is you are, so it's not worth two orets. But I thought you should have it anyway." She held out her arms. Marilia took what she offered—a habithra sash of blue and gold, woven through with verses from the Book of the Gods. It was exquisitely made.

"It's beautiful," Marilia said in a choked voice.

"I've really taken to needle-work," Nyreese said, shrugging. "Might have made a good apprentice in another life."

Marilia stared at the sash, winding the silk absently through her fingers. It was more than a garment—it was a work of art. She remembered her own art, the water-script paintings she had done back in Karthtag-Kal's villa. She recalled the feeling that work had given her, the warmth of creation. For the first time in years, she could picture each piece clearly, as if she were seeing them for the first time: *mountain, flower, galley, my fathers standing among the hills of Svartennos.* She might have taken to water-script painting the same way Nyreese had taken to needle-work...had it not been for Karthtag-Kal. But her life had turned down a different path. She felt a lump form in her throat.

"Thank you, Nyreese."

"I should let you rest," Nyreese grunted, looking uncomfortable at the show of affection. "You look tired." Marilia had the sense that now that she had done what she'd come to do, Nyreese was eager to be gone. She understood; the air felt too close between them. There were too many spirits crowding there.

Long ago she and Nyreese had been friends. But some things could not be carried over down the river of time and plucked un-changed from its waters. Some things were of the past, and that was the only place you could leave them.

Marilia did not leave the pillow house the next day, or the one after.

"My lady, the men weep," Septakim told her. "They fear that you are crippled, disfigured, and that is why you hide your face," he said.

"They're not all wrong," she replied. Though the physicks told her that her sprained wrist was healing well, she still bore a mark on her chest where the Graver's sword had pierced her, and another, more obvious scar on her face where his gauntlet had torn her cheek and the physicks had sewn her back up: a raised furrow of skin that reached from the middle of her cheekbone to the bridge of her nose. "Let them weep."

"They say that this is the gods' punishment, what you spoke of back on the hill by the riverbank—that the gods have taken their Lady Chrysathamere from them because of what they did. That further wrath awaits."

"Is that what they think?"

"Many of them, my lady."

She faced the wall. "Let them think it, then. I do not wish to go out, Septakim."

"My lady..."

"That is all."

How could she go out, when every time she closed her eyes, she dreamed of the night the city fell? Each dream was different; the only constant was the sense of horror they left her with when she woke afterwards, wide-eyed, her neck ringed in sweat, her night-gown stuck to her skin like the pale, webbed fingers of a dremmakin.

In one, she saw Annuweth crawling towards her through a red room, across a pool of blood. Her first realization was that the blood was her mother's, dripping from the ends of her drained and lifeless fingers as she lay on the birthing bed, covered by a dark sheet. Her second realization was that the blood was not her mother's after all; it was her own. She was wounded; a sword had gone right through her, and her spirit was running out of her on both sides, front and back, twin ribbons of red silk winding to the floor.

In another, she watched herself transform into a grave beetle, her limbs lengthening, twisting, as she kicked helplessly against a current that pulled her over the edge of a waterfall.

In a third, she wandered among the books of Karthtag-Kal's library, only this time the books were tall as city walls, towering above her. The smell of those books—old vellum and musty leather—filled her nose and throat until she gasped for air and felt bile rise in her gut. Slowly, the books tilted, and she marveled at the immensity of them, the weight contained in all those ancient pages. They fell, around and upon her, crushing her to the earth, and she woke screaming.

As she lay there, shivering in the cool night air, she thought again of those books. Karthtag-Kal's library had been the temple of her childhood, a second shrine no less important than the one with the pit of white sand where she knelt and lit candles. Its gods were the heroes of long-ago battles; its holy psalms told of the wheeling and charging of horses, the shattering of shield walls and the sight of banners waved from atop a hill. The fall of cities, one man's triumph over another, the rising of one star and the fall of his enemy, steady and constant as the sun chasing away the moon.

The Valdruk reigned nine and thirty years on the isle of Svartennos before Queen Svartana rose up against them, casting them down from their high castles and driving them to the northern shore, surprising them in their own homes.

...Governor Sullyn returned to the Sunset Isles, and his men subdued the local populace with some difficulty.

... Emperor Vergana passed into the land of Kanadrak, and they carried great wrath with them.

...And the armies of Svartennos and Antarenne, led by Marilia Sandara, who some called Lady Chrysathamere, passed into the city of Tyracium, a great and sudden victory, sweeping aside all opposition, and so revenged the treacherous attack the Tyracians had performed upon the harbor of Svartennos two months prior.

How many forgotten lives, she wondered, were contained in the spaces between those letters, in the gaps between words? How many like Saleema and Damar and the children of the pillow house, how many like her own mother? Thousands of common, simple, everyday lives that, but for chance, might have been her own.

Unable to fall back asleep, seized by a feeling of restlessness, driven by an impulse she could not explain, she had her men bring her a piece of paper and several vials of colored ink. For the first time in years, she took a brush in her hand.

She paused, staring at the blank page before her. Once, it had seemed a promise. Now, there seemed to be something threatening about that stark emptiness. It was waiting for her to fill it, demanding that it be filled.

She closed her eyes. She tasted Tyrace—the dust of its streets, the aged wood of the floorboards beneath her feet, the sharp, pillow house smell that could never entirely be washed out.

She let the spirits guide her hand, as Nelvinna had taught, writing words from the Book of the Gods. Or maybe it wasn't the spirits, but just her, as it had always been—her hand knowing exactly where it was going.

When she stepped back to study what she had painted, she saw that it was two children, a boy and a girl, standing on the deck of a ship. Black lines formed the silhouette of mountains and the bodies of the children themselves; blue for the line where the sea met the far-off, wind-swept clouds.

Tyrennis Castaval, who had been marching south to relieve the siege of Tyracium, halted in his tracks.

None had expected the city to fall so quickly; Tyrace was thrown

459

into confusion. Letters flew between King Damar and Emperor Vergana. A truce was called, while each side took stock of its losses, and all wondered whether the war would go on.

Annuweth's war against death did go on. And through it all, Marilia stayed beside him. Finally, good news: the physick (with some qualifications; nothing could be certain when it came to such matters) told her that it looked as though her brother was on the mend. Annuweth had woken twice and taken water. He had even tried to speak. He continued to slip in and out, but most of the danger, the physick informed her, had passed.

She nodded, but she couldn't let herself relax; not until he stood again on his own two feet.

She sat beside him. The light through the curtain was thin and golden.

"I'm sorry," she said. "I never meant this. I just...I want you to wake up, 'Weth. That's all." She took his hand.

She knew he couldn't hear her; maybe that was why she felt the words pouring out of her, all the thoughts she'd held inside, all the things she couldn't forget—the sight of Saleema crawling on the floor, One-Eye's last breath, the trampled girl in the plaza, the cost of her victory.

"I keep thinking about what Andreas said...no one *cares*. All they care about is that I got hurt, that I'm in here, refusing to go out and make some speech to make them all feel better. Not the rest of it. Not what happened. I saw Nyreese about to be raped. I saw a boy beaten to death; I saw a little girl ridden down. The girl—she looked just like me. And I saw Saleema and Damar..." she broke off, her breath shuddering. "The only ones who cared were us, 'Weth."

There was a sound like a dry wind scraping over sand; it made her jump. It was Annuweth's voice. He had awoken and was staring at her with glassy eyes. "It wasn't supposed to be this way. It *shouldn't* have been this way." His hollow eyes fixed on hers and for a second something flashed there—something hard and cold as aeder drawn on a stormy morning. His sorrow turned to anger, and his anger set its teeth in her. "I tried to stop you," he said through gritted teeth. "I told you not to trust the Graver. I tried to stop you from killing Aexiel. But you didn't listen."

She swallowed. "I'm sorry. You were right."

Even that brief display of anger seemed to have cost him more strength than he had; his eyes fluttered closed, his breathing slowed, and for a second, she thought he'd passed out again. Then—

"All my life, I thought I'd kill the Graver. I trained for it, swore to it. And when the moment came, I couldn't even avenge them." He opened his eyes, staring up at the ceiling. She realized from the look in his eyes that he was only half there, and half somewhere else.

"You did save some of them," Marilia said, giving his hand a reassuring squeeze. "We saved Nyreese and her daughter, and Raquella. We beat the Graver."

"You beat him. Now they call you Graver's Bane, or so the physick told me."

"We did it together."

"No; you did it. I failed. I suppose…I suppose at least that must be some consolation to you."

She drew back as if struck. "What does that mean?"

"Come on, sister." The cords of his neck stood out as he grimaced, easing himself up onto the pillow. "You told me back in the tent that I was jealous of you, and you were right—I was. But you're no different."

461

"That's not so."

"No? Look me in the eyes and say that."

She got to her feet, shocked, staring down at him. She tried to speak the words, but a knot formed in her throat. He lay there, waiting.

But after everything that had happened, she could not bring herself to lie to him.

He nodded and closed his eyes. The silk that covered him rustled as he let out a long sigh, his body deflating, shrinking into the bed. His voice was slurred; sleep was coming for him again. "I was the golden child, Karthtag-Kal's heir. I know you hated me for that."

"I didn't hate you."

"Yes, you did. That's why you wanted to beat me. That's why you pushed me away. And I know it wasn't fair—you didn't ask to be born a girl. But you don't know what it was like. You don't understand." His eyes opened again. He stared at the ceiling as if a corpse-white childhood monster was waiting there, splayed across the wooden beams of the pillow house's roof. "He was always there...our father, the prefect...*staring* at me, watching every move I made, waiting for me to turn into Nelos Dartimaos. Always watching…and I kept trying and trying, but I couldn't give him what he wanted." He swallowed, and she wasn't sure the shine in his eyes was only from his sickness. "I couldn't, because he wanted me to be you."

"'Weth...'" she began.

His voice was faint. "That is not my name."

His breath evened; his hands fell limply to his sides. She stood there watching him for a while, surprised to feel tears in her eyes. She returned to her room and sat staring out the window for a long time.

CHAPTER THIRTY-NINE

Slowly, Annuweth grew stronger. *He has the strength of a tiger,* the physick told her, admiringly. *I think he will live.*

With Annuweth on the mend, Marilia finally allowed both of them to be moved to a villa that had once belonged to a Tyracian noble, not far from the city's northern gate. At first staying in the pillow house had seemed the right choice—an act of defiance against all those who had forgotten that her story began there, a gesture of respect to those that had died there. But the longer she stayed within its walls, the more the memories began to crowd in on her, until she felt that she was breathing in the spirits of the dead each time air entered her lungs; until she felt that she was choking on them.

She made the trip at night, avoiding the crowds, moving almost as furtively as she had done when she'd entered the city in the first place. She found a room with a shrine overlooking the villa's garden, and there she stayed; things returned to the same routine, she in her room, Annuweth in the one next door.

On the seventeenth day after the battle with the Graver, Septakim came to her as she stood at the window, looking out over the city streets. "My lady, the men are growing uneasy. Tempers are fraying. I think we've already seen what can happen when soldiers get restless, when tempers rise..."

"Fine," she said, squeezing her eyes shut tight. "Fine; I'll go out."

And she did. She stepped out into the hot Tyracian sun, transported in a yoba-drawn carriage, surrounded by the men of her Flower

Company, shielded from view as she made her way to the main plaza and stood atop the dais where, during the year's Solstice Festival, yoba were sacrificed in honor of the gods. The bronze statue of the First King upon his winged horse gleamed in the sunlight.

Her men parted so that she could be seen, so that she could give them the news that had come to her the previous day, delivered by a rider from Emperor Vergana's army.

The street was full of people—the knights and shield-men of Svartennos, filling the square, waiting for their lady to speak.

The scar on her face was still swollen around the edges, and the splint on her wrist had not yet come off. None of that seemed to matter. The way they stared at her, she might have been a figure as proud and flawless as the bronze rider behind her.

She saw Antiriel, looking gaunt and humbled; saw Leondos, noble and impassive as ever, freshly returned from holding the pass against Castaval's army; Laekos, the one who had never doubted, looking at her with bright eyes; Aerael, skulking at the back, expressionless.

"Men of Svartennos," she said. She raised a letter in her left hand. "Word from Emperor Vergana. The Tyracians have agreed to a treaty." She breathed in and hurled her next words across the square. They echoed in the still air. "In a fortnight's time, we will give back the city. In return, they will abandon Dane and destroy what is left of their fleet so that they cannot threaten Navessea's shores again. They will release their prisoners and we will release ours. We will have our princes back." Among the Tyracian prisoners were Ilruyn, heir to Naxos, and— as it turned out—Ben Espeleos, Prince of Svartennos.

Another debt they owed her.

She let the news of the treaty sink in, let her army realize what it meant before she spoke the words aloud, confirming what everyone was thinking.

"The war is over. We won."

The cheer went on and on. Her knights had brought her a new aeder sword, perhaps not as clear or flawless as the broken one that Karthtag-Kal had given Kanediel, but a fine blade nonetheless. She drew the weapon and held it aloft, the sword sparkling in the sun, a smaller piece of the bright, cloudless blue sky that stretched overhead as far as the eye could see—the same color as the flower in the middle of the black banner that was raised over the square.

"Chrysathamere!" Her army shouted. "Chrysathamere!" They smiled and sang and cheered.

But as her men bore her back to the villa inside the carriage, their cries ringing on all sides like the waves of a restless sea, she realized that she was weeping.

Marilia returned to the villa and made her way into the shrine. She took a stick of incense from the pot on the dresser and made to light it.

"My lady." One of her knights knocked on the doorframe. "There's a letter come for you. It's from the Lady Paetia."

Marilia slipped the stick of incense into her pocket, her plan to light candles for the dead forgotten. She made her way back inside her bedroom and found the letter waiting for her on her bedside table. She broke the familiar seal—two crossed swords, the emblem of House Paetos—and began to read.

Dear Marilia,

My mother has made a full recovery. I think even the physicks were surprised. Maybe it was Kanediel's spirit, lending her strength, or maybe it was your candles. I like to think it was both; I like to think all that candle-wax wasn't a waste.

I'm so sorry for what happened in Tyracium. I know those words aren't enough. They never are.

I wish I was there with you. I wish you could look into my eyes so I wouldn't have to write this letter, but although I'm traveling to see you, I'm still miles away and so words are all I have. So I'll do my best. I never told you this, but before I became obsessed with horses, I used to try my hand at poetry. Zev used to mock me for it. He thought I was terrible, which I guess means I must have been decent, because when was Zev ever right about anything? I suppose only once—when he gave you Kanediel's sword.

I wish more than anything I could be with you because I know you, and I know that right now, you'll probably be sitting alone in your room like a prisoner in a cell, telling yourself that it's all your fault, wishing you could go back and do things differently. But if you blame yourself for the things that men like the Graver do, guess what? Then they win all over again, because they get to make you suffer, too.

I'll tell you what's your fault. It's your fault that when everyone lost hope—even me—you gave it back to us. I don't know, because I wasn't there, but I can imagine what your first victory meant to the soldiers in Dane, with the Tyracian army closing in, and I can imagine your last victory will mean for the knights on the decks of Governor Ikaryn's ships and the oarsmen beneath his decks when the chicayas finally come to the far west to let them know the war is over. I can imagine what it will mean to all the wives waiting beside their candles for their husbands to come home, to all the children who will get to see their fathers again, and all the villagers who no longer have to fear fire and the sword.

I know what you mean to the people here on Svartennos. I've spent most of the time since I left helping them rebuild Svartennos City and the Harbor. It's hard and painful work, sifting through the ashes of our burned cities, but thanks to you we get to do it instead of gathering up the ashes of our dead.

I'll tell you what you are to all those people, from Dane to Svartennos to Ulvannis to the farthest reaches of the west. You're the stories their mothers used to tell them as children. You're the first light that comes at dawn and the rising star that cuts through the clouds. You've been that light for thousands of people since the day you first lifted that banner over Chrysathamere Pass.

You can go on being that light—or don't. It's up to you.

I remember you told me once that when Karthtag-Kal came to take you from Tyrace it felt like a whole new world had opened up to you. It was new, and exciting, and a little frightening. Back then you'd barely set foot outside Tyracium's walls. He took your hand and told you that you had a chance to travel farther than the sands go, farther than you'd ever dreamed of going. You didn't know what you would find there, but you trusted it would be something good. And you threw yourself *forward, the same way you threw yourself off that cliff with me (I hope you enjoyed that as much as I did).*

I know it might be hard to see, but that's the same choice you have now. You can't just run away and escape from your past or your wounds. I know because I never managed to run away from mine, and I've always been faster than you, Chrysathamere or not. I'll never forget what it was like watching my brother and sister die. But if you throw yourself forward and you run fast enough and long enough, I know you can at least get a good lead on them. A few strides. That's all it takes.

Until we meet again,
Camilline.

Marilia set the letter down. There were tears in her eyes. "Thank you, Camilline," she whispered.

A knock sounded against the open door behind her. "My lady," Septakim said. "There's someone here to see you."

She wiped at her face, brushing the tears away before she turned to face him. "Who?"

His mouth twitched. "Oh, come now, my lady. You wouldn't want me to spoil the surprise, would you?"

She entered the next room to find Karthtag-Kal waiting for her. She stared at him, open-mouthed.

"How?"

"The emperor let me leave the Order to come visit you. He said it was the least he could do, after you saved his son Ilruyn from the Tyracians' dungeons." His brow furrowed with concern. "Where is Annuweth?"

"Asleep in the next room." She had already written him a letter informing him that Annuweth's injuries were no longer life-threatening and that he was expected to recover—but Karthtag-Kal, who had already been traveling from the Neck of Dane to visit her, had missed it. So now she told him all that had happened since he had parted ways with Emperor Vergana.

Karthtag-Kal let out a long sigh, closing his eyes briefly. "Thank all the gods. I was afraid to lose him. And you."

He embraced her, and she folded into his warmth, feeling for a moment like the little girl she had been when she'd first come to his villa, letting him rock her in his arms.

"I can wake Annuweth," she offered.

"No; for now, let him rest. I am sure he needs it. I would like to speak with you, my daughter." He put his hands on her shoulders, studying her wonderingly from arm's length. "I never thought to find you here. You have done incredible things."

She smiled, but it felt forced. She looked away from him. "And terrible things. Do you know what the men of Navessea say about me out there in the streets? That I am a hero, invincible—that I cannot be defeated. And yet I couldn't even control my own soldiers."

Karthtag-Kal's smile dimmed. "I heard what happened when the city fell," he said. "But Marilia...you can't blame yourself for that. You tried to stop it."

"Camilline said something similar." Marilia felt a knot form in her stomach. She turned from him and walked to the window, staring out at the garden, where, despite the city's heat, the flowers grew bright and tall, fed by water that was pumped through pipes beneath the moss lawn. She let her eyes wander beyond the garden, to the roofs of the city beyond. Not too far away, the Tower of Tyrace rose into the sky, its teeth touching the sun. She felt Karthtag-Kal's hand on her shoulder again as he came up to stand behind her.

"Think about what you have done. You ended the war. You stopped the fighting. You saved Dane City, rescued Ben Espeleos and Prince Ilruyn. Do you remember the words of Neravan Vergana? *We all must do our duty—we do what we can for the good of the empire.* That is what you did, and did better than anyone could have hoped."

"No," Marilia said quietly. "My duty was to sit and light candles. To bear Kanediel's children. To wait with Camilline and Catarina on Svartennos."

Karthtag-Kal looked at her strangely. "That is one way to look at it."

"They don't sing songs or put my name in the books or cheer because I did my duty," Marilia said. "They cheer because I'm the blademaster." Her jaw trembled. "Because I beat Tyrace; because I *won* and Castaval and King Damar and the Graver lost. And because I did it all with a sword in my hand. That's the truth of it."

"You draw a curious distinction," Karthtag-Kal said.

"Curious, but true. I see that now. This city is full of thousands of dead who did their duty. Who never had the chance to do anything more. I could be dead and burned like Saleema and Damar and the rest of them. Except for luck."

"Luck?" Karthtag-Kal shook his head. "No. There was no luck in this, girl. You are different from those others, and you always have been."

"Am I? I thought you once told me that the Fates didn't plan our lives for us. That we were put on the earth as the threads spun out. That it was all *chance*."

"I was wrong. I never much believed in prophecy, but to deny that

470

every so often, the gods guide us to shape the world to their will...that they choose some among us as their instruments...even the stoics acknowledge that this is the case. You were *meant* for this war, girl. And you are meant for more."

"Meant for more?" At last she turned to face him fully. "What does that mean?"

"Have you given any thought to what happens next? Where you go from here?"

She wished she had an answer for him. But she searched inside herself and found none. She wasn't sure whether she longed more to return to Svartennos or longed more to run far away. On Svartennos lay her friends—Catarina and Ben. Camilline. Thousands who honored her, who sang songs about her.

But on Svartennos lay also the memory of Kanediel's death, lay thousands who had betrayed her and helped cause the deaths of her friends in the pillow house, lay the slow, inevitable pain of watching Camilline—who was now the lady of House Paetos—marry, watching her bear children, grow old in another's arms.

But if not Svartennos, then what?

"I don't know," she said.

"I think I do," Karthtag-Kal said. "I am growing old. I cannot do this forever. Someday not too far from now, my legs will grow stiff and I will not be able to make the climb to the prefect's villa. But you are young, daughter. And when the time for me to step down finally comes, I can think of no name I would rather pass along to Emperor Vergana than yours." He reached to his waist and drew his sword. The green aeder blade caught the light and glowed like spring grass.

"This is my sword. The one I used to kill Kanadrak."

He offered it to her.

471

She stared at him, speechless. Whatever she'd been expecting, it was not this. *Prefect of the Order of Jade.*

Prefect.

Me.

"You want me to be...prefect?" she said. Her voice was hoarse. "The emperor...he'd never...it's impossible."

"The emperor is a man of tradition," Karthtag-Kal admitted. "It might take some work to convince him. But he made me prefect, and I have the blood of a barbarian. He did it not because of my birth, but because I impressed him with my skill and my loyalty to Navessea. As for you...outside this room is the Imperial Chronicler himself. He traveled all the way from Dane with me so he could speak with you and take your account of the war. He means to put the story of the last few months down into a book that will be studied for centuries. What you've done...Marilia, it has changed everything."

"I'm still a woman. Emperor Vergana...he..." she found herself at a loss for words.

"Emperor Vergana is first and foremost a stoic. He will do what he thinks is right for Navessea. He'd want to test you first, of course, and I imagine he'd have many questions, but he respects my judgment. I believe I could convince him. If that's what you want."

"What about Annuweth? He always wanted to be prefect."

Karthtag-Kal sighed. A little frown tugged at the corners of his lips "Annuweth is a strong spirit and a fierce fighter—when he's a little older, he'll be one of the best swordsmen of his age. And he's clever enough to make a fine commander. But a prefect...a prefect is meant to represent the very best of us. When I step down, I am required to pass to Emperor Vergana the name of a person—*one* person—who I believe best suited to succeed me. Do you understand? In good faith, I can give

472

him no name but yours."

Of course he couldn't. It was, after all, his duty.

But this went beyond duty; she saw the eagerness in his eyes, naked as the drawn blade in his hands.

"You have the spirit of Nelos Dartimaos inside you," Karthtag-Kal said. "Your brother has inherited Dartimaos' weapon. But this sword...my sword...belongs to you."

She closed her eyes.

She wanted it—of course she did. To be the prefect—the first and only woman to serve as prefect in the history of the empire—to hold Karthtag-Kal's sword at her side. The sword she had won, had *earned*. How could she not want a thing like that?

She felt a deep, familiar hunger pulling her onward, upward, like an eagle had gripped her in its talons and was carrying her to the clouds, where the air was light and dizzyingly thin. And it would be simple, so easy, to just close her eyes and hold on.

But she opened her eyes and the eagerness in Karthtag-Kal's face was still there, along with his pride in her, a warm glow like a room full of prayer candles, and for the first time in her life that glow made her feel sick.

And she saw it then, clear as day. She and Annuweth...a circle that went on and on without end—the two of them bound together by their need for that warmth, each straining against the other, burning bright like a pair of blazing galleys circling each other on the open sea as they bled smoke into the sky. And in the center of the circle was him, Karthtag-Kal, their father. It had always been him.

Gently but firmly, she closed her father's fingers around the sword. She already had her own sword; the one that had belonged to Kanediel, and then Zev, and finally to her. The one that had shattered against the

Graver's blade. Now it lay broken in the bottom of her dresser; and she realized, with a feeling that was like waking, that there was no reason it couldn't stay there.

There was no reason she ever had to lift a sword again.

"I'm sorry, father, but I can't do it. I can't be the prefect."

Karthtag-Kal's brow furrowed. "Then what will you do? Where will you go?"

"I don't know yet. But I will figure it out."

She saw his disappointment.

It hurt less than she'd thought it would.

In fact, as she turned from him to make her way out into the garden, she felt almost relieved.

She spoke with Vergana's Chronicler for four hours, sitting with him until the sun was setting. She answered all his questions and insisted that he mention the fall of the pillow house and the deaths of her friends in his account. From the look on his face, she didn't think he planned to, but she had to at least try.

She told him of the burning of Svartennos Harbor (*who could have foreseen such treachery?*), of Kanediel's death (*so terrible, my lady, so sorry for your loss*), of the Battle in Chrysathamere Pass (*extraordinary, such a victory*), of the disaster in the Bay of Dane (*the gods must have been watching over our ships...how incredible that you were able to escape!*) and finally came to the moment when she and Andreas and the strategoi of Svartennos stood in a tent on the banks of the River Tyr, wondering what to do next.

"And I understand it...from talking to Leondos, that it was your idea to attack Tyracium?"

474

"Yes," she said.

"And you thought of the plan to take the city, all on your own?"

Yes, she almost said. The Chronicler's words would make her legend; the whole of Navessea would know what she had done.

Then she stopped. She thought of her brother, lying maimed and broken in a room not far away, of the little frown of disappointment on Karthtag-Kal's face when she had spoken Annuweth's name. She thought most of all of the moment she had stood before the Graver, the lives of Nyreese and her child in the balance, and felt the world crumbling down around her, felt herself slipping at the edge of a cliff. He had stepped forward to help her, and, just for a moment, the world froze in place, and she stopped falling.

"No," she said. "Not on my own."

The Chronicler paused with his pen in the air. "No?"

"That was what we wanted the strategoi to think…we agreed it would be better if it seemed as though it was all my idea. If I came up with everything myself. We wanted the men to believe I was invincible. To give them hope."

"We who?" the Chronicler asked.

"My brother and I. We made the plan together. The details of the attack were mine—where to strike, and when, and who would lead…but the idea of diverting the river and crawling in under the walls…that was Annuweth's idea."

The Chronicler frowned. "But the plan to enter the city…diverting the River Tyr, the use of Daevish acid to create a breach in the city's walls…the strategoi of Svartennos are insisting you came up with it right there in the tent before their eyes."

"It wasn't so. My brother and I spoke about it the night before in my tent. He remembered the gap in the city walls; we used to swim

475

there as children."

"Are you absolutely sure, my lady…?"

"Yes," she said, feeling her chest flutter, feeling a sudden, incredible sense of lightness. "Yes, I am sure." She looked him right in the eyes. "The strategoi didn't know. No one knew but me and Annuweth. But I am telling you—the plan belonged to both of us. So, you see…we all owe my brother a great deal."

After she had finished speaking with the Chronicler, she lingered a while in the villa's garden. She walked to the parapet. There, below her, the waters of the River Tyr flowed on their steady pace to the sea.

She realized that she was still holding the stick of incense in her pocket, one she'd been planning to use to light the shrine's candles when Camilline's letter had arrived and distracted her.

She held it between thumb and forefinger for a moment, turning it back and forth, studying it as if somehow it might reveal its secrets. Then, with a shrug, she snapped it in half. She touched one end to the other and tossed both pieces over the parapet into the river. She leaned forward to watch them fall.

But a sudden gust of wind swept in from the south; it caught them mid-tumble and hurried them along, past the river, over the northern wall of Tyrace, out among the fields of sand until they vanished from sight.

Author's Note:

Thanks for reading *Marilia, the Warlord*. The story will continue in the second installment, which has been drafted and is in the slow but steady process of being edited. This is the part where I share my life story and, if you enjoyed the book, politely beg for a reader review.

It's been a long journey. I'd be lying if I said it was a pleasant one. When I first came up with the initial spark for this book (over a late-night fireside chat with my brother about how, if we could, we would remake the Star Wars prequels), I was still in college, pursuing a double-major in history and creative writing in the mistaken belief that this would open doors for me as an author (spoiler alert: it didn't). I suppose I can admit I was one of those "snowflake" millennials the media loves to hate so much. As a child, I'd been exposed to one too many motivational posters. "Follow your dreams," they read. "Shoot for the moon. If you fail, at least you'll land among the stars."

I shot for the moon, and I landed in a dingy apartment in the small-town Midwestern United States spending six hours a day applying for jobs on Indeed.com and the rest in an unpaid internship as a Spanish-English interpreter. Not exactly the stars I'd envisioned.

It didn't help that I suffered from crippling self-esteem problems and was convinced that I was entirely terrible at anything besides writing fantasy novels. Job interviews were a real drag: *where do I see myself in five years?* Unclear, but is the sweet release of death too much to hope for? It's got to beat Cleveland in the winter, at least (sorry, Cleveland).

Over the course of several highly unpleasant and financially unstable years, I managed to find and lose an Honest-to-God literary agent. After speaking with the Big Fantasy Publishing Houses, this agent let me know my book was too cross-market—since Marilia's age changes over the course of the story, the powers that be weren't sure how to best market the thing. Young adult? Adult? In short, the age range of the protagonist (not uncommon in "literary fiction," but less so in recent fantasy) made the book a somewhat risky bet.

Hang on, you may be thinking. *Is this just one of those bitter rejected authors taking the opportunity to rant about the shallow fools in the publishing industry who didn't appreciate their brilliance?* Yes, kind of. Ranting is fun. Don't ever let anyone take that away from you.

Maybe I'm a bit of an unreliable narrator. Maybe the publishing industry just really sucks. Probably, the truth is somewhere in between. If you yourself are an unrequited writer, sent me an email, and maybe we can swap sob stories.

Since I always had a knack for making my life as difficult as possible, I declined my agent's suggestions and found myself back at square one—no agent, no publishing deal, no writing career in sight, and no belief that anything better was on the horizon.

But it did. Is life perfect now? No, there's still a troublingly high statistical likelihood that we're all sliding towards a bleak, post-apocalyptic future. But it could be worse.

Hey, at least I finally finished this book. It only took nine years.

If you found it entertaining, inspiring, or at least a better way to pass the time than watching the latest dubious slew of Netflix offerings, I'd appreciate a review. I try to take my readers' feedback seriously, and since there are two more books on the way…seeing a review also lets me know that the struggle wasn't all for nothing, that the story that kept me afloat during some of my darkest years was able to touch someone else's life and make it just a little bit better.

That's all, folks. Morgan Cole out.

Made in the USA
Coppell, TX
18 March 2020